Dallas
WOLFEMAN
AN MC SERIES: BOOK TWO

ANGERA ALLEN

Copyright © 2021 by Angera Allen

No part of this book may be reproduced, distributed, or transmitted in any form or by any means, including photocopying, recording, or other electronic or mechanical methods, without the prior written permission of the author, except in the case of brief quotations embodied in critical reviews and certain other noncommercial uses permitted by copyright law.

All rights reserved. Except as permitted under the U.S. Copyright Act of 1976, no part of this publication may be reproduced, distributed, or transmitted in any form or by any means, or stored in a database or retrieval system, without the prior express, written consent of the author. This book is intended for mature adults only.

For questions or comments about this book, please contact the author at authorangeraallen@gmail.com.
Printed in the United States of America

Angera Allen
www.authorangeraallen.com

Publisher's Note: This is a work of fiction. Names, characters, places, and incidents are a product of the author's imagination. Locales and public names are sometimes used for atmospheric purposes. Any resemblance to actual people, living or dead, or to businesses, companies, events, institutions, or locales is completely coincidental.

Editor: Ellie Mc Love at My Brother's Editor
Formatted by Champagne Book Design
Cover Design by Clarise Tan at CT Cover Creations
Cover Photo by Reggie Deanching of RplusMphoto
Cover Model Blake Sevani
Proofreader: Jennifer Guibor | Kim Holtz | Michelle Kopp

Dallas / Angera Allen. - 2nd ed.
978-10-936287-9-1 Paperback

Dedication

To all of us that made it through this last year! This is also to remember the ones we've lost. To the people that welcomed my beautiful baby girl and me into your bubble during this fucked-up pandemic. What a scary, life-altering, mind-blowing experience. I've learned what true friendship means. If it weren't for my friends and family, I would have gone crazy. So, thank you for loving my daughter and me.

FUCK COVID!
Please be safe and love each other.
Love, Angera

Dallas Playlist

"Sure Thing" by Miguel
"Bullet With Butterfly Wings" by The Smashing Pumpkins
"Song 2" by Blur
"Big Booty Bitches" by Bombs Away
"Your Little Beauty" by Fisher
"Losing It" by Fisher
"Take It" by Dom Dolla
"Stop It" by Fisher
"Boneless" by Steve Aoki, Chris Lake and Tujamo
"Be Yourself" by Audioslave
"Hey Man Nice Shot" by Filter
"American Girl" by Tom Petty and the Heartbreakers
"Landslide" Remastered by The Smashing Pumpkins
"With Arms Wide Open" by Creed
"Walkin' On The Sun" by Smash Mouth
"La Grange" by ZZ Top
"Ride It" by Regard
"Free Your Body" by Chris Lake, Solardo
"All I Need" by Shiba San, Tim Baresko
"Right Now" by Anti Up, Chris Lake, Chris Lorenzo
"Turn Off The Lights" by Calvin Harris, Disciples, Chris Lake

Note to Readers

Disclaimer:

TRIGGERS –This book is not suitable for young readers. It has strong language, adult situations, and a lot of violence.

SPOILER ALERT – I recommend that you read the Spin It Series to fully understand and enjoy all that's discussed in Dallas. This book talks about all situations that happened in Alexandria, Ginger, and Izzy's story. If you have not read those books, I would hold off on reading this until you do.

LISTED IN RECOMMENDED READING ORDER
Alexandria (Book 1)
Ginger (Book 2)
Firecracker (Prequel to Quick)
Izzy (Book 3)
Quick (Book 1)
Dallas (Book 2)

Dallas
W🐺LFEMAN
AN MC SERIES: BOOK TWO

1 | The Light

Dallas

"**M**R. CARSEN, CAN YOU HEAR ME?" A FEMALE VOICE calmly asks.

I struggle to open my eyes, concentrating on the voice near my ear. I repeatedly blink, trying to adjust my eyes, but the lights are so bright. When I'm finally able to focus, I see hands flying around, pushing and prodding. My body feels so cold.

Wh-What the fuck. Where…

"Mr. Carsen, stay calm and try to stay awake for me," again, that female voice says, a little louder this time.

Fuck, I'm cold.

I scan the people hovering over me when someone pushes hard against my side. I groan, gritting my teeth as the pain shoots through me.

Motherfucker!

"Mr. Carsen, can you focus on me?" a petite woman asks as she leans over me, blocking the lights. I try to suppress the pain and focus on her sweet voice. My gaze lands on her beautiful face to see the most stunning light golden eyes sparkling back at me.

Angel eyes. She's beautiful.

She can't be real. The shimmering gold twinkle pulls me in as tears pool up before cascading down the sides of my face. Not wanting to lose eye contact with this woman, I blink faster, trying to eliminate my tears.

Jesus, the pain. I'm so fucking cold.

"That's it, look at me." She smiles, and my heart constricts.

1

Darkness slowly lines my outer vision, making everything blurry.

"No, stay with me." The woman with angelic eyes rushes out with concern. It's the last thing I see before the darkness consumes me.

"Ms. Rogers, please calm down. He's going to be alright. It will take some time for him to come around, but I promise you he'll be okay." A female voice hums next to me.

Goddamn, that voice. Where the fuck am I?

I try to open my eyes, but they feel so heavy, like something is restricting them from opening. I hear a faint sound of crying.

"He has to be okay," a voice quietly cries out.

Legs.

The sound of Izzy's muffled voice jolts me into a protective mode. *She's crying.* I try to move my body, but it feels like a Mack truck hit me.

I groan.

The room goes silent.

I feel a cool rush move up my arm as my body relaxes, sagging weightlessly against the bed. My head is foggy, but flashes of what happened come flooding in—

Going to Izzy's old apartment.

Being caught off guard by her previous kidnapper, Miguel, and his brother.

Protect. Izzy.

My heart starts to race.

"Mr. Carsen, you need to relax," a familiar voice whispers softly.

"Dallas. Please wake up," Izzy cries.

But the memories keep coming like I'm still there.

Dallas

Nick, my club brother, was shot in the head.
Jumping in front of Izzy.
Protect. Izzy.
Several gunshots hitting my body.
Izzy shooting Miguel.
Me shooting his brother.
My club brothers rushing in, guns drawn.
My head becomes hazy as my last thought fades away...
Protect. Izzy.

A hand grips my wrist, stirring me awake, and when I grab the hand in mine, the person gasps.

"Mr. Carsen?" a female voice, sounding startled, questions.

My eyes flutter open, trying to focus, but everything is blurry.

"Alec," the soft, sweet voice says. I keep blinking my eyes, clearing my vision without turning my head in her direction.

"Dallas," the woman's voice says louder, demanding, sounding sexy as fuck. Grabbing my attention, I tilt my head toward the alluring voice, blinking slowly.

"Can you focus on me, Alec?"

A dark-haired woman leaning toward me starts to come into focus.

"I'm Dr. Hart. You're in the hospital," she explains.

When my eyes finally focus, I'm the one taken off guard. Sucking in a deep breath as I lock eyes with my golden-eyed angel.

Fuck me. She wasn't a dream.

She straightens, smiling down at me as she pulls something from her white coat.

"Mr. Carsen, can you follow my fingers?" she asks, leaning over me again while flashing a light in my eyes, sliding a finger in front of me. I blink, not moving my eyes off hers.

"Can you tell me the last thing you remember?" she questions, straightening without breaking eye contact. I blink another slow blink.

"Are you fu-real," I rasp, my voice scratchy and dry.

She laughs, squeezing my hand, sending a wave of electricity through me. I break our stare to glance down at our joined hands. I squeeze back.

"Good!"

I snap my eyes back to her, seeing her smile widen. *Who the fuck is this bitch?* Christ, she looks like a goddamn angel standing there in all white with her brown hair flowing softly around her face and those fucking eyes. *She can't be real—this has to be a joke.*

"Let me get the nurse, and she'll get you some water. You lost a lot of blood…" I don't hear anything else she says because I can't take my focus off her angelic eyes glistening and her perfectly shaped mouth.

Well, I must have enough blood pumping in my lower region. My cock stirs to life, making me chuckle. I wince in pain, gripping her hand tighter.

She places her other hand on my shoulder, telling me to relax. *How the fuck can I relax with this bitch touching me?*

I look up to see the concern in her sparkling eyes. I'm transfixed on them. They're so light, I can't stop looking at her. Suddenly, the door flies open, both of us snapping our heads toward the entrance, breaking our connection. I feel her hand quickly leave my shoulder as she releases my hand.

I groan loudly.

Fury erupts inside me for the interruption until I hear Izzy cry out. "Oh, God. He's awake."

Izzy moves to the other side of my hospital bed, grabbing my hand. She's crying, but when she locks eyes with me, she suddenly becomes angry.

Dallas

"Dallas, don't you *ever* fucking do that again. Or *I'll* shoot you myself," she scolds me as tears fall from her eyes.

I chuckle, but my throat is so dry, I cough.

All my brothers filter in behind Izzy, full of smiles. My heart constricts as the love of my brothers fills the room.

I sense the doctor tense next to me but only for a split second before she masks it with a smile. I don't think anything of it since that's the typical reaction we get from people that don't know us.

"I'll send the nurse in with some water. I'll let you visit for a bit, but I'll be back to check on you later," the doctor says to me before slightly bowing her head. I can tell she's uncomfortable as she starts to maneuver her way around the men. "Mr. Carsen still needs his rest, so please try not to overwhelm him with too many visitors," she states once she's at the end of the bed.

I become irritated watching her leave. I try to stop her, but only a low groan escapes me as I watch her disappear out the door. Once she's gone and the door closes, I snap my head to Shy, the president of the Wolfeman MC and longtime friend, as he takes the spot the doctor just left next to me.

"Is she my doctor for real, or are you fucking with me?" I demand.

Shy nods his head, answering, "Oh, she's for real, brother."

The room booms with laughter.

"Christ. She *is* fucking hot. Redman, you weren't lying." Worm laughs.

My eyes snap to Worm as an overwhelming desire to beat the ever-loving shit out of him consumes me.

Jesus Christ, these drugs are making me lose my mind. I need to get my shit together.

"Easy there, lover boy." Shy laughs next to me.

I relax into the bed, closing my eyes, listening to my brothers start to give me shit about how hot my doctor is, and I smile.

2 | The Thrill

Dallas

I'M GOING BATSHIT CRAZY BEING IN THIS FUCKING HOSPITAL BED. To make things worse, I haven't had any alone time with the hot doctor. Someone has always been in my room when she comes to check on me. I'm obsessed with her. The way she smiles when she walks into the room and gets nervous seeing the boys here. The way her hair smells of strawberries and, most of all, her fucking hypnotic, shiny golden eyes.

I need to know more about my angelic doctor. I begged Mac to bring me my laptop, but everyone told me no, that I needed to rest, so I put the guilt-trip on Izzy that I took a bullet for her. The least she could do is bring me my laptop. I need to do what I do best, and that is hacking into people's lives. I know it's wrong, but there isn't anything I can't hack into, and I need to learn more.

The bitch short-circuited my brain. I can't think about anything but her. Just looking at me, she has my body temperature rising and my heart racing, making me feel like a fucking teenager. It could be that I'm horny as fuck, being as I haven't had sex in almost a week, but I feel different inside when she's around me.

Mac has been in here easing the tension between us, but goddamn, each time she touches me to check my incisions, my dick instantly hardens. I can't hide it either, so I just smile and lay some cheesy line on her, making her laugh.

Today's the first day I've been left alone. Most of my brothers are heading to Los Angeles to help another brother, Quick,

Dallas

and his girl Ruby. I was supposed to be going with them. They're doing club business down there and moving Ruby to New York.

Mac, the vice president of our New York chapter, and Gus, a prospect, are staying behind to watch over the clubhouse and ol' ladies. I told them to go take care of business, so I have a few hours to myself before they return. Now I just need Doc to come in.

Anxious, I try to preoccupy myself with watching ESPN, but nothing is working. I'm all amped up. I'm never this excited about seeing a girl. Yeah, getting pussy maybe, but not like this!

The door slowly swings open. "Mr. Carsen, how are you feeling today?"

Fucking finally!

Christ, that voice of hers, it's like a siren calling my dick to attention.

"*I* would be better if *you* told me *your* name?" I say with a smile. I place my hands over my lap and lift a leg slightly, trying to hide my growing erection.

The doctor looks up from her device and notices we're alone. She smiles, moving to the side of my bed, placing her tablet next to me. I hold my breath, anticipating her touching me. Every time she lays a finger on me, a jolt of electricity shoots through my body.

Her eyes lock with mine, she places her hands into her lab jacket pockets. I let out my breath, slightly disappointed that she didn't touch me. She smiles the biggest, most beautiful smile ever, making her eyes twinkle.

Goddamn, this bitch is fine.

"My name? Is that your question for the day?" she teases. Mac and I have been making bets, questioning her about her personal life, trying to get some information on her.

I raise an eyebrow, amused. "No, Mac will be here later for that question. I just want to know your name."

Her face is flushed. She licks her lips, making me groan.

"Do you have to be so fucking beautiful?" I breathe at the same time she answers me.

"Lee."

We both smile.

I shift my bulging cock, wincing in pain as I try to move my torso. She moves to check my injuries, but I stop her. "Doc, you touch me, and I swear to God, I'll bust a nut."

She stops instantly, shocked eyes snapping up to meet mine, her mouth forming an 'O.'

I chuckle.

Her face turns a darker shade of pink. Nervously, she swipes her loose strands of hair that have fallen from her long ponytail behind her ear.

"Mr. Carsen."

I correct her, "Dallas."

"Alec," she replies stubbornly, waiting to see my reaction.

I don't say anything because I like hearing my real name rolling off those voluptuous lips of hers.

She chuckles. "Alec, why don't you tell me why everyone calls you Dallas. Maybe that will preoccupy your mind so I can check your injuries. Because I need to touch you to do my job." Her voice is low and sultry, not hiding that I affect her just as much as she does me.

I give her a seductive smirk. "I don't think it will help, but don't say I didn't warn you. My buddy has a mind of his own."

The doctor gives me a curious look as her eyebrow raises in question, but the good doctor doesn't bite and ask me if I just called my dick *my buddy*.

Leaning back, I lower my leg, removing my hands from my lap, releasing my cock that I've been holding down against my stomach.

Instantly a tent forms as my dick pops up, leaving nothing

Dallas

to the imagination. I'm not shy. My dick's a good size, with more girth than average.

My hottie doctor's eyes grow wide, licking her lips, showing me just how much I affect her.

Smirking at her, I ask, "What was your question again?"

She half coughs, half laughs, shaking her head. When she finally moves her lustful eyes from my cock up to meet mine. I give her my pearly whites and chuckle.

She clears her throat. "Dallas."

I smile. "Yeeees," dragging out the word.

Raising her brow, she says, "That was the question. Why the name Dallas?"

She reaches out her hands toward my gown, but instead of pulling the gown up on the side, she pulls it down from my shoulders to inspect my wounds.

"Dallas is my road name. I've been Dallas most of my life." I chuckle but instantly stop when I smell her strawberry-scented hair as she leans slightly over me. I take a deep breath in, making it evident that I'm smelling her.

When her tiny delicate fingers touch my skin around one of my wounds, I suck in another deep breath. She tilts her head toward me, darting her eyes to me.

"Did you just smell me, Mr. Carsen?" she asks in a flirty voice.

I smile, showing her my *come fuck me* smile. "Why, yes, Lee. *I did* smell you, just like I do every day. It's one of the highlights of my day," I reply warmly.

She smirks, moving her fingertips over the tattoos covering my chest, and my body automatically tenses.

"Try to relax, Mr. Carsen," she says calmly.

Yeah, right, Doc, like that's going to happen.

"What's the meaning behind this tattoo? Who's the woman?" she asks, pointing to my shoulder tattoo with the picture of a woman inside a wolf's mouth.

"The woman is my mom, and the wolf is our club's insignia, symbolizing protection over her," I say emotionlessly, even though every ounce of me wants to punch something. I don't like talking about my mom. It brings up too many memories.

When she slides her fingers down my side to the gunshot wound lowest on my waist, goose bumps trail behind them, tensing every muscle along the way, making my cock jolt up. I guess her plan to distract me didn't work. One touch from her, and my brain goes to one thing—fucking.

She giggles. "Mr. Carsen, can you please control yourself."

"Jesus Christ, Doc, I've been trying, but when it comes to you, he's got a mind of his own." I chuckle.

All I want to do is grab her, pull her down on top of me so I can devour those fucking lips of hers.

The door flies open as Mac strolls in with his phone to his ear, listening to someone talk. He takes in the scenery with Doc leaning over me, hands on my lower hip, and my dick standing straight up, making a very noticeable tent. He smiles, turns around, and exits without a word.

Lee recovers first, standing up straight, adjusting my gown, not making eye contact. When she starts to pull away, I grab one of her wrists, stopping her from retreating. She looks up in surprise and says, breathily, "Mr. Carsen—"

I cut her off, "Call me Alec or Dallas, but please stop calling me Mr. Carsen."

When I release her wrist, she slides her hands into her lab coat pockets. "Okay, Alec."

We stay with our eyes locked to one another for a few seconds that feel like minutes before she clears her throat, breaking eye contact. Smirking, she picks up her tablet off the bed that's lying right next to the tent my penis is making. I see her smirk as she picks up her device.

Dallas

When she finally looks up from her tablet, which is for only a second, but in that second, I see how I've affected her. *She wants me.*

"I'll have the nurse come check on you soon. Let her know if you need anything. Otherwise, I'll be back to check on you at the end of shift." She says softly, moving toward the door.

"Doc?" I ask, needing to see her eyes one more time.

"Yes, Alec?" she asks, stopping midstep with the door cracked open. She looks back to make eye contact with me.

She's good. I thought she would have looked at my still erect cock. Fuck, I wanted her to look at my cock again. The tent's still standing strong, and I know she can see it in her peripheral vision, so I say, "Can you swing back by here in a bit?" I pause, grabbing my buddy over the sheet, giving it a couple of tugs, trying to calm it down. "I'm sure Mac and the girls will want to ask you your question for the day." My voice is thick with desire as I grip my dick.

She smiles big, giving me her sparkling eyes. Right before she turns to exit the room, she glances down where I'm slowly tortuously stroking my cock, and with a laugh, she leaves, calling over her shoulder, "I'll see you later, Mr. Carsen."

I grip my cock even harder. Fuck, I need to relieve myself. I haven't had to take care of myself in a long time. I usually have one of the girls service me at the clubhouse.

I hear Mac outside the door say, "Doc, don't forget to come back for your question."

When Mac walks in a few minutes later alone and still on the phone, he smiles big, saying, "Brother…"

When he sees I'm stroking myself, he pauses, covering the phone, and says, "You need a minute?"

I need Doc back in here, but I just nod and say, "Yeah, give me a couple, I'll whistle."

Mac laughs. Walking over to the counter, he picks up the box of tissues and throws it at me. "If you keep this up, you might need a chaser to come in and handle this for you. I got the door."

I don't say anything but nod in agreement. This bitch's going to give me blue balls by the time I get out of here.

I throw the sheet off me, licking my palm. I grip my rock-hard cock and groan as I'm about ready to explode. I use my pointer finger to rub my precum around the tip of my cock as I start stroking myself.

Christ! It's not going to take much. My buddy's ready to combust. I'm so fucking hot for my girl.

My girl? What. The. Fuck.

I lean my head back against the pillow and close my eyes, picturing her leaning over me with that intoxicating scent of hers. *Fuck.* I see her like she's right here. Those shimmering golden eyes twinkle down at me. Her honey-brown hair cascaded around her face. *Fuck yeah.* My strokes quicken as my body goes taut. Clenching my ass, I thrust into my hand. Making pain shoot through my wounds. I groan. *Yea, Doc. Suck my dick.* I imagine her wet, warm, voluptuous lips as they slide down my cock. "Fuuuuck!" I groan my release as warm cum jets from my shaft going all over. I don't care that it's getting everywhere. Sated, I sag into the bed with relief.

Mac's voice booms from outside. I quickly use the tissue to wipe up what I can, and as soon as I throw the sheet back over me, I hear Mac say, "Legs, what're you doing here?"

I whistle, letting Mac know it's okay. I'm gathering all the tissues when the door opens, and Mac walks in first, making sure I'm good. When he sees the wad of tissue, he smiles.

"Hey, brother, guess who I found in the hallway?"

Before I can answer, in walks Izzy with two of my favorite things in the world, my laptop and my ball cap. She's chatting away with someone, and that someone ends up being none other than Doc. I chuckle to myself, make those three of my favorite things.

Dallas

My buddy stirs to life again, but I have my hands over him. *Fuck me!*

Mac's laughing, Izzy stops talking as they all look over to me. I'm holding a wad of tissue, and I'm probably a bit sweaty from overexerting myself.

My eyes lock on Doc when Izzy speaks first. "Dallas, you okay? You congested?"

Never breaking eye contact, I give her a devilish smile and, with a laugh, say, "Nah, just needed a good blow. I'm all better now."

Mac booms with laughter.

Doc's face turns beet red. She knows what I just did, *and* she knows I did it thinking of her.

Izzy, who is clueless about what's happened, moves toward the bed. "Well, I brought your laptop, phone, raggedy hat, and all the other shit you asked for."

I still don't take my eyes off Doc, when I answer her, "Thanks, Legs."

Doc, still standing by the door, says, "Okay, you got me here. What's your question? Ask it now so I can get back to my rounds."

I fire back, "Is that why you came back so soon?" I pause. "I thought it was because you missed me." I tease, making a sad face.

Amusement is etched across her face. I know she's affected by me, and deep down, she loves our questions just as much as we like asking them. It's become a game.

Mac starts to ask, but Izzy blurts out, "It's my turn to ask."

All of us in the room look over at her as she picks up a wastebasket, motioning for me to throw away my tissue. Before I do, I look over to Doc and smile. "Thank you," I say, having a double meaning to that. Izzy says you're welcome, but my eyes lock on those shining golden ones. She knows my 'thank you' was also directed to her. Her cheeks turn a slight pink, which I only notice.

13

Mac groans from the corner. "It better be good. So, whatcha got for the doc today?"

Izzy grips her forefinger and thumb on her chin like she's thinking. Izzy beams with excitement when something comes to her and asks, "I want to know what you do for fun. I know you work like crazy, but what do you do when you're off?"

Good fucking question, Legs.

I pipe up, egging her on, "Yeah, Lee, what do you do when you are not being a doctor?"

Lee looks over at me with a devilish smirk. "I like to go running, work out, try new restaurants, maybe go dancing—"

Izzy interrupts her, "Oh, my God. Where do you go dancing? You should come to the club when I'm DJing?"

Now that has Doc snapping her head in Izzy's direction.

"You're a DJ?" Doc asks, sounding shocked, but she recovers quickly, adding, "I mean, where do you DJ? I had no idea."

I caught her reaction. It was a flash of emotion that lasted for a split second, but I saw it. Now I just need to understand it—fear—pain—sadness? And why? She's hiding something, that's for sure.

We're all looking at Doc like she's nuts because Izzy's well known around the world, but Izzy answers sweetly, "Yes, Doc. I'm known as Legs to these big boys, but I'm known in the music world as DJ Izz. I've played all around the world, but lately, I've only been playing locally."

Doc looks still uncertain of this information as her face slips between emotions again, but this time not trying to hide it like before.

Izzy continues, "You should come to see me DJ, or go out with us when we all go out. Ginger, that comes here to see Dallas, is DJ GinGin. We're both with Spin It Inc record label."

As Izzy keeps talking, Doc still hasn't spoken. Her brain is somewhere else mentally but snaps out of it, plastering a smile

Dallas

that I'm pretty sure is fake, but they wouldn't know. But for me, who stares at her all damn day, I know she's hiding something.

Something terrible has happened to my Doc.

"That's awesome. Yes, I need to come see you perform. I love music and have traveled with some friends—"

Doc's cut off when the door flies open, almost hitting her. Nurse Cheryl rushes in. "Oh, thank God. Dr. Hart, we've been paging you. We need you."

Without another glance, she's in doctor mode and leaves quickly with the nurse, saying, excuse me over her shoulder.

Everyone in the room is quiet for about two seconds before we all start talking at once.

"She *so* likes you," Izzy blurts out.

"Brother…" Mac booms.

"Give me my laptop," I exclaim.

I need to tap into my girl's life.

There I go again.

My girl.

Jesus Christ!

3 | The Challenge

Dallas

"WHAT DO YOU MEAN YOU STILL CAN'T FIND ANYTHING on her?" Izzy asks, walking into the bathroom, gathering my things here at the hospital. I'm so ready to get the fuck out of this hospital. The only reason I haven't left yet is that I want to keep seeing Doc, but I'm getting released today.

I'm going nuts not being able to find anything more about my hot as fuck doctor. Before college, Lee Hart didn't exist. I think that's what's bothering me the most. Someone has erased her life. Or, she isn't who she says she is. But being a doctor, you would think they would do complete background checks or some shit. It's pretty hard to falsify your identity. Well, unless you're me, who can create anyone. Either way, red flags are flying, and she's hiding something.

With all the questions we've asked her over the last two weeks, I can't find anything. I've hacked the hospital files, emails; you name it, I've searched it. She isn't telling me the truth. I can't very well call her out on her shit because she'll want to know how I know. I need to get to my office, where I can do a more thorough investigation.

When I asked her what Lee was short for, she said it wasn't short for anything. The bitch is good, I'll give her that, but I'm better. I didn't push it, but now I've got to know. I pride myself on my ability to find shit out about people, especially the people that want to stay hidden. I just need to find that missing piece so I can find out more about her.

"Doc is hiding something. I'd bet my life on it," I declare.

"Maybe you shouldn't pry, especially if you *actually* like her and want to keep fucking her. Since we all know you *will* fuck her. Maybe she's just a good girl. Plus, I don't think she'd like you digging into her shit either." Izzy explains.

On paper, she seems to be a workaholic. She lives alone in an upscale penthouse, owns a Range Rover, and has a butt load of money, from what I can see. It seems she only has a work cell phone that the hospital pays for and a home phone, but no personal cell phone. I've hacked everything. Now I just need out of here to do some physical recon.

"I'm going to ask her out," I announce, but Izzy ignores me. I think she's over my obsession with the doctor. We walk out to the nurses' station, where Nurse Cheryl has all my paperwork.

When I hear her voice, my body instantly tenses up, making my cock hard. "Mr. Carsen and Ms. Rogers, I'm sad to see you leave, but I'm glad you're well enough to go," Doc says, walking up with a smile. We've all come to terms with her calling us by our formal name when she is in the presence of other staff. But when she's been behind closed doors, she calls us by our first names. "I'm going to miss your daily questions."

We all laugh.

Doc puts down the chart, looking at me, and asks happily, "Whatcha got for me today? You only get one more."

Before I can answer, Izzy's mouthing off, "Today's a two-part question. The first part is, do you think he will ask you out, and the second part is, will you say yes if he does? *Annd,* today Doc, the stakes just went up from twenty to fifty." She laughs, but I'm so pissed off, I'm shooting daggers in her direction.

Everyone laughs, including the nurses standing behind the doctor, just as Ginger walks up, handing me my cut.

Doc folds her arms, looking between all of us and then to the nurses. Just when I think she's going to answer, a nurse asks if they can put money down too.

Doc laughs. "No, it's rigged." She pauses, looking to everyone but me, and adds, "You put him on the spot, so you know he's going to ask me now. When he does ask, you'll think I'm going to say no, but I could say yes to win my money back. Sooo…" My sexy as fuck Doc puts her hands on her hips, showing me her tiny-sized waist. "Y'all need a new question for the day. I've got rounds."

What the fuck? Fuck that.

I throw my cut on as she's about to walk away, firing off, "You're right. Fuck it. All bets are off. My only question to you is, will you go out with me?"

Standing next to her, I tower over her.

Fuck me. She's tiny.

I've only stood next to her a few times, but now that I'm standing up tall and so close, I'm a giant compared to her. I smile a devilish smile as I look down at her magnificent body. My cock's pushing against my jeans.

Fuck it.

I want her.

She knows it.

And, I want an answer. We've been pussyfooting around for weeks now.

Doc looks up at me, giving me her golden eyes before she slowly scans down my body, stopping to look at my name on my cut for a brief moment before looking farther down to my strained pants, knowing damn well that my cocks hard for her.

She continues back up my body, locking eyes with me again, and says with a sassy smirk, "Nah, I don't date my patients. It's against my rules."

What the fuck. Did she just. Oh. Hell. No. This bitch…

Dallas

I'm shocked, silent. I just smile at her. I know she wants me just as bad as I want her. I can feel it in my bones. I stand there as she starts to walk away from me but stops halfway. She turns and says, "But, I have seen you naked already, so…" Pausing like she's thinking about me naked, a seductive grin spreads across her face. *Oh, she wants to see me naked again, alright.*

When she blurts out, "Yeah, no. I don't date my patients."

My body wants to react to her defiance. I want to throw her up against the wall and shut that lying little mouth of hers with my tongue shoved down her throat. Then bend her over my knee to spank the ever-loving shit out of her deviant little ass.

My Doc's a fucking little tease. Game on. I turn and laugh. "Goddamn, that woman gets me harder than I've ever been. Fuck yeah!" I look back to see her almost turning the corner and yell, "Challenge on, Doc!"

Motherfucking game on. You will *be mine.*

I hear the girls laughing, but I don't care. I pull out my cell phone and send my first text.

Dallas: Doc, you forgot to give me your personal number. You know, just in case I need you for any medical issues.

Lee: How did you get this number?

Dallas: I have my ways. So, can I have your number?

Lee: I don't date my patients.

Dallas: Lucky for you, as of right now, I'm not your patient anymore.

When she replies with the hand-over-her-face emoji, I laugh.

"Dallas, come sign your shit. The guys are waiting downstairs," Ginger snaps.

I place my phone back in my pocket and walk over to the counter with a massive grin on my face. All the nurses laugh, taking off back to work, but it's Nurse Cheryl that says something, "Alec, you know you are the first man that has gotten a spark of life from her." She pauses to look around to see who is listening. I do the same. Seeing Ginger and Izzy heading to the elevator, I know we are alone.

When I turn back to face Cheryl, she continues, "I like you. I think she likes you too. Never seen her beam or hang around a patient's room as she did yours." She stands up from behind the desk with my paperwork and walks around to stand next to me. Setting the clipboard on the counter, she points to where I need to sign and keeps going. "I think she works too hard. Several men and doctors have asked her out, but she has declined all of them. She tells me she's just too busy, but I know that isn't it. I hope you can get through to her. You don't seem the type to give up easily, so please don't. If you need any help, just call me." She points to a small piece of paper within my paperwork that has her handwritten number on it.

I nod with a smile. I start to sign my name on all the documents. Cheryl heads back around the desk. I pull her number out, slipping it into my pocket, handing her the paperwork back. She moves to make a copy when I ask, "So, she doesn't date, never married, no ex's of any kind that you know of?"

Cheryl shakes her head. "She's only lived here for a couple of years."

"No friends that come visit her?" I question.

Cheryl stops to think and beams when she remembers something. "She does have a couple of girlfriends, but they don't live in New York, so it's infrequent when she sees them, and if Lee does, she flies to them."

Dallas

Now that I can work with. I know she went to med school in Chicago, so they must be from there.

I reply, "Well, Cheryl, don't you worry, I'm not one to give up so easy."

Cheryl hands me my copies, and when I go to reach for them, she pulls them back. "But you listen here. If you just want to fuck her and leave her, don't bother. If you hurt her, I'll come after you myself. She's a good girl and needs someone to watch out for her."

I smile. "Looking for more than a fuck and don't plan on hurting her. You have my word," I say, grabbing my copy of the documents before walking away.

The girls must have gone down to the main floor because they are not at the elevator. I push the button for the elevator; when it hits me, she said, 'she needs someone to watch out for her.' *What the fuck does that mean?*

I look back at the nurses' station, which is now empty. I debate going to look for her but know everyone's waiting on me downstairs. Plus, I don't want to look like I'm crazy or stalkerish. I have Cheryl's number. If after I dig some more and can't find anything, I'll get ahold of her.

Once I'm downstairs, I move toward the girls who are waiting for me.

"Are you alright? What's wrong? Why do you have that look on your face?" Izzy blurts out, looking concerned.

Ginger laughs. "Maybe he's sad, or his pride is hurt, after the doc—" She raises her hands to make air quotes. "Denied him."

I laugh, lifting an arm around Izzy's shoulder, I feel my wounds still hurting, but I throw my other arm around Ginger, pulling both girls into me and reply, "Snow, my pride is fine. I'm definitely *not* sad. She just fueled my interest even more. Now, let's get the fuck outta here and get a motherfuckin' drink."

When we exit the hospital, I'm shocked to see my bike there. I look over, and Ginger smiles. "Doc said it was okay. That you just need to go slow, so we thought you might want to get some air."

My heart speeds up, seeing my brothers sitting on their bikes. I release the girls and clap my hands together. "Fuck yeah, my baby missed me, didn't she?"

Mac laughs. "At least one bitch loves you."

Gus fires right after him, "Is *me boi* heartbroken?"

I laugh, letting them tease me, but nothing will get me down today. Izzy heads over to Gus, jumping on the back of his bike. While Ginger goes to her bike, I approach mine.

I feel my body tense and look around, I don't see her, but I know she's around. I can feel her. *I'll be back, Doc.*

4 | The Obsession

Dallas

THE FIRST WEEK HOME FROM THE HOSPITAL, I SPENT ALL MY time determined to get over Dr. Lee Hart. I drank myself into a stupor and fucked anything around me, but nothing worked.

I was in unfamiliar territory. I've never been consumed by one woman before. I've had years of one-night stands, nameless faces, and countless sexual encounters. But I've never fixated on one woman. It's nerve-racking, and to be honest—scary as fuck.

Since my old techniques didn't work, I tried something different and threw myself into my work. With most of the guys gone, I decided to do some digging on a few of our shady associates. I locked myself up in my suite upstairs at the clubhouse. My suite is my private domain, where my personal computer, servers, and all my high-tech stuff is.

There are a few computers downstairs in the office, but that's for everyone to use. I've also set up a security system throughout the building with monitors everywhere. If someone were to infiltrate our facility, they would think they found our entire operations in the office. But all the main stuff is in my room.

I have two places off-site, where I store all of our backup servers for emergencies, that only Shy, Mac, and myself know about. Plus, no one besides club officers or their ol' ladies has been up here in my room. So, I know that in no way, anyone, including bitches, could tempt me or distract me from my work.

I know doctors work endless hours, but who doesn't have

social media nowadays? She doesn't have any that I can find. Nothing is linked to her name except the hospital. She doesn't even have a picture in her biography. I did a scan for facial recognition, and nothing came up. It's like she doesn't exist. Who does that? Someone who's hiding from something or someone.

I'm the treasurer here at the MC, but I'm known for my IT and hacking skills. Depending on which alias I'm signed into, I'm known all over the world. The dark web is an endless pit of bad motherfucking people and the best of thieves. I contract myself out to people for my hacking and tracking skills. Which is why I'm obsessed with finding out who the fuck Dr. Lee Hart really is.

I started texting her again once I knew I wasn't getting over her anytime soon. She hasn't told me to leave her alone, but she hasn't agreed to go out with me either. I still can't get her to open up about anything personal.

I was going to talk to her the other day when I saw her in front of her penthouse, but something about her facial expression made me stop. Repeatedly looking over her shoulder like someone was there. But I didn't see anyone or anything out of the ordinary. Maybe she sensed me watching her. I've watched her run around the hospital a couple of times. I didn't approach her then either, because seeing her in that sexy running outfit had me beelining it back to the clubhouse to fuck the first bitch I saw. Christ, her body's all muscle, firm, tight, and perky.

She hasn't shown any interest in any man. I see men flock all over her, but she doesn't know how beautiful she is. She keeps to herself, but I can see the sass in her eyes. She was feisty when people were in my hospital room. But when we were left alone, I can tell I got under her skin, making her sexually flustered.

When I went in for my follow-up, the good doctor was out for the day. I lost my shit. I've waited long enough, I'm going to start pursuing her. My dick strains against my jeans just thinking

Dallas

of her. Goddamn, this bitch has gotten to me like no other woman has before.

My feelings have me running around like a fucking preteen with my hormones all out of control. I feel frantic, like something terrible is going to happen to her. The need to protect her is weighing heavily on me.

I make my way downstairs to the bar where Maze is restocking items. Before I even make it to the bar, I hear laughter coming from the front door.

"Hi, y'all," Dixie and Trixie say in unison as they enter the clubhouse.

Maze looks up from behind the bar.

"What're you doing here?" she demands.

"We're going to practice some new stuff. Shy said it was okay," Trixie says while Dixie licks her lips, eye fucking me.

Goddamn, her lips are dick-sucking material all right. My buddy twitches again. Jesus, it's been too long since I got my dick wet. I'm an everyday, few times a day kind of man, and it's been over a week since I came. My obsession with Doc has been the only thing on my mind.

Fuck it, —time to release.

I give Dixie the nod—the nod that lets her know I want to fuck around. She smiles with excitement. I stop next to the bar as the girls walk up. Dixie's eyes go straight to my cock that's straining against my pants.

Bitch, this isn't for you, but you'll do just fine.

"Dallas..." Maze laughs.

I glance over at Maze and shrug before walking toward Dixie. Trixie tells her she'll meet her up there, sensing her friend has other things on her mind now. Dixie follows me to one of the clubrooms.

"Dallas, it's been over a week. Where have you been? I haven't seen you around. I've been worried about you," Dixie says, sliding past me into the room. I shut and lock the door. I start to undo my pants, just enough for my buddy to spring loose.

I point to the ground in front of me and say with a smirk, "Oh, yeah? Well, I'm here now, sugar." I lean back against the desk, resting my ass against it as I slide on a condom. I've never touched a bitch without being strapped, even for a blow job. I don't want no shit touching my buddy.

I grab the base of my cock and wait for her. She smiles, gripping my thighs, lowering herself down between my legs.

Christ, I need this.

I watch as she replaces my hand with hers and slowly starts to lick the rim. Her eyes look up at me as she tries to be sexy, but all I can see is how much she isn't my Doc. I close my eyes, tilting my head back, imagining my beautiful Doc sucking my cock.

Dixie thinks I'm excited for her as she slides my dick in and out of her mouth, milking it. But all I'm thinking about are those angelic eyes swirling with lust.

Fuuuck yes. I groan.

Dixie starts working her mouth faster, up and down my cock, like the pro she is. I grip her hair tighter with both hands, making her suck harder. She starts to moan deeper, sending vibrations around my dick. I picture Lee's soft pink lips around my dick. Her mouthwatering strawberry scent as she leans over me, calling me Alec. I push off the desk, taking control, gripping her head so I can ram my cock in deeper. *Yea, Doc. Fuck yeah.*

When I open my eyes, irritation washes over me that it's not my girl.

Feeling frustrated, I fuck Dixie's face harder, increasing my thrusts, holding her head still so I can hurry this along. It seems this little encounter wasn't the best idea, but I need a release. I try and concentrate on just the feeling of my cock being sucked to get this over with. Dixie's eyes are closed, moaning as she fingers herself while suctioning around my cock.

Dallas

Christ. I'm close. Come on, buddy. Come. Fuck!

My balls listen to my plea to come as they tighten, and all my muscles tense.

"Fuck yeah. Suck my dick, sugar. Take me," I grumble with each pump.

Dixie orgasms with a long moan, gripping her lips tighter around my dick. A deep, guttural groan escapes me as I explode into the condom.

Releasing her head, she leans back on her heels as I pull the condom off, tying it before disposing of it in the trash. Pushing my cock back into my pants, I turn around to see Dixie standing up, wiping her face off with a big smile.

"Damn, Dallas, that was intense. I want more, baby."

"Yeah, that's not happening today. Sorry, sugar, but I need to be somewhere," I lie with a smile. I try to hide my frustration. I don't want the poor girl to think I'm disappointed in her performance. But she must see something because her smile drops.

"Well, if you need anything, you know how to find me, just give me a call. You got my number," she says in a soft voice.

I smile, but don't say anything. We both exit the room. Dixie heading upstairs to practice her pole moves with a massive smile on her face, while I head to the bar for a stiff drink. Frustrated, I take my ball cap off, gripping the brim. It's something I do when I'm overwhelmed, pissed off, or just in deep thought. It helps soothe me. I place the cap on the bar, running my hands through my messy hat hair.

"What—did that not go as planned? Ya look like someone stole your cookie. What the fuck?" Maze laughs with a tease.

"I'm pissed off that I'm not satisfied after getting my dick sucked. Frustrated, and just overly mad at myself for letting one woman affect me like this." I pause, grabbing the beer Maze hands me before continuing. "You know me, I love women. *All women.* Any shape, size, color, as long as she has a pussy, I like it. I've never been a one-woman man. Never. But goddamn, the doc has it in for my cock. *Buddy* only wants her, and *he* ain't even been inside her yet. What the fuck?" I admit, sounding defeated and a little bit crazy.

"Buddy? Are you talking about your dick?" Maze asks, sounding amused.

"Yes!" I shout. "*He* has a mind of his own. Anything I do, and I mean anything—thinking, talking, or seeing the doctor—*he* does this fucking shit." I point down to my erect cock.

Maze just stares at me for a beat before throwing her head back, arms flying up in the air, as she laughs uncontrollably.

Pissed off, I growl, "This isn't fucking funny, Maze."

"Dallas, you seriously need to talk to a brother about this shit because I just can't. I can't sit here and talk about your dick like *Buddy's* a person. The boys are back next week, and everything will be okay. You're just bored. Go ask her out instead of stalking and texting her. Just have your buddy" —she points to my dick—"nut the fuck up. Use those balls of *yours* and ask her out in person *again*," Maze states with laughter.

I stare at my friend a beat, throwing back my beer. Once it's finished, I slam it on the bar, grab my hat and turn toward the door. I call out over my shoulder. "Fuck it. I'm done with this pussyfooting around. I'll be back."

A half hour later, I'm sitting a few blocks away from the hospital on my motorcycle, listening to "Sure Thing" by Miguel when I get a call.

"What're ya doing right now?" Mac bellows through the phone.

"Nothing, just handling some business. Why? What's up?" I ask, sounding irritated.

Dallas

"Well, Maze tells me you're having a problem with some dick named Buddy. That he won't do what you want, and you're pissed off or some shit, she wasn't making sense," Mac replies, sounding genuinely concerned.

Maze, that fucking bitch. Motherfucker.

"She's talking about my dick, Buddy. I was pissed off earlier and vented to her about how he only wants Doc," I say, trying to hold back my laughter.

Silence.

"Mac?" I pull the phone away from my ear to see if we got disconnected.

Mac barks into the phone, "Hold on." Before he says to someone, I'm assuming is Maze, "Were you talking about Dallas's dick?"

Laughter's heard across the bar as Maze answers, "Yes! He was talking like his dick was a person. I couldn't handle it."

"Bitch, you got me all amped up thinking someone was giving our boy a hard time, and it was *his dick* the whole time?"

I try to hold back my own laughter because I can see Mac getting pissed off. Good, she deserves it for telling him my business.

I hear Maze whine through the phone, "What? He was seriously upset."

"About *HIS* DICK!" Mac yells.

I look over and see Lee coming around the corner on her run, so I tell Mac, "I gotta go. I'll call you back."

He doesn't even say anything before he hangs up. I laugh, knowing damn well he's going to lay into her for making him get worked up.

Taking out my earbuds, I turn off the music that was playing before Mac called. I slide my phone in my pocket and watch her head out on her typical Thursday run. I've memorized her schedule. On Thursdays she's here all day for almost twelve hours, so she takes a long jog around the hospital.

I shift on my bike, readjusting my buddy as he fights against my jeans to be released. I whisper to myself, "Down, boy. Ain't happening, buddy." When she turns suddenly, going off her regular course, I sit up straight, trying to figure out where she went. I've watched her do this run a couple of times, and she never goes down that alleyway. I wait a few more minutes. When she doesn't surface, I become agitated. Pulling my helmet off the handlebars, thinking I'm going to look for her. I came here to talk to her, not stalk her.

"Are you following me?" a woman's voice huffs out behind me.

Startling me, I jump, snapping my head back, seeing her walking toward me from the other side.

What the fuck? How did...

"Where did you come from?" I demand.

Lee stares at me, out of breath, with her hands on her hips. I take her in as she walks toward me wearing her tight black yoga pants, sports bra-type top with a band around her arm to hold her phone. "I asked you a question. Have you been following me?"

Yes.

"No, it's not following if I'm sitting here in the open. I came here to talk to you," I half lie to her.

She tilts her head, not believing me. "You could have called or texted me. Are you sure you haven't been watching me? Like, every day?"

The worried sound in her voice has me coming clean. "Yes, I *watched* you run a week ago. I sat right here, hoping to talk to you. I wasn't hiding. I also *watched* you go into your building the other day. I was going to talk with you then too, but you looked stressed out, so I left you alone. Those are the

Dallas

only times I've actually *watched* you. So, my answer is still no, I haven't been *following* you, but I have *watched* you. Today though, I did come here to talk to you in person, not watch you."

"You know where I live?" She huffs, out of breath, looking quite angry before bending down, placing her hands on her knees, trying to catch her breath.

I don't answer, letting her catch her breath. I watch her take in big, long, deep breaths as her olive skin glistens with sweat. *Fucking beautiful.*

"Alec, how the fuck do you know where I live?" she demands, standing upright to look at me before she bends back over, grabbing her hip like she has a cramp.

"What the fuck did you do, sprint around the block to get here? Where did you go? One minute you were right there, and the next, you were gone," I ask.

Still bent over, she replies, "I cut through the alleyway and then through the parking lot." She stands up, raising her arms above her head, locking her fingers. She motions her head. "Back up that sidewalk back there. I wanted to sneak up on you. Now, answer my question, how the fuck do you know where I live?"

I don't look toward where she's talking about because I'm entranced watching her chest rise and fall. Her tits are smashed together with sweat rolling down her cleavage in that fuck-me athletic bra she's got on. My mouth begins to water.

Praise Jesus!

God was generous as fuck the day he made this beautiful woman. Her scrubs don't do her any justice. She's toned everywhere. Voluptuous, mouthwatering breasts. Tight as fuck ass. It's not like the bitch needs any more help looking angelic with those eyes, but put a body with it, and goddamn, you have a motherfucking goddess.

"Alec!" Lee yells, snapping me out of my lustful trance.

I shake my head.

"Shit, sorry. What did you say?" I reply apologetically.

"Quit eye fucking my tits and tell me how you know where I live and what the fuck you want. I need to get back to work."

Damn, she's kind of bitchy today. I smirk.

"I have my ways of finding things out. Why weren't you at my follow-up appointment?" I demand.

Lee rolls her eyes, placing her hands on her tiny waist that I can't look at, or I might get caught eye fucking her again.

"Look, you seem like a nice guy, but I don't date patients or bikers. I don't appreciate patients following me home. Now, if you need medical assistance, call the hospital."

"Damn, Doc. Who pissed in your Wheaties today? And, for the record—I didn't *follow* you home." I laugh.

She starts to turn toward the hospital, looking irritated.

"Why don't you date bikers?" I ask.

Lee turns around to face me, and without thought, she fires back, "They're liars, assholes, shady as fuck, and their only loyalty is to their club."

Well, goddamn. Someone fucked my girl over.

I'm about ready to disagree when her phone rings.

"Dr. Hart here."

Watching her listen to the caller, I'm looking at a whole different woman right now. One that makes me want to protect her. She's not the confident doctor, more like a scared, pissed-off kid. She's acting all bitchy, but her eyes tell me something different. She's tired, worried, or scared, but what I do know for sure is she ain't no bitch.

"Yes, I'll be right there."

When she's off the phone, she looks at me and says, "Sorry, I have to go. If you need me for anything, just call my phone. But, please quit following me."

I cross my arms over my chest and answer her with a big

Dallas

smile, "Lee, you will be hearing from me again. I'm not going to promise you that I won't try to see you again. But I promise I have not and will not hide from you. If I'm sitting here waiting for you, that's not following. I will be coming for you again, but it won't be on a day you're working, that's for sure. Have a good day, Doc."

She doesn't say anything, nodding her head in understanding before turning to run toward the hospital. I just sit here and watch her fine ass run away. Something's going on with the good ol' doctor, and I'm going to find out what it is.

Dallas: I'm sad to see you go, but damn, you look good going. (emoji with the tongue sticking out) Have a nice day and think of me.

Lee: I'm glad I could make your day. (smile emoji) Sorry for being bitchy. I just don't like feeling that I'm being watched. (stressed out emoji)

Damn, she's paranoid.

Dallas: Well, you need to get over that because I really like watching you. (emoji winking with his tongue out) But I promise I won't do it from afar. Dinner?

Lee: No. (emoji laughing and emoji with tongue sticking out)

Dallas: I won't stop asking until you say yes. (emoji winking with a kiss)

When she doesn't reply, I put my phone back in my pocket and get ready to head back to the clubhouse. Just as I'm about to leave, I feel the hairs on the back of my neck rise. My instinct is lethal. I might not be the biggest of my club brothers, but my fighting skills are on point. I do a peripheral check around me, not seeing anyone out of the ordinary, but I can feel eyes on me.

Maybe Lee isn't imagining someone's watching her. Or are they watching me? Fuck, this just got more interesting. No one stays hidden forever. They always seem to show their face sooner or later.

5 | The Brotherhood

Dallas

"**Y**OU KILLED THOSE FUCKERS, DIDN'T YOU?" CHIV, ONE of our brothers that just got out of jail, asks Quick. We're in West Virginia at the mother chapter, where it all started for me. When I moved to West Virginia from Dallas to live with my deadbeat dad after my mom died of cancer, I became friends with Mac in school.

When his uncle Wolfe, the original president of the Wolfeman MC, found out my hacking abilities, I was welcomed into the family. I've never looked back. I hated my ol' man, so once I became eighteen, I officially moved into the clubhouse.

Since the guys got back, things have been hectic at the clubhouse. First, we had the celebration of life for our boy Nick that was killed the same day I was shot. We did a long ride from New York to West Virginia. We partied for three days straight. Quick got engaged to Ruby at our party in New York.

But all good things came to an end when a few days later, we get a call from our biggest rival—The Black Crow MC. They wanted a sit-down. Now, this is bad because we've had beef with them since I can remember, and a few years back, they almost killed Shy, and two of their men were killed. We've called a truce since then, but it's never a good thing when we're called for a sit-down.

Our meeting is tomorrow, so everyone's partying tonight, trying to get some pussy before we head out. I'm sitting at the bar, the party is in full effect.

"Chiv, you were there, brother, you know what happened. Shit, you went to jail, for fuck's sake," I say, sitting next to Quick.

Chiv leans forward to look over at me, giving me one mean motherfucking stare down. He's tatted up, which is completely opposite of his twin brother, who doesn't have a mark on him except for the Wolfeman insignia that's tatted across his stomach.

"I know, motherfucker, but I didn't know Quick that well, and he was in New York. I didn't know shit except they fucked up Shy, two Crow bitches were killed, and they were hot on our asses for it," he hammers.

"As Shy said, you know two things, he saved him, and he got his name Quick. End of the story," I rasp out.

"I spent my time in jail. Had to be a kiss-ass, pussyfooting motherfucker in there to get out on good behavior. So, I think I deserve more fucking details than that." Chiv glares over at me.

Quick tenses up between us before blurting out, "Yeah, I did it."

Well, fuck me. He admitted it out loud.

Chiv and I both look at Quick as he takes a swig of his beer, neither one of us saying a word, so he continues in a calm, controlled voice, "You saw the photos. You know what I did. You know how I got Shy out. What else do you need to know?"

Chiv looks at Quick a beat before throwing his head back, raising an arm to grip Quick's shoulder. "Not a goddamn thing, brother. I have been waiting years for you to own up to that shit. I started thinking they made that shit up about you. You were a scrawny little fucker back then too. It was hard to believe before, but the fucker in front of me today, now that I can see." Chiv chuckles.

I laugh.

Quick laughs.

"Dallas!" Wolfe yells. I look over my shoulder, seeing him

Dallas

and Shy standing there, motioning me over to them. Shy yells, "Grab your shit."

In other words, grab my laptop. Well, there goes my plans of getting my buddy some action tonight.

When I enter the chapel, where no one but club members are allowed, Wolfe tells me to shut the door.

"What's up?" I ask, sitting down, placing my laptop on the table. Usually, we're not allowed any electronics in here, but that's only for when we have an all-member "church" meeting. I never bring it unless I'm instructed to.

Wolfe speaks up first. "Have you heard anything new from our insiders about this meeting?"

Sitting back in the chair, I shake my head. "Nah, dude told me they don't know why. Only Knight and officers seem to know."

I've got people all over the world that spy for me. Everyone owes me something for favors I've done for them.

"I want you, Chiv, and Blink next to Quick at all times tomorrow. I don't give a fuck if he goes to take a shit. I want you next to him, do you understand. I don't feel right about this," Wolfe barks out.

I nod. "You got it, Prez."

John Wolfe started this motorcycle club along with three of his best friends and is still our original president. I will always call him prez because it shows my respect and loyalty to the man. Shy understands and respects me for still calling him that even though Shy is officially my prez.

"If that motherfucker Ronny tries anything tomorrow, I'm taking him the fuck out," Shy rants.

"If he starts it, we'll fucking finish it. We're stronger and ready for this shit if it comes to it," Wolfe replies.

"Keep your ears and eyes open. You tell us the minute you hear or see something," Wolfe tells me.

They know my worth, and that's why I'll love my club brothers till death. Like our motto, Wolfeman for life, and I wouldn't have it any other way. Most people look at me like I'm the boy next door who's a computer nerd. Or, that I'm some scrawny biker white boy, which is why they never see me coming. I might not strike you with my fist at first, but I can turn your power off, freeze your accounts, or cancel your credit cards. I can fuck your life up without even showing you my face, but if I do show my face, you will remember me. I don't fight fair, that's for sure.

"Anything else? Why did you want me to bring my shit?" I ask, wondering what else they have for me.

"Yeah, I wanted to see if you had any more information on why Ronny has been entering our territory? I know you said he visits these two guys, but do you have anything else to report? I want to have something to give Knight if he gives us shit about crossing in his territory," Wolfe explains.

I power up my laptop before answering, "Nah, these two dudes have no affiliation to any motorcycle clubs. I've put surveillance on their shops, as you can see." Turning my laptop to show them live feeds of the men's shops. "But from what I can see, they're just normal dudes. I mean, one has an automotive garage. The other one has a convenience store. So far, nothing has come up. They have no connection with us, the Crows, or any business of ours. I'll let you know if I find anything else out."

Shy looks up from the screen. "Have you cased their homes? Anything there?"

I shake my head. "Nah, I've only been surveilling their shops. I thought if shit was going to go down, it would happen there, not their residence. But I can get some equipment together and wire up their homes."

Wolfe nods his head, and it's quiet for a few seconds. Shy breaks the silence, leaning forward, placing his forearms on the table. "Next time any of them come into our territory, I wish

Dallas

you would let us intervene. They wouldn't give us this pass. Why are we?"

We both look over to Wolfe, who looks deep in thought. "I want to know what they're doing. Are they moving in or trying to set us up? Why the fuck would they break the truce between us? That's what I want to know. Tomorrow we'll find out if Knight even knows about this and what he'll do when I mention it."

"Anything else to report with the new search?" Wolfe asks.

"You mean Frank Mancini?" I clarify.

Frank is one scary motherfucker, and I've seen my fair share of scary fuckers. I have a feeling his link to the Italian Mafia is more significant than we thought, but I'm not going to say that until I have my proof.

When Wolfe gives me a nod, I continue, "Well, I've only dug into his travel activity, and he's been in the States more than we thought. I don't know how much Luc knows about his whereabouts, but I've tracked him all over the state. I'm still digging. I'll have a full report for you by next week."

"Do you have any idea if Luc and Frank are, in fact, estranged, or is that all for a show? I want to know if they communicate," Wolfe says.

"Do you think they're hiding something?" Shy asks, sounding shocked.

"I don't know. Luc definitely hates Frank and has for years, but that family is linked together somehow. Luc and I have been friends for a long time. I know for sure all his businesses are entirely legal, while Frank's empire is altogether illegal. Luc and Beau have always come to me when they need anything on the unlawful side done. In all my time knowing Luc, I've never dealt with or met Frank. Luc's always been firm on his hatred for his uncle, so I've never really dug too deep, but..." he trails off.

"But... since meeting him, you think differently now?" I question.

Wolfe rubs his jawline, nodding his head. Shy and I both nod back, understanding.

"Well, I'll make some calls and do some digging to see if I can find anything else out," I say, powering down my laptop.

Wolfe stands up, pushing his chair back. "Let me know what you find out. I need a motherfucking drink."

I follow Shy out of the chapel and head toward my old room—the room I used to live in for years before I moved to New York. I need to have some privacy to do my investigation. Hopefully, I can finish in time to get some much-needed partying in before tomorrow.

6 | The Sit-down

Dallas

Hawk, the treasurer of the West Virginia chapter and one of the original five members, has been my mentor of sorts through the years. We both work together to get intel for the club. He showed me the ropes and how the structure of a club worked while I did most of the hacking for them.

We've been close and still work side by side to handle all the searches and so forth for the club. We helped Wolfe decide where to have the meeting since Knight, the Black Crows president, called the meeting, we got to pick the place.

Wolfe picked Shooters Bar and Grill, off the beaten path in the middle of nowhere. It's on the border of Tennessee and Virginia. Bristol's the owner of the bar and a good friend of the club. He welcomes all bikers and is not affiliated with any club. I've met the dude more than a few times, and he's one big motherfucker. The nicest guy you'll meet, but don't fuck with him or his bar.

He has one rule and one rule only, no fighting inside his bar. If you need to fight or do business, you do it outside. If you fuck up inside his bar, there will be consequences.

As of this morning, I still haven't heard anything new from my sources regarding this meeting. Everyone's on edge, feeling like we might be walking into an ambush.

Wolfe's at the head of the table across from Knight. Only the presidents and vice presidents are sitting at the table, while the rest of us stand behind them.

I haven't left Quick's side like Wolfe told me, with Chiv and Blink flanking us. Knight starts the meeting, but I don't pay any attention to them. I'm looking at every Crow in here, taking mental notes of all their names and ranks.

I know that everyone has noticed that Ronny isn't here, which has me even more on high alert because that motherfucker should definitely be here.

The room becomes restless when Wolfe explains to Knight about our exchange in their territory, but when he tells Knight about his men entering our territory unannounced, he becomes irritated. Knight looks around the room and says, "Well, I wish you would have informed me because that's not okay. We have an agreement, and if I am to uphold my part of the deal, I need to know when my men are not doing their part."

Wolfe nods just as the door to the room swings open, and in walks Ronny along with five other Crows. Knight becomes enraged, yelling, "You're late. Again."

Ronny, who isn't even fazed by his president's outburst, replies sarcastically, "Hit traffic."

Knight apologizes for the interruption.

I don't take my eyes off of Ronny, who's scanning our group. Knight and Wolfe keep discussing shit, but I have tunnel vision on Ronny and his men.

Ronny snaps his head to Wolfe, who just smiles at him, pissing Ronny off even more.

Quick shifts his weight, letting me know he's anxious with Ronny here. Chiv and Blink move in closer to us, sensing the tension as well. Fuck, the whole room is ready to explode. There is so much pent-up shit.

Ronny blurts out, "It's going to happen again. If that motherfucker doesn't leave my cousin alone."

Wait. Is he pointing at me? What the fuck? Cousin?

I look to Quick, who's looking at me just as shocked. I look

Dallas

back toward the room and come face-to-face with every motherfucker in the place. I don't like attention on me, much less a whole room of motherfuckers I don't like, so I do what I do best—deflect by talking shit. Firing back, I say, "Um, you're going to have to be more specific because I fuck *a lot* of bitches. Like one or two a day."

I start to calculate all the bitches I've been with lately, and none of them have been a Crow. *Who the fuck? Fuck this!*

Of course, my shit-talking only infuriates Ronny more. He lashes out, "Motherfucking cocksucker, if you touch Harley I'll fucking kill you."

Harley? Who the fuck's he talking about?

I look over to Quick, but he looks just as confused as I do when Wolfe announces, "Knight, what's this all about?"

I look over to Knight for answers myself because I don't know any bitch named Harley, and I sure as fuck don't know any Crow whores.

Knight, looking more irritated than mad, says, "This was the other business that we need to discuss. Ronny brought to our attention that one of your Wolves has been pursuing one of our Crows. We wanted to make sure it wasn't in retaliation or anything. I had no idea Ronny had been breaking the agreement going into your territories." Knight looks to Wolfe. "I take it New York is where Ronny's been going too?"

Retaliation? What the fuck?

I'm lost thinking of the plethora of bitches that I've fucked, trying to figure out who the fuck they're talking about.

Suddenly Ronny growls, "Wait a fucking minute," moving toward us. I turn my body, ready for him to make a move, praying he will make the first move so I can end this motherfucker for good.

My brothers move in behind me, ready for anything.

Ronny points at Quick, "Rocco said it was you, but I didn't

believe it, but it is. This motherfucker is Jake Reeves. The bartender we fucked up because he wouldn't tell us who killed my brother."

A couple of Ronny's brothers hold him back, stopping him from charging over to us. Knight stands up, looking pissed off, yelling, "Ronny, back the fuck off, or I will remove you from this fucking bar myself. You've caused us enough drama to last us a fucking lifetime. Christ! Rash, you better lock that fucking down before I strip all of you of those fucking patches."

Ronny ignores both his presidents and charges toward us again. "You either killed him, or you know who did, motherfucker. Either way, I'm going to get it from you."

I can't get my mind wrapped around this bitch, so I ignore them, questioning who Quick is. I'm fixated on who the fuck they're talking about.

Harley. Har-ley. Har-lee. It can't be…

"What bitch am I fucking that is a Crow?" I ask loudly.

Knight ignores my question, turning to Wolfe, asking him about Quick and why he's a member now. I ignore them as my irritation starts to boil up inside me.

Fuck this!

"What girl?" I demand, yelling, pissed off.

"She's Ronny's cousin. Her name is Harley Donovan." The guy who was shooting daggers at Ronny, turns and now that I can see his cut, is named Rash and is the president of the South Carolina chapter.

"I don't know any Crow bitch named Harley Donovan," I state, feeling better that I don't know this bitch. They must be mistaken.

Rash fires back, "You know her as Dr. Lee Hart."

My heart stops hearing her name. *My Doc?*

"She changed her name when she moved away. She has no ties to the Crows, but Ronny's still protective of her."

Dallas

My beautiful Doc is Ronny's cousin? But how? It can't be. Is Lee, Harley?

Fury rages inside of me. "My doctor, Dr. Hart, is Ronny's cousin?"

No. No fucking way.

My mind starts to replay all the conversations we've had when Rash nods his head. I mentally close down as I try to figure it all out and put the pieces together.

She can't be a fucking Crow.
She's property of the Black Crows.
She was hurt by a Crow.

Infuriated, I growl.

I don't listen to the rest of the conversation because the only thing my brain is processing on replay is that my Doc is a Crow.

Knight pulls me from my thoughts when he states, "Dallas needs to leave Harley alone. She's a Crow."

Fuck them!

"She's *my* doctor, *and* isn't that up to *her* to decide?" I say through clenched teeth.

Knight narrows his eyes at me. "She is Crow's property."

I don't back down, firing back, "She's my doctor. I have to do follow-ups."

Knight looks at me. "She better just be your doctor and leave it at that."

My whole body tenses up, and I'm ready to kill all of them, but I don't say a word.

I need to get the fuck out of here, and I need to get home. Lee has some explaining to do.

Turning to head out of the bar, I rant, "She's a motherfucking Crow. But why change her name?"

Quick follows, along with Chiv and Blink, but none of them answer me or say a word.

I need to get some air, I'm about ready to flip the fuck out, and the last thing my club needs is for me to flip out inside Bristol's bar, causing us more issues.

Slamming the door open, I feel the brisk air hit my face, and I take a deep breath.

"Brother, you good?" Chiv asks behind me.

NO! Fuck no.

"Fuck!"

I hear the boots of my fellow brothers following me. I just keep clenching my fist and taking deep breaths.

Why lie?
Why change her name?
Why hide?
Is she in trouble?
Does she hate the Crows?
She hates bikers.
No, he said she is *a Crow!*

So many questions flood my brain, and no one can answer them but her. I need to get back to New York now.

Making my decision, I turn around, heading toward my bike but stop when I come face-to-face with my brothers. Quick, Chiv, Blink, Mac, and Shy standing there waiting for me to respond. Ready to have my back as usual. I take a deep breath.

"I'm heading back," I bark.

Shy steps forward, saying in his usual 'calm the fuck down' voice, "You should cool off, stop overnight at the mother chapter before heading back. Give it some time to set in before you fly off the handle after a long, hard ride. You'll freak her out."

"Fuck that!" I yell, pacing in a circle. I continue ranting more to myself than anyone else, but I know they're all listening. "She's a fucking *Crow* and didn't say anything. Why did she change her name? Does she know we hate them? Is she scared of them or us? I need to know. *Now!*"

Chiv and Blink both say in unison that they'll ride back with

Dallas

me. Quick steps forward, too, and agrees with me, "I get it. You need answers. I'll head back with him too. We'll make sure he's good before he confronts her." The last sentence, he says to Shy.

Shy lifts the beer that he's been holding to his lips, finishing the rest of it before speaking. "Nah, we'll all head back. I've been away from my ol' lady for too long. Give me five to talk to Wolfe, and then we'll head out as a group." Shy pauses, asking me, "Is she worth all this trouble?"

I snap my head, giving my closest friend a death glare.

Shy put a hand up, "Whoa, brother. I'm just asking, is she more than a doctor to you? I'm just trying to understand."

Clenching my hands, I say through gritted teeth, "She's more…"

Shy nods his head. "Well, let's go figure this shit out, brother. Give me five."

For a second, I feel relief my brothers are riding back with me, but it fades with all the 'what-ifs' building up inside me. My brain's on overload with so many scenarios of why. My first instinct is to grab my computer and lock myself in a room to find all my answers. But, my heart and body are telling me to go and protect her.

Protect her…

I've never felt so drawn to someone before. It scares the fuck out of me. I think that's what's shaking me to the bone more than anything. Scary as fuck. I don't care what her answers are. I just need to hear her tell me her story instead of reading about it on the computer screen.

I mount my bike, pulling my phone out. I need to zone out so I can have my head on straight for this long ride. I stick my earbuds in; that way, I can listen to music. Music will calm me down and let me get my thoughts in check. Thank fuck. I have a good ten hours of hard riding.

I have playlists from Ginger and Izzy. Ginger's playlists are all different with a lot more old-school shit. While Izzy's are more modern EDM, house, and soul shit. The way I'm feeling right now, I need some fast-paced shit to keep me alert, so I play one of my go-to riding playlists. When I click the play button, "Bullet With Butterfly Wings" by The Smashing Pumpkins blares into my ears. I bounce my head, letting the song sink in.

Fuck, I still want her. Despite all my rage…

Within an hour, we're on the road, and if traffic is good with only stopping for gas, we should arrive back in New York by ten or eleven p.m. No one has pushed me or questioned me, which I thank God for because I don't think I could handle it. I'm a pretty quiet guy, and when I'm hacking or searching, my brothers know to leave me the fuck alone. The only time I like to be the center of attention is when I'm dominating a bitch naked in front of me. Otherwise, I want to be in the background, watching and analyzing.

With the wind to my back, music blaring, and my brothers flying free next to me—I'm at peace for the moment.

We're about three hours away from the clubhouse, and we've stopped for our last gas fill-up.

"Brother, talk to me—you good?" Shy asks me while I pump my gas.

"I'm better. The ride has given me time to calm down, but my imagination is still getting the best of me. I need to see Doc and find out what the fuck is going on," I answer truthfully.

"Brother, I had no idea you and her were even a thing. I knew you wanted to fuck her, but you want to fuck anything that's hot. But, *that* look in your eyes is telling me something different." Shy leans against the gas pump, crossing his arms over his chest.

"I didn't know it either," I reply.

Dallas

Quick moves around the gas pump, joining us with his phone to his ear. Finishing up his call, I hear him say, "Okay, Rube. I'll meet you there. Love you."

Shy turns to him, narrowing his eyes, and I look between the two men and see they exchange a look.

"What?" I snap.

Shy turns back to me. "Nothing. All of *our* women are at White Wolfe Lounge."

Quick adds, "Rube's managing some girl, and she's playing there tonight, so all the girls and brothers are there. I guess it's packed."

I lose interest when they start talking about music, women, and shit.

"I'll run by the hospital and then her house. If I can't find her, I'll come to the lounge." I tell them about my plans.

Shy and Quick both get quiet. Sensing something's off.

"What the fuck?" I demand this time.

Shy lets out a long breath. "She's at White Wolfe with all the girls."

"Who?" I ask, even though I know who.

"Your Doc's there. I guess she knows the girl DJing tonight," Quick answers.

"What the fuck? You're just now telling me. Who the fuck—" but before I can finish, Shy cuts me off.

"Brother, you need to calm the fuck down. This bitch isn't even your ol' lady. You've been flipping the fuck out over her since you've met her. Christ, you haven't even fucked her yet."

I snap, firing back, "Watch it, *Prez*." Giving him a warning.

Shy pushes off the gas pump. "Relax. I'm just saying you can't just lose your shit on her because what if *she is* in good with the Crows. You need to calm the fuck down and pull yourself together. All of us will pull her aside." He pauses, placing his hands on his hips, "To answer your fucking questions, I just found out when we pulled in here, and I saw my text. *And,* I'm sure he" —he points to Quick—"just found out on the phone too, so chill brother."

"Did you tell the girls about what we found out?"

Both men answer in unison, "Fuck, no."

Shy continues, "I don't want her taking off before we can get some answers from her."

I get protective. "I'll be the one asking her questions."

"If you stay fucking calm. You can't fly in there all hotheaded. Christ, this isn't like you," Quick states.

Putting the gas cap back on my bike, I try to keep my shit in check, but I'm close to losing it. I have no control over myself, and I'm treading on a thin line of sanity. I'm anything but calm. I put my earbuds back into my ears before grabbing my helmet.

"We ready to roll?" Mac says, walking up with Chiv and Blink in tow. When they see my face, they all ask what's up.

Shy answers them. "Doc's at the lounge with all the girls."

Mac's face turns shocked. "Really? Why?"

I mount my bike. "Just more fucking questions that we need answers to. Let's roll."

Everyone jumps on their bikes, and I press play, letting "Song 2" by Blur fill my ears. Another perfect song.

Whoo-hoo. I do need my fucking head checked.

We file out behind Shy and Mac. The closer we get to the lounge, the more my adrenaline starts to flow through me, amping me up.

7 | The Girls

Lee

I'VE HAD MIXED EMOTIONS ABOUT THIS EVENING EVER SINCE THE moment I agreed to come with Ray and Vi to the White Wolfe Lounge. For over a month now, I've been battling with myself about what to do with my current situation and my newfound friends. I know the consequences, but now that my two best friends are involved, I can't say no anymore.

Not like I was going to anyway.

The instant Izzy told me in the hospital that Ginger and she were DJs, I knew my life was about to change. Adding Alec into that mix was only going to increase the catastrophe that was undeniably going to happen.

I reached out to my two friends, Raydene and Violet, who're known worldwide in the music scene as DJ X-Ray and DJ Vixen. Even though Vi hasn't DJ'd in a while, she's still well known.

DJ X-Ray is Dexter and Raydene, who DJ as a couple. Dex had some family business to attend to, so he didn't fly out here with the girls.

"LeeLee, we *gotsta* blast, ya ready?" Vi asks from the kitchen where she and Ray have shots.

"Yea, just finishing up," I call out, tying my Puma's. I'm in comfortable clothes for tonight so I can dance my ass off, and tonight should be unbelievable since Vi's tag-teaming with Ray since Dex isn't here.

It has been a whirlwind of sorts since I told Raydene about Izzy. It turns out she's been on tour with this couple, Alexandria and Maddox. Which, come to find out, they are from the same label company that Izzy and Ginger are signed and managed by. *And*, they're all really close friends. Talk about a small world.

When Izzy found out, she flipped her shit and has been texting me nonstop since. Right about the same time, Dallas, or I mean Alec, stopped texting me. It's been over a week since I confronted him on my run.

Christ, he was smokin' hot!

I was a complete bitch to him that day. Which is another battle I've been having with myself. From the moment he was brought into the ER, I've been drawn to him. I can't stop thinking of him. Yes, he's hot as fuck, but he also reminded me of...

Don't go there.

"Lee, *bouta* kick your ass if ya don't come on," Vi practically screams from the doorway, scaring the shit out of me, making me jump.

"Goddamn Vi! You scared the shit outta me!" I exclaim, holding my chest.

Vi just laughs. You would never know Violet was half Latin with her pasty-ass white girl skin. She does have long jet-black hair, and of course, her signature red lipstick. She's always showing off her beautifully thick as fuck body and celebrity smile.

When men are around her, they're immediately enthralled by her exotic looks. But, besides her gorgeous looks, Vi's got a mouth of a sailor and can drink anyone under the table with her straight-up tequila. *And*, she's scary as fuck if you cross her. She's one mean bitch. She's lived a hard life coming from a Latin familia that has ties to one of the most significant gangs in Chicago and then marrying into the biggest Italian Mafia.

"Guurl, you know I ain't got time to be sitting around. I *gotsta* be making some bread and drinking some tequila. Which reminds me, why didn't you stock up on tequila when *ya knew* I was coming?"

Dallas

"Vi, I didn't have time to get any with work and everything this week. If you finished what I have, then we'll get some more." I answer her, grabbing my leather jacket and head past her out of my bedroom.

"*Wherr* Ray at?" I say over my shoulder. My Chicago accent's always thicker when I'm around these two. I moved to Chicago after college to attend medical school, so I picked up some of their accent and slang. I moved here from Chicago, little over two and a half years ago for work.

"She's in the *frunchroom* on the phone with Alex. *Dey* swinging by *herr* to grab us before heading out," Vi answers in her thick Chicago accent. I smile as we head down the hall to my front living room, where Ray's sitting on my couch, talking on the phone.

Hearing the name Alex has me thinking of Alec, wondering where he is right now. Izzy promised me he was out of town with most of the club, but Izzy's man and a couple of other members were going to be there tonight. I was sad at first, wishing I could see him without it being a date. But, I know it's for the best. He's too tempting, and I don't think I can say no to him again if he asks me out.

When she sees us entering the room, she ends the call with a huge smile. "Someone's ready to slay the dance floor. Get it, girl!" Ray says, looking at my fit.

All three of us have some sort of hat on, me wearing an army-style hat that matches my green attire. I have on a pair of jeans, my green Puma suedes with a matching tank top. I'll top off my ensemble with my black leather jacket and gray scarf. Tonight's about getting out and dancing.

"Ray, you know I need to get my therapy in while you two are here." I laugh but am totally serious.

The girls went to Spin It Inc. and met up with Izzy, Ginger, Alexandria, and a girl named Ruby to talk about music while I was working. Raydene and Dexter have a particular style of music they always play. Even though they can mix just about any form of music, they usually stick to one style when they're together.

Now Ray, by herself, is a whole different vibe. One not too many people see since she and Dexter mostly DJ together. I don't think this group is ready for what's about to go down, especially since Vi's jumping in the mix.

Vi mixing tonight is very rare. Vi stopped doing public events a few years back, only making special appearances. So, that makes tonight that much more special. They've been sending out encrypted messages on social media to their 'lifers.'

Lifers are considered fans that have followed Ray and Vi since the beginning. So, if any of them are in New York tonight, you can guarantee they'll drop whatever they're doing, and they *will* be at the lounge to see them perform no matter what.

I know if I saw their social media messages, I would know Vi was going to be there with Ray. I need tonight, it's been a long time, and I need to escape mentally. Music and dancing are a form of meditation for me, and with these last few months, I need this.

"LeeLee, ya gonna be okay being around *dese* bikers or if we *kickback* after with *dem* at the clubhouse? Ginger, Izzy, *an* Ruby are ol' ladies, *an dey* mentioned us maybe hangin' after, but I don't wanna stress ya out," Ray asks, sounding concerned.

Vi's body stiffens next to me, but when I glance over at her, she just smiles. They've been with me through all my shit. They're actually the reason I got away from my family, so they know how I feel about motorcycle clubs. Even if this isn't my family's club, it's still a club.

"Nah, I'll be fine. Most of the men are gone, and they seem cool. Plus, Alec won't be there, so I'm good," I reply honestly.

I've heard of their motorcycle club before, and they don't know my past, so I'm good with hanging out but not getting close.

"You mean Dallas, the guy *you* saved? Izzy and Ruby were telling me how much he's into ya," Ray says, sounding excited.

Dallas

Both of my best friends have been trying to get me to go out and start dating. I can't use school, work, or my residency schedule as a reason not to date anymore. I'm settled into my new job, and my life is good right now. I could start dating again, but I haven't been ready.

Until Alec.

"Well, he definitely woke up my lady parts. *Dem* cobwebs might need some dusting off. The man's fine as fuck, period!" I say with a laugh.

"Dayum... oh-kay. Well, hopefully, we get to meet him before we head back." Vi laughs, moving toward the kitchen, saying over her shoulder, "Now let's drink."

I follow Vi into my kitchen, hoping they don't get to meet Alec because I'm trying to not want him. He's dangerous for me to be around. If they find out…"

"I'm so happy you came out tonight, Lee. It's so crazy that we all know each other but didn't know each other. If that even makes sense." Izzy laughs next to me.

"I know. It's crazy," I say, grabbing my shot, slamming it back.

We're standing at the bar in the White Wolfe Lounge, and my head is spinning with so much information they just crammed into me on the way over here.

I found out Shy, Ginger's fiancé, who I guess I met in the hospital but seriously didn't remember because there were so many of them, is also the president of the Wolfeman MC. He's the co-owner of this lounge with Mac, who I do remember from the hospital while Alec was there.

Christ, I feel like the ride over here was a cramming session with a pop quiz at the end. I glance over Izzy's shoulder and see Redman, her man, talking to a group of security guys. He's never

55

too far from her, and after what she's been through, I wouldn't blame him.

I heard what happened to her while she was in the hospital. She wasn't my patient, but I heard the stories. She hasn't brought it up, and I haven't asked. She seems to be doing okay, but I can tell her body tenses when her man isn't around.

She told me everyone's club name, which I knew Izzy's was Legs from her visiting the hospital, but I guess Ginger goes by Snow, and Ruby goes by Firecracker. Also, Ruby's man's name is Quick. It's like these ladies live two different lives. It's crazy.

"I can't believe you're best friends with DJ Vixen. She's badass." Izzy beams next to me. I follow her line of sight to Vi, standing next to Alex and her man.

"Yea, I'm lucky. They both are truly amazing DJs and even better friends," I answer. My chest aches with the thought of how much I love my girls. They truly saved me.

From what I've heard from Raydene, their tour was cut short, so Alexandria and her man, Maddox, could return to help with the search for Izzy.

Maddox, who they call Madd Dog, and Ray calls him Madds, has a crew of security men that hang around him, but I can't even remember their fucking names. I probably won't even be able to remember half of these people's names as it is, plus all the multiple names. I'm picking one of each and sticking to it.

"Christ, I feel like I'm in school again," I say, exhaling as I scan the lounge. I guess they're expecting more people than usual because the guys Redman was talking to start to move tables and chairs out. They left an area roped off for probably VIP or the club members. I'm sure we'll stay close to the DJ area since they have their own little room. The less I'm around the club members, the better off I'll be.

"Doc, these *me* brothers, Tiny *an* Worm," Redman introduces

Dallas

the two men that just entered the lounge, followed by a handful of members.

I turn my body to face them, recognizing them from the hospital. I smile and say, "Yes, I met you both when you came to visit Al—" I stop, correcting myself. "I mean Dallas. But it's nice to meet you guys officially."

They both smile big and say hello back to me. The man they call Tiny—which is entirely opposite because the man's taller and more significant than most fucking men—keeps his eyes locked on me for a beat longer than the other man. He seems friendly enough, but I can tell his mind is running like he's trying to figure something out. Suddenly he turns his head slightly toward Redman. "Does he know?" he asks. While keeping his eyes locked on me.

Does who know? Oh, God! Do they… No, they couldn't. Fuck, do they know who I am?

I shake my head slightly.

What the hell was that? I haven't panicked in years.

But panic does start to race through me when Redman answers, "Nah, they haven't stopped."

Wait. What? They?

"Does who know?" I exclaim, sounding pissed off, but inside I'm freaking out.

Both men are smiling at *me*. I try to calm myself, but when neither of them says anything, I'm about ready to lose my shit.

"Dallas," Izzy says next to me. "Tiny asked if Dallas knows you're here."

I turn to Izzy. "Why would he? Does he need to know I'm here?"

She smiles bigger. "Girl, that man's obsessed with you. If he knew *you* were here—*he* would flip his shit."

"Puh-leeze. Why would he get mad?"

"*Cos* he's not here," Redman huffs out with a laugh. The man's Irish accent would usually have me excited, but I'm too irritated.

The three men all laugh, but I'm anything but happy. Why would he be mad? It's not like we've even gone on a date or anything.

I'm not his. Not yet...

Rather than argue with these men, I grab my drink from the bar and excuse myself, needing to get the fuck away from them. Maybe I *can't* handle being around bikers without being paranoid. I'm here to dance, not get more obsessed with Dallas.

Damnit, now I'm calling him Dallas.

Ginger has been DJing for a couple of hours. She's good, and I like her style. As long as I can move my body, I like it. I'm not as good of a dancer as Vi and Ray, but I can get down.

The place is filling up. After I left the guys at the bar, I haven't really seen them. All of us girls have been dancing and drinking in the DJ booth.

The booth is like a room with a big bay window but without the window part. From the dance floor, you can see the DJ mixing. You can talk and interact with them but can't touch them or get near them. You have to go through a door, down the hall a bit to another door that leads you into the DJ room. I like it because we have our own privacy and bathroom. The place is so packed that it's getting hot out on the dance floor, but we can cool off back here while we drink.

There are about ten of us girls back here now, and Ray's getting ready to go on, so the lounge is jumping with excitement.

"Gin, you got a mic?" Ray asks.

Ginger smiles, nodding her head as she grabs a mic from a nearby shelf.

Dallas

Ray plugs it in and starts messing with the mixer as she puts her headphones on over her newsboy cap. I know she's getting into the zone. My heart starts to pump with excitement. I haven't seen Ray and Vi DJ together since I moved here, so over two years.

Fading the song down, she picks the mic up. "Are all you naughty little fuckers ready for an unforgettable night of nothing but dirty, sexy, panty-dropping vibes?" The crowd cheers. The lounge is shoulder to shoulder with people everywhere. They had to stop letting people in due to capacity.

"Well, I wanted to thank you all for coming out tonight. It was a spur-of-the-moment gig for me, but I couldn't resist since we have the legendary minx herself DJ Vixen in da house."

The place erupts in screams and whistles, including me.

"I haven't seen this place this packed and lit up since we opened it," Ginger says, ecstatic next to me.

I laugh. "Girl, you haven't seen anything yet."

Raydene laughs. Looking over her shoulder. She asks, "GinGin, can we turn some lights down *cuz* it's *bouta* go down."

Ginger smiles, nodding her head.

All of us girls scream with excitement.

Ray turns back to the crowd. "Okay, are you ready for us big booty bitches?"

When the cheers vibrate off the wall as Ray drops her first song, "Big Booty Bitches" by Bombs Away, Raydene jumps up and down with an arm in the air, pumping the crowd up before turning around to all of us girls. I raise my drink to cheers everyone. "We want big booty bitches!"

All the other girls scream, "Cheers, biatches!"

Violet moves next to Raydene and they start to move together, getting in sync. Ray is preparing for the next song as Vi smiles big out to the crowd, bouncing her upper body with the beat of the song.

All the ladies back here are moving to the song, drinking and laughing our asses off. My smile couldn't get any bigger. I'm so happy. Clubs are the only places I would go out with my girls to. I love crowded places where I can just get lost in the crowd and not worry about anything.

Ray mixes her next song by Fisher, "Your Little Beauty." Vi goes crazy, pumping up the crowd. When she starts to do footwork, I know she wants to bust a move.

I start to move but need to get out on the dance floor to really move. I look over to the group of girls and say, "Okay, who's ready to slay the dance floor with me?"

Ruby and Ginger both scream, "Hell yes!" Ginger takes us over to the VIP area, so we have room to dance. I see Izzy dancing with her man, along with a group of members with girls grinding up against them. I don't pay attention. All I want to do is lose myself to the music, closing my eyes and just feeling the beat vibrate to my soul.

I've had my share of tequila tonight, so I'm feeling really good and relaxed. I feel high just from the music coursing through my body, add alcohol, and you got a pretty fucked-up girl here.

When I feel a pair of hands grip my hips, I just keep moving but try to move away from the hold. The hands are suddenly ripped from me, and I hear a thick Irish accent growl, "*Feck* off. Dallas will *bust ya* crown."

I want to get mad, but a sense of calm washes over me. Something I haven't felt in a very long time. I keep my eyes closed and move away, raising my hands above my head, losing myself in the music.

"Lee, I'm so sorry, but I need to tell you something." Izzy's voice breaks my trance. When I open my eyes, the lights in the lounge are even dimmer, and I'm sweaty from dancing. Seeing Izzy's face, I stop dancing. "What's wrong?"

I become alert. My fight-or-flight instinct kicks in, ready for anything.

Dallas

She looks freaked out, with Gus behind her. I look at the DJ booth, where both girls are grooving. Then look to my watch, realizing I've been dancing for over an hour but it feels like only minutes. '

Jesus, I was lost in the music.

When Izzy doesn't say anything, I ask again, "Izzy, what's wrong?"

"He's on his way. He should be here anytime." Izzy looks like she's freaking out, but her man has a huge smile on his face.

"Who?" I ask, even though I know who.

"Dallas! He's coming here. He knows you're here," she replies apologetically.

I play it off by replying slowly, "Oh-kay, so what's the problem?"

Izzy's face lightens, and she smiles, "You're not mad? I told you he wouldn't be here, but they came back early. I didn't want you to feel uncomfortable."

"Izzy, it's fine," I lie.

"Oh, thank God!" she raves.

I give her a hug just as Vi announces, "You ready to lose it, only to take it and then stop it?" The crowd cheers. "Oh-kay, here you go. Remember, be kind, and grind your neighbors."

The crowd moves closer together as she drops "Losing It" by Fisher. I whoop and holler as I move closer to Izzy, making her move to the music with me. We both laugh.

Gus has one of his hands securely placed on her hip from behind her, moving with us. Izzy has her hands on my hips as I move my hands up my body, pulling my hat lower on my face before raising them above my head.

"Lee, they totally turned this place into a full-on rave! I love it." Izzy screams with delight.

I turn around, putting my back to her, and we all look out

over the crowd. It's just a mass of people moving as one. It does look like a big rave.

A few minutes later, I notice a crowd of men moving from the door. It's like the red sea opening up as two massive blond bikers move toward us, followed by a man I recognize but don't know who he is, and then I see him.

Holy. Fucking. Shit.

My nipples harden as tingles go off all over my body like it's fucking Fourth of July. My senses heighten, and for the love of God, my pussy spasms just seeing him. He looks so… so fucking *yummilicious.*

Jesus. Gorgeous + Bad boy + Biker = Iwannafuckhim.

Gus releases Izzy, heading toward the men. Leaning into me, she tells me what I already know. "He's here."

My God, he's mouthwatering. I watch him move through the room, searching the crowd as dominance radiates off him, making him feared by those that don't know him and respected by those that do. He wears a hat low, covering his beautiful emerald eyes, but emphasizing those lips I've dreamed of kissing—shags of wild hair sprout from under the cap.

Jesus, he looks good with all his leathers on. My body aches between my legs.

Yep, my lady parts are definitely awake!

When he starts to turn his head in my direction, it takes everything I have to spin around to face Izzy. I begin to dance seductively toward her. "Well, let's give him a show." I smirk.

I'm all sweaty in just my little tank top that shows off my stomach and tits.

"You read my mind. He'll go nuts." Izzy beams, grabbing my hips again, pulling me closer as "Take It" by Dom Dolla drops.

We both laugh.

This song is the perfect song. It's so dirty, grimy, and a

Dallas

completely sexual song. It's perfect. It would drive any man nuts watching us dance.

We start to move together, with our hips moving in sync. I feel Alec's eyes on me as we move seductively. I glance out the corner of my eye, seeing Ginger and Ruby move next to us with their men in tow, but I don't see him. I keep my hat low on my face so I can peek around.

Gus returns behind Izzy, pulling her back up against his chest. I release her, spinning around to face the DJ booth. Keeping my head down, I get lost in the song.

Vi drops her next song, "Stop It," by Fisher. When I start to move up and down, as the song says, the hairs on my neck stand at attention, sending goose bumps down my body, letting me know he's close. Oh, God, I feel him watching. Vi and Ray are looking straight at me, or actually behind me. I smile from under my hat, letting them know I know he's behind me.

Vi mouths, 'dayum girl.'

Ray laughs as she starts to dance again, looking for another song.

A strong masculine hand slides around my waist just as he murmurs in my ear, "Damn, Doc, you look *real* fucking good."

I smile, letting a throaty moan escape my lips.

Christ! He even smells yummy. Kill me now!

Alec closes the distance between us, gripping me tighter, so I move my hips in a torturous motion, knowing it will affect him.

The song's beat is perfect for us.

I move from side to side.

Up and down, in sync with the lyrics.

His arm coils against me, moving with me as one. I let out another gasp, feeling his rock-hard cock press up against my ass through his leathers. I've already seen his dick and have actually been dreaming about it this last month.

God, why have I denied this man again?

"What, Doc, no hello, you're not happy to see me?" Alec's deep, husky voice breathes into my ear, sending chills down my body. Feeling his soft lips against my skin and the brush of his few days' stubble has my body coming alive after being dead for so many years.

I'm speechless. My body's humming pressed against him. "Boneless" by Steve Aoki, Chris Lake, and Tujamo sounds through the lounge.

I turn around to face the massive man that I've been trying to forget. Alec looks pretty rugged right now. He's beautiful, but I know better—he's dangerous. He looks like he rode hard for hours with his windblown hair and a couple of days' growth on his face. He usually keeps his beard trimmed short, more like a chin-strap style than a full beard, but he has a few days' growth, looking more rugged than usual.

Being held in his arms gives my body a sense of hope—hope I haven't felt in many years, if at all. I've dreamed of being held tight, feeling safe, but never have I ever felt it to my bones. Only dreams.

Fuck, it feels good, though.

Alec's a good bit taller than me, so I slide my hands up his body, resting them on his chest, pressing my body even closer to his as we move as one. I smile under my hat that still shades my eyes.

Alec's voice drips with desire. "Doc, I need to see those golden eyes of yours."

As I glance up, he licks his lips, biting the lower one, giving me a salacious grin once he sees my eyes. My knees almost buckle. He's so goddamn gorgeous.

I want him! God, do I want him.

"There's my Doc," he says with a devilish smile. He moves his hips, rubbing his erection right up against me.

Dallas

Keeping my gaze on him, I smile. "Hi, Dallas." My voice is low and seductive.

His smile grows ear to ear, hearing me call him by his road name.

"What, Doc, no Alec anymore?" he says, sounding hurt, but his smile says differently.

I answer, "I thought that was the name you wanted me to call you?"

He laughs. "I did, but now... I kind of like hearing you say my name."

I fire back, "I'll call you whatever you want me to call you."

Just kiss me!

He throws his head back with a deep, full belly laugh. I look around to see all the men watching us, but the girls are lost in the music.

Why are the men staring?

When Alec stops laughing, he asks, "What should I call you?"

Immediately, I know because I've been dreaming of him calling it out while fucking me. I try to answer calmly, "I like Doc."

"Why not Harley? That *is* your name, isn't it?"

"What?" I gasp. *Did he say, Harley?*

"Har-Lee. Isn't that your name?"

Shocked, I stop at the sound of my real name. A name I haven't heard in over ten years.

Fuck! He knows.

I look around the room, but everything becomes blurred as fear consumes me.

8 | The Truth

Dallas

MOTHERFUCKER! SHE'S GOING TO RUN. I SEE THE FEAR CROSS her beautiful face before she looks around for an exit. She pushes against my chest, trying to get away from me, but I hold her tight.

"Let me go. I need to leave," Lee demands.

Holding her firmly against me, I say calmly, "No, we need to talk, *Harley*."

Seeing her reaction to me calling her by her real name changes everything. Tears fill her eyes, and that's when I know instantly that my gut was correct—she's been hiding.

She snaps, "Don't call me that name."

When she yells, everyone around us notices she's stopped dancing and looks distressed. My brothers know why she's reacting this way, but the girls don't, and Izzy tries to come over to us, but Redman pulls her away. We hear her start to fight with him. Lee begins to panic, seeing all the members move closer around us.

She tries to look over at her friends in the DJ booth, but I know Chiv and Blink are over there, distracting the girls.

Her voice cracks. "Please. Let me go. I need to leave."

I almost let her go, hearing her pleading. Fuck, it has me all in knots. I lift my cap so she can see my eyes when I lift her chin. When I make eye contact with my golden-eyed angel, I smile.

"Doc, I'm not going to hurt you. I just need to talk to you. *Please*."

Dallas

The sincerity in my voice stops her from squirming in my arms.

Tears finally escape, sliding down her cheeks. "Why? How? Fuck!" She cries out the last word with defeat.

When she pulls her hat down over her eyes, I whistle, getting Shy's attention.

"Come on, Doc, let's go talk. I need some answers."

When she nods in agreement, I grab her hand, pulling her through the crowd, making our way toward the back office area.

Once inside the conference room, I motion for her to sit down. "Doc, I just need to ask you some questions, and I need you to be honest with me," I say calmly.

When she notices the other men follow in behind me, she wipes her eyes, squaring her shoulders back with confidence.

There's my beautiful Doc.

I introduce Tiny, Worm, Shy, Mac, and Quick as the officers, even though she knows everyone. While Tiny and Worm look confused, the rest of us know what this meeting is all about.

She looks around the room at all the men and gives each one her attention with a nod, showing no fear.

Please. Please don't be a Crow.

Landing her eyes on me, she asks without emotion. "What do you want to know?"

"Is your name Harley Donovan?" I ask.

Both Tiny and Worm's mouths fall open in shock.

"She's a fucking Crow?" Tiny seethes.

Shy gives him a look, and he shuts up.

Lee fires back, "Used to be. I left when I was eighteen for college. I changed my name later legally to Dr. Lee Hart," she answers truthfully.

Fuck!

I fire off my next question. "Are you related to Ronny Donovan of the Black Crows?"

I don't look up but hear my brothers scoff at Ronny's name. She tenses, wringing her hands in her lap. She tries to hide it, but I can see right through her. *She's scared.*

"Not anymore. They're all dead to me," Lee answers with venom in her voice.

Shy jumps in, asking, "Why?"

She snaps her head to Shy, looking him in the eyes when she answers, "Because he killed someone I loved."

Hearing her say she loves someone has me clenching my fist like a jealous little schoolboy. I demand, "Who?"

Lee just looks at me, but I can see in her eyes that she's thinking. Probably wondering what we know, and sure enough, a minute later, she asks. "How did you find out my name?"

Mac answers, "Let's just say we had a meeting today with the Crows."

Fear and what looks like total, utter terror fill her eyes. "You told them where I was?"

She looks around the room frantically. She's like a caged animal wanting to escape. Lee's whole body language changes from the solid independent doctor to a fearful child ready to run.

I slide forward in my chair, grabbing her knee to calm her down, "No, Doc. *They* told *us* about you."

Shock spreads across her face as she shakes her head in denial. She starts chanting no, over and over again.

Pounding on the door breaks the tension in the room.

"Open *dis* fucking door right now," a woman screams from the other side.

Shy tells someone to open the door, but my eyes don't leave my Doc's face. I want to see every single emotion that crosses her face to make sure she isn't lying, but deep down to my bones, I know she's not and that she needs our help.

Protect her. She needs someone to watch over her.

Nurse Cheryl's voice keeps going on repeat in my head.

Dallas

The door flies open with Redman trying to hold off all the girls who storm in full force. In files Lee's two friends, followed by Ginger, Ruby, Izzy, and Alexandria, with a handful of men on their tail.

"*Wherr* she at? Lee, you okay?" her tall friend bellows, trying to get past Redman at the door.

But before anyone can answer, her dark-haired friend threatens everyone. "I'll fucking kill whoever hurts her." Her voice is deep and lethal.

I stand up, blocking anyone from getting by me. I don't want anyone near Lee, including her girls. I still need to get her story.

I hold up my hand, stopping them. "Lee's not hurt, and we didn't do anything to her."

"The fuck you didn't. She's crying," the skinny bitch fires back at me.

"Calm the fuck down. We're not here to hurt her," I demand.

"They know."

I hear Lee say from behind me, but it's low.

The big bitch snaps, "What?"

Lee says in a clear and louder voice, "They know who I am."

Both bitches go stone solid, but the other people that don't know anything ask, "Who? What?"

"They know my name and where I am," Lee tries to explain.

Ginger, frustrated, looks to Shy, demanding, "Shy, you better explain what the fuck is going on for those of us that are *not* shell shocked."

I turn to face Lee, squatting down to be at eye level with her. I ask, "Who did Ronny kill, and how long have you been running?"

When she looks up, tears are falling from her eyes, and I lose my shit. In that instant, I know I would do anything for this woman. My heart constricts.

I say in a hoarse voice filled with emotion, "Doc, baby, I can't protect you if I don't know what the full story is."

Suddenly Ruby shrieks, looking to Quick, "Wait! Ronny, in like the Black Crow Ronny, the one that wants you dead, Ronny? The same Ronny you have issues with?"

Lee looks up to Ruby just as Quick pulls Ruby into his side, kissing her on the head. "Yeah, Rube, that would be him."

Lee's eyes sparkle with hope, but for only a split second, before Shy announces, "Okay, there are too many people in here, so everyone out. Let the two of them talk. The questions can wait."

Maddox speaks from behind Alexandria. "Obviously, no one is going to hurt Lee. Why don't we let them talk, and we can discuss this after the bar closes."

People start to filter out, but her girls haven't moved. If anything, they've moved closer to us. They both shuffle up behind me, I'm sure trying to figure out what Lee needs or wants.

Lee plasters a fake smile on and says to her girls, "Ray, Vi, it's okay. I need to talk to Al—I mean Dallas. Go DJ, and I'll be out soon. Let me just have a moment alone with him. I promise I'll be out."

I get up, moving behind Lee's chair, giving the girls room to hug their friend, knowing they need to ask her if she's okay, and sure enough, I hear them whisper.

"Are you okay?" the girl I think is Ray whispers.

Then.

The scary bitch with dark hair, I'm guessing, is Vi says, "We can run. We've got you."

I chuckle to myself.

My girl isn't going anywhere.

Lee laughs, squeezing both of them

"He won't hurt me. I need to find out what happened."

They both pull away as Lee says, "I promise. I'll be out soon."

Standing up, Vi points to me. "I'm trusting you."

I squeeze Lee's shoulders with a laugh. "I got her. I promise you that."

Dallas

I follow the girls to the door, shutting and locking it. When I turn around, Lee's buckled over, crying into her hands. Immediately I pull her up into my arms, pressing her against my chest. Letting her cry, I try to soothe her, caressing her back.

Picking her up altogether, I sit down with her cradled in my arms as I begin rocking her.

"Doc, you have to tell me what happened. I can help you. I can protect you, but I just need to know what is going on."

"I can't do this again. I can't put everyone in danger. I can't. I need to run," Lee slurs through her sobbing.

I'll kill the fucker.

A few minutes later, she pulls away, wiping her tears away.

"I have only told a handful of people this story. I don't understand why I feel compelled to tell you. I don't even know you."

I try to lighten the mood by teasing her. "Well, I'm a lovable kind of guy."

"Yeah, well, that's also a problem. You're too lovable. I've known men like you my whole life. You feel too good to be true. I'm sure you leave behind a string of broken hearts. But..." She pauses as my heart aches, hearing her say that, but it's true. I haven't been committed to anyone. My mother's the only woman that held any part of my heart. When she died, a part of me died too.

"But?" I breathe.

"It's all so painful. You make me feel things I haven't felt in years." She sobs.

"Feel what?" I ask softly.

She whispers, "Safe."

Thank fuck!

When I don't say anything, she turns to me. "Why me?"

The question catches me off guard. "What do you mean?"

She moves off my lap to sit in the chair next to me, and my body instantly misses her.

"Why me? Why do you want me?"

My heart explodes. It's like she's talking to my soul. I'm spellbound, looking into her eyes.

"I don't know. From the first day I saw you, I've been drawn to you. I have this undeniable need to protect you. I can't explain it. You're right about me, though. I've never committed to anyone—like ever. I don't understand it either, but there's something about you, Doc. You got me. Maybe it's that you saved my life or something, but you got me, and I will protect you." I answer truthfully, and it even shocks me how truthful I am. I sit back in my chair, stunned. I take my hat off, running my hands through it before putting it back on.

Lee asks next. "How did you find out? What happened today?"

I clasp my hands together. "Crows requested a sit-down. We thought it had to do with club business but low and behold, Ronny flipped out, saying I needed to stay away from his cousin."

Lee's face hardens but doesn't say anything, so I continue.

"As I'm sure you can understand, I was shocked to find out it was you. They threatened us to stay away from you, that you were Crow's property."

"What!" Lee yells.

I sit forward, resting my elbows on my knees. "They said you have no ties to the club, but Ronny's still protective over you since your family and all."

Again, she demands. "What?" Her voice is dripping with hatred.

There's a knock at the door, and when I hear Shy announce it's him, I unlock and open the door to a handful of people.

Great! Here we go again...

9 | The Story

Dallas

SHY, LOOKING APOLOGETIC, SAYS, "THE GIRLS WANT TO BE IN there. Everyone has questions that I think need to be addressed. I only brought those that are involved."

Looking over his shoulder, I see Ruby, Quick, Ginger, Vi, and Ray standing there waiting for me to open the door. When my eyes lock on her friends, Ginger orders, "Alex is DJing right now. They need to be in here."

I look over my shoulder, seeing that Lee is okay, so I open the door, gesturing for them to come in.

Ginger jumps in full force once everyone is seated. "Did you know we had a beef with the Crows? Why didn't you tell us your real name?"

Lee answers without hesitation. "I didn't know about your beef. I did know of your club, though. I was hoping that would keep Ronny away. I was praying you didn't know them. I left for college and didn't look back."

Ruby's face relaxes, knowing she didn't know anything about Quick.

Shy goes next, "Why change your name? Why hide?"

Ray grabs her hand, giving her the courage to continue. "I grew up among the Black Crows. When my uncle was killed, everything changed."

I ask, "Uncle? Who's your uncle?"

Lee lets out a long breath. "My mom was a drug addict, and I never knew who my father was. My mom's brother, Big Ben, was the enforcer for the Black Crows many years ago. He took us in, and my mom became a club whore. I was left alone and was raised as one of theirs. My uncle married a woman who had a boy named Ronny. They had a kid together, Tommy."

Murmurs sound around the table, stopping Lee from continuing. Everyone is taking all this information in and putting shit together.

Shy asks, rubbing his chin as he remembers. "Wasn't your uncle killed, and no one knew who did it?"

Lee nods her head. "The clubhouse was having problems within the ranks. It was dividing. I only knew small details because I was dating a member, and he was furious with some of his brothers."

I react when she mentions dating a member. "Who did you date?" I practically barked at her.

If that motherfucker is still alive...

"Scooter was his road name. He was just a member, not an officer, but he was good friends with Tommy," she answers.

Shy gets frustrated, leaning forward, resting his forearms on the table, asking, "What happened that made you want to leave and change your name?"

Lee looks over at her friends, then me, and says, "I'm pretty sure Ronny had Scooter, Tommy, and my uncle killed. He was jealous of them and fought with them all the time. He's crazy."

This information has everyone firing off questions at once.

Quick, "Why do you think that?"

Shy, "Do you have proof?"

I ask, "Scooter's dead?"

The scary friend, Vi, starts to laugh, getting all of our attention, and the room gets quiet. I look over at Quick, who I know is freaking out, thinking the same thing I'm thinking—that Scooter could have been the other Crow that he killed when he killed Tommy.

Dallas

"I've known this girl for years. *Dese* motherfuckers are ruthless." Her thick Chicago accent drawing out the last part of the sentence.

Ruby pipes up, "How did you three meet?"

Quick looks up at the ceiling. I look over at Shy, who's looking between Quick and myself. So yeah, we're all thinking the same thing. But I pray to God that Scooter wasn't the other guy because Lee might not ever forgive him if he was. Which means she would never forgive our club.

Fuck! I need to ask.

"She saved my cousin from dying in a nightclub one night. *Dere* was a fight. He got shot. She came to the rescue. She's been in our family ever since, but that story is for another day," Vi says, looking at Lee.

Shy speaks, "Lee, why did you change your name?"

"At first, Ronny was there for me, comforting me after Scooter was killed."

I ask, cutting her off because I need to know, "When and how did he die?"

"He was with—"

Oh, God, please don't say Tommy.

"My uncle on a run when they were found dead on the side of the road."

Thank fuck!

Relief washes over me as I let out a deep breath. I can see Quick and Shy do the same.

"What?" she asks, seeing my reaction.

"Nothing, continue. Why did you change your name?" I rush out, trying to move on.

Lee shakes her head, not believing me, but continues anyway, "Ronny started getting overly protective with me and not in a cousin kind of way. I was never close with either of my cousins, but Ronny was the worst. Tommy always followed Ronny like a puppy dog. It used to piss off Scooter because Ronny was such a dick.

"My uncle favored Tommy, of course, since he was his flesh and blood, and Ronny hated it." She pauses, lost in an old memory for a second, before snapping out of it. "Anyway, he started talking crazy talk like he wanted to *be* with me. He would kill anyone that came near me again. I told him I was going away to college, and he forbid it. Without my uncle there to protect me and the clubhouse split, fighting among themselves, I didn't feel safe."

I ask, "Did Knight know about any of this?"

She shakes her head. "No, Scooter, Tommy, and my uncle had talked about going to Chattanooga for a sit-down with Knight, but it never happened."

Ginger speaks up, "Why didn't you go to Knight with all of this before you took off? Couldn't he have helped you?"

"No, I didn't know him like that. They have different rules for women. Women don't speak out, or else you'll pay for it. Plus, I was told it was against the rules to ever go against your chapter president."

Ruby asks, "Where was your mom?"

"She didn't care. I think she's still there. I disowned her a long time ago. She never wanted me. She was never a mother to me. I had nothing to lose when I took off to college."

"The only thing I had on my side was my brains and scholarships. Scooter knew I had applied to a lot of colleges and was accepted, but he died before I actually got to pick one.

"Ronny was crazy. I was scared of him, and Tommy wouldn't do anything to help me. I felt so alone, so I told them I was moving to Austin, Texas, for college.

"At first, Ronny said no, but I told him I was going. No one knew that I accepted a full-ride scholarship to a University in Tennessee. I knew I needed to plan this carefully and hope he would just forget about me.

Dallas

"It just made Ronny more protective of me. He started getting aggressive with me. One day, I just picked up and moved to a small apartment in Austin, where I got a job waitressing.

"Within a few months, he found me. I think he let me stay because he watched me and knew I had no life. Back home, he was fighting men left and right at the clubhouse. He said I was safe away from all the guys, so he let me stay. He said that I needed to let him know where I was at all times. He would visit me as much as he could, that I was his family.

"Just crazy shit. I told him I would become a doctor and help the club. I fed into his lies just so he would leave me alone. I planned and bided my time. Finally, I moved to Tennessee for school at the last minute, leaving all my belongings behind in Austin.

"That time it took him longer to find me, but he did. He found me for the second time, and that time it was much worse."

I grab her hand, needing to touch her. I want to kill the motherfucker even more now, hearing how he terrorized her.

"Lee, I'm so sorry. I can't believe you've been through all of this. How did you finally get away from him?" Ruby asks.

"Well, after the first time, I became a pro at becoming invisible. I moved around a lot. The first year and a half of college, I bounced between hotels and dorms. I just studied my ass off and worked. I learned to use cash only, burner phones, and get jobs that paid cash. I created mailing addresses all over the United States. I even changed my hair color a few times.

"But, when he found me the third time, police were involved since he beat me up instead of just raping me."

"Motherfucker!" Quick yells.

Slamming my fist down, I jump out of my seat. "What the fuck? He raped you?" My body shakes with rage. "More than once!"

Lee jumps at my outburst, and the girls tear up. Shy stands

up, ready to grab me, but I calm down. I take my hat off, running my hands over my face and through my hair before putting it back on and sitting down.

"I'm sorry, but he's a dead man," I vow to her.

"Yes, he is," Shy confirms.

Lee's eyes twinkle, but what she says next guts me. "I've had someone promise that to me before but it backfired."

"Who? How? What happened?" I huff, sounding like a fucking owl.

"I called Tommy after he found me the second time. That's when he raped me for the first time. Tommy flipped out, vowing to me that he would never let that happen again. He promised me he would keep Ronny from finding me again. Tommy did keep his promise, and that's when I got away from him, moving to Chicago.

"I met these bitches, they made me feel safe, and I thought my life was going great. I was in medical school and was, for once in my life, happy."

When she paused, the girls ask, "What? What happened?"

"I think Ronny found out Tommy was helping me and killed him. A little over a year after Tommy died, he found me," she says sadly.

Quick murmurs precisely what I'm thinking, "Fuck me."

Ray speaks up. "Well, after our girl here saved Vi's cousin, we all started hanging out. One night she didn't show up to go out with us, so we went by her place to pick her up. But, it was surrounded by cops and an ambulance. Someone called the police, and they found her beaten and bloody. Vi's cousin and his friends took it the hardest, and they went after Ronny but couldn't find him." Ray pauses, looking around the room.

She's hesitating.

"Go on," I encourage her.

Ray looks over at Lee before she continues, "After hearing her story and him finding her again, I took it into my own hands.

Dallas

I have connections with some high-ranking people, so we made her disappear."

"What do you mean—disappear?" I ask.

Who is this bitch?

"We had all her records erased, changing all of her transcripts into her new name. Pretty much gave her a new life," Ray says proudly.

"Well, I'm a professional hacker, and I knew she had a false name. I just didn't know her past. Whoever gave her a new life was good, but they should have given her life before college. She didn't exist before college. Which is a huge red flag," I explain.

I make a mental note to contact Ethan and Luc regarding these two. Luc doesn't just let anyone around Alex.

Lee sits up straight. "I haven't heard from or seen him since that night in Chicago. How do you think he found me?"

I shrug. Still thinking of her friends and who they might know.

Shy speaks, "Well, they know, and it sounded like they've known for some time. New York is our territory. They're not supposed to enter without permission, so Ronny's breaking their rules. Knight wasn't happy with him, and it seems Ronny has been causing problems for the club."

I jump in, saying, "We've been keeping an eye on him, but he hasn't been anywhere near you, so we didn't put two and two together."

"Who does he visit?" Vi questions.

I answer, "Two guys that own businesses, but they have nothing to do with either of our clubs."

Lee pinches her thumb and forefinger at the bridge of her nose, thinking. "He couldn't have known where I've been until recently. He would have tried to contact me. Especially after all these years."

Ray leans toward her, grabbing her hand. "You need to let Greg know immediately. We can—" I cut her off.

"Who's Greg? We will be protecting her from now on, and we will handle Ronny ourselves."

Pounding on the door has everyone jumping in their seats.

Quick barks, "What?"

A muffled, "it's me" sounds through the door.

Quick opens the door just as Brick, our Chicago chapter president, barges in, looking overly pissed off. Before anyone can say anything, he scans the room, locking eyes on Vi, he points. "What the *fuck're ya* doin' here?"

Vi's eyes go wide in surprise. She groans, "Fuck."

"Fuck is right. Did you not think I would find out that you were here? Two of my club brothers own this fucking place."

The fuck is this?

Vi yells, "Who the fuck cares if I'm here or not. I don't answer to you."

Shy stands up, slamming his fist on the table. "Enough. Explain what the fuck is going on."

Everyone in the room, including Ray, looks clueless as to what is going on. Brick wasn't even with us when we rode back from our meeting. He had stayed with Wolfe, which makes all of us clueless about why he's here—making this situation even weirder.

Brick, who's fuming, explains, "Vixen and I…" He pauses, looking around the room and then back to Shy before continuing, "I'll explain later. We—" He moves his fingers between him and Vi "need to chat in private."

Ray protests, "The hell you do. She ain't going anywhere with you."

Vi stands up, grabbing her shoulder. "Ray, I got this. You all keep talking. I'll go check on Alex."

Brick gives Shy a look that says he'll explain later as Vi moves toward the door.

Dallas

I turn to Lee. "Who's Greg?"

Irritation spreads across Lee's beautiful face, then she asks, sounding worried, "Is she safe with him?"

When the door closes, Ginger asks Ray, "How does she know Brick?"

Looking at the closed door that her friend just went through, Ray answers, "I have no fucking idea."

As if Brick and Vi's little scene didn't even take place. Shy says, rubbing his face, "We need to talk to Wolfe, and we need to have a vote."

"Fuck a vote. I'll do this myself," I exclaim.

"I'll be right there with you," Quick adds. "The motherfucker needs to be *dealt* with."

A smirk crosses Shy's face when he asks, "You claiming her? Are you putting her under your protection?"

I know what he's getting at—that our clubs don't start a war for just anyone. Especially the Black Crows.

Without hesitation, I answer, "Yes, I claim her."

The room goes quiet. All my brother's eyes are on me. Lee's the first to talk. "No! Alec, I can't bring this problem to you guys. You barely know me. I can't ask—"

I shake my head, cutting her off. "Doc, we've been fighting the Black Crows for almost as long as you've been running from them. It was fate that you saved me, so now let me save you. Plus..." I look to Quick, then Shy before saying, "We're the reason he found you the last time."

Lee's watery eyes go big. "What does that mean? You didn't even know who I was until today."

"Our beef with the Crows got Tommy killed. If our fighting didn't happen, he would still be alive and keeping you safe," Shy explains.

"Ronny had Tommy killed. Even his club thinks that," Lee argues.

Jesus Christ, can this get any more complicated.

Shy begins talking as he looks between Quick and me. "It's late. We just rode for ten hours to get here. We've had a rough couple of days. I need to talk to Wolfe. I need to find out what the fuck is going on with Brick. I need my ol' lady naked, and then we need to have a club meeting."

Shy pauses and looks from me to Lee. "Lee, I think you need to come stay with us at the clubhouse or go to the Mancini building, where we have a shit ton of security. Half of them are out there." He points toward the door. "That is until we figure out what to do or what he's about to do. Ronny was out of his mind today and he stormed off. I would feel safer if you would stay under our protection."

Lee is about ready to say no, but both Ray and I protest.

"I'm not leaving your side," I finish.

Ginger speaks up, "Lee, my father is the founding president of the Wolfeman, and when he finds out about this, he's going to take action. He will protect you, I promise."

Ray adds. "LeeLee, Ruby was going to have us stay there until I told her we were staying with you. I would feel better if we stayed at one or the other too."

Lee gets tears in her eyes. "I'm so sorry. I've caused you all so much trouble. It's all my fault."

Quick jumps up, taking two strides over, pulling her from her chair. The fucker's so fast, I didn't even have time to respond.

Lee is in his arms in a matter of seconds. "We got you, Doc. I promise you on my life. We'll keep you safe."

Ruby moves up behind him, wrapping her arms around him, crying her agreement.

I pull her from Quick, kissing her forehead. I try to lighten the mood like always. "You're *my* doctor. *My* Lee. *My* girl. Now let's try to savor the night and go dance so you can get dirty rubbing that fine ass all over me."

Dallas

"Your girl, huh?" Lee laughs.

Oh, Doc. You have no idea.

"Well, I'm hoping so, but I need to see your dancing skills first," I tease, and everyone laughs, standing to head out of the room.

Shy snaps his fingers at Quick, giving him the head nod, letting him know what needs to be done. It's usually my job to contact everyone, but tonight I have my girl in my arms, and I'm not letting her go.

Ronny is a dead man walking.

10 | The Vote

Dallas

"**C**ALM THE FUCK DOWN!" Shy booms across the room, trying to get the men to shut up.

"Shut the fuck up!" Wolfe yells, silencing the chatter around the table.

I pace the chapel, feeling caged. It's over capacity, with so many members crammed in here. Plus, I've only slept for a few hours. After leaving the conference room last night, I tried to get Lee to dance, but too much had happened, and everyone was in a piss-poor mood. Luckily it was close to closing when we emerged from the room, so we ended the party.

When we went to Lee's place to get the girl's stuff, we found it trashed. She doesn't think it was Ronny, it wasn't his regular routine, which was to wait for the perfect moment to take her. My guy on the inside said he had eyes on Ronny too. It could have been either of the two men I'm surveilling, but I won't know until I check the security cameras.

We took the girls to the Mancini building, where Lee cried herself to sleep next to me on the couch. I had Mac send over my laptop so I could get to work. I reached out to Ethan and Hawk in regard to the girl's background. Making sure their stories were correct.

My mind hasn't stopped running, and now I'm overthinking everything. My body is tired and aching to be near her again, touching her. I feel like a goddamn tweaker needing a fucking fix.

Dallas

Quick contacted everyone, including Wolfe, who was already on his way after hearing I freaked out and left to come home. Wolfe, Cash, and a group of them wanted to make sure everything was okay, so they headed our way. Now the clubhouse is packed with members.

"Calm down, my fucking ass. He needs to die and by our hand," Cash, who's Wolfe's VP, and one of the original five demands.

"We need to reach out to Knight. We need to have a sit-down with him," Wolfe explains.

"Fuck that!" Mac yells at his uncle.

"Knight's weak. The bastard doesn't even know what his chapters are doing, for fuck's sake," Cash chimes in again.

This meeting isn't going too well. We're supposed to be voting on protecting Doc, but it has only become an arguing match about killing Ronny so far.

"Silence!" Wolfe stands, pounding his fist to the table. The whole room goes silent.

"Now shut the fuck up and listen. We have rules for a fucking reason. Ronny will be dealt with in time. We need to reach out to Knight first. End of story! We're here right now to vote if the doc is welcome into our protection. That needs to happen first."

Ayes are hollered throughout the room.

Wolfe stands up straight, folding his arms over his chest. "Any nays?"

The room goes silent. "Alright. Doc is under our protection. Now I only want the two heads of each chapter to stay behind. Everyone else, get the fuck out. I need to call Knight."

Chatter begins as everyone exits the chapel, where we have our meetings.

"Dallas, stay," Shy demands.

I wasn't planning on leaving.

"Cash, grab my phone," Wolfe says, taking a seat as the room empties.

Cash comes back, shutting the door, and hands Wolfe his phone. We all take seats around the table.

"If anyone speaks up during this call, you'll deal with me, and it won't be pretty. I want complete silence in this fucking room. Do you all understand me?"

Everyone nods, giving their word.

Wolfe grabs his phone, dialing Knight before putting it on speaker.

"Wolfe."

"Knight."

"I was just about to call you. I'm surprised it took you this long to call me."

It was Ronny! He trashed Lee's place!

My blood boils.

He continues, "My men are dealing with the situation. I promised you yesterday I would deal with my men, and I will."

Hearing that has everyone sitting forward on high alert.

"What the fuck are you talking about, Knight?" Wolfe asks.

There's a long silence before you hear Knight exhale a long breath. "Ronny has gone rogue. He beat the fuck out of a couple of members last night and was talking crazy. Saying you took Harley."

I stand up, clenching my fist, but Wolfe's death glare has me holding my tongue. Mac moves to stand next to me, and I can see he is just as amped as I am.

"We do have her, but it's not what you think. She's here under our protection. That is why I'm calling. The doc's place was trashed last night. Do you know what's really going on between Ronny and her?" Wolfe answers.

"What do you mean under your protection. I told you

Dallas

yesterday that she was Crow property and who trashed her place?" Knight's voice booms through the phone.

Wolfe fires right back, "Well, she is *now* under *our* protection—*from* Ronny. Are you aware of him beating, raping, and terrorizing her for over ten years now? Is she *that* kind of property to you?"

I growl, pacing the room.

"What the fuck are you talking about?" Knight barrels through the phone.

"I think you need to do some research on your boy. Harley has three different restraining orders on him in three different states. He found her again, and now her place is ransacked. He's fucking crazy. Either you need to deal with this shit, or I will."

"Rash, get the fuck in here now!" Knight screams. "No! I didn't know any of this fucking shit. I knew he was crazy protective, but not that crazy. You have the girl? I need to talk to her, and we need to sit down."

"Agreed—"

"Fuck that!" I yell. Each of my brothers shoots me a death glare.

If he thinks he's getting anywhere near her, they're all fucking crazy.

"I agree. We need to meet up, but the girl isn't going anywhere near your guys. You coming here?"

"Yeah, we think Ronny's headed your way, so we're coming to deal with him. Let's sit down tomorrow. Text me a location to meet. And, if you find him first, hold him so we can deal with him. This is an in-house matter."

"I can't promise you anything. If Ronny comes for her, we will protect her at all costs. She's been claimed by one of our own."

All eyes shoot over at me, waiting for a response.

There's a long silence.

"Knight?"

"Who?" he snaps.

"We'll discuss details when you get here," Wolfe replies.

"Yeah. Well, I hope we find Ronny before he finds whoever claimed her. See you tomorrow," Knight says before hanging up.

Let him come for me.

Wolfe's voice booms across the room at me, "What the fuck did I say about making a motherfucking noise when I'm talking on the phone?"

I'm back to pacing the room, and I don't fucking care if he's mad. I want to kill all those fucking Crows.

Shy stands up, moving to stand in my path, stopping me from pacing, with Mac flanking him. My two best friends are probably the only two that can talk me down. Shy says calmly, "Brother, look at me. You need to rein that shit in. You, of all people, need to keep your head on straight for the doc. We will deal with this and protect her."

Shy grabs me by my shoulders. I look up at him, my president. I respect him more than most. I know he means it, and I trust him with my life.

"Yeah, okay," I reply, giving him the answer he wants to hear, but I'm anything but good.

"Wolfeman for life," Shy says.

The room erupts as everyone replies, along with me, "Wolfeman for life."

Mac slaps both of us on our backs with a huge smile.

Wolfe announces. "Now, we need everyone in lockdown until this shit is over and the Crows are out of our territory. I don't trust them. Everyone, go deal with all your chapters and make sure they're secure. Send members home if you need to, but we need as many as you can spare to deal with them." He pauses. "Here we go again. It's going to be a long few days."

Everyone nods in agreement.

Dallas

The room clears out, except for Cash, Mac, Shy, and Wolfe, I stare at them, waiting—waiting for them to tell me the actual plan—the plan that ends with Ronny dead. Wolfe, who's still sitting, motions for us to sit.

"Look, I know what *needs* to happen and *will* happen, but I need to go by the rules first. We don't need a full-blown war if it doesn't have to happen. Now that Ronny has gone rogue, we can deal with him. Just keep the girls here and your eyes open," Wolfe explains.

"Like you're going to be able to keep Snow here, or Doc for that matter. Good luck with that. Doc will want to go to work. We need to have a plan," Mac states the obvious.

"I'm not leaving her side. If she has to go to work, then I go with her," I tell them.

Wolfe, looking tired, rubs a hand over his face. There's a knock on the half-open door as Brick pokes his head in before entering. Unfortunately, things were so hectic last night we never did get the time to find out what was going on.

"Got a minute?" Brick says, leaning against the doorframe.

Wolfe nods his head. Brick closes the door before taking a seat next to me.

"What's up?" Wolfe asks.

Brick looks to Shy and me before answering, "Well, I thought I would kind of explain what happened last night."

"I don't understand. Were you with them last night?" Wolfe asks, confused.

"Yes, one of my prospects called me after the meeting, informing me that Violet had left Chicago and was here in New York. She left without any security. She's under my protection."

"Who is, Violet?" Wolfe interrupts, sounding irritated.

"Violet is Lee's good friend, who came here with Raydene to DJ," Shy answers for him.

"Okay. What does this have to do with us?" Wolfe again asks.

Shy and I just sit there wanting to know as well. Brick had said he'd explain later, it wasn't the right time, it was a long story. Given all that the girls went through and how tired everyone was, I let it go.

Brick takes a deep breath. "Violet's husband was Anthony Manetti, an underboss of the Chicago Outfits. He ran one of the largest crews in Chicago."

"Vi's husband?" I blurt out. *Are you fucking kidding me!*

"Thee Anthony Manetti as in Salvatore Manetti's son?" Wolfe draws out.

Jesus Christ! Can this get any more complicated?

Brick nods his head. "Yeah. When he was murdered a few years back, I put Vi under my protection. Manetti and I were good friends."

"Protection from who? Why am I just now hearing of this?" Wolfe demands.

"Well, you do know all my business with the port shipments, my relationship with the Outfit, and the Reapers, but what isn't club business is my relationship with Vi," Brick explains.

We're all quiet, each of us in our thoughts. Brick takes a deep breath before he continues to explain. "My relationship with Vi has been on the down low. Before her husband died, he introduced us, told her to come to me if anything happened to him. Vi's connection with both the Outfit and the Reapers is why she's under my protection. He hired me to be a ghost, follow her and watch just in case. Manetti asked me to protect her at all costs if something was ever to happen to him. Seeing as her cousin's the leader of the Reapers gang, and her in-laws are a part of the Outfit, he was worried for her safety."

Dallas

"Her cousin, the one Lee saved, is the leader of the almighty Reapers gang?" I question. *Motherfucker! I need to talk to Ethan.*

"Yes, Marcus Rios, he's dangerous and a feared man throughout Chicago. I just wanted to explain why I flipped out last night, pulling her from the room. Vi isn't supposed to go anywhere without a bodyguard. Her cousin is pissed off. That doesn't have anything to do with our club besides her being my responsibility," Brick explains.

Wolfe rubs his chin in deep thought. "Manetti's wife? I thought her name was—"

"Ambrosia Manetti was her married name," Brick interrupts Wolfe. "She kind of lives multiple lives as a DJ, slash Mafia wife, slash gangster familia. Yeah, it's a clusterfuck. She keeps her lives separate for the most part, but it hasn't been easy."

Everyone sits silently, taking it all in, nodding for him to continue, Brick adds, "I've kept it secret to help in protecting her. If no one knows I'm protecting her, they won't see me coming. Lately, she's been acting up, so it's been making it harder for me to keep it quiet. I promised to keep her safe, and that's how Vi came under my watch. No one's ever mentioned the Crows to me. The first I heard of all of this was last night. Vi also mentioned last night that Marcus has a soft spot for the doc and feels protective of her too."

I scoff, not wanting to hear about anyone else favoring my girl.

"Well, he can rest assured she's safe with me. I'm not letting anyone near her," I hammer out, letting Brick know she's mine.

"We don't need the Reapers coming here. Either you or Vi needs to contact her cousin and handle that," Wolfe declares.

"Already did, but I'll have Vi contact him too."

Shy fires off, saying, "Well, it explains her fearless attitude last night."

"You have no idea, brother. That woman is one of the bravest, badass bitches I know," Brick replies, shaking his head with a chuckle.

Yelling's heard from down the hall toward the bar area.

"Seems the ladies have arrived," Shy murmurs.

All the men stand up, heading toward all the commotion at the bar.

"You can't keep us locked up," Ginger yells at Tiny.

When I clear the hall, entering the room, I see six women all standing there, but only one is furious with her hands on her hips—Snow.

Here we go.

11 | The Lockdown

Lee

FOLLOWING THE GIRLS INTO THE WOLFEMAN CLUBHOUSE, I'M taken aback at how nice the club is compared to the Black Crows clubhouse. The place's filled with bikers, so I try to focus on the building's cleanliness and newness rather than Ginger yelling at these men. I don't want to start panicking or freak out, so instead, I look around the massive room.

"Where are my dad and Shy?" Ginger demands.

"Snow, you need to calm down," a ginormous man they call Tiny says to her.

"Princess! What the fuck?" someone yells.

I turn to find an older man stocking toward us, followed by a handful of men and none other than Alec.

Christ, he looks just as *yummilicious* as he did last night. My heart skips a beat as I intake a deep breath.

God, I want this man. It's been so long.

"Why do you have us all on lockdown? These ladies have to get home, and Lee's a doctor. She can't be on lockdown," Ginger exclaims.

I'm in shock. I knew Ginger was pissed off when they told us earlier this morning, but I can't believe she's talking to him this way in front of all these men.

Jesus, has club life changed that much since I've been gone?

When I was in the club life, women were never seen or heard. There's a protocol for women, how they can speak to members, or at least there used to be. They were usually only good for one thing—sex.

I hold my breath, waiting for him to reprimand her for speaking to him that way, but instead, his face softens when he speaks to her.

"Princess, you need to calm down."

Holy shit!

Shy steps up next to Ginger, placing his hand on her back. "Angel, why don't we all go into my office and discuss this." He turns to us all. "All of us. Please."

What the ever-loving fuck? Did he just say please?

I look to Vi and Raydene, who both are shocked too.

Alec—I mean, Dallas walks up wearing that sexy as fuck ball cap low, hiding his eyes again, making me look at his voluptuous lips. He probably does that on purpose—he does have nice lips. *Fuck!*

I need to train my brain to call him Dallas. The girls told me no one calls him by his real name, and some don't even know it. So, I've been trying to remember to say Dallas.

"Hey, gorgeous," he rumbles, making my nipples hard.

Dallas. Dallas. Dallas.

I smile but don't trust myself to answer him. Instead, I just follow him down the hallway. Ginger, the man she yelled at, Shy, Mac, and another guy I don't know, lead all of us into a room. Following behind me are Raydene, Vi, Brick, Ruby, Quick, and Izzy, with her man closing the door.

When the large man's eyes turn on me, I glance down to see he's a president, and his name is Wolfe. I look back up to meet his eyes. Brick is next to Vi, with Raydene in the middle of us girls and Dallas on the other side of me.

Wolfe speaks. "I take it you're the doc?" I nod before he turns, pointing out each girl, "Raydene, and Violet, am I correct?"

Dallas

We all nod in agreement, so he continues, "I'm Wolfe, Ginger's dad and president of the Wolfeman." He motions to the man standing next to him that I don't know. "This here is Cash, and you seem to know everyone else in the room."

My eyes go to Cash's cut, seeing it says Vice President. When we still don't say anything, Wolfe continues, "Seems we have a mutual problem that needs to be dealt with before we can let you go anywhere."

Ginger starts to say something, but her dad puts his hand up, stopping her. "I have spoken to Knight. Ronny went rogue last night and is possibly headed this way. It seems he didn't trash your house last night, but that doesn't mean he wasn't behind it. Knight and his men are on their way here to meet with us and to deal with him. That is if we don't find him first."

My body tenses hearing the Black Crows are on their way here, but knowing Ronny's on his way, terror slithers through me. He's coming for me. Memories flash before me, making me shiver. I close my eyes and tell myself I'm safe, *They will keep me safe*, before opening them again. *Be strong. I'm safe.*

"Until we find Ronny, you are under our protection," Wolfe says to me, then turns his gaze on the girls. "Now, I understand if you two need to get back home, and seeing as Ronny isn't after you, Brick will make sure you get home safe and are protected."

Both women shake their heads and Brick groans.

"What does your lockdown entail?" I ask at the same time Vi announces. "I'm not leaving my girl," she says, more toward Brick than anyone.

Brick fires back at her, sounding pissed off, "Vi, ya need to go home. Marcus isn't going to be happy, and when he hears Ronny's on his way here, you know he'll come, and we don't need that."

95

Vi puts her hands on her hips. "Y'know he'll come anyway with Lee being in trouble."

It's Dallas's turn to grunt.

Shit!

"You need to tell Marcus we have it under control. She's well protected. Did you see all those men out there? We have her covered. I'm not letting anything bad happen to her *again*." Dallas promises, and my heart does a flip hearing him say that. I don't know if I should cry or be pissed off. I did see all those men out there, but I've come from a club where women are not cherished, only used.

Raydene announces. "I'm not leaving her here alone. *We* don't know you. She is *our* family. And bikers have done nothing but bring terror into her life. We are *not* leaving."

Ginger fires back from beside the table. "We protect what's ours. Doc *is* our family now. She saved Dallas, just like she saved Marcus. She *is* our family too."

Oh, God. Please done fight over me.

Tears well up in my eyes hearing her say that, and I genuinely feel the love in this room.

Dallas pulls me into his side, kissing the side of my head before murmuring into my ear, "I got you, Doc. Trust us to protect you."

My emotions have been all over the place since he uttered my real name last night. I don't know how to act or what to think. I want to believe him and let him protect me, but at what cost? I can't fathom anyone dying for me or because of me.

"I'm so sorry," I say softly, looking around the room.

Wolfe shakes his head.

"Don't be sorry. We've had a problem with Ronny for many years, and it's been coming. You are just the extra push we needed to end this feud. We *will* protect you, Doc, I promise you that," Wolfe says from across the room.

Dallas

I give him a soft smile along with a nod because my throat is clogged up with so much emotion, I can't speak.

Brick grabs Vi's shoulders, turning her to face him. "*You* know *me*—*you* know *my* men. Well, these men are my brothers too. *We* all are a family, and *we* will take care of this."

"Well, I don't know you or them," Raydene spouts out, sounding irritated. I think more toward Vi keeping Brick a secret than anything.

"How does your 'lockdown' work?" I ask for the second time.

Dallas turns to face me.

"Doc, if you need to work, I'll go with you. You need to have someone with you at all times. That someone—being me." Dallas says to me and then turns to the girls. "If you two want to stay, that is fine with me too, but just know you're all stuck with me."

"And if you stay, I'm glued to you." Brick tells Vi.

I nod at Dallas and then look to Wolfe, asking, "What do you need me to do? How can I help in ending this without any of you or the people I care about getting hurt?"

Wolfe smiles. "Well, if you can take some time off work, that would be great, but if not, then we need to speak with your head of security there at the hospital, and you need to have someone from our club—"

"Which will be me," Dallas interrupts him.

"As I was saying, someone from our club that knows what Ronny or even his men look like, so that way he can't grab you without us knowing."

I nod. "Do you lock us up here? Can I call Greg?"

Wolfe laughs, "Doc, we don't lock you up, but we do keep you here at the clubhouse or at the building you stayed at last night. We just ask you to stay inside so that we can protect you, and yes, you can call whoever you want."

Relief washes over me, hearing I'm free to do as I want, but when I look over at Dallas, I tense.

Dallas's face hardens. "Who is Greg?" he asks through clenched teeth.

Aw, he's jealous. I laugh to myself.

I want to give him sass for being jealous, but right now is not the time, so I just smile at him. "He's my boss and colleague. He's the reason I'm here in New York. He knows my situation and who I really am. He'll give me time off even if I didn't have vacation and sick days available, which I do. I just need to go in and speak with him in person."

Before Dallas can say anything, Wolfe announces, "Great! Can you give him a call instead of going there? We don't know where Ronny is, and the next few days are going to be pretty hectic with all the Crows coming here."

Not looking away from Dallas, I nod with a smile.

"Perfect. Let's go meet with the men and form a plan," Wolfe says to the men in the room.

I look to Dallas, asking softly, "Can I speak with the girls alone, and then can we talk?"

Dallas smiles. "Of course, you and the girls head to the bar after your talk. I'll come find you after our meeting so that we can talk. How does that sound?"

I nod with a smile in response, and he leans in, kissing my forehead. My body ignites with the touch of his lips. I intake a deep breath and close my eyes as he releases me to leave with the men, whispering, "I got you, Doc."

Once I hear the door close, I open my eyes to a furious Raydene.

"What the fuck?" Raydene exclaims.

Ginger, Ruby, and Izzy all move to my side as Raydene turns her anger toward Vi and me.

"Ray, I understand you're upset with me, but like I said

Dallas

last night, this is not the time to discuss it," Vi says, completely calm.

Ignoring Vi, Ray folds her arm over her chest and says to me. "I need to call Dexter and my family if I'm staying with you. I need to cancel my next couple of events." She pauses, taking a deep breath. When she opens her eyes, they are focused on Vi. "I'll let this go for now, but I can't believe you held this information from me," Raydene finishes, sounding more hurt than angry.

"This is why I didn't tell *you*, Ray. You don't let things go, and it is *my* business, *not* Dexter's *or* your family. We will discuss this later after we've dealt with this situation first," Vi fires back at her best friend.

Raydene huffs, turning to walk away, pulling her phone out.

I turn to my newfound friends with tears in my eyes, "I'm truly sorry for all of this, and I pray Ronny won't cause too much trouble."

All the girls shake their heads, but Izzy answers. "Girl, we got you. *Believe me.* These men here can handle *a lot* and *will not* let you down. We have a great team of security men along with all those Wolfemen out there to protect you."

Tears now escape, streaming down my face, with a sense of security overcoming me. The girls surround me, giving me a big hug, along with words to comfort me.

Gathering myself together, I say, "I need to call Greg so he can re-arrange my schedule."

The girls disperse around me. "We'll let you girls call who you need to, and we'll be at the bar waiting with drinks for you," Ginger says cheerfully.

Vi goes with the girls, not calling anyone, as she looks over at her best friend Raydene, who is already on her phone. So, I grab the burner phone Dallas gave me last night and call my good friend and boss.

Greg answers on the first ring, sounding frantic. "Lee, where are you? I heard your place was broken into last night. I've been calling and texting you. Are you okay? Where are you?"

If Greg didn't live in the same building, I would question how he knew, but I do know—our bellman. I didn't even think to tell him to keep quiet about what happened.

Last night after the police left, we took off in a hurry. I'm sure the other two doctors and three nurses that all live in our building know as well. Great, I'm sure I'm the buzz of the hospital.

Wonderful!

12 | The Drive-by

Dallas

WE'VE BEEN IN CHAPEL FOR ABOUT AN HOUR, AND I'M GET-ting antsy. I want to see Lee and pull her away so we can talk. Hearing all the plans and everyone's thoughts about the subject has me on edge, and I need to be near my girl.

Wolfe's voice booms from across the room, pulling me from my thoughts. "Dallas, you stick with the doc. Now, let's get this place locked down before Knight gets here."

Wolfe's voice is cut off by shouting and alarms going off. Everyone is on their feet, rushing for the door. The clubhouse is packed with girls screaming and members running for the door with their guns drawn. I look toward the video screens that show what's outside the clubhouse. I see members running for cover and at least four men down in the parking lot.

"What the fuck happened?" I demand, running toward the bar. Scanning the area quickly, I see all the women, except Doc. She's not here. I become enraged.

Tiny is yelling from behind the bar. "I'm going to pull the video." Someone else says, "I think it was a van."

I'm trying to hear all the chatter when more shots are fired.

"Where the fuck is Doc?" I cry out to Maze, as she jumps over the bar with towels and a shotgun.

She points to the outside, and my heart stops.

Please, God, don't let her be hurt. Please don't let her be hurt.

I rush to the doors just as Cash is dragging in a prospect,

yelling, "Stitch!" Stitch is the road captain of our West Virginia chapter and is also considered our doctor.

Stitch yells from behind me, "Over here. Bring him over here to me."

Next through the door is Redman helping another member into the clubhouse, who's hobbling in with a gunshot wound to the leg. Maze is next to me, grabbing for him. Once outside, I just see a mass of people. Members are running down the street. As other members get their bikes started, they take off in the direction the van went.

"Where the fuck is Doc?" I scream out to the madness.

"I'm here!" I hear her angelic voice. The voice I heard when I was getting carted into her hospital. I see her on the ground, leaning over someone. I'm about to lose my shit when I see who she's working on, Chain. *Fuck!*

Chain's one of our prospects and a good motherfucker.

"We need to get *him* inside, and we need to get *you* inside. NOW!" I demand.

When I reach for her, she gives me a look that stops me in my tracks. "No, I'm helping to save your brother's life. I need my bag. Now help me or go the fuck away."

That look is something fierce, and I fall for my Doc even more. The scared, upset girl is gone, and the demanding in-charge doctor is here barking orders.

"LeeLee, here you go, girl." Vi hands Lee her medical bag. "What do you need help with?" Vi's calmness has me just as shocked. This bitch is calm as fuck, like this shit happens every day.

"I need to stop the bleeding. Help me roll him over."

Chain grunts, crying out a slur of curse words, which snaps me out of my daze. I bend down, helping the two women roll my brother.

"I got you, Chain. You're going to be okay."

Dallas

Chain doesn't speak. He just tries to smile as he grits his teeth in pain.

I help pull off this cut and hold on to his legs so I can steady him while the girls examine him.

"Okay, there are two exit wounds, but this one you still have in you. I need to get you inside and get it out," Lee demands, looking at me from behind Chain.

Shy comes up behind me. "How is he? What do you need?"

I stand up, looking at him. "We need to move him inside so that Doc can work on him."

Lee looks up, asking Shy, "How many men are down and need medical attention?"

Shy replies, "Five wounded. Besides Chain, there is one other guy who is hurt pretty bad. How bad is Chain?"

"I'm fine!" Chain spits out as he tries to get up, grunting in pain.

"The fuck you are. You are not fine," Vi yells at him, standing up trying to help get him up.

Shy bends down to grab Chain, just as I see a Honda drive up slowly from a different direction. I see the window roll down, with guns pointing—*fuck, pointed directly at us*. My instinct kicks in, pulling my gun, I push Lee to the ground just as Brick appears with his gun out, pointing toward the car.

The three of us start firing toward the car while moving in front of the girls. We put our bodies between them and the shooters. Brick gets hit but keeps going. More gunfire goes off from behind us. *Fuck, are there more shooters?* I keep my focus on the car, and their guns pointed at my Doc.

"Vi, what the fuck?" Brick yells.

I turn to see Vi next to Shy with a gun in her hand pointed at the car as well.

"What the fuck *ya* think? *Ima* let *dese* motherfuckers shoot at me? Hell nah," she yells, shooting.

The car slows, hitting the curb. We all stop shooting, but keep our guns drawn. As we approach the car, we see no movement. Brick moves around the back side of the car, working his way toward the driver's side.

"Vi, stay the fuck back." He barrels toward us. Yanking the door open, he curses. "Goddamn motherfuckers!"

When Brick drops his gun, we all lower our weapons.

"What?" Both Shy and I ask.

Brick looks straight at Vi. "Now do you think I'm paranoid? It's the Chingas."

"Fuck!" Vi breaths out.

"Who the fuck are the Chingas?" Shy demands.

"They're a rival gang in Chicago. They have been making vital threats toward my family and me since my husband passed away," Vi answers somberly. Turning to Shy, she says, "This is on me, and it will be dealt with. I'm sorry."

Brick is moving toward her when Shy answers, "Them attacking our club isn't on you. That's on them. We'll figure this out, now let's get everyone inside. I need to call some people to get this mess cleaned up."

I turn to find Doc has gone inside, and the parking lot is full of Wolfemen trying to clean up the damage. Brick embraces Vi, holding her to him as she inspects his shoulder wound. Wolfe is by the front door on his phone just as Raydene and Ginger come out running, looking relieved seeing their loved ones are okay.

Fucking shit show.

My heart aches when I don't see Doc, but I know she's working on my brother. The last thing she's worried about is me.

I turn back toward the car, to double-check that they're dead and search them for IDs.

"Are they all dead?" I jump, hearing her voice, hitting my head on top of the doorframe. Withdrawing from the car, I rub

Dallas

the top of my head to see my girl smiling, with her gloved hands on her hips.

Christ, she's like a fucking angel.

Taking my hat off, I rub my head a little more and smile. "Yah, they are. Why, were you gonna try to save them or something?" I tease.

Lee drops her hands. Moving toward me, she reaches up, shooing my hands away to look at my head. "No, I came out here to see if *you* were okay. I was worried you might have gotten shot, the way you went all guns a blazing."

She was worried about me.

My heart skips a beat, hearing her words of affection toward me. I pull her against me. "You were worried about me, Doc?" I inch my head closer, just inches away from hers. When I hear her breath hitch, I close the gap without hesitation, finally kiss my girl.

Doc slips her fingers through my hair, clasping them behind my head, pulling me down, deepening the kiss. *Fuck yes!* We both moan in unison, intensifying this long-awaited kiss. It feels so good to have her in my arms. Squeezing her closer, I slide my hands down over her ass cheeks, gripping them tightly. Reality hits me when Redman yells, "Doc, we need *ya*. Stitch needs *yer* help with Chain. He isn't doin' too good."

Breaking the kiss, we're both breathless. "I'll be right back. Don't forget where we left off," she teases, moving toward the clubhouse.

Christ, down buddy, it's not the time.

I stand up straight. My jeans stretch to the max with the extremely erect hard-on I have, along with an ear-to-ear smile. "Oh Doc, when you're done, you'll get lots more where that came from, I promise." Shifting my cock, she licks her lips before turning to jog back inside. Ginger is right behind her, asking her what she needs.

Fuck yeah. My Doc. My girl.

I look over my shoulder to see Vi attending to Brick's shoulder.

"You okay, brother?" I ask, turning to them.

I see Wolfe approaching Shy, and I stop, waiting to hear what needs to be done.

"Just got off the phone with Knight, and it wasn't them," Wolfe states.

"We know it wasn't directed at us," Shy starts to explain when Vi interrupts him.

"It's because of me. They followed me here, they're after me. This is on me," Vi says remorsefully.

Shy fires back, "The fuck it is. I told you they came here to our clubhouse. How did they know you were here at this clubhouse?"

"Who the fuck are *they*? What the fuck is going on?" Wolfe demands.

"They" —I point at the car—"are members of a gang called the Chingas. A rival gang in Chicago. Brick identified them," I explain.

Vi squares her shoulders, turning to face Shy. "It all makes sense now. I bet my life they're the ones that ransacked Lee's apartment looking for us. I guarantee they knew where I was and how to hit us. I made my plane reservations last week. We've been secretly promoting on social media. If someone was really watching me, you would know where I was. Plus, they know about the clubhouse because" —she points to Brick—"they probably know about him."

"Jesus Christ!" Wolfe exclaims, running his hands through his thick hair. "We don't need a fucking war with—"

Vi interrupts him again. "I'll leave today, so there won't be any more problems, and my people will deal with this matter when I get home. Worry about Lee and make sure she's safe. Ronny is your main concern. I'm so sorry."

Shy, squaring off with her, interjects, "With all due respect,

Dallas

we don't take orders from you. Even if you do leave, which I don't think would be a good idea right now, we are not letting this go. Yes, they may have come here looking for you, but Brick is our brother, and if he's having issues, then we all have issues. No matter who they were aiming at, we don't let shit like this go." Shy pauses to look over at Brick before adding, "As Brick said, you are under Wolfeman protection. They came to our town and fucked with our people. We will handle this. If we need to work with your cousin, so be it, but we will deal with it."

Vi opens her mouth to talk, but Shy lifts his hand to silence her. "Don't. Listen, you're not in Chicago, where you can just go around ordering us to do shit. Things don't work that way here. No disrespect, but let us handle this our way. Why don't you go check on the girls while we talk."

Brick squeezes her hip and whispers, "Go, Vi. We'll handle this. You are not leaving to go anywhere."

Vi gives him a look, biting her tongue as she walks away. All three of us watch her in silence as she makes her way toward the clubhouse. That bitch is one badass woman, with her gun half hanging out the waist of her pants.

"Fuck, Brick, you got your hands full with that bitch right there." I chuckle as we all watch her head into the clubhouse.

Brick scoffs, "You have no idea. She is a force to be reckoned with. Christ, you should see her go toe to toe with her cousin. They're like brother and sister, they fight so bad."

Once she's inside, we all turn to face each other. Wolfe pinches his brows before rubbing his temples in thought.

Brick begins to explain, but Wolfe puts his hand up, silencing him.

"Look, we'll deal with why you haven't told us ANY of this shit later. What we need to do right fucking now is figure out what we're going to do about this fucking clusterfuck of a mess right now."

Wolfe puts both hands on his hips, squaring his shoulders, showing his authority over all of us. "We're dealing with a lot of fucked-up shit, and we need to deal with it in order and together as one. So, the first thing we need to do is damage control of this situation right here, before authorities get involved. Then we need to deal with Knight and his men, who should be here tomorrow. Most importantly, we need to keep the girls here. No fucking questions. No fucking lip from any of them."

Wolfe looks to me, "You need to get to work. Find out what you can on these fucking guys here." Turning to Brick, he says, "You need to call Marcus and deal with him. I don't want him coming here and bringing his war to our fucking town. Handle that first and foremost. Make sure your clubhouse is on lockdown, leaving what men you have there to hold down the club until we get there." And last, he looks to Shy. "You need to handle cleanup, have your prospects handle bike damage. We need to be able to ride. I had already called in other chapters before this fucking shit happened, so they should be here soon, and I want all this fucking cleaned up before then. Once everyone is here, we'll sit down and deal with all the other issues at hand. Once we've dealt with Ronny and all our other issues here, we'll head over to Chicago to deal with the Chingas. Hopefully, Marcus can hold them down till we can deal with them."

We all nod our heads to Wolfe, letting him know we heard him loud and clear. We get our shit together and handle business.

"Shy, cleanup crew's here," Mac announces from behind us.

13 | The Talk

Dallas

MY PHONE RINGS, AND I SEE IT'S MAZE. I LOOK TO MY SEcurity monitors and see her at the bar with the phone to her ear. I pick up. "What's up?"

"Um, Doc's looking for you. You coming down, or should I tell her you're busy?"

Just then, my phone chirps, notifying me I have a text. I see it's from Doc.

Doc: Where are you? Did you leave?

I smile.

"Maze, show her where the elevator is and send her up to the third floor. I'll greet her at the top. How is it down there?" I ask, looking at the monitor. The place is at total capacity, with more members arriving every minute.

She looks at the camera. "What? You want me to send her up to your room?" Maze says, shocked.

I laugh. "Yes, send her up to my floor."

Maze pauses a few seconds, still just staring at the camera, knowing damn well I'm watching her. "Okay. And it's a fucking goddamn mess. Everyone's antsy. We need to get some girls here to calm them down or something."

I chuckle. "I'll handle it. Just keep the alcohol flowing. Thanks, Maze."

Dallas: Doc, go with Maze. She'll lead you to the elevator. I'll see you when you come up.

Lee: Ok

I head out of my room to the elevator to meet my Doc. I have been keeping an eye on her, but when she goes into the spaces where we put the wounded, I wasn't able to see her. I finally had to turn off the screens so that I could focus on my work.

When the doors to the elevator open, my stomach does a flip with excitement. Her smile has me grinning from ear to ear. You would think after all the bad shit that's happened today, we both would be distressed, but no, here we are, grinning like we just won the lottery.

"Doc." I reach for her.

"Dallas," she replies seductively.

I pull her to me, and just before I'm about to kiss her, she blurts out. "Why was everyone tripping out that you had me come up here? What am I not understanding?" Lee questioned with a smirk.

I go the last two inches, giving her a brief kiss before standing back to my full height.

Releasing her, I grab her hand, pulling her to my room. I say over my shoulder, "I've never brought a woman up here before. We don't usually have people, especially women, up here. This floor is home for a couple of us and is our personal living space."

Doc stops in her tracks, yanking her hand back just before I reach for my bedroom door.

Her face turns livid. "What do you mean? That's bullshit! Don't tell me you've *never* had a woman here at the clubhouse?"

Turning around to face her, I reach behind me, pushing my door all the way open. "Come sit down and let me explain. I need to be at my computer right now, making sure my scans are still going."

Before I retrieved her from the elevator, I closed out or hid stuff she shouldn't see, or that is club stuff. The only things up that she could see are a few of the security cameras and a few

Dallas

scans she won't understand. We don't want anyone to know everything we have.

I back up into my room, letting her see my room isn't just a room but a suite. There are eight of them up here. Doc's eyes widen as she takes a few steps inside, with her arms still folded across her chest. "Be Yourself" by Audioslave is playing in the background.

I move to the corner of my suite, where I have all my computer stuff set up.

"Holy Shit! What is all of this? You have so many monitors. What the fuck?" Doc releases her arms, wandering over to the monitors.

I laugh, shutting my bedroom door.

"This is why I don't have women up here. It's like my own apartment and the only place I can be alone. Yes, I've had plenty of women at the clubhouse, but in one of the rooms downstairs. None of us that live here really let anyone up here. It's our private quarters," I explain, moving up behind her.

Christ, she smells so fucking good.

She scans all the monitors. "What is all of this? Why is this in your room?" She's so enthralled with all the TV's she doesn't care that I'm right behind her. Or that I'm checking her ass out in those tight as fuck jeans. I can't wait to have her long, luscious legs wrapped around me.

I grab a chair, setting it right next to mine, gripping her hips, I motion for her to sit down. I take my seat next to her and check my scans to make sure they are still running before turning to her. "Doc?"

She keeps looking at all the monitors.

I grab her chair and turn it toward me, making her face me. "Doc. You need to pay attention to me."

Doc's golden eyes are wild with questions bouncing around in her beautiful little head.

"I'm head of security, and I'm the treasurer of the MC, so I have all the computer stuff here in my room."

Doc's eyebrow rises. "What about those two offices downstairs?"

I laugh at my girl and how observant she is.

"Yes, those are for club members or anyone that needs to use a computer. The other one is Shy's office. This is my office and my workplace."

Doc looks back over at the monitors and then back to me.

"Is it okay that I'm up here? Was everyone acting weird because I'm not supposed to be up here?" Doc says, sounding nervous. You can see her brain overthinking everything.

"Of course, you can be up here, this is my place. This suite is my home, where I live. The clubhouse is separate. No one can come up here unless you have an access code or you're escorted by one of us that live up here."

Doc fires back, "Then why was everyone acting so weird?"

I chuckle. "Because I've never had anyone up here. I usually go down and meet them. You're special."

It finally clicks in her head, and she forms an 'O' with her mouth.

My computer dings and I turn to the monitor.

"Are you some kind of hacker?" she asks, looking at all the coding.

"Yes," I answer, finishing what I need to do before closing out of everything.

"When you said you *looked into* me and couldn't find anything before college. That meant you *really* looked into me," she says softly.

Turning to face my girl, I say, completely serious. "Yes, I look into anyone that comes into our lives. I do complete background checks on every single person that enters this clubhouse. I make sure anyone that comes in contact with a club member is

Dallas

thoroughly investigated. We've had some fucked-up shit happen, and I'm overly protective of my people."

She asks shyly. "So why me? I'm just your doctor. Why investigate me?"

"Well, I wanted to know more about you. Then when I saw someone fucked with your identity, I became more intrigued," I reply softly.

"So, I was a challenge for you? A mystery?" she says sarcastically.

I turn my chair toward her, scooting to the edge of the seat, so I can get as close to her as I can. Then, with her legs between mine, I slide my hands over her thighs, gripping her hips.

"It probably started as a challenge, but now I'm just obsessed with you. I want to know it all." I smirk, trying to ease the tension.

Doc raises her hands, placing them on my biceps. "No one has truly known me. I've hidden who I am for years. Ever since Scooter died, I've closed myself off and became who everyone wanted me to be. I play the role really well. I don't think I've ever really felt like I've belonged anywhere. I've been on the run and terrorized for so long. I don't even know what a real home feels like or how to belong anywhere."

Hearing her dead boyfriend's name makes me groan.

"The only time I'm truly myself is when I'm in doctor mode. I throw myself into being the best. It's what I love to do, and when I'm a doctor, all my troubles go away. It's probably my fight-or-flight mentality, but I'm good at it."

"Well, there will be no more fight or flight. You are not running anymore, and I'll protect you from Ronny. It's because of..." *Shit.* I still haven't told her about our involvement with Tommy's death.

Doc questions me, "Because of what?"

I can't get into this right now with her. Without thinking, I shake my head and snap out, "It's because of us, so we'll protect you. I can't talk about it, but because of our club business, Tommy isn't protecting you anymore."

My statement comes out unintentionally harsh. *Goddamn it!*

Lee instantly straightens her shoulders, snapping, "I'm not some charity case, and I don't *need* you to protect me. I've been taking care of myself all my life. I don't understand why you claimed me anyway. I'm not your problem."

There's my spunky Doc...

I laugh, which only makes Lee even more defensive. "We haven't fucked. We're not even dating. Why claim me? I—" I lift my hand, cutting her rant off.

"Doc, I am going to protect you and for a lot of reasons. But none of them are because you're a charity case. The main reason is—" I lean into her personal space. "I *want* to protect you. *Because* I like you *a lot.*" I drag out the last two words, ending with a huge smile.

Lee's shoulders relax some, but her face is still stern. I know she's hiding her real feelings. When she doesn't say anything, I sit back, giving her some space before continuing to speak. When I do continue, it's with a calm but stern tone, "I'm only going to say this one more time, so please listen. Like I said last night and just a few minutes ago. I've liked you since I first laid eyes on you, and I didn't even know who you were. So, I have been trying to get to know you. Yes, at first, it was a game trying to figure you out, but it became so much more. And to be honest, I became infatuated with you. Plus, you always turning me down only fueled the fire. And, you know what?" I pause, waiting for her to reply.

"What?" she murmurs.

"I did all of that before I even knew who you were or how we were linked together. I think it's fate, and this situation that we're in is only icing on the cake. I know you don't *need* me, but I'm here if you *want* me. Now I want to keep you safe, and last night you said, '*I make you feel things you haven't felt in years,*' which

Dallas

was safe. So please, let me do what I do best and protect you, not because *we* have to, but because *I* want to. Can you do that?" I finish, folding my arms over my chest, watching as my words chip away at her wall.

We sit in silence as she thinks over all that I have just said, and I give her time to let it all sink in.

She shakes her head, obviously fighting within herself. She wrings her hands. I know that look, and it's not a good one.

"Stop!" I shout, leaning into her, grabbing her thighs, which scares her a bit, making her jump in her seat. Instantly I'm sorry for scaring her and say calmly, "Please, stop overthinking this, Doc. It's simple. Do you like me?"

"Yes, but—"

Cutting her off, I fire another question. "Do you want to be with me?"

Again, she exclaims, "Yes, but you're a biker. I don't want to get hurt."

Anger rises inside me, but I control it knowing she's only known the fucking Black Crows.

Through gritted teeth, I explain, "I'm not a fucking Crow. I would never hurt you. We don't treat our women like they do. We cherish our women. So, Doc, the last question. Do you feel safe with me?"

Lee's eyes fill with tears and she whispers, "Yes."

Finally, a fucking yes with no 'but' after it.

I exhale, "Thank fuck." As I grab the back of her neck, pulling her head closer so I can kiss her, she instantly grips my neck with both hands, deepening the kiss.

I have her in my arms within seconds, gripping both ass cheeks. Lifting her, she instantly wraps her luscious legs around me as I walk to my bed. Her body is firm, muscular, and these fucking legs—legs that I've fantasized over while watching her run.

Christ, I want to be balls deep in her.

But I don't want to scare her by falling on top of her, trapping her. I don't know how messed up she is from being raped by Ronny, so I need to take it slow. I need to let her control what happens. So, I twist in the air as we descend to my bed, with her landing on top of me.

We both moan as our kiss deepens, engulfing each other, our hands move across one another like wild animals.

Fuck yes. Finally.

Lee starts to move her hips over my rock-hard cock. She inhales sharply, liking what she feels. I grip her hips, holding her firmly against me, connecting our bodies as one. I let her control the pace, and she quickens her movements, rubbing her clit up and down my shaft, faster and faster.

Fuck! I'm going to come in my pants.

"Oh, God. Alec," she pushes out, letting lust and desire take over.

We both heave our bodies against each other like we were two teenage kids messing around for the first time.

My muscles coil. "Fuck, Doc." I huff, "I'm gonna come."

Gripping her hips tighter, I take control of our movements, increasing the sexual frenzy happening between us.

Christ, feeling her sweet heat against me has me losing my fucking mind. I can't believe I'm going to come in my jeans.

Panting breathlessly, Lee grinds down hard, taking back the control. A groan slipping from my throat has her moving her hips in swift rocking motions, faster and more demanding.

"Fuck yeah," I grit out, every muscle in my body taut, ready to snap. Doc bites my neck, murmuring shit I don't understand because I'm chasing my climax.

My phone dings. *No. No. No. Fuck… don't stop.*

Ignoring it, I move to flip us over, but she clenches her legs, crying out. "Don't move. Fuck. I'm so close."

My phone dings again. *Goddamn it. Fuck this.*

Dallas

Knowing we need to finish this soon before someone pounds on my door, I want to get her off. "Hold on, Doc. I got you," I say before flipping us over, pinning her to the bed.

I press my steel rod exactly where she needs it and start pummeling her with short, hard, quick pumps hitting her clit just perfect. Lee grips my biceps, throwing her head back, screaming yes as she falls off the climactic ride.

Yes. Fuck. Almost, buddy. Oh, God.

I clench my teeth, pumping faster, making wild noises as I come hard. It takes quite a few pumps to release all my cum, filling my crotch with wetness. Seeing her under me, breathless and sated, makes it all worth it.

My phone dings again. *Jesus Christ. Give me a second.*

As I lean over Doc, trying to catch my breath, only inches away from her face. I scan her expression, hoping, no praying, she doesn't regret this or feel embarrassed.

What I find are happily lustful eyes looking back at me with a devilish grin. I lean down, placing a soft kiss on Doc's lips before moving to her neck. I choke out, "Goddamn, Doc," I cough. "You've got me over here creaming my pants." I half cough, laughing and trying to clear my throat, "Like a goddamn teenager."

"Hey man, nice shot," blares through the speakers. We look at each other, not saying anything, and when it repeats again, we both start laughing, as "Hey Man Nice Shot" by Filter plays in the background.

"Why, thank you," I say in a deep, raspy voice.

We both continue to laugh, embracing each other. I go in for a deep, passionate kiss, and my body instantly reacts, ready to go again. My brain and cock are on the same page for once. *More.* We want more.

Just real quick. I can slip it in. Yes. Real quick. I can do this.

I slip my hand under her shirt and start to move up her torso, but my phone rings this time, interrupting the moment.

Lee pulls back, laughing. "I think you should get that. It's been beeping. It might be important."

I lean my head down, irritated. "This fucking better be important," I rant.

Jumping off the bed, I adjust myself before grabbing my phone. "What?" I snap.

"Answer your fucking text, and I wouldn't have to call. Get your ass to church now!" Mac yells into the phone.

Doc is already up adjusting herself. I let out a groan. "I'll be there in ten." I hang up the phone before he can argue.

I throw my phone to the bed, grabbing Doc into an embrace, I tell her, "I have to go downstairs. Are you okay?"

Doc smiles, "I'm fine. I should check on the guys downstairs too."

Doc sits down as I move around the room, grabbing clean pants. I drop my jeans right in front of her, and she smiles big, biting her lip. I pull away, looking down, seeing that my pants are wet. Doc doesn't look away as I clean my still fully erect dick before slipping jeans on.

Doc laughs. "What, no underwear?"

I smirk seductively. "Nah, fewer things to take off later."

She raises an eyebrow. "Later, huh. You that confident?"

I drop to my knees in front of her, spreading open her legs. I run my hands up her thighs, cupping her cunt. She gasps with a moan before I kiss her seductively. I end the kiss by sucking her lower lip and say, "Oh, I'm confident I will be deep inside this pussy tonight."

Before she can reply, I'm up on my feet, moving around the room again, turning off my computers, grabbing my shit so we can head down to meet with my club. When I turn around, ready to leave, I catch her staring at me with a smile. I reach my hand out to her. When she grabs it, I pull her up out of the chair into an embrace.

Dallas

"You good?" I say with a smile.

She nods, biting her lip.

Damn those fuck-me lips.

"I need your words, Doc. You good? No running, right?" I ask, lifting her chin so she can't look away.

Doc smiles. "I'm good, Dallas."

I smile, hearing my name across her lips. I nod back, "Good, because tonight I want you. I want all of you." I place a kiss on her lips, adding, "that is if you'll have me?"

Doc's eyes tear up, and she smiles. "Yes, I'll have you."

I give her another quick peck on the lips before turning toward the door.

"Alec?"

I stop and turn around, hearing my name. "Yeah, Lee?"

Softly she says, "Thank you."

I just smile back, reaching for her hand again, before leaving my room.

14 | The Clubhouse

Lee

IF A MONTH AGO OR EVEN A WEEK AGO, YOU ASKED ME IF I WOULD be sitting in a clubhouse having a drink with my friends, I would say you're fucking crazy. I would have never imagined myself being here in this situation again, but here I am, sitting at the bar having a drink with my girls and a shit ton of bikers.

After leaving Dallas's room, we came downstairs to a club full of chaos. I got pulled away to help the bikers who were wounded in the drive-by, while Dallas got pulled into church for a club meeting, which was most likely about me.

An hour later, I went searching for my girls, it didn't take long to find them at the bar. Vi, Ray, Ginger, Ruby, Izzy, and Maze, the bartender, were all sitting at the end of the bar laughing, talking shit.

When I walked up, they had a drink waiting for me. My heart ached with longing to belong again. I've missed that feeling when Scooter was alive. I can feel it here too, but so much more.

I've been here all day, over ten hours. Throughout the day, I've been watching the members interact with each other and the women here. I haven't seen one girl or guy fight, and not one girl has been slapped. They don't even have naked girls running around, which is rare in a clubhouse. This place just keeps surprising me. I've had mixed emotions all day with flashbacks to when I was living at the clubhouse.

"Earth to Doc? You want another?" Maze asks, standing across from me at the bar.

Dallas

I smile. "Yes, Maze, that would be great. Thank you."

I turn to listen to Vi and Ray talk shit back and forth about who knows what. I've zoned out a few times, but I'm glad they are back to their usual shit-talking selves, but I can still see Raydene is bothered. So many secrets were revealed yesterday and today. I've been trying to keep my feelings under wraps, but the more I drink, the more emotional I'm feeling. So, I'm doing what I do best—I become quiet.

I feel a nudge next to me. "You doing okay?" Ginger asks low enough only I can hear.

I scream in my head, *Fuck, no, I'm not*. But I give her a quick smile, then turn to look at my glass on the bar. I need to get my emotions under control before looking at her because I don't want to cry. She's been so good to my friends and me through all of this.

Izzy yells, "Fuck that! Are you serious?"

Everyone laughs. They're so enthralled with Vi's story that I decide I'm going to let go and trust these ladies.

You can do this.

I take a deep breath and turn slightly away from the group toward Ginger, giving her my full attention.

"I'm just shocked and confused. Being in a clubhouse again has rocked me, good and bad, I guess you could say. Being here has brought back a lot of old memories. I thought all clubhouses were the same, but being here has proven me wrong." I pause as Maze walks up.

Maze hands me my drink, giving me a smile and a wink. I smile back, saying a thank you before she walks off.

I look to Ginger, who is still full of smiles, waiting for me to continue. So, I take a huge drink and say, "I've just been waiting for a bar fight or naked girls to be walking around."

Ginger laughs. "Doc, just wait. I'm sure at least one, if not both, of those things will happen. Maybe not today because everyone is on high alert, but sweetie, that shit happens here."

Not like the Crows.

I laugh, taking a drink. "Yeah, but I'm sure your members don't abuse the women or smack them around."

Ginger's face hardens. "Fuck no. My dad and all his members respect, if not worship, women. Yeah, they might have some patch chaser running around here naked, but everyone is consenting adults. There is no forcing or any mistreating of the ladies here or at any of our chapters. It's all about making money, fucking bitches, and brotherhood. And, I say bitches in a good way."

We both laugh, taking drinks.

I sigh. "My biggest fear is Ronny walking through that door."

Ginger turns entirely toward me, looking serious. "That will never, and I mean never, happen. And, if it did, which it wouldn't, but if it did, it would be a planned meeting. So, please trust me when I say it would never happen. We hate him just as much as you do."

I nod.

"Doc, I know this is hard for you, but know this—the Wolfemen will never let you down. No matter if you and Dallas become a thing or not, we got you. You're one of us now, and we girls have to stick together. I know Dallas has been kind of a lot for you lately, and your life has turned upside down, but it will get better, I promise. You just have to believe and trust us."

Tears well up in my eyes, hearing her tell me I'll be okay.

My voice cracks with emotion. "I've just been so alone. I'm tired of being scared. I'm tired of running. I'm tired of lying about who I am."

Ginger grabs my knee, squeezing me. "We got you. It'll be over soon. Just trust us, and we'll keep you safe. No more running, living alone, or in fear. That ends today."

I lower my head, hiding the tears that run down my face. "In ten years, I've only trusted a handful of people with my true identity."

Dallas

Ginger pulls me in for a hug. "Well, you can add a few dozen more now. I don't see Dallas letting you go anytime soon, and you're stuck with us girls." She squeezes me. "We know where you work. You can't hide."

I laugh with a sob. "How do you keep your DJ life separate from your MC life? Is it hard to keep them separate?"

Ginger scoffs, "Lee, when we have time, we'll sit down, and I'll tell you my journey, but for now, I'll say this—It's going to be hard, and if you really want both in your life, you'll make it work. If Dallas is into you like I think he is, well, he'll stop at nothing to make you happy. Shy and I work together to keep both lives together. He is my biggest fan. Plus, what bikers don't like free liquor and a club full of women?"

We both laugh as I wipe my eyes. We turn to the bar, grabbing our drinks. Vi, on the other side of me, whispers, "You good?"

I smile.

Ginger smiles.

I take a deep breath and answer, "Yeah, I will be."

"Fuck yeah, you will, LeeLee. Ride or die, bitches, for life," Vi says with a huge smile.

"Oh. My. God. I love this song," Ruby exclaims, jumping up, "Oh yeah, Alright. Take it easy, Izz."

We all laugh as Ruby sings "American Girl" by Tom Petty but changed a word calling out to Izzy.

Izzy follows suit, popping off her chair. She joins in as they both sing into an imaginary mic, "Make it last all night!"

Everyone at the bar laughs and screams, "She was an American girl!"

I watch the girls bounce around, singing and laughing. I feel happy, and my heart swells with emotions.

"Shots, biatches!" Maze yells across the bar.

Everyone screams, "Shots. Shots. Shots."

I smile, watching my two best friends laugh along with all my newfound friends.

When everyone has a shot, all of us girls scream, "Cheers, biatches!"

Slamming the empty shot glass down, I hear, "Maze, you getting our ladies drunk?"

I would recognize that husky voice anywhere now. I turn around to see Dallas with about twenty-plus men walking toward us. My mouth and pussy both instantly go wet. I clench my legs together, needing friction to ease the tingling that's erupted between them.

Most of the men are smiling, but you can see who the officers are by their facial expressions. *Stressed the fuck out.*

All the ladies turn around to face the men approaching. Each one of us starts making catcalls, others whistle and scream.

I smile. *Yes, I think I'm going to be okay.*

"Dayum, ya man is stalking toward ya like you're his next meal." Vi laughs.

God, I hope so.

"He can eat me anytime. I'm ready to be taken," I respond.

Am I really ready?

"Get it, gurl!" Vi exclaims.

Without a word, Dallas walks straight up to me, giving me a mouthwatering kiss. I wrap my arms around his neck, pulling him closer to me.

Someone says from behind us, "Dallas, get a fucking room, brother."

I break our embrace, asking him, "Do you want something to drink?"

Dallas smiles down at me. "Yeah, I'll have one, but really you're all I'm thirsty for, Doc."

His eyes are a darker green, filled with mischief, and desire has my heart rate increasing.

Dallas

I chuckle, feeling my face redden. My body is hot and ready for him.

"Well, that's good because I'm as wet as a dry martini, ready to suck you dry."

Dallas's face lights up, but I can see I shocked him.

"Yes! Our girl's back!" Vi yells to Raydene.

"Well, fuck. I'll take that martini to go. Finish your drink," Dallas drawls with a seductive smile.

I grab my drink, finishing it in one big gulp. I turn to Vi. "You girls staying here tonight or going back with Ruby?"

Vi answers, "We're staying where you're staying, so I guess we're here for the night."

I look over her shoulder as Brick nods his head. Then I look over to Raydene, who's huddled together with, I think, their VP Mac.

Feeling weird about leaving my girls, I look to Ginger, who is watching me. She smiles. "I promise. I got you and your girls. Don't worry. Go have fun. You're safe. My suite is on the same floor as Dallas's, so if you need me, I'll be right there."

Dallas whistles. I look to see who he is whistling at when Mac looks up, giving him a nod without a word. Shy laughs. "We got the girls covered."

Is Mac going to try to mac on Ray?

Dallas extends his hand out for me to take it. I exhale, letting my fear go, taking the first step. He pulls me into his chest, whispering into my ear, "I got you, Doc. Trust me."

"Let's go." I smile. *I can do this.*

As we head to the elevators, we pass many members, all giving him a head nod, showing him respect. *Not like Ronny. His brothers feared him.*

Then suddenly, two blonde model-looking girls start walking toward us, eyes locked on Dallas. "Hey Dallas, will you be around later? We miss you," one of them says as they approach us.

Dallas squeezes me closer to him. "Sorry, ladies. I'm off the market."

What the fuck?

Both of their faces drop in shock, firing off simultaneously, "What? When?"

Without answering them, Dallas glides us right past them with a smile.

I'm about to protest when Dallas leans toward my ear. "Don't. Let's talk upstairs."

I snap my mouth shut as he punches in a code, closing the elevator doors. Dallas turns to face me, caging me against the elevator wall. "Fucking finally, we're alone. I've had to share you all goddamn day," he rushes out before smashing his mouth against mine and not letting me say a word.

When the door dings, he pulls me out of the elevator and heads straight for his room. When we approach his door, I'm surprised when I see he doesn't have a regular lock. No, this door, you can either use your thumbprint, a keypad, or like ordinary people, a key.

Dallas puts his thumb to the pad, unlocking it. I stand there in shock as his door swings open. I start to get nervous. It's been a couple of years since I've actually had sex with a man. I've used toys and maybe ground on someone at a club, but full-on intercourse, it's been a while.

It will be fine. I want him.

My body comes alive every single time I'm near him. It clearly knows what it wants, and that's him. Earlier today, I didn't think I could feel that aroused. It felt so good to feel that euphoric high.

What if he doesn't like it? What if I suck? I start to panic as we enter his room. Dallas has been with so many women and so frequently. My mind is starting to overload when Dallas pulls me to his chest.

"You okay, Doc?" he rasps out.

Dallas

I don't lift my eyes. Instead, I place my head on his chest and take a few deep breaths.

"Doc, talk to me. What's going on in that pretty little head of yours?" Dallas asks, lifting my face.

"There's my Doc. Talk to me, beautiful."

Tell him.

Tears fill my eyes as I try to explain. "I'm just so overwhelmed. So many emotions."

Liar. Tell him.

Dallas smiles down at me, wiping away my runaway tears. He doesn't say anything but just watches me.

"I'm nervous," I blurt out.

Dallas's face becomes serious. "Why are you nervous? I would never do anything you didn't want to do. I have all the time in the world. As long as you're next to me, I'm good, Doc."

I smile. *Is he for real?*

When I don't say anything, he starts to worry, "Are you afraid of me?"

Fuck no.

He starts to pull away from me, but I grab his biceps, pulling him back to me. "No, I'm nervous because you're so experienced and well... it's been a while for me."

God, that sounds ridiculous out loud.

Dallas's face softens, wrapping his massive arms around me. He engulfs me in an embrace. I sink into his warmth, placing my head on his chest as he rests his chin on my head.

Jesus, he smells so fucking good. My inner thighs spasm.

"Doc, I know we have a lot to talk about. We hardly know each other, but I want you to know. I'm all in. I want to be with you and only you," Dallas murmurs into my hair.

Can this be real? Is this really happening?

I start to pull away, but he keeps his grip on me. "I've never been in a relationship before. I lost my mom when I was young and just never opened up to anyone before. I've never treated a woman bad, but I've never cared about any of them either." Dallas rubs my back, soothing me, as he tells me how he feels.

He pauses, kissing the top of my head. "I've had lots of women. I'm sure we will run into a lot of them like we did tonight, but just know that no one has ever made me feel as alive as you have these past few months. Just being around you makes me high on life. I can't get you out of my fucking head." He chuckles.

Me too. I feel the same way.

I slide my arms down his chest, wrapping them around his waist.

Dallas keeps talking. "So, I think we're both nervous, but I probably hide it better."

I laugh into his chest, and he releases his hold on me so I can lean back and look up at him.

He smiles. "So, we don't have to do anything tonight. I just want to be with you. You've had a rough couple of days."

I smile.

He leans down, placing a quick kiss on my lips before leading me to his bed. "Go ahead and lie down. I need to do a couple of things on the computer."

Fuck, I want him.

My body instantly misses his touch as he moves away from me to his computer as I sit down on the bed to take my shoes off. He keeps his back to me, clicking away on his keyboard. I strip down to my panties and bra as soft music starts to play, but he changes the song a few times, finally deciding on "Landslide," but I don't recognize the band.

"Who is this? It isn't Fleetwood Mac," I ask, climbing into his bed, getting under the covers.

"You good?" he asks over his shoulder.

God, he is so sweet.

"Yeah," I answer, feeling less nervous.

Dallas

He turns around, answering me, "It's 'Landslide' but remastered by The Smashing Pumpkins. Do you like it? If not, I can put on whatever you want."

Fuck, he looks so good. Just do it. Take him.

So, I do it and ask, "What I want is for you to come lie with me. Do you really have to do work right now?"

Dallas smirks, "No, but I wanted to give you some space."

The next song, "With Arms Wide Open," by Creed starts playing, and I laugh to myself because it's the perfect song,

I smile, patting the bed. "Get over here." I extend my arms wide open and sing along, "My arms are wide open."

Dallas chuckles. "Alright." Shaking his head, he turns to his computer, clicking on something, making the screens go black. He strides his muscular body around the room, turning a couple of dim lights on before turning off the main light. I lie there in awe as my mind and body finally get on the same page. I want him, and he wants me. When he starts to take his clothes off, I watch, eyes glued to him.

He's mine.

Dallas lays his cut over his chair, kicking off his shoes. He knows I'm watching him, so he goes torturously slow. When he turns toward me, he slips his shirt over his head, showing off his tattoos I've admired several times while in the hospital. I lick my lips, wanting to touch him. Feel his body on mine, skin to skin.

"Doc, you like what you see?" he drawls.

"You know I do." I giggle. "But Christ, hurry up."

Courage builds inside me, and I sit up, letting the sheets drop down to my waist, showing him my breasts sitting firmly in my top-shelf bra.

Dallas groans, "Doc, that's not fair."

I smile.

"Well, you're taking your sweet ass time getting naked, so I thought I'd give you the incentive to hurry up," I sass back, unsnapping my bra, letting my girls bounce free.

Dallas moves next to my side of the bed, unbuttoning his pants. That's when I remember he went commando. I lean back on my elbows, kicking off the sheets, showing my lace thong.

Dallas drops his jeans, letting his cock spring out. "Doc…"

"Hmm," I answer, licking my lips.

Dallas moves onto the bed, leaning over me. He engulfs one of my breasts into his mouth. I moan, arching my back up higher.

He's on top of me in seconds, and all hands are on deck. We are both groping, clawing, feeling every inch of each other.

"Dallas, please," I rasp out. "I want you so fucking bad."

Dallas pops one of my breasts out of his mouth and moves up my body to face me. "Are you sure you want to do this?"

"I've never wanted anything more than I want your dick inside me. Please hurry the fuck up." I groan, frustrated.

Dallas smiles a wicked little smile. "As you wish."

He slides a hand down between my legs, using his fingertips to circle my clit. "Fuck," I intake air, making a hissing sound.

Dallas positions himself between my legs, lowering his hand, slipping a finger into my sex.

Fuck, this is going to be quick. I'm so aroused. I'm about ready to burst.

"Fuck, you're tight. Don't come until I tell you. Wait for it," Dallas demands.

Shit. Fuck.

Slipping two fingers inside me, I clench the bedsheets as every nerve in my body is about to explode, and he's only inserted fucking fingers inside me.

"Fuck me, Doc, you're so wet." Dallas exhales.

"Hurry. I'm about ready to…" I stop midsentence, clenching my teeth, holding back a scream as he slips three fingers in and out. I move my hips in sync with him as my breathing becomes erratic.

Hold on. Don't come.

Dallas

"That's my girl. Fuck, you're so fucking wet, baby." Dallas's breath soothes over my pussy.

He moves up my body, positioning himself at my entrance but pauses. "Doc, look at me, babe. Eyes on me." I open, locking onto his vibrant green eyes, grabbing his ass. I pull him down hard, forcing his cock inside of me.

"Fuck!" we both cry out as his cock slips halfway in.

Dallas starts to move in and out, slicking his dick inch by inch with each push.

I watch as he concentrates on his movement. I grip his chest. "Fuck baby. I'm not gonna last long, your pussy is so fucking tight. Goddamn," he mumbles, breathless.

Goddamn, he feels so fucking good.

I start to move my hips, meeting him thrust for thrust.

"Yes, Alec. Fuck. Yes," I grind out, gripping his forearms.

"Yeah, baby. Come for me. You feel so fucking good," he says through clenched teeth, increasing his motion.

I close my eyes, losing myself as my climax builds higher and higher.

"Doc, eyes on me," he demands.

I open my eyes, again locking eyes with Dallas, but this time his eyes are wild, filled with lust and desire. "Alec, please. Faster. I'm so close," I pant, out of breath.

Dallas pounds me faster. "Yes, come with me, Doc. Fuck. I'm close."

Oh, God.

I cry out, "Yes." Throwing my head back, letting the wave of ecstasy ignite through my body.

Dallas follows me over the edge, groaning his release. He slows his motion but doesn't pull out. He keeps going, slowly torturing my clit with each push, and his cock isn't going soft. My body's spasming, coming again as my high intensifies.

Jesus. Yes, more. Keep going.

"Christ, Doc. You feel too good to be true. I don't want to stop... Fuck," he breathes into my neck.

He moves a few more times inside me, finishing again, but he doesn't pull out. He lowers his body down onto mine, giving me his full weight. I'm lost in bliss but whine in protest when he pulls out, moving next to me.

Every nerve in my body is humming with excitement. I'm on such a high that I can barely move my body. When I feel Dallas get off the bed, I panic, reaching for him, but he's not there. Slightly opening my eyes, I call out to him, "Alec?"

He answers, "I'm here, just throwing the condom away."

Condom? Fuck, I didn't even think about protection.

I'm exhausted. I just lie there sated. The bed shifts and I'm being pulled against his body. Dallas places my back to his front, spooning me.

Dallas whispers into my ear, "Sleep. You've been through a lot. I got you."

"Thank you," I rasp out.

He kisses my head. "Always."

Seconds later, I'm out.

15 | The Feeling

Dallas

I DON'T KNOW WHAT THIS FEELING IS, BUT GODDAMN, THIS WOMAN has a hold on me. I'm lying here watching her sleep with a fully erect hard-on. Her pussy was the tightest and most fantastic pussy I have ever had, and I've had a lot. It seriously was by far the best sex I've ever had. Every spasm her cunt made, I almost nutted each time. I've never had to try *not to come* during sex. I need to calm down. I focus on the lyrics of "Walkin' On The Sun" by Smash Mouth, that's playing in the background.

Don't think of her warm body. Don't do it.

Today with her was like experiencing sex for the first time again—first, dry humping, coming in my pants like a fucking eager teenager. Second, telling my buddy not to come, that I needed to last a bit longer. Now, I'm high on Doc, wanting more. I'm counting down the minutes until I can slip back into heaven. I know it's sad, but I want her. No, I need to be inside her again.

Fuck it.

I snuggle up behind her, placing my dick right up against her ass cheeks. She coos, wiggling her ass, and I slide down a bit so my cock can slip up between her legs.

Christ, she's fucking soaked. I feel the wetness running down her legs. I stay lying behind her but move my hand from her belly up to cup one of her breasts.

"Alec…" she breathes out, still sleeping.

I know I need to let her sleep, but fuck, I crave her, needing more. I don't have a condom on. I need to get a condom. But if I move, I'll lose the moment.

Fuck.

I've never debated wearing a condom. I've always wrapped buddy up. Lee moans, moving her hand over mine, gripping her breast as she motions her hips back.

Fuck, I need a condom. Fuck. Fuck. Fuck.

I'm panicking.

My buddy's slipping.

Fuck, he's sliding between her folds. If she keeps wiggling or moving her hips back, my cock will just slip right in, and goddamn is it inviting.

I start to think of all the ways around wearing a condom or why it will be okay not to wear one *just this once*. I can pull out, and she's a doctor, she's probably protected. Plus, she has to be clean, and I'll pull out to be safe. It will just be this once. *Liar.*

"Alec, please." She swoons.

Fuck this.

I release her breast, only for her to replace it with her hand tugging on her nipple.

"Jesus Christ, Doc," I grit out.

I grip her waist and slowly thrust my hips up, gliding my overly ready-to-combust cock into her wet folds. I take a deep breath, leaning forward, I suck on her shoulder before asking, "Ready?"

Instantly she replies, "Uh-huh." Shoving her ass back, colliding with my cock.

"Oh, fuck. Yes," I sputter as my eyes roll back from the overload of sensation that I feel as my buddy slips into heaven. I see motherfucking stars. I don't know if I will ever be able to wear a condom again. Lee's tight, her hot sheath envelops my cock, like nothing I've ever felt before. I slowly inch my way into her slippery channel, stretching her until I'm grounded deep inside her.

Dallas

Once seated deep inside her, I pause, enjoying the feel of her creamy pussy coating my dick. Lee wiggles her ass, and a guttural moan escapes me.

"Christ almighty," I grit out as I slowly start to move in and out of the depths of heavenly bliss.

My God, what have I been missing? Christ!

"Alec, more. Please." Lee looks back with wanton eyes, begging me for more. I snap out of my heavenly bliss and start pumping into her magical pussy.

Gripping her hips, I smash into her like I'm a ravenous madman. Lee sputters nonsense, mumbling into her pillow, making it hard for me to hear her.

"Christ, I'm going to come. Fuck," I push out, feeling frustrated and satisfied at the same time.

Slow down. I need to last longer.

I pull out. "Ride me. I need to see you, Doc," I demand, pulling her with me as I lie on my back.

"I'm so tired," Lee whines but moves to mount me.

I watch as her long golden-brown hair flies around her face. It's better than any wet dream I've ever had of her. She flicks her long locks over her shoulder, letting it cascade down her back. As she sits on me, devouring my cock back into the abyss, I sit up, gripping her ass. I start moving us slow and tortuously. Lee's head is tilted up, looking at the ceiling with both hands running through her hair, slicking it out of her face.

"Jesus Christ, you're so beautiful. I can't get enough of you," I croak out, sucking a breast into my mouth.

Her response is a long moan as she picks up pace, rocking my cock with a deep, long, hard thrust. When Doc finally looks down, her eyes are glowing with desire.

My Doc knows what she wants.

"Take me. Ride me hard, Doc." I release her ass cheeks, lying back down. She grips my chest, licking her lips with a smile.

"Are you sure?" She motions forward and back, slow and deep.

"Fuck yeah." I groan.

Lee starts moving, working my cock, leaning forward. She picks up the pace. I grip her hips, holding on for the ride of my life. I watch her facial expression.

"Yes, ride me. Fuck yeah," I encourage her to let go.

Her tits start flapping as she increases her rhythm. I reach for them, pinching her nipples between my thumbs and forefingers. She purrs in ecstasy.

"Dallas. Oh, God. Yes. Harder," she exclaims.

She encourages me to pinch harder, gripping her breast full handed. When she digs her nails into my chest, I know she's close. Her slick walls spasm around my dick, becoming a vise grip.

Fuck. I can't hold it much longer.

"Come for me, Doc. You're so fucking tight," I plea with her to come. "Christ, I can't hold it much longer."

A clapping sound gets louder while she bounces her ass up and down on my cock. Lee's breathless as she cries out when her release washes over her.

Thank fuck. Slow it down.

I flip us in one motion, hurrying so that I won't miss a beat slamming inside her. I kiss her passionately with a moan of approval as I continue pumping into her with a slow, controlled, deep, long thrust. I want to savor the feeling of my buddy skin to skin. Just in case she freaks out.

Oh, God. Yes. Almost, buddy.

"Doc, your pussy is the tightest fucking thing I've ever felt. Fuck. It. Feels. So. Fucking. Good." I pummel each word like my life depends on it.

She laughs.

I smile down at her. I pump into her deep, then circle my

Dallas

hips, making her feel my cock even more profoundly. "You like that?" I grunt.

"Yes," she gasps.

I clench my ass, pushing my buddy deeper into the abyss. She arches her back off the bed.

"Are you sure?" I tease.

"Fuck yes," she cries out as her sweet little cunt milks my cock.

"That's it, Doc. Come one more time," I order, pulling my dick almost entirely out, before ramming her hard, bottoming out inside her.

I vigorously continue doing this over and over—pulling out and then instantly ramming back in.

Fucking heaven.

I unleash all I have, fucking her senseless. I want her limp and breathless when I'm done with her.

I lift one of her legs over my shoulder, hitting her perfectly. She combusts with a shriek that could shatter glass. My body slickens with sweat as I pound into her, giving her another orgasm.

Don't come inside. One more thrust into heaven. *Oh, God.*

Don't come inside. But it feels so fucking good.

Don't come inside.

"Fuck. I'm going to come," I declare.

Every muscle tenses up as I plow harder into her.

Don't come inside.

I lower her leg, leaning over her, pumping erratically into her as sweat drips from my body onto her.

Don't come inside.

I can do this. Yeah, buddy. Fuck. Yes.

Just as I'm about to pull out, she locks her legs behind me, pumping up hard and fast, keeping my cock inside her.

"Fuck. Oh, fuck." A guttural roar escapes me as the best

climax I've ever had erupts throughout my body. Every single muscle in my body is taut and tingling.

Cum bursts from my cock inside her.

One pump.

Two pumps.

Fuck!

Panicking, I sit back, breaking the lock she has on me, pulling out. I keep pumping my hips like a fucking dog in heat. I instantly grip my buddy, jacking him off with my seed flying everywhere. I throw my head back, breathing heavily as my release keeps spewing from me.

Jesus Christ. That was un-fucking-real.

I keep jacking my cock sitting on my heels, not wanting to see her face once she realizes I'm condomless.

"Alec, that is the fucking hottest thing I've ever seen," Lee says breathlessly.

I snap my head back to look down at her lying there watching me as she caresses her breast.

"What?" I croak out, feeling light-headed.

"You fisting your cock is hot as hell." She giggles.

"You're not mad at me?" I question, still holding my dick in my hands.

"Why would I be mad? That was the best sex I've had," she explains with a smile.

"I didn't use a condom. I'm mad at myself. I've never, and I mean never, done that before. I wrap my buddy up even for blow jobs," I confess.

"Buddy?" she asks, raising an eyebrow.

"Oh, I call my dick my buddy sometimes." I chuckle, embarrassed.

She laughs.

I move to lie next to her. "So, you're not mad I took you without a condom?"

Dallas

Lee turns to me, lying on her side. "No, I'm not mad. I'm protected. I mean, I might have asked if you were clean, but since you just confessed you've never gone bareback, then I think you're clean."

"Thank fuck, because I think I came inside you a little bit. It took everything I had to pull out. And, I've never been tested because I've never gone bareback. But, I can tell you this, you've ruined me," I say with a chuckle, pulling the sheets up to cover us.

Lee slides up to my side, laying herself half on me. "Ruined you? For what?" she teases, knowing damn well what I meant.

"Doc, your girl down there is so fucking wet, warm, and cozy. It's goddamn heaven. I can't see my buddy ever going into any other pussy again," I confess to her as I caress her shoulder.

Lee giggles against my chest, and I join in laughing with her.

"So, what you're saying is *your buddy* found his forever home with *my girl?*" Lee jokes.

Fuck yes, he did.

I poke her, making her laugh harder. "Don't joke around about my buddy."

"I'm sorry. I would never want to hurt *Buddy's* feelings." Lee yawns against me.

"You need to get some sleep. I promise not to let my buddy bug you until morning," I tease her, running my hands through her hair.

"Hm, he can bug me anytime," she replies sleepily.

"Nite, Doc," I whisper.

She murmurs, "Nite."

Within minutes, she's asleep, and I'm left holding her while I'm wide awake. My brain runs amuck with Ronny and the Black Crows coming into town and now the Chingas. Our club has a lot to deal with, and I should be on my computer researching, monitoring, diving into the black web, hacking, but my body won't move. It's happy right here holding this remarkable woman.

I can't even imagine what she's been through all these years, running from Ronny. I know how horrible the Crows are with their women. I know Lee and I will need to sit down and honestly discuss everything in depth. I want her to really understand I'm not going anywhere and don't want to be with anyone else.

I never believed my brothers when they said you'll know when the right one comes along. I've been with so many women that I never thought it could happen to me. I thought maybe I was broken or something. I never really cared about women unless I wanted to get my dick wet.

I was so lost after my mom's death that I never wanted to put my heart out there again. It still pains me to think of my mom and all she went through. Her strength to keep going, keep working, keep going through treatments. She said it was all for me. She didn't want to leave me, and she gave it her all until the end.

Lee reminds me of her. Her strength to keep running, keep hiding, to better her life by going to school even though she got dealt a shit hand. Well, her struggle is over. I promise on my mom's memory that I'll do everything in my power to protect Lee. I'll be there by her side to make sure she is truly happy.

I lie holding her for about another thirty minutes before my brain overrides my body, and I slide out of bed, powering my screen alive. It's time to do my job. Before I do, though, I glance over, and for the first time in my life, I feel complete seeing my beautiful Doc sound asleep in my bed. She's the first and only one that will be in that bed—my computer beeps, drawing my attention away from my girl.

16 | The Storm

Lee

It's morning, and I'm sitting in one of the rooms downstairs, making a list of all the supplies we need to get from the hospital. I'm exhausted, but for a good reason. After yesterday's mind-blowing sex, I passed out in Dallas's arms. It was the best feeling ever, being held in solid arms, feeling safe.

That is until the dreams of Ronny came flashing through, making me restless. It's been years since I've had a full-blown nightmare. I think being back in the club life, being here in the clubhouse and, of course, Ronny stalking me, has triggered a lot of old memories.

I woke up once last night to an empty bed. At first, I was startled. I wasn't home, but I relaxed when I saw Dallas sitting at his desk. Dallas was on his computer with headphones on, doing work. I snuggled into his bed, enveloping myself in his scent. Smelling his pillows as I lie there watching him work.

He crept back into bed sometime later, pulling me into his chest, securing me to him. All I could think of was how safe I felt being with him, and that's a feeling I'm not used to, so it was overwhelming.

His buddy, as he calls his dick, was poking me again early this morning. I thought he was trying to slip him in when I realized he was fast asleep. So, I decided to show him my appreciation by giving him a little wake-up blow job.

But when Dallas woke up, he stopped me from sucking him off. I was initially upset, feeling self-conscious, so I tried to get off the bed, but he pulled me back down, covering me with his body. I thought… maybe I wasn't doing a good job, but he explained that he wanted to be balls deep inside me.

When I told him he could come inside me that I was protected, he went ravenously mad. I think *his buddy* is addicted to *my girl*. I'm not complaining, but I'm sore as hell today.

"LeeLee? Earth to LeeLee?" Vi demands, snapping me out of my lust-induced daydream.

"Sorry, what did you say?" I turn, giving her my full attention.

"Raydene and I need to run to the studio with the girls and Maddox. Are you going to be okay here?" Vi asks.

"Yeah, I'm good. Just waiting for the guys to get out of their meeting. Then hopefully, we're going to head to the hospital to get some supplies." I pause, realizing Brick is in that meeting, and he hasn't left her side since he arrived. "Who's going with you? Won't Brick flip out that you're gone?" I ask, hoping she'll give me some more information on Brick.

"That is why I'm taking off while they're in church. Like they say, *Madd Dog* has just as many men on his security team as this club does members. Plus, I need to get away for a bit. Going to work on some music with Ray at the label. It will help me clear my head," Vi explains.

I can see in her eyes she's upset. She feels responsible for the men getting shot.

"I get it. Go have some fun and release some stress. I'll deal with the guys when they get out," I say, hugging her.

"Doc?" Chain grumbles from the room.

"Okay, we'll be back in a few," Vi says, kissing me on the cheek.

I watch as she takes off through the crowd of people. Since last night, the place has filled up with other chapters and, of course, women. I've stayed back here with the guys that were wounded, mostly Chain.

Dallas

Shit. He called for me.

I rush to the room where Chain is supposed to be lying down, but when I turn the corner, I see he is trying to get out of bed.

"What the fuck? Chain, you can't get up. You'll split the stitches open," I demand.

Chain, gritting his teeth, clearly in pain, groans. "I've got to get out of this fucking bed and do something."

"If you don't get back in bed, I'm going to flip out and have someone come put you back in bed. Now lie back down!" I move next to him, standing my ground.

"Doc."

"Chain."

"Fuck!" he roars but does what I say, getting back into bed.

Redman rushes in, "*Wat* the *feck* is goin' on?"

I turn, folding my arms across my chest, holding my ground. "Your brother over here was trying to get out of bed, but that ain't happening on my watch."

"Redman, I need to get the fuck outta this bed," Chain pleads to him.

Redman's face relaxes. "*Bloody hell.* I thought something happened. Chain, brother, *ye* need to stay in bed. Look how long it took Dallas to recover. *Yer* lucky we got the doc here, and *yer arse* isn't in the hospital."

Chain throws his head back against his pillow. "Dallas had Doc to inspire him. I can't flirt with Dallas's ol' lady."

I laugh. *Ol' lady.*

Redman coughs. "Well, brother, I'll find a nurse *fer ya*. One *that'll* give *ya* a good *ride.*"

Chain's head pops up with a smile. "Now that's what I'm talking about, and maybe give me some medicine that's named Jack."

We all laugh.

"I'm okay with that, but you have to stay in bed. I'll be getting more supplies later. Until then, I can't do anything except keep you from popping those stitches and bleeding out."

Chain's face becomes serious. "I promise, Doc." He salutes me. "I won't get out of bed or do anything that will pop my stitches."

Redman and I walk out of the office and head toward the bar.

"*Ya alright?*" Redman asks, guiding me through the crowd.

We're almost at the bar when an older woman enters the club with a handful of women following her. "Where's my niece?" the lady yells. "Snow?"

"Mother of Christ. Hold on." Redman rushes over to the group of women. Most of them have property leathers on, but I'm not close enough to see names. I move to the end of the bar, keeping my eye on the group.

Memories flash through my mind of Beaver smacking my mom around for talking out of line. I panic for a second, worried this lady will get the same punishment my mom did.

I know Redman is a good man, so is he rushing over to shut her up?

"Where's Snow?" she demands.

I know Snow is Ginger's road name, and she's with a few other girls in the kitchen getting food together.

Redman and this lady conversate before the ladies head for the kitchen. I just watch as they move through the clubhouse. What I didn't realize was that three men followed them in.

"Doc, you need anything?" Maze asks, making me jump.

"Shit, you scared me." I breathe.

Maze smiles. "Sorry. You good?"

I wish everyone would quit asking me that.

I smile. "I'm good. Can I have a beer? I need a drink."

She slaps the bar. "Hell yeah, you can have a beer."

When I turn back to look for the women, they're all gone, but two men have moved to the bar, joining a group of other members. They're a little older but good-looking. One is like a giant, while the other has a medium build.

"Haven't seen you around. What's your name, little mama?" I hear a deep rumble behind me.

Shit.

I turn slightly to see a very massive, very brawny man smiling down at me. He's got a bandana on with wild hair flipping out from underneath like he's been riding hard for days.

Christ, he could be a lumberjack with that beard.

When I don't say anything, he laughs. "Cat got your tongue?"

I smile, locking eyes with him. I'm about ready to tell him my name, but Maze announces. "This is Doc. Doc, this is Bear."

Damn, he is a bear. Perfect name.

Bear looks over my shoulder at Maze. "Aw, the infamous Doc."

I look to his cut where his patches are. One says Sergeant at Arms, and the other says his name, Bear, with an original patch above it.

I hear Bear laugh, "Does she talk?"

I shake my head, snapping me out of my daze, and finally, speak up. "Yes, sorry. I'm Lee, or as everyone seems to call me, Doc. Nice to meet you, Bear," I say, lifting my hand to shake his. Then, I add, "Nice name, by the way, it suits you."

Bear laughs, a deep heart-filled laugh as he tilts his head back. When his eyes land back on me, he pulls me in for a hug saying, "Darlin, I'm glad you like it. It's good to meet you."

"Boyd Bear Harding, you better let that girl go before I cut your balls off," a woman yells from behind me.

I cringe. Bear releases me.

"Woman, you best rein that shit in, or I'm going to take you down that hall and smack that ass of yours," Bear says over my shoulder before looking down at me. "I apologize for my ol' lady. She's having a hormonal day."

I hold in my laughter.

"The fuck I am," she fires back.

I turn to come face-to-face with the woman who charged in here minutes ago with her entourage.

I smile as Maze yells from across the bar. "Storm, this is Doc. Doc, this is Storm. Bear's ol' lady and Ginger's auntie."

Storm looks over at Maze and then back to me.

"Aw, sweetie, you're the doc everyone's talking about?" She pulls me in for a tight hug. "We gotcha, girl. These men here will protect you," she releases me with a huge smile, "and if they don't, us bitches will handle it."

Maze yells across the bar, "Fuck yeah, we will."

I laugh. "Thank you. That means a lot."

Storm turns to her entourage and introduces them, "Ladies, this is Lee, aka Doc. Doc, this is Felicia, Hawks ol' lady. Sissy here is with Stitch, and these beauties are Gigi, Lolli, Peaches, and Coco." I nod and smile to each lady as they give me a warm smile in return. They all seem nice. I don't feel threatened at all.

I wave like a weirdo. "Hiya."

"Lolli!" a high pitch voice calls from behind all the ladies.

Storm rolls her eyes, looking over to Maze. She asks, "Why are these bitches here?"

"We need girls to entertain," Maze replies, sounding just as unhappy as Storm.

All the ladies turn to watch the two blonde models from last night.

Great. I spoke too soon.

Their eyes are not on Lolli anymore—now they're on me. And to my luck, their smiles are gone, replaced with hatred.

Fucking great.

I square my shoulders back, ready for a confrontation, but Storm moves in front of me. "What do you two want? Aren't

Dallas

you two supposed to be upstairs or taking care of a member somewhere?"

Damn, I love this woman already.

"Yes, we came down here to get ready for Dallas once he comes out."

This bitch did not just say his name. I slide to the right, moving out from behind Storm, making eye contact with the blonde bimbo.

"That's right. You heard me right. We're waiting for Dallas." The one that spoke last night steps forward.

Stay calm.

Storm takes a step toward her, but I grab her arm, stopping her. "Oh, I heard you. Do I care?" I shrug my shoulders. "Not so much. You can try all you want with *Alec*—I mean Dallas. But I know where *his buddy* will be laying his head tonight and every night after." I grab my crotch with a smile. "So good luck to you."

The blonde turns red and fires back, "You can't even get his name right, and who the fuck is Buddy?" She cackles like a hyena, looking around like she's making a fool out of me.

I laugh. *Stupid girl.*

"This bitch don't even know." Maze laughs from behind me.

Again, the bimbo laughs her hyena laugh. "I know, Maze, this bitch is stupid."

I take a step even closer to the blondes, who are a good bit taller than I am. I give them a wicked smile. "She's talking about you, dumb fuck." I take another step, getting right in front of her, and look up. "Dallas's real name is Alec, and if you *really* knew him, you would know he calls his *dick buddy*."

Both girls' mouths drop open as I fold my arms over my chest, standing my ground. I'm waiting for one of them to make a move, but both just stand there clueless.

"That's right, bitch. Walk. Away," Storm announces behind me.

"What the fuck are you two doing down here? We don't pay you to fucking sit around. Get your asses upstairs and work that pole for those men," Ginger walks up, barking orders.

Ginger sees all of us standing around and reads the room. "What the fuck did you two do now?" Ginger snaps.

I smile, feeling the support from these women.

Maze, the commentator, interjects. "Dixie tried to pull rank on Dallas, but our Doc here pulled the *buddy* card, and Dixie lost."

All the ladies laugh, and I grab the beer Maze got for me. Ginger laughs, looking at me. "Dallas must like you if he told you he calls his dick *buddy*," she says.

I smile. "Yes, Dallas told me his *buddy* found his forever home."

The girl I was talking to, Dixie, huffs loudly, grabbing the other girl's arm, shoving her toward the stairs.

Everyone just watches and laughs as the two girls walk away.

Storm turns to me with a glimmer in her eyes. "Why, Doc, I think you'll fit in just fine around here."

"Damn, I was hoping for a catfight!" Bear announces behind us.

Storm's face turns from happy to furious again. "I'll show you a catfight. Let's go. I need to fuck the shit out of yah or beat yah. But I need to get it out of my system. Let's go," she orders him, and I'm shocked when he lights up, slamming his beer, following her toward the hallway of rooms.

Holy. Fucking. Shit.

Ginger walks up beside me, laughing. "That's my auntie and uncle for you. You'd think, at their age, they would slow down, but they fuck like rabbits."

I just stand there watching them grab each other and head to a room. If any women did that in the Crows, they'd get their ass beat. Tonight, I have seen a whole different side of club life.

Dallas

Yeah, naked women are running around here, but no one is being mistreated. Ginger was telling me the truth. This place is different.

"You good?" Ginger nudges me.

"I'm in a bit of shock, and other than everyone asking me every two seconds if I'm okay—yes, I'm good," I answer, still looking in the direction her aunt and uncle went.

"Shock? Because of my aunt and uncle?" Ginger asks, confused.

I chuckle, "Nah, I'm shocked at how different it is here."

Ginger throws her arm over my shoulder, squeezing me. "Girl, like I said last night, we've got you. Plus, you haven't seen anything yet."

I give Ginger a side look with a smirk, drawing out, "Greaaat."

"Shots!" Ginger yells, squeezing me again with a smile.

My heart aches. Can this place and these people become my family? God, I hope so. I need to trust them and take the leap. I turn to Maze and scream, "Shots!"

All the girls join in chanting shots.

17 | The Low-down

Dallas

"Okay, so everyone has the lowdown on what is happening, what they need to do, and when we're meeting back here, right?" Wolfe announces to the room of officers.

All the officers reply, pounding on the table.

"Let's finish this shit. Meeting adjourned," Shy declares.

I stay seated as everyone exits the room. My brain's on overdrive, and I'm trying to put all the pieces together without frying my brain. My life is like a code or, I guess, a puzzle. Every element or number has to fit perfectly. If one thing is out of place, it fucks up everything.

That is how my brain is functioning right now. All the pieces are not matching up. I thought Ronny was the key to all this clusterfuck happening, but now I don't know. The mystery men Ronny meets with are MIA. Lee's place was ransacked. The gang who did the drive-by is linked to Vi—who is linked to a shit ton of trouble, and Doc. Is it just a coincidence that Vi and Doc are friends and connected to us separately? Is it really that small of a world?

"Dallas," Mac asks, across from me. "You alright, brother?"

"Huh?" I huff, keeping my eyes tranced on the notes I took during our meeting.

"Dallas?" Mac demands.

"Sorry, what did you say?" I answer, snapping out of my thoughts.

Dallas

"I asked if you're okay? You seem out of it," Mac says, sounding concerned.

"I'm good. I'm just wondering if Doc's magical pussy has me overlooking something. Like, am I spellbound and missing something?" I reply automatically without thinking as I underline their names—Vi, Ray, Lee—over and over on my paper.

Mac booms with laughter. "Did you just say the doc has a magical pussy?"

"He sure did." Shy laughs from the front of the table.

Quick joins in, adding his two cents. "I remember when I had my first talk with myself about Ruby's voodoo pussy. It happens, brother."

The room erupts in laughter. I swivel around to see who's still in the room with us, seeing Shy, Quick, Mac, and Cash.

"Yeah. Doc has me hooked for sure. I'm not fighting her magical pussy. I'm fighting its effect, wondering if it's clouding my vision of the whole picture," I explain.

"You think something's linking all this together?" Cash asks, leaning back in his chair.

"You mean besides Doc?" I throw out there, adding, "Yeah, something just feels off."

Shy sits back down, looking around the room, and asks, "Well, let's lay it all out there. What do we know for sure about Vi and Raydene?"

All eyes land on me because I am the club's hacker who finds out all the secrets—secrets like hers. I should know all of this, but I don't. Not yet anyway.

"I've put a call into Hawk, Luc, and Ethan. I know Luc doesn't let anyone near Alexandria without them getting vetted. So, I know Ethan's involved too. The only mystery here is Vi, but Brick should know if anything is off there. I won't know until I do the looking myself. I'm pulling all my intel from them, and

I'll lock down and figure this out. Someone is linking them all together," I say, looking around the room.

"Well, even if the girls are clean and there are no red flags, it doesn't mean someone around them or in their life isn't linking it all together. Brother, this is your expertise," Quick chimes in, tapping his fingers on the table.

"Raydene does have a red flag, that's why I've asked Luc and Ethan about her. Her record is too clean for my liking—kind of like how Doc's was squeaky clean. I don't know." Frustrated, I throw my pen on top of my notepad, grabbing my cap that's on the table, and push my chair back to stand. "All I know is I need a computer. I need to take Doc to the hospital with Stitch—"

Mac cuts me off, "And you need to stick your *buddy* inside that magical pussy and get your head straight?"

All the men get up laughing, making their jokes.

I smile.

"Fuck yeah, I do." I look down toward my dick and say, "You're hooked and claiming that girl, aren't you, buddy?"

The whole room booms with laughter as we file out of the room. We're all talking shit about my dick when Storm and Bear turn the corner, grabbing onto each other.

Mac groans, "Ma, stop groping Pops."

When they see us, they both laugh at their son. "How do you think we got you, boy?" Bear says to his son.

Mac ignores his parents, who are still groping each other.

Bear turns, making eye contact with me, and says, "You got a keeper, that Doc of yours."

Followed by Storm. "I like her. She's going to fit in here fine. She's a feisty little thing, doesn't take no shit."

"What the fuck happened?" Shy groans.

"Was there a catfight?" Cash asks, getting all excited.

Bear's smile falters. "Nah, I was hoping for one too, but Doc shut that shit down."

Dallas

Then it sounds like a bunch of owls sounding off with all of us asking, "Who?"

So, I ask again, "Who did Doc—"

Storm, obviously wanting to hurry this along, blurts out, "Long story short, the tall blonde, Dixie, came up talking shit like she was going to fuck you. I was going to handle the bitch, but Doc moved me out of the way—called you Alec and something about your buddy finding his forever home. Dixie ran off, pouting. Your girl's at the bar taking shots." She grabs Bear's shirt, pulling him away, "Now let's go. We'll see you boys in a few."

"Fuck, we missed it." Mac pouts.

"Fuck is right," I say, moving toward the bar. "I'll pull the video for you," I call over my shoulder to Mac and Cash.

Simultaneously, they both get excited, calling out, "Fuck yeah!" Mac says along with Cash, "Yes, brother!" Then I hear them high-five each other. They're like two little kids.

The front room is packed with members and girls. As I head toward the bar, I see Hawk, and he gives me a head nod.

Goddamnit. That's not good.

I give him a half man hug, slapping him on the back greeting him, "Hawk, glad you made it, brother."

We release each other. Hawk replies, "Dallas. Good to be here, brother."

After our hellos, I give him a head nod. "Whatcha got for me?"

Hawk looks around the room before leaning in close. He says, in a hushed voice, "Talked to E—Vi's husband was working with the feds."

I lean back to face him, shocked. "The feds?"

Jesus Christ, can this clusterfuck of a mess get any more confusing?

"Yep," he says, leaving me hanging for more information.

When he doesn't give me anything more, I demand, "What

the fuck, Hawk? You can't just say that and not give me any more details."

Hawk shrugs. "I don't have anything else. E just called and said Luc was on it and that he would get back to us."

"What the fuck is Luc going to do?"

Hawk shrugs again. "Again, brother, I don't know."

Motherfucker.

I slap him on his shoulder. "Okay, I'll get on it and figure it out. Thanks."

Hawk gives me a nod and heads back to the bar, leaving me standing there with my thoughts that erupt into a million—what-ifs.

"You ready?" a voice asks from behind me.

When I turn around, Stitch, Sissy, and my Doc are standing there.

Shit. No.

"Yes," I reply with a smile. Pulling Lee against me, I say before kissing her. "I was just on my way to get you."

She giggles. "You were, were you?"

I kiss her again, this time deepening the kiss. "Mm-hmm. I heard you were out here causing some problems," I tease.

Doc leans her head back to look me in the eye. "Um, I did not start anything. That—"

I cut her off with a kiss, shutting her up, and when we break, I explain, "I know. I was teasing, Doc. I'm sorry about Dixie. I'll have a word with her."

Doc's face tells me she isn't too happy about that.

I ask, "What?"

"Uh, no, you're not. I handled it," Doc replies, feisty as ever.

"How much have you had to drink?" I question her because I'm starting to realize that she becomes sassy and bold when she's had a few drinks. The only other time she is outspoken is when she is in Doc mode.

"A beer and a couple of shots. Why?" she replies defensively.

Dallas

I kiss her forehead. "Just wondering." I turn to Stitch and Sissy, who are entwined together, having their own conversation. "You ready? I need to get back."

Stitch turns his head but doesn't let go of Sissy. "Yeah, let's go."

We both grab our girl's hands and lead them to our underground garage, where we keep most of our bikes.

"Who's going with us?" Stitch asks from beside me.

I look around to see who isn't busy when I see Brick charging toward us. I give him a head nod. "What's up?"

Brick looks past me right at Doc. "Where the fuck did she go now?"

Doc comes up to my side as we stop in front of Brick, and she answers boldly, "She went with the girls and Maddox to the studio to work on music."

Oh shit.

"Motherfucking bitch. I told her." Brick exhales, frustrated.

"Look, Brick, I don't know you or what your situation is with Vi, but I do know her, and she doesn't like being told what to do," Doc throws her two cents out there, shocking us all.

I look down at her with a smile. Storm wasn't lying when she said she's a feisty little thing. "I think you need to drink more often," I say with a smirk.

Brick just huffs and walks away.

Cash and Mac walk up next.

Stitch rants, "Damn, are we ever going to get out of here?"

"Where are you going?" Mac asks while Cash stares at Doc.

"We're headed to the hospital." I bribe them, "You two want that video—you'll come with us."

Cash smiles. "Are there any other hot doctors like Doc there? Or nurses?"

Mac jumps in, answering him, "There are some hot nurses, but I didn't see any other hot doctors."

I pull Doc and say, "Let's go. I need to get back."

Following behind me, Doc asks, "What video?"

Mac laughs. "The video of you and Dixie."

Doc shrieks, "What video? Why do you want to see that?"

I say over my shoulder, "They like girl fights."

"We didn't fight. Now, if she tries touching you, then there might be a fight," she says confidently.

She's possessive and jealous.

I stop, turning to Doc as they go around us. "Are you claiming me?" I say, giving her a devilish grin.

My heart aches as I hold my breath, waiting for her to answer.

She smiles up at me. "If your *buddy* can claim *his* forever home. Don't you think I should be able to claim him back?" she replies sweetly.

"Buddy *definitely* likes you claiming him," I say, rubbing him up against her, showing her how much he *likes* her. My cock strains against my jeans, hearing her claim him. I lean down, giving her a soft, sweet kiss.

"See? He misses you," I tease, pulling away. "That's why we need to get this fucking hospital trip over with, so he can jump back into heaven."

It was the first time I had Doc on the back of my bike, and fuck me. It was like seeing a kid run free on a playground. She still has an ear-to-ear grin on her face.

We left two prospects with our bikes as the six of us walked into the hospital. I'm walking hand in hand with Doc as everyone eyes us. I watch her as she walks with confidence through the hallways. I'm waiting to see if she will let go of my hand, but so far, she hasn't.

Dallas

When we get to the elevator, I ask, "So, what's the plan? How are you going to get all this stuff we need?"

She turns to all of us, showing a mischievous grin. "Well, I was thinking you three" —she points to Mac, Cash, and me— "can distract the ladies at the desk while us three head to my office where we'll figure something out."

Mac and Cash both agree with shit-eating grins. The elevator dings, and we exit to the floor where I was treated. When we get to the nurses' station, I see Nurse Cheryl.

At first, she eyes all of us in leathers, but when she sees Doc and me holding hands, she shrieks. "Lee! Oh. My. God! Alec!"

Cheryl hurries around the desk, giving us both a big hug. "Lee, are you alright? I heard your place got broken into."

Lee replies, "Yes, I'm fine, Cheryl. I wasn't there, thank goodness."

Cheryl puts her hands on her hips, looking back and forth at us. "I'm so happy you two finally got together. What are you two doing here? No one hurt, is there?" Cheryl asks, looking around at all of us, inspecting us for injuries.

Lee laughs. "No, we're all good. I just needed to get some stuff from my office since I'll be taking some time off."

Cheryl lights up. "Are you going away together? Hmm?" She nudges me.

Doc laughs as she heads to her office, with Stitch and Sissy right behind her. Great, this is where I'm supposed to distract.

I follow Cheryl to the desk and lean up against it. Mac and Cash are already chatting it up with the other nurses. So, I turn my attention to Cheryl.

Finally answering her, I say, "No, we're just taking some time to get to know each other."

Cheryl looks around the office before leaning in to whisper, "I heard someone's been looking for her. And that's why her place was broken into. I hope you are protecting her."

I smile and say reassuringly, "I'm not letting her out of my sight. Hence the reason we're all here with her. I promise nothing bad will happen to our Doc."

Cheryl beams. "I knew you'd be good for her. I miss her around here, but I agree she needs some time off."

"Cheryl, can you take a sample bottle into room four, please?" A male voice says from behind me.

Cheryl looks up, and her eyes widen. "Yes, Doctor."

A tall, slender male doctor in his early fifties with glasses walks our way when I turn around. He's looking down at a chart, and when he looks up to see us, he stops in his tracks, pushing his glasses up. He looks to my cut, and I look to his name tag—Dr. Gregory Wilson.

Fuck, this *is her boss.*

I smile.

He's older. Thank fuck.

He returns my smile and asks, "Hello. I'm Dr. Wilson. Can I help you?"

I'm leaning against the desk, but push off, extending my hand to him. "Hey, I'm Dallas. We're here with Doc. I mean Dr. Hart. She's getting some stuff from her office."

He shakes my hand back, giving me a firm grip.

Good, he's not a pussy.

"Oh, she's here?" he asks, looking over my shoulder for her.

"Yeah, she's in her office."

I stay quiet as I watch him look for her. When he's done looking around, the good doctor's appearance slips, becoming serious. He looks me in the eyes, firing off questions. "You're protecting her, right? Is she okay? Have you found that fucker yet?"

I'm shocked, speechless. I just blink and stare at him.

When I don't say anything, the doctor tilts his head to the side for me to follow him into a room. I glance over at the guys, whistle and motion where I'm going. Mac gives me a nod. I follow

Dallas

the doctor to an empty room. When he shuts the door, I stand there and wait for him to talk.

"Dallas, I'm taking a chance here with you since Lee obviously trusts you. I know all about Lee's past. I was the doctor on duty when she was brought in after her attack the last time in Chicago. After hearing her story and everything that she'd been through, I pretty much took her in as one of my own. She's a brilliant doctor." He pauses but quickly continues once I don't say anything. "I've tried to keep her hidden all these years, but he found her. I need to know you will do whatever it takes to protect her. He needs to be taken care of, the piece of shit," he says, frustrated, running his hands through his hair.

At least I know how they met and why they're so close.

Finally, I speak, "I agree."

He looks over at me with hope as his face softens, looking thankful.

"When she took your case, I asked if she was okay with it. She said yes, of course, that she was fine. Then when she called me and told me she was with you when her place got broken into, it freaked me out. She said you could help her. I was not too fond of it, but she needs someone who can protect her," he tells me like I don't know him. "Ronny is a crazy motherfucker."

My phone dings. It's probably the guys.

"I know," the doctor snaps his head to me in shock. I continue, "I've known Ronny for many years, and we've had beef for as long as she's been running. So—yes, I can protect her, and I will," I say, moving toward the door, reaching for my phone.

"Well, whatever you need, you just let me know. Lee's like a daughter. I just want her safe."

With my phone in my hand, I grab the door. Turning, I say, "I'm glad she had you all these years helping her hide, but she won't need to hide any longer. I promise it'll be over soon."

I put my phone to my ear as I open the door. I find Lee

looking frantic while everyone is huddled around her, looking at something.

"Dallas, we got company," Jammer, our prospect, announces in my ear.

Christ, what happened now?

I bark back, "Who?"

When she sees me come out of the room with her boss behind me, she runs over to me. As soon as she's within arm's reach, I pull her against me, embracing her with one arm. She wraps her arms around me, holding me as if her life depended on it.

I got you, Doc.

"There were a couple of guys on bikes, but no colors. When they spotted us, they took off," Jammer explains.

"Okay, keep an eye out. We're on our way down," I say, ending the call.

Wrapping my other arm around her, pulling her against me. "Lee, what happened?" I say softly into her ear.

Doc doesn't say anything, but Cash hands me a piece of paper. I reach for it with the phone in my hand. Her boss, Greg, moves in closer to me so he can see.

> Harley,
> You can run, but you can't hide.
> Remember that.
> See you soon.

Dallas

"Motherfucker!" I breathe out.

Greg asks before I get a chance. "Where did you get this?"

Stitch looks at me, and I nod, letting him know it's okay to answer him. "It was in her office on her desk, sitting there in an envelope."

Greg curses under his breath, mumbling to himself, "I need to talk to security, we need to call the police, and I need to pull the video."

When I hear police, I snap my head to him. "No. No police. I'm taking her out of here, but I'll call you with what I need from you. You can start with the video. I'll be needing that first."

Greg looks down at Lee in my arms, completely beside herself, and nods his head. I look to Stitch and ask, "Did you get all the stuff she needed?"

Stitch holds up a bag.

Greg hands me a business card. "Here's my numbers. You can reach me at any time."

"Okay, let's get the fuck outa here," I growl, moving Lee to the elevators. "Jammer thinks we may have company but doesn't know for sure."

Cheryl calls out behind us. "Take care of our girl. Call me if you need me."

Within ten minutes, we were on the road with no signs of trouble.

The ride back snapped Doc out of her panic attack. When we pulled up to the clubhouse, she was back in Doc mode, ready to take the supplies and take care of my brothers. I guess I'm lucky for that. Otherwise, I would have had to spend more time that I don't have, making sure she was okay.

Instead, she gave me a phenomenal kiss, grabbing my ass, and told me to go handle business, that she was okay.

She told Stitch that he could help me, or whatever, that she had it under control. Sissy kissed Stitch, and the girls left us standing there speechless.

Mac speaks first. "Christ almighty, was that the same person from ten minutes ago. The one that freaked the fuck out?"

"Yeah, I mean, that's hot as fuck—Doc being all bossy but, fuck—is she okay?" Cash chimes in next.

"My girl's a fighter, been surviving for years. She's been getting beat down and bounces right back up. She's good, but if she's not, I'll be there to catch her," I say with pride.

"You better lock that one down," Stitch says, slapping me on my back. "She's a keeper."

"Both of you fuckers better lock those bitches down because, if not, I will. Dumb motherfuckers!" Cash says over his shoulder as he walks to the door of the club. When the door opens, music blares out.

"Fuck yeah! I love this song!" Cash shouts, getting pumped as he walks in singing, "You know what I'm talking about. Just let me know if you want to go…"

As "La Grange" by ZZ Top sounds throughout the club.

Mac laughs, joining in. "They got a lot of nice bitches. Haw." Of course, changing the words.

Everyone watches as Cash hops around, throwing his hands in the air, playing the drums, and Mac joins in with the electric guitar behind him. The club erupts in laughter as people whistle and shout for the guys. Then we all join in singing, "A haw, haw, haw, haw."

I laugh. Another reason I love my brothers. No matter what's going on, they live for each moment—They live life free.

18 | The Black Crows

Dallas

WE DECIDED TO HAVE THE SIT-DOWN WITH KNIGHT AT THE White Wolfe Lounge. That way, we could control the setting. After our meeting to discuss how this was going to go down, we called Knight. He was in Brooklyn at a hotel, while most of his men were out looking for Ronny.

Once we told him where to go, he let us know he would only be bringing his officers and the officers of Ronny's chapter. We agreed to do the same, but we will still have members out of sight around the building just in case this goes sideways.

I didn't particularly appreciate that he wanted to hear from Lee herself what the story was and what had been happening. I protested, of course, but once Wolfe silenced me, he laid down the rules. She will be hidden from everyone until the time was right where only Knight, the president of Ronny's chapter, and their VPs were present. Everyone else had to wait outside. Then we'll bring out Lee to explain her story to Knight.

Still, I wouldn't say I liked it, but I understood that Knight needed to hear from Lee about what was going on. When I explained it to Lee, she freaked out a bit, but she understood. She kept saying as long as Ronny wasn't there, she would be fine.

They still haven't heard from or seen Ronny, and neither have any of our people. It's like he vanished, which didn't make me happy bringing her out in public, especially with the Crows around.

After we got off the phone with Knight, we headed out to the lounge to get ready. Mac, Shy, Wolfe, Cash, and I are seated around a table waiting for them to show up. They should be here anytime now. Lee is in the back office area with Brick, Tiny, Ginger, Vi, and Raydene. Bear and Hawk are hanging out at the bar, while Chiv and Blink are outside waiting for Knight and his men to show up.

"You need to keep your cool, brother. If you can't, I'll need you to leave the room. I don't want a war with the Crows if we don't have to. Knight seems to want to squash this shit, just as much as we do," Wolfe says from across the table.

Fuck that.

"Dallas!" Shy yells.

I look up from the table where I'm in deep thought. "Yeah, I get it. I will try my hardest but—"

Shy cuts me off. "No buts. Do you *really* think I'm going to let anything happen to Doc?" he exclaims, laying his forearms on the table.

I shake my head no in response.

"Exactly. Now let us do the talking. We all know what we want here, and that's for Ronny to be gone. So be cool, brother," Shy says, sitting back into the chair, taking a swig of his beer.

Brick pokes his head out the door, from the hall of offices where the girls are. "Can we get some drinks back here. Doc needs to calm her nerves."

Hawk answers before anyone, "I'll bring you a bottle."

Mac spouts off, "Tequila." He looks around the room and scoffs, "Those bitches can drink tequila like it's water."

The table erupts in laughter, and Hawk hands Brick a bottle of tequila with some glasses. Just in time, too, because a whistle sounds from the front door, and everyone sits up on high alert.

When Knight enters the lounge, we all stand up and watch his men file in behind him. Right behind Knight is a big black man. I recognize him as one of the men that dragged Ronny out of the last meeting we had. Then Rash, the president of Ronny's chapter

Dallas

in South Carolina, and another huge man. He's the man who sat next to Rash at the last meeting, so I'm assuming he's the VP.

Wolfe walks up to Knight shaking his hand and every man that follows. I don't move from my spot at the table.

"Would you like something to drink before we get started?" Wolfe asks, moving to the head of the table on our side.

Knight says as he sits down at the opposite end of the table, "Yeah, we'll all have a beer. Thanks."

Hawk and Bear hand out beers to all of us before heading back behind the bar to watch over us.

With Wolfe at the head of the table, it goes Cash, Shy, Mac, and myself on one side of the table. Then Knight is at the other end with the big black guy, and his cut says Big Black Original VP. Next is Rash, who is the president, and his VP is Rocco.

Rocco was the name Ronny said was the guy who told him he thought Quick was the bartender, that started Ronny's outrage at the other meeting. Both Rocco and Big Black helped drag Ronny out that night. Interesting, I wonder if they're close with Ronny.

"Wolfe, I did some digging on all the shit you said yesterday, and you were right," Knight says, looking at Rash and Rocco. "Seems they've been keeping a lot from our meetings."

Rash jumps in, "I didn't know about the restraining orders or the rapes. I just knew he was obsessed with her."

"There's *a lot* you didn't know *or* haven't told us," Knight grits out, looking furious.

I feel myself start to boil, but I keep a lid on it.

"Have you found him yet?" Mac asks next to me.

"Nope. Not a word. He's gone dark, he has *a lot* to answer for, not just about Harley," Knight explains.

"Ronny and two other members are missing. They've been unhappy with our business dealings lately and thinking of going nomad—" Rash tries to explain, but Knight cuts him off.

"Look, we're—" He pauses for a second, gaining control of

165

himself. "Or I should say, *I'm* finding out Ronny's been doing a lot of shady shit on the side. Doing bad deals using our name, then blaming other people, which starts fights with other clubs. It leads us all the way back to when we had issues." Knight pauses, rubbing his temples. "Once we put all of this together" —he looks across the table to Wolfe— "we need to sit down and discuss shit, but right now, we need to deal with Ronny."

"Agreed," Wolfe says from across the table.

When none of us speak, Rash leans forward, placing his forearms on the table, clasping his hands. "Okay, so I knew Harley. I watched her grow up and I knew how possessive Ronny was with her. I knew her uncle and Scooter. I really would like to talk with her and hear her side of this."

We all become silent.

"What is your endgame here?" I ask, rubbing my chin.

"You claimed her?" Rocco spits out, pointing his finger at me, "Even though you knew she was a Crow."

"Yes," I reply instantly. "She's mine."

"She's a Crow," Rocco says through clenched teeth.

"I was a Crow," Lee shouts, startling us all.

We look around for her, but she's nowhere to be seen. Suddenly, the door from the DJ booth opens to the hall, where she enters the room with Ginger by her side and her entourage right behind them.

Everyone stands up, when I start to move to her Mac grabs my arm, stopping me. "Wait," he whispers.

I do as he says and watch as my Doc, my girl, my Lee, walks in, shoulders back and head high. I fall even harder for her as pride fills me, seeing her be so strong.

Christ, she's beautiful.

She repeats herself loud and clear. "I *was* a Crow."

Ignoring her, Knight says, "Harley," greeting her.

Dallas

She moves toward me, and when she reaches me, I pull her into my side, claiming her.

"Like I said. She's mine now," I declare to the room.

"Why don't we all sit down and let Doc explain herself, then you can ask her questions," Wolfe says to the table. Then he looks to his daughter, "Snow, why don't you and the girls go to the bar and wait there with Bear and Hawk."

Ginger nods and the girls head over to where Bear and Hawk are sitting. I'm in shock that neither Vi nor Raydene protested, but they see the seriousness in this meeting, and they know I won't let anything happen to her.

Doc looks up at me with a smile and whispers, "I got this."

My heart swells. Doc is one badass bitch, and she's mine. I nod, letting her sit down next to me, which places her right next to Knight.

She turns to Knight, "What do you want to know?"

Knight shifts in his seat and looks over at Rash before looking back to Lee. "I'd like to hear your side of the story from the beginning."

"Right now is the time to explain everything from the beginning," Rash throws out there simultaneously.

Lee takes a deep breath and begins, "It all started back when my uncle Ben and Scooter were alive. Ronny was crazy jealous back then. Ronny and Scooter were always fighting, but Tommy always got in the middle."

Rash interrupts, "Yeah, everyone saw that he was a dick, but it was out of brotherly love. He's always taken on the big brother role with you, even though you were cousins. Anyone would be protective of his family. Shit, we all thought of you as a little sister."

Rocco scoffs, shifting in his seat.

Lee ignores him and keeps going, "When Beaver got sick, and the club started fighting within itself, Scooter and my uncle wanted to go to you, Knight." She looks over at Knight, "and tell you what was going on. Ronny was furious with them. Telling them it was an 'in-chapter issue' and not to bother you."

Knight adds, "And what was going on?"

"Nothing," Rash exclaims. "We were trying to figure out who was going to be president."

Bullshit!

I look over to Wolfe to see if he'll chime in because we know it was more than that. They were fighting with us over territory and doing shady shit.

Rocco snaps his head, giving Rash a look, telling him to shut up.

Ha! See, motherfucker.

Lee ignores Rash's outburst.

"I don't know. All I know is that my uncle and Scooter were killed a week before they were supposed to see you. Ronny didn't seem upset, and that's when he started talking crazy, saying I was his and no one could have me. He was fighting with members when they would just look at me."

"Is that why you stopped coming around the club?" Rocco asks softly.

Lee looks over to Rocco and nods her head. "You know how he was. I mean, you were one of the guys he was always fighting."

Wait. Is that why he's pissed at me, because he wants her?

I growl.

"Why didn't you come to me?" Rocco leans forward, placing his forearms on the table. "Once Rash was elected, shit settled down. Why didn't you come to one of us?"

"I was told women are never to be seen or heard, and only there to fuck. I didn't feel safe. Ronny threatened me and said you would believe him over me," she says to all of them. "Plus, I was long gone by the time you both got voted in. I needed to get away, so I picked up and left for Austin, without telling anyone."

Dallas

"He said you were getting ready for college, and that's why you weren't around," Rash explained.

"I thought something was up, but when he said you were going to college, I thought maybe it was true since you always talked about going," Rocco added.

Why didn't you look for her, you stupid motherfucker?

"Yeah, well, he found me in Austin. He flipped out, smacking me around a bit. Then he said it was for the best, because he was fighting all his brothers over me. I told him I got a full-ride scholarship to Austin. He left me alone for a while. He would text or call and check in on me daily, but he wasn't around. Finally, right before school started, I left with just a bag and moved to Tennessee, where I *actually* had a full ride," Lee tells them, folding her arms over her chest.

I rub her back, letting her know I'm right here for her. All of us keep our mouths shut, letting her tell these motherfuckers her story.

Rocco and Rash look at one another.

"What?" Knight questions his two men. "What are you not telling us? No more fucking secrets." He pounds his fist onto the table. "It's bad enough we're airing our dirty laundry here in front of the Wolfemen. This fucking shit needs to end."

"Ronny wasn't happy when we got voted in as president and VP. He was one of Beaver's boys that didn't like our new ruling. He still answered to Beaver, even though he wasn't president anymore. Tommy was in favor of us, and it started a feud between them. Ronny went off the deep end, wasn't seen for a couple of weeks. We think this was around the same time. Because when he came back, he acted differently, more to himself, and always on his phone doing something. We thought it was him rebelling against us," Rash explains to Knight.

"If only I'd known, Hay," Rocco says to Lee in a soft voice.

Hay? What the fuck is that, her nickname?

169

"He found me a little over two years later in Tennessee, and that's when he raped me," she announces to all of us, but looking straight at Rocco.

"Motherfucker," I sputtered through clenched teeth. The whole room reacts to her words, so I wasn't alone in my outburst.

Lee kept going. "I didn't report the rape because I didn't want them to go looking for him. Instead, I made a report to the police telling them my story of abuse, and they granted me a restraining order."

Obviously, by their faces, none of them knew about this.

"Was he alone? Or were there any other members with him?" Knight questions.

"I don't know. I didn't see anyone with him. He was always alone, just waiting for me in the dark," Lee says, squeezing herself as memories surface.

I can't take much more, so I lean over, pulling her into my arms for a hug.

"You're doing great, Doc. I'm right here, babe," I say into her ear before kissing her.

She smiles at me once I let her go.

Knight asks, "Then what happened?"

"I finally called Tommy. I told him what happened. He flipped out. He was upset I didn't come to him sooner and said that he would take care of it, and he did."

"Tommy didn't know where you were? Why didn't you go to him sooner? Did you not talk to Tommy at all?" Big Black finally speaks up.

"Tommy wasn't in a good place after his pops passed," Rocco answers for Lee.

"I left everyone and everything behind. I knew Ronny was psycho. I truly thought he had my uncle and Scooter killed. I was scared to talk to anyone in the club, including my cousin Tommy." Doc pauses, wringing her hands together. When they don't say

Dallas

anything about her suspicion that Ronny killed them, she keeps going. "Tommy checked in with me every few weeks for a year. I told him I was moving away again to attend medical school. He said he was proud of me but not to tell him where. That he would keep me safe, and he'd always be there if I needed him, but he wouldn't contact me anymore unless it was life or death. And I shouldn't contact him unless I needed help. Those were his last words to me."

"Jesus Christ, and you two didn't know anything about this shit? Tommy didn't tell anyone?" Knight looks to his men.

Rocco and Rash get quiet.

"What? Goddamnit, spit it out," Knight shouts.

"Tommy came to us, letting us know Ronny was bothering Harley at school, and he wanted to keep him from screwing up her chances of graduating. He asked us to tell him if we heard of him going to see her or trying to have anyone find her," Rash explains.

"But Ronny never asked or said anything to us about Harley," Rocco finishes.

"Well, a year after Tommy died, he found me for the third time in Chicago. I was admitted into the hospital after he raped and beat me half to death. If the cops weren't called, he probably would have," Lee declares to the room.

"Motherfucker!" Rocco yells.

"When was this?" Knight demands.

"Was he arrested?" Rash asks next.

"No, he got away. It was a little over four years ago."

Rash looks at Rocco. "He said he got into a bar fight in Chicago, and that's why he had a warrant for his arrest."

"You didn't miss him when he was off doing this fucking shit?" Knight asks them.

"No, after Tommy died, you knew we were dealing with the Wolfemen, and Ronny was a loose cannon. Never around, and if he was, he was always getting into fights," Rash tells Knight.

The men start hammering back and forth about Ronny and Tommy's fights with each other. Also, Ronny's attitude changing toward many of them, and how he started going down the rabbit hole.

"I also think Ronny killed Tommy because he found out Tommy was hiding me," Lee announces, shutting all of them up.

Oh, shit. This could go badly.

I look around the table, and everyone has gone silent.

Knight looks to Wolfe and drawls out suspiciously, "Why do you think that?"

"Because I got an email from Tommy a week before he died telling me that he hoped I was safe and that he would always love me," Lee replies quietly.

Knight snaps his head to Lee.

"And?" Big Black adds, wanting more of an explanation.

"And, I replied with a smiley face." Lee wrings her hands together.

"And?" Knight leans toward her.

"And when I reread the email, I just knew it wasn't from Tommy. I started to panic, praying if it was Ronny that he wouldn't be able to find out where I was from an email," Lee further explained.

I close my eyes. *Fuck, Doc. Yes, you can. Christ.*

I bet all of my brothers are shitting themselves right now. If we could get them to think it was Ronny, all our problems would be gone.

Curious, I blurt out, "How did you know it wasn't Tommy?"

"In the email, it said he would always love me. Tommy never spoke the word *love* to me, or anyone, for that matter. He didn't believe in love. I used to tease him. He would always say, '*I will always be here for you.*' Or, '*I am always with you.*' I prayed I was wrong, but a year later, I ended up being right," Lee explains.

Dallas

Knight curses under his breath and looks to Wolfe and then back to Lee. "Harley, tell me the rest."

"After that, I changed my name. I relocated but still stayed in Chicago. I had great support there, and once they knew about Ronny, we all worked together to change me into Dr. Lee Hart. When a colleague offered me a job here in New York, I took it. I started my new life as a doctor here. I didn't know you knew about me until Dallas told me a few nights ago. Ronny hadn't reached out to me until the letter."

"What fucking letter?" all the Black Crows say at once.

She pulls out the letter she got and hands it to Knight.

"For fuck's sake," Knight says, handing it to Big Black.

Each one reads it and curses under their breath.

"But, I haven't *actually* seen him," Lee says, cheerfully.

The table's quiet.

"So, now that you know the full story, we need to work together and figure this out," Wolfe speaks up.

"This helps us fill in a lot of the blank spots," Rash says, looking at Rocco, who is nodding his head.

"Well, we don't know where he is, and we'll keep looking for him, but we need to know what you have on those men he sees while here. It might help us connect more of the dots," Knight says to Wolfe.

"They both went dark yesterday after we got hit here," I answer.

"The drive-by?" Knight confirms.

"Yeah, it seems they can't be found, and they're not at home or their shops."

"Can you share your intel with us? We'll stick around for a couple more days doing our searches, but if we don't find anything, we'll head back to our chapters," Rash says, grabbing his beer.

"We need to do some housecleaning," Knight says to Wolfe, who nods his understanding.

"As long as we're on the same page about Ronny. If he comes here for Doc, we'll try to keep him *around* for you," Shy speaks up for the first time.

"We would really like to deal with him ourselves, given the new information we've received. We want to interrogate him before you have him *dealt* with because I need answers," Knight explains.

I'm about ready to protest when Rocco interjects. "If he comes for her, we won't hold it against you for protecting her, but we would appreciate it if we could at least see him before you do anything *permanent*."

"If he comes for her, I *will* deal with him," I declare.

"He'll come for me. I know him," Lee throws out, all eyes landing on her.

"Hay, I'm so sorry this has happened to you," Rocco says sadly.

"Me too." She smiles. "But, I'm safe now. I'll be okay." Lee grabs my knee, squeezing me.

That's my girl.

I smile back at her, squeezing her back.

"I don't know about you all, but I need a stiff drink," Cash announces as he gets up.

Big Black follows suit. "You read my mind."

As everyone is getting up, I pull Doc into an embrace and say into her hair, "I'm so fucking proud of you. Do you want me to take you back?"

Lee lifts her head with a smile. "Nah, I'm good. I feel better knowing they didn't know. That it wasn't all of them behind it."

"We didn't know," Rocco says from beside us. "I would have hurt him a long time ago if I did."

Dallas

Doc and I release each other, turning to face him as I tuck her into my side. Rocco extends his hand out to me, shocking us all. *What the fuck?*

"I'm sorry for jumping the gun on you. I'm glad you've been here for Harley and keeping her safe. Something we all failed to do," Rocco says genuinely. "She was like everyone's little sister. We all watched out for her while she grew up. We thought he took his brotherly role a little too serious but never this. It's why we didn't come looking. We thought Ronny protected her, and if he needed us, he'd ask."

I shake his hand. "I get it. We feel that way about Snow over there, so we get it."

When he releases my hand, he looks to Doc. "Hay, we'll find him, and he'll pay for what he's done. Not just to you but to our brothers too."

What the fuck does that mean—his brothers?

She releases me and steps to hug him. I tense up, not liking his arms around her, but I have to give them this. Obviously, they were close, but fuck that. If Snow ever picked up and left, which she did. There would be more than just one of us going after her. I mean, we all went after her and *watched* her from a distance. No one would just let her leave. And no one would believe she just left.

I guess that's the difference between the Crows and us Wolves. We ask questions, and then we follow up on the answers. We check and recheck all the answers. We don't just let it go.

They break their embrace, and Doc steps back into my side, wrapping her arms around me. Rocco smiles and heads to the bar, leaving us there.

"Now, isn't that a sight? Never in my wildest dreams would I have thought we'd be drinking at a bar with motherfucking Crows," Mac says from behind us, startling us both.

"Hell no, brother. Never." I chuckle.

19 | The Search

Dallas

SINCE OUR SIT-DOWN WITH THE CROWS—IT'S BEEN A WEEK AND a half of searching for Ronny, only to come up empty. I've been working with a guy named Buzz, who does all their intel. He's new, and he's good—not as good as me, but he's good. I uncovered they are indeed cleaning house. They have a lot of new prospects and they've stripped more than a handful of members of their cuts.

The Crows went home yesterday, and if we find him, we're to keep him alive until Knight or Rash can interrogate him. If they find him, they'll give us the same courtesy.

Wolfe and Knight met up a couple of times discussing the timeline and swapped details of what intel was given to them at the time of our brutal war. We did kill Tommy and that other member, but we're finding out Ronny orchestrated most of the issues we had leading up to that fight and everything after.

Ronny has been biding his time, gathering men to do his bidding, hence the two men he's been seeing here in New York. They told us that Ronny has been dabbling in hard drugs, using and selling. When Wolfe told Knight that we knew Ronny was transporting drugs, Knight flipped out—asking why we didn't say anything. Wolfe just answered—we thought you knew and were okay with it.

We think Ronny is using those men that we still haven't found to transport drugs, but how is the question. I've been holed up

Dallas

in my room, on my computer nonstop, trying to find them and doing what I love to do—uncovering secrets.

Most of our other chapters took off throughout the week, but Wolfe and Cash stayed behind until we figure shit out. So, today it's been pretty quiet around here.

Doc has made herself at home here at the clubhouse. She's been helping around the clubhouse, getting to know the girls while taking care of our brothers. I don't know what I'll do when she decides to go back to her place. We've been back to her place to get stuff and a courier brought over some of her files so she could work.

I love seeing her in my bed every day, and the sex is beyond heavenly. I can't get enough of her. I don't think I've ever hung out with the same bitch this long. I mean, my brothers' ol' ladies or club girls, yeah they're around me daily, but not in my bed, in my business all day long.

Thank fuck it hasn't bothered me. I mean, *I want* Doc hanging around here, and *I want* her in my bed. And, to see her jump into Doc mode, being all badass, just adds fuel to my fire.

"Cheryl, can you schedule him for next Thursday? That'll give me enough time to follow up on all his tests," Doc says into her phone, interrupting my daydreaming.

I look over, and my dick instantly gets hard seeing her in my bed with all her patient files spread out around her. She's so goddamn beautiful, even now with no makeup on, wearing yoga pants, and her hair is in a messy bun on top of her head. Perfection.

Damnit! Turn around. I have work to do.

Doc doesn't notice me staring at her as she scans the file.

Get back to work.

Doc's heading back to work after this weekend. Life must go on, so I'll be escorting her to and from work. She'll always have someone with her and men stationed around the hospital until we find Ronny. Beau, Redman's boss at BB Security, has stepped up and coordinated with her boss Greg about security. Redman has his group of men, so he's handling all of that for us.

I hear Doc drop her file onto the bed and giggle. Not sure if she was still on the phone, I turn to find her smiling at me, but she still has her phone to her ear.

She says with a smirk, "Yes, he is very charming." She pauses to listen. "And, yes, he's good-looking too."

I smile.

She laughs, "Yes, Mac does have a way of getting what he wants."

Mac? What the fuck...

I frown, thinking she was talking about me.

She blows me a kiss.

I smirk, raising an eyebrow.

Doc laughs harder, tipping her head back.

My mouth waters seeing her exposed neck, ripe for the taking.

Fuck me.

I grumble to myself, "Down, buddy. We got work to do, and it ain't the doc—not yet anyway."

Turning to face my computer again, I laugh and think to myself. She has no idea what Mac can get away with, that motherfucker has a way with women. I think Mac will be a little sad to see Raydene go, even though she does have a boyfriend.

Vi and Raydene have come to the clubhouse to hang out every night, sometimes staying here and sometimes going back to the Mancini building. It's funny that Doc has told us several times that Raydene has a boyfriend, but we've not heard it from Raydene. I'm pretty positive my brother is secretly hitting that on the side.

An email pops up from Luc regarding the security for Doc. Luc and Maddox have been working with us since all the girls are staying at the Mancini building. Maddox and Alex toured with Raydene for a while, so they all felt comfortable being there with

Dallas

them. Luc has been trying to sign them, from what Doc has told me.

Doc went with Ginger and the girls one day to get out of the clubhouse. I was deep into my shit and needed to concentrate so I couldn't go. I knew she was in good hands with all of Maddox's men, Redman, and his men, so I was comfortable with her going.

She came back happy as can be, rambling nonstop like a little kid, all excited. She said Izzy was dealing with some anxiety, so she was working on music most of the time in the studio. She met Bella, Ruby's little girl, and fell in love. Ruby was talking to Vi and Raydene about signing with Spin It, Inc. label. Doc said it was a long, entertaining day. And this Saturday, her friends are DJing at Club Spin one night before they both head back to Chicago.

Brick had to go back to Chicago to deal with what happened here the day after our meeting. He and Vi had the biggest fight about her not coming back with him. She called her cousin Marcus and dealt with him, and Brick knew we could keep her safe, so he had to leave. Brick said he would be back to travel home with the girls, so he should be back tomorrow.

Vi's actually been chill since he's left. I catch her watching me and everyone around the club. I don't know if she's trying to figure us out and see if we're good enough for Doc. But I'm good at reading people, and I can tell something's been on her mind because she hasn't been all loud and aggressive. The only person I see her with besides the girls is Chiv and they're usually smoking weed.

Ethan and Luc are getting me the intel on her late husband. They assured me she wasn't linked to the feds. And, seeing as she helped kill the men who did the drive-by, I think she's good.

But, as I said before, we check and recheck everything. I'm just swamped with Ronny's shit right now. I'll be diving into her story once I get Ethan and Luc's intel.

Between diving into the dark web, searching for the truth,

unraveling secrets, and most of all, how it's all connected while trying to spend as much time as I can with Doc, I'm fucking fried.

"How did Izzy's appointment go?" Doc questions, again catching my attention, I don't turn around this time, as I continue to read Luc's email.

Izzy and Ruby haven't been around too much this week. Having little Bella, Ruby didn't want to bring her around until it cleared out around here.

Redman and Quick have stayed with their girls over at the Mancini building. We've kept Quick out of sight while the Crows were here. We didn't want any questions being asked to him or about him. So he's been helping Redman with the security detail and watching over the girls.

Stitch, Hawk, and Bear took off midweek with their ladies because Hawk's ol' lady had to get back to run her strip club.

"That's good. I'm glad. Okay, well, if you need me, just call. Otherwise, I'll see you Monday," Doc replies, ending her conversation with Cheryl, the head nurse at the hospital.

I try to keep my attention off Doc as she moves around behind me, when I start to reply to Luc's email, her angelic hands slide over my shoulder and down my chest.

I smile, taking in a deep breath, and close my eyes.

I don't move or say anything as she cups my chest and whispers seductively into my ear. "Alec, I'm done with my work." Nipping my ear. "Do you have anything you need me to do for you?" She lets her hair down. It's cascading around me as she continues her assault, sucking my earlobe.

My buddy stands to attention, hollering, *me, me, do me.*

I laugh to myself.

"Doc, I can think of a few things you could do *to* me." My voice is a low rumble.

Doc moves, suckling down my neck, slowly positioning herself to my side as she runs her hands down my stomach, gripping

Dallas

my cock. I take her mouth, sliding my chair back just a tad so she can move in front of me.

"Hmm. Well, I think *your buddy* needs my attention the most, don't you?" She giggles, licking her lips, moving into a seated position.

Yes. He. Does.

Before I can even reply, Doc has my pants open and my buddy popping into her mouth.

"Fuck yes, Doc," I breathe, gripping her head, sliding my fingers through her hair, securing it out of her way. And, of course, out of mine, so I can see every inch of my cock slip into her mouth.

Doc moans, and I swear to God I almost come on the spot.

"Jesus Christ!" I groan, sagging into my chair, throwing my head back.

A sound comes from my computer, but I don't look up. I know it's an alert. I should look at it, but *fuck*, her wet, warm mouth is skin to skin, and it's just as divine as her heavenly pussy.

My eyes roll back, lost in each pump going up and down. *Don't come yet.*

Doc grips my thighs, taking all of my cock, letting it hit the back of her throat.

Holymotherofchrist.

Unfamiliar noises escape me as she moves faster, sucking my cock like a fucking pro.

Ding.

"Yes, Doc. Fuck, baby. Ya—" Ding. "You're killing me."

Jesus.

The dinging from my computer increases, mimicking Doc's motions as she pumps my cock faster. I know it's crucial from the increased dinging sound.

Ding.

"Oh, fuck. Y-yes, Doc."

Ding.

Come on, buddy.

Doc moans, sending a vibration through my cock straight down to my balls.

"Shit, I'm going to come." I grip her head, trying to pull her off my cock, but she persists faster.

Ding.

"Fuuuuck," I moan.

Ding.

"Doc," I choke out.

I bust the hardest nut down her throat as stars erupt in the back of my eyelids.

Ding.

My God. I crack one eye open, seeing her finish me off, slowly swallow every last drop.

Ding.

"Christ, Doc. It just keeps getting better and better with you." I say breathlessly.

Ding.

Doc pops my cock out of her mouth, wiping her face with a big grin.

Ding.

Fuck!

"I think you need to get that." She giggles, sliding up my body and placing a quick kiss on my lips.

Ding.

I grip the back of her head and pull her back to me, deepening the kiss.

Ding.

"It's my turn." I move her to sit on me.

Ding.

"First, let me turn this fucking alarm off." I move her slightly to the side so that I can turn off the alarm.

Dallas

Ding.

When I click on my computer, I see the alarm is coming from my facial recognition search.

"Shit," I say, gripping her ass.

Standing with her wrapped around me, I lay her down on the bed.

"These." I grip her leggings "Off. Now," I say with a quick kiss.

She giggles. "Okay."

I run my hand down her body before turning back to my computer, where I come face-to-face with one of the men we've been looking for, Lenny Costello.

Fucking finally!

I lean closer to the computer, grabbing my mouse to adjust the screen, zooming in on him, and I can see he's at his auto body shop.

Gotcha, motherfucker.

He opens the big door to the garage. To let five motorcycles pull in. I lean even closer to the screen, hoping to see if they have colors, but my eyes lock on one person.

"Fuck!" I exclaim, grabbing my phone. "It's Ronny."

Doc springs up, shouting, "What? Where?"

Doc is at my side in seconds. When she sees him on the screen, she gasps, "Oh, God."

I pull her to my side, instantly wanting to protect her and give her assurance she's safe, as I put my phone to my ear.

The phone rings once, and Shy answers, "Whatcha got?"

I grit, "Ronny."

Shy answers instantly, "Let's go."

20 | The Discovery

Dallas

"**W**HAT THE FUCK ARE THE DEVIL DUOS AND DEVIL'S Dames doing with Ronny?" Wolfe demands.

"I don't know, but we knew that Ronny and the Devil Duos were working together to bring us down before when we were dealing with the Scorpions," Cash replies.

We're all in the conference room now watching the surveillance cameras, where I connected all the TVs, that way we can watch them as we prepare to figure out what they are doing.

I asked Doc if she wanted to come down, but she decided to stay upstairs and wait for me to return. She said she felt safer upstairs where you have to have a code to get up the elevator.

"Look! There..." Tiny points to the TV projecting the live video, so everyone in the room can see while I try to grab more intel. "The bike parts they are unloading are filled with bricks."

"Where?" Wolfe moves closer to the TV.

"See the gas tanks? They're pulling out bricks," Tiny explains.

I don't take my eyes off my screen with my baseball cap sitting low on my face, keeping my focus. I keep working away at getting more footage of the building and the outside surrounding area. We don't want to rush into an ambush or be outnumbered. We still don't know where the other Crows are or the other guy, Rayaan.

"You better get that motherfucker." I hear Raydene announce from down the hallway.

"Oh, we will, darling," Mac says confidently.

Dallas

"The girls are here," Redman announces from the doorway. "I'm going to take Ruby and Bella upstairs to my room." I hear Quick say.

Not taking my eyes off the screen, I shout as I keep typing, "Doc and Ginger are up there too. Tell her I'll give her an update soon."

Mac throws himself into a chair next to me. "I think all the girls are going to go hang out upstairs with Doc and Ginger."

That gets my attention. Yanking off my baseball cap, I grip the brim before putting it on backward. I look Mac in the eyes, giving him my full attention. "I don't want any of those bitches in my room, I have too many things exposed right now. Go make sure my room is closed up," I rush out.

Having Ginger, Izzy, and Ruby up there is one thing, but Vi and Raydene are another. I don't trust them or know them, and I don't want them in my room.

Just as Mac's about ready to get up, my phone rings, and it's Doc. I answer on the first ring. "What's up?"

She clears her throat. "Um, I'm going to close up your room, but I don't know how. You usually lock it up, and I've never been up here this long without you. You rushed out of here. Do I need to do anything to make sure it locks?"

I close my eyes as relief washes over me, and I relax, motioning for Mac to wait a second. My heart fills with pride and shame at the same time. I should have known Doc would protect the security of my room since she knows how private I am. I mean, she is the first bitch I've had in there.

"Dallas? You still there?" She says nervously.

I let out a deep sigh, "Yeah. I'm sorry, Doc. I've got a lot going on. It means a lot to me that you're making sure it's locked up. All you have to do is shut the door, and it locks automatically."

She's quiet.

"You okay?" I breathe.

"I just…" She pauses. "I just can't take my eyes off all the surveillance cameras. Ginger's been coming in and out, checking the footage. I know you don't mind her entering your room, but now I see all the girls coming up here, and I don't want them in your room. So, I'm going to head out to the living area and wait for them. But…" she trails off nervously.

"But?" I encourage her to keep going as I take the key to my room off my chain.

"But, if your door locks automatically. That means I won't be able to watch Ronny's video."

Looking at Mac, I hand him the key as I speak to Doc on the phone. "Mac's heading up, and he'll give you my key. That way, you have access to the room when I'm gone. Ginger's like a sister and can come into my room. But, while all the other girls are up there, I would rather you kept my room locked or just you going in there. Okay? I'm trusting you."

"Dallas, you don't have to do that. I just wanted to check on you through the video. I know how private you are, and I don't want to intrude, and I won't let anyone in there," she says softly.

I click on my laptop a couple of times, sending the feeds to another TV.

"Lee, I want *you* in my room, just no one else. So, I'll feed this to the big TV upstairs in the living area, and I'll have Mac set it up for you. That way, all of you can see what is going on. Just be careful with Bella around."

Shy yells from across the room, "That motherfucker's importing this fucking shit, and we need to figure out how and when."

"I need to let you go. I'm sorry," Doc rushes out.

"Doc, you're fine. I'll be up there soon to check in with you before we leave. So, don't worry. I've got you. Okay?" I try to reassure her.

"Okay," she replies softly.

"See you in a few," I say before hanging up.

Dallas

Mac moves behind me, waiting for instructions. We've been friends the longest, and he knows the drill. My fingers fly across the keyboard, trying to hurry, so I can get back to what I was doing.

Fuck yes. Easy as pie.

"Can you put it on HDMI 3?" I say over my shoulder. "And, show them they can switch between HDMI 1, our building security that plays on all TVs, and HDMI 2, which is regular TV."

"Got it," Mac replies, exiting the room.

"Jammer's in place," I tell the room, seeing his camera pop up on my feed. I've had people taking shifts on all the places Ronny's met up with these two men. Jammer happened to be close to the auto body shop, so I sent him over to video the situation, or if they left before we headed out, he could follow them.

I split the screen so they could see Jammer's video from the outside. When his camera focuses, we see massive bikes.

"Motherfucker!" I say under my breath, but the room erupts in curses as we look at a parking lot full of both Devil MC clubs' members.

Wolfe says, "Something big is going down. Dallas, can you—"

But I cut him off, already knowing what he wants. "I'm downloading now, and I'll send it over to Knight."

The room is full of Wolfemen now as we all watch this auto body shop fill with Devil members.

"That's Karma, president of the Devil's Dames, next to Ronny and her brother, Blaze, the president of the Devil Duos." Worm points at the first screen. "She used to date a few Scorpions back in the day, and she's one lethal bitch. She and her brother are into all kinds of illegal dealings."

"It's like they're having a meeting," Chiv chimes.

"They've never had this kind of meeting before, especially here in our territory," I answer.

"Shy, look." Quick rushes to the TV, pointing. "Isn't that the motherfucker that was with Tommy and Royce the night they jumped you?"

Shy moves closer to the screen. On my laptop, I screenshot it, trying to get a closer glimpse of the man's face.

"He's not wearing colors. I don't know," Shy answers.

"They've got incoming," Jammer announces over his live feed. "They look connected." He focuses on the two black SUVs that just pulled into the parking lot.

"Knight. Do you see this fucking shit? What the fuck are they doing?" Wolfe demands into the phone. "Did you know about any of this?"

Silence.

"Don't send your men there. We need to know what the fuck they're doing. There are too many of them, and we still don't know who the fuck is in the car," Wolfe yells into the phone.

Knight left behind five men to help in the search for Ronny.

"There's Lenny, the owner of the auto body." I point to Jammer's feed as the guy walks over to one of the SUVs. I'm trying to pull the plates for information.

When the window rolls down, everyone becomes quiet in the room. Lenny says something to the person and then points to inside his shop. Lenny steps back as the window rolls up. The door opens up, and three men in suits exit, moving toward the second SUV.

"Fuck!" I yell after seeing the report that just popped up. "The SUVs are rentals. Both rented under Lenny's name."

Two men and a woman exit the second car, and the room explodes with everyone talking at once.

"Jesus Christ. That's Russian Bratva," I say, grabbing my phone.

"What? Who?" Wolfe shouts.

My fingers fly across the keyboard with my phone lodged between my shoulder and chin. "E, we got a problem."

Dallas

"We always have a problem. Can you be a little more specific?" He chuckles.

"Russian's are in town." Ethan curses as I continue. "Viktoriya Petrov, Leo Aslanov, and an unknown."

"Where?" Ethan exclaims.

Typing as fast as I can, I say, "Sending you the link now. Get over to the clubhouse as soon as you guys can."

"On it," Ethan replies before hanging up.

"Jaysus, the girls!" Redman shouts across the room.

I flip over to the feed I have running upstairs and interrupt it, so the girls won't see the Russians enter the building. Thank God we are the only ones who can see Jammer's live feed.

Izzy was abducted just months ago. We don't need her going back into hiding. At least not until we figure out why they're here.

They might not even know they're Russian. I was the one who did all the digging on Dominic after we found out he was a Petrov. That's when I did a full background on all the Petrovs, finding out that Kirill has a sister. They call her Viktoriya the terror.

"This is bigger than just Ronny now. We need to figure out what is linking everyone together." Wolfe slams his hands on the table. "This shit stays here in this fucking room."

"What did Knight say?" Cash asks.

"He said he has no idea what is going on, and he wanted to send his men in there to talk to Ronny. I told him it would be a death sentence, and no one is getting through that line of defense without a plan and more power."

"So, we wait, we watch, we follow, and we make a plan," I reply.

"We need to get a few more eyes on that place," Mac says from the door. I hadn't even realized he was back from going upstairs.

"I need to find the other guy Ronny was dealing with, Rayaan

Bhasin, because if something is going down, what part does he play in all of this?"

I start a search on the unknown Russian, but my brain is starting to go on overload. I need help pulling information, so I bark out orders. "Redman, get on the phone with Luc and Beau. We need them to join forces again, and I need their intel on Vi and Raydene. Have them come here to do a brief. I have already contacted Ethan and his crew. Cash, get on the phone with Hawk and fill him in. We're going to need all hands on deck here."

"We've got movement." Jammer's voice booms through the live feed.

Everyone looks up to see the three Russians, followed by their security detail, enter the building just as another SUV rolls up. Three men get out without any hesitation and stroll up to the building.

Wait a minute. What the fuck—isn't that guy...

"*Lay off,*" Redman says, with an Irish slang meaning shut up, as he walks up closer to the TV.

"Who the fuck are they?" Wolfe asks the room.

"Is that who I think it is?" I ask Redman.

"*Aye.*" Redman pulls his phone out, saying to the room. "We *dinna* see this comin' did we?"

"Who the fuck is it?" Wolfe demands, losing his temper.

"I believe it's Raydene's ol' man, Dexter," Shy confirms.

"What? Where? Which one?" Mac demands, moving closer to the screen.

I point to the white guy about my height and size, and he's the more diminutive guy of the three.

"Beau, ya need to get over here now," Redman barks into the phone.

Pause.

"*Aye,* but we got a bigger problem. Just get here." Redman listens for a brief second before hanging his phone up.

Dallas

"Can the girls see any of this *shite*?" Redman asks me.

"No, I cut all surveillance."

Wolfe announces with a clenched jaw, "We need to keep those girls in our sights. Get them to go dance or get drunk, but I don't want the Chicago girls going anywhere that we don't have eyes on them until we figure this shit out."

I respond. "Yeah, I agree."

Shy speaks up next, looking over at Mac. "I want eyes on all exits and send a couple of guys in cages without colors on standby to follow each one of these motherfuckers."

Mac, who hasn't taken his eyes off Raydene's man, answers, "I'll go with a couple of guys. Keep the feed going to my phone. I want to know what is going on inside."

Shy looks to me and then back to Mac. "Are you sure, brother?"

Mac turns to the room of members. "Fuck yeah, I'm sure."

"I'll go with him. No one's seen me in years," Chiv says, coming up behind Mac.

Shy turns to Worm. "Do you think Phil'em-up Phil will be spotted if any Scorpions or Devils see him?"

"Naw, Phil would be good, and I'll go with him. That way, each of us isn't riding alone," Worm says, getting up to move toward the door and yells down the hallway. "Someone get Phil'em-up."

Phil is another member who was patched over from the Scorpions. He's been loyal to a fault, so I know he'll do what's needed.

Jammer announces, "Trey just got here, and I've got my brother Cam and cousin, Josh with me too, so we'll be covered if they all decide to leave at once."

I rush around to get the earpieces for the men, so they can all be linked in like Jammer. Once the men are hooked up and linked in, they head out.

A loud ding sounds through the room, and I know what that means, we've got facial recognition on our mystery Russian. A loud dinging sounds again. This time I click on it right away and announce to the room, "Maxim Semenov, also known as—Maks the Muscle. Christ, Viktoriya has some major protection with her."

Wolfe's on the phone with Hawk. Shy's speaking to Luc as we watch the group move around the shop, with Lenny moving his hands around talking to them. He's probably explaining how they move the drugs. Ronny just stays off to the side as Lenny does all the talking.

"Did you see that? Viktoriya just gave Dexter a nod. It looks like they know each other," Tiny says, motioning toward the screen.

Shy, who is standing next to him, nods his head. "Yeah, you can see that they're more familiar with the Russians than they are with the bikers."

I start another search for the two other men with Dexter, just as Shy says, "We need to find out who they are."

"I'm on it," I answer.

A loud whistle comes from the hallway. Someone must've put a member on the elevator, letting us know if one of them came down.

The girls. Shit.

"Close the door. I don't want any of the girls getting wind of this. We need to keep them preoccupied," Wolfe explains, heading for the door.

"Why did you turn off our cameras?" Ginger yells from down the hall.

Here we go.

Redman is on the move as well, heading for the door, asking, "Bloody hell, is it all of them or just Snow?"

Tiny, standing next to the door, pops his head out to see, then replies, "All the girls, minus baby girl." Meaning Bella is still upstairs, but the Spin It girls, as we call them, are on the move.

Dallas

Shy, Quick, and Redman all step outside the conference room to handle the women. I want to go to my girl, but I can't stop searching. My job is to protect my club. *Protect her.* I need to find out who those men are and what the fuck's going on, but my brain keeps going back to Doc. Wondering if she's okay. Is she scared?

"Fuck!" I shout, hitting my fist on the table.

Cash, who I didn't even know was behind me, says calmly, "Brother, take a break. Get a beer. Go check on your girl. I got this. You've been going at this for how many days now? We've got eyes on them, and if something happens, we'll holler." Cash puts a hand on my shoulder, squeezing me.

Wolfe turns from watching the TV. "Dallas, go handle the girls. Get a drink and bring us back one too."

I sigh, pushing my chair back to stand up. I feel like I'm letting them down. I should know all of this already, and I'm not fast enough.

"Brother, you've done a great job. All these fucking curveballs are not your fault. Fuck, not one of us saw this coming," Cash says, stopping me as I turn to leave the room. "We'll figure it out, but we can't do that with you half out of your mind from exhaustion."

I give him a nod.

Just as I'm opening the door, Wolfe says, "Bring back Jack and Jameson. It's going to be a long night."

21 | The Waiting

Lee

"What the fuck happened to the surveillance? It just turned off?" Vi announces from the couch.

Ginger and I round the kitchen counter to see the TV, sure as shit, the feed is gone and the TV is white as snow.

"Shit, they cut us off," Ginger exhales.

I turn to her. "What's that mean?" sounding panicked.

"It means they don't want you seeing what the fuck they're doing," Raydene answers dramatically.

"Thank fuck Izzy and Ruby are in the room with Bella. We need to hurry," Ginger grunts, moving fast to the TV.

"What are you doing?" I follow close behind her.

"I'm switching it back to our security cameras so at least we can see what the fuck is going on downstairs."

The four of us girls sit and watch as the men go in and out of the conference room while other members mingle around the building. Nothing seems different than earlier. I can see the men are anxious, but I don't understand why they cut our footage.

I start to bite my nails. My stomach is all in knots, knowing Ronny is in the same city as I am. I'm trying to keep my cool, but I was in a full-blown panic attack before the girls got up here.

"Stop, LeeLee. You are safe," Vi declares across from me. "We got you. They've got you. It ends now. No more hiding."

Ginger puts an arm around me. "Agreed. We got you, girl. Don't let Ronny control your life. Live for today."

Dallas

I start to cry, letting my wall fall a little. I can't hold it in. Ginger pulls me into a full hug, and Vi and Raydene circle us too.

"What did I miss? Did something bad happen, or are y'all having a moment without me?" Izzy teases as she enters the room.

The girls pull away from me, laughing as Izzy prances in with a massive smile on her face.

I wipe my eyes. "I was having a moment, that's all." My voice cracks.

"Lordy lordy, don't we all. You should have seen me a few months ago. Shit, I wouldn't even leave the apartment, and I still have at least one meltdown or panic attack a day. Thank God for Redman, he whips me right back into shape," Izzy says, plopping down on the couch.

Dallas. I wish I could talk to him.

"So, what's going on? Why haven't they left yet? And why is the TV showing our security cameras?" Izzy questions, finally realizing the video of Ronny isn't up.

"*Dese* motherfuckers cut our feed off," Vi replies, waving her hand toward the TV.

Raydene jumps up off the couch. "Fuck this. Let's drink. We can't do anything about it, and we're safe here, so fuck it. Let's have some fun."

"Absofuckinlutely!" Izzy bounces up, following Ray into the kitchen.

Vi is next to follow. "Oh-kay. It's *bouta* go down."

Ginger and I look at each other and smile.

"Ruby-Rube! Fuck me till Tuesday, girl. Let's go," Izzy hollers from the kitchen.

Ginger and I jump up when Ruby runs out of Quick's room like the room is on fire. She starts whispering, but by the time she's in the kitchen, she's yelling. "For the love of God. Finally, baby girl's asleep. You betcha—fuck me, it's time!"

195

I start laughing. Firecracker is the perfect nickname for Ruby, she goes from quiet mom to party girl in seconds. I love it.

After my third shot, I finally feel relaxed. We're all sitting around the table taking shots, bullshitting about music. Just as we're about to take our fourth one. Ray demands, "Where the fuck are they going?" as she points to the TV.

We all snap around to see Mac, Chiv, Worm, and other guys I don't know storm toward the front door.

Ginger is out of her seat first, grabbing her phone. "Where are they going?" She pauses. "What do you mean, no one's talking? Maze, for fuck's sake, find out!" she says, hanging up her phone to text someone.

Oh, my God. They're going after Ronny.

I start to bite my nails, and just like that, my anxiety is back. *Fuck!*

Raydene slams her phone. "He's not picking up. It's going straight to voice mail."

I turn back around. "Who?"

"Mac."

Ginger looks to the TV and then back to us. "Fuck this. I want to know what the fuck is going on, I'm going to head down there. We can drink at the bar, they can't keep us locked up here."

Ruby jumps up. "I'll get my baby monitor."

I laugh nervously. "Shouldn't we stay up here? Won't they get mad if you ask about club business?"

Ginger laughs. "This is about you. You have every right to know what the fuck is going on. Shy is my man, Wolfe is my daddy, and Mac, who just stormed out of here, is my cousin. So, fuck yes, it's our business."

"Dayum, girl! I like you more and more." Vi laughs, standing up.

Raydene stares at her phone like it's magically going to ring.

I can do this.

Dallas

I start to pace in front of the TV while all the girls move around. I murmur to myself, "I do have the right. I do want to know what is going on. Are they going after Ronny? Alec did say he would come to update me, and it's been forever. It is about me." I stop pacing to see all the girls standing in silence, watching me. "Fuck it. Let's go."

I know it's the alcohol talking, but I want to know what is going on.

"*Attagirl!* Wait, we have to finish our shot," Vi demands.

After taking our shots, we head to the elevator.

I can do this. He won't get mad. I am safe.

I tell myself this all the way down the elevator, down the hall, heading toward the bar. When Ginger starts yelling, I stop in my tracks, letting the girls go ahead of me. Just in case the men do come out roaring, I have time to run.

Just then, Shy, Quick, and Redman file out of the room, closing the door behind them. My heart drops. He didn't come out to check on me. Is he mad? Did he leave with Mac, and we just didn't see? I start to panic.

I'm still near the elevator and can't hear what the men are saying, but they steer the women toward the bar away from the conference room. I'm debating going back up to Dallas's room and locking myself in there until he comes and finds me. I watch the men struggle to get the girls to move. Then Quick looks over at me, smiling, before leaning down to kiss Ruby.

Okay, he doesn't seem to be mad. Maybe I'm tripping? Perhaps Dallas is just really busy. I should just go back upstairs where I said I'd be. I head back down the hallway, pausing when I get to the elevator.

Why can't I go to the bar? He won't be mad, will he?

Suddenly two arms wrap around me from behind, and I cry out.

"Lee, it's me, baby," Dallas says, trying to calm me down. "Calm down, it's just me."

I turn around to face him, and when I see it truly is him, I throw myself at him—wrapping my arms around his muscular neck, kissing him hard and frantic. I don't know what has come over me, but I need him.

He's safe.

Dallas grips my ass, lifting me so I can swing my legs around him as he presses me up against a wall. My hands are all over the place, gripping his shoulders, grabbing his biceps, clawing his back.

"I need you inside me," I demand.

Dallas groans, moving to the nearest open room, slamming the door shut with his foot. He places me on my feet, breaking the kiss. He leans down, practically ripping my jeans off. I flick his baseball cap off, running my fingers through his wild hair, tugging at it.

"Alec, fuck, I need you." Pushing his head into my crotch. My body is ready to explode.

Dallas rips my panties down, moving his skilled tongue swiftly over my clit. He sucks my swollen bud before suckling it gently. "Fuck." He groans, moving up my body. "I don't have the time I need to worship that heavenly pussy of yours," he says with regret while moving up to grab my breast through my shirt. "I promise it will be soon, though." Dallas spins me around to face the bed, bending me over. "I'm sorry, but this is going to be rough and quick." Dallas's voice drips with deep desire.

"Fuck me," I beg.

Dallas moves his hands up my back and down over my ass before gripping my hips, slamming into me. We both cry out instantly.

"Heaven," Dallas says, gliding into me over and over again. "Fucking heaven."

Oh, God. Yes.

I'm lost chasing my orgasm that's at the brink of

Dallas

bursting—slamming my hips back, meeting him thrust for thrust. I clench the bed, giving me more leverage.

"That's it, Doc. Fuck me. Fuck me hard," Dallas grunts breathlessly.

"Yes. Yes. Yes," I cry repeatedly.

My climax is right there.

Yes, right... Oh... Oh...

My muscles contract as tingling explodes down to my toes, instantly curling them.

I cry out his name, drawing it out as my orgasm washes over me.

"So fucking beautiful. Keep coming, Doc." Dallas grips my hips harder, his fingers pinching into my skin, but I welcome the pain as it intensifies my high.

Dallas pulls me up against him, putting one arm around my chest while his other hand pushes hard against my mound. He slips his fingers down between my folds, playing with my clit.

A gut-wrenching moan escapes me when another orgasm ignites.

He pounds up into me with deep, long, hard thrusts. Each slam increasing his pace. *He's close.*

I can't move. My body is like butter. Dallas kisses my neck, nipping it, before fully sinking his teeth into the crevice of my neck, jump-starting my body again.

I reach up, pinching my nipples.

"Yeah, buddy. Come on. Claim her. Make her yours," Dallas chokes out, his voice deep and raw, dominating me.

"You're mine, Doc. No one will ever have this pussy again."

My eyelids shut as those words resonate to my core, and just like that, I'm forever his.

"Yes. God, yes." I swoon. "I'm yours."

In one motion, Dallas flips me over onto my back, slamming

right back into me. Leaning down, he takes my mouth ravenously, caging me in with his hands at my shoulders.

"Look at me, Doc." He pounds into me faster and faster. Our bodies slap against each other as I grip my breasts, holding them from flying around.

Sweat's dripping from his forehead, our eyes are locked. I can see his orgasm knocking at the door, ready to bust out.

I smile.

"Yes, Alec."

He smiles.

When he grips my shoulder, holding me in place, I know he's close. I moan as another orgasm springs to life. "Oh, fuck. Yes."

His neck veins bulge as his body tenses against me. His breathing becomes erratic as he pants louder.

I reach my hand between us, flicking my clit as he hammers me harder.

I look into his eyes. "Alec, come with me. Fuck. Yes."

Dallas leans down, giving me a sloppy kiss as he cries out his release, biting my lip, sending me over along with him. I slam my tongue into his mouth, we're devouring each other's guttural moans. His rhythm starts to slow, emptying every last drop into me.

Dallas breaks the kiss, dropping his face into my neck as we try to catch our breath. He relaxes, putting his weight on me. He rotates his hips a few more slow torturous pumps, letting the climax run its course through us.

A few seconds later, Dallas pops his head up, giving me his beautiful green hooded eyes.

"Fuck, baby, I needed that." His voice is dry, scratchy.

I don't say anything because I'm thinking the same thing—how I needed him inside me to calm my anxiety.

Dallas takes my silence wrong. "Are you okay? Did I hurt

Dallas

you?" He moves to stand, but I grab his arms, pulling him back down onto me.

"I'm fine. I was thinking the same thing. I needed you to calm my nerves." I smile.

"Doc, you have no idea how stressed out I am, and all I can think about is you," he groans, dropping his head down to my chest.

"I'm sorry," I whisper.

He snaps his head up. "Don't be. If it were under any other circumstance, I would be elated, and we probably wouldn't be leaving my room for like a week, but your safety and the club's safety are in my hands. I need to work to get this resolved," he explains to me, sounding torn between the two.

I reply softly, "You have me. Don't worry. I'll be okay. Do what you need to do, just know I'll be here." I cup his face in my hands, rubbing my thumb over his scruffy beard.

He closes his eyes, so I continue. "You don't have to babysit me. I've been through worse. As long as you tell me the truth, keep me in the loop, and tell me what you need me to do, I'll be okay."

He still doesn't move or open his eyes. I start to panic and ramble even more.

"I just can't handle the unknown. The worrying and not knowing kills me. I understand I can't be in there with you but at least keep me in the loop with what you can."

Fuck, did I piss him off?

Dallas opens his eyes.

"I need you to keep what you see and hear to yourself. Can you keep what I tell you between us and not tell any of the other girls?" he says in a low voice.

"Of course," I reply instantly. "This is my life we're talking about."

He takes a deep breath, probably thinking of what he can tell me.

"Please just trust me." Dallas's phone rings, interrupting him. "Fuck. I got to go back in there. Just know we have eyes on Ronny, but we can't go after him yet because curveballs are being thrown at us from different directions. We're waiting it out to see who's all involved."

Great, a baseball chat.

"What do you mean, who all is involved?" I fire back.

Dallas's phone rings again. This time, he stands up to answer it. "Yeah?"

He pauses.

"Yeah, I'm just down the hall. I'll grab the bottle and head back in. Give me a couple." He puts his cock back into his jeans, then grabs mine off the ground when he stands up. I lie there propped up on my elbows, watching him.

"It's that bad? This isn't all about me, is it?" I ask softly, seeing the worried look on his face.

Dallas squats down, slipping both of my feet back into my jeans. He pushes them through one by one, looking like he's lost in thought. I don't think he's going to say anything, but when he looks up, our eyes lock, and he crawls up to me slowly.

Goddamn, he's beautiful.

Alec's hair falls into his eyes. His facial hair's long again since he's been working nonstop these past few days.

"It's a clusterfuck. So many things are linked together, and we don't know who's pulling the strings. We have to be sure who's involved before we pull Ronny. I promise you, though, you're safe with me. I just need more time." Kissing me on my forehead, he pulls me up to a standing position.

I wrap my arms around his neck as he pulls my jeans up over my ass.

"I trust you, I know you'll figure it out." I smile. "Just don't leave me in the dark. I hate the unknown."

"I'll tell you everything once I figure out a few things. You're

Dallas

right, it isn't just about you anymore. The club is involved now, but I'll talk to you before we do anything. I've got you, Doc." Dallas leans down, engulfing my mouth with a deep, passionate kiss.

When we break, I whisper, "I've got you just as much as you've got me. I can handle it, and I'm here for you."

He kisses me again, quickly.

We both finish straightening ourselves out before heading out the door. Dallas goes out first, holding my hand, his body blocking my view. We're both lost in thought when I look up to see who's greeting us at the other end of the hall, stopping me in my tracks.

What the ever-loving fuck!

Maddox, Luc, and Beau are standing around with a bunch of their men next to them. Some I know, and some I don't. All of them are standing around the conference room.

I yank Dallas back, so we're face to face. "What the fuck is going on?" I demand.

Dallas smiles. "I got reinforcements. Like I said, a lot of curveballs, I need help finding out who's throwing them."

I'm speechless. He leans down, kissing me before hauling me down the hallway.

I don't like baseball.

22 | The Secrets

Lee

"**A**RE YOU OKAY?" RAYDENE ASKS, SITTING DOWN NEXT to me.

I shrug. "I don't know. Half of me is relieved we're away from the clubhouse, but the other half feels scared not being there. I really hate the unknown."

After Dallas dropped me off at the bar, he went back into the conference room, only to return half an hour later with Redman, Quick, Maddox, and Shy on his tail. They decided it would be best if we all went to the Mancini building where Maddox's men, along with Beau's men, could watch over us while all of them figured stuff out.

I was the only one that protested, but when I saw the pleading look in Dallas's eyes, I knew shit was bad. He needed us girls gone so they could stay focused and for me to be safe.

Plus, Ruby had already gone back upstairs to be with Bella, so taking Bella home made more sense.

Redman, Maddox, and a guy named Eli drove us to the Mancini building where practically all the security men and people from the label live.

The plan is to head up to Mia and Luc's penthouse, where we'll have dinner, and the girls can work on music.

I went with Vi and Raydene to the apartment they were using while they're here. Luc always has an apartment or studio for DJs who are from out of town.

Dallas

"Yeah, I get that. I wish Mac would text me back," she says, looking at her phone.

"What the fuck is up with that anyway? Shouldn't you be more concerned with why *your man* hasn't returned your call in two days?" Vi asks, plopping down on the other side of me.

Raydene looks over to our friend. "Why do you have to be such a bitch?"

Vi laughs. "Says the girl dropping shitty comments left and right toward me."

Fucking great. Here we go.

I lean back, folding my legs up under me on the couch, and let the two girls have it out.

Raydene turns her body so she can look straight at Vi and me. "Goddamn straight. I want to know what is going on. Why don't we just get it all out right now." Raydene huffs, folding her arms over her chest.

I look over to Vi, waiting for her to respond, but she doesn't reply. Hell, she doesn't even look over at us. She stays slumped into the couch where she landed, just staring straight at the TV, which isn't on.

Raydene scoffs.

I touch Vi's arm. "Are you okay, Vi?"

Vi leans her head back, closing her eyes, and starts to cry.

Holy shit.

"What the fuck?" Raydene exhales.

I unfold my legs and turn to my friend, pulling her into an embrace.

"Oh, my God. Vi, what's wrong?" I say softly, holding her. I look over at Raydene, who is just as shell-shocked as I am.

Raydene snaps out of it, moving to the floor in front of us. She wraps her long arms around us both. "Vi! Girl, I'm sorry, and we don't need to talk about it."

We're both in shock because we hardly ever see Vi cry—like

never. She is the strongest woman I know, and we both just hold her while she unleashes whatever she's been holding in. When Vi is upset, she doesn't cry—she hurts someone. Like physically.

Vi releases me, sitting up straight, wiping her eyes.

Raydene and I sit there waiting for her to talk.

"I'm so tired. I'm sorry," Vi croaks out.

Raydene jumps up, rushing to the kitchen, retrieving some tissue and water.

Vi smiles, reaching for the items. Once she has cleaned up her face, she takes a deep breath and says, "I think we're going to need lots of tequila for this conversation."

Again, Raydene bolts up and, within seconds, is back with a bottle of tequila and three tumblers. Not shot glasses, but glass tumblers you usually use for whiskey.

Once our glasses are full, we all take a sip and wait.

Looking down into her glass, Vi announces, "I had two miscarriages before Ton' died."

Raydene and I just look at each other in shock. It's been a little over three years since her husband, Tony, was murdered. That was another time she lost it in front of us two, but she held it together in public and at the funeral. She rarely talks about him anymore.

Those were some rough times for us all. After I got out of the hospital, they moved me to Marcus's place until I could find somewhere else to live. They kept me hidden because the last place Ronny would think to look for me would be with the leader of the Reapers. So, I was lying low while Raydene was getting help to change my identity.

Six months later, I moved in with Greg and his wife—becoming Dr. Lee Hart. Two months later, Tony was killed, and it changed everything for us girls. Between me being in hiding, Raydene working and trying to help me, and we didn't even notice something was going on with Vi. Then after the funeral, Vi went into hiding.

Sonovabitch.

"Why didn't you tell me?" Raydene asks softly.

"Ton' didn't want anyone knowing we were having a hard time getting pregnant. We went through fertility treatments." She wipes away the tears. "He had a low sperm count and not very good swimmers."

"You could have told us, and we wouldn't have told anyone," I said, squeezing her arm.

She smiled. "I know. It was just a tough time for all of us. You two were dealing with what happened to you, Lee. His family kept pushing us to have a baby. A lot was going on in his family business, and he was stressed out all the time. He felt like he was letting me down, but I kept telling him we didn't need to have kids."

"His family ended up finding out, or at least his father did. I don't know if he told anyone else, but his father flipped out. Said it had to be me that was the problem because his son was fertile. Ton, of course, defended me, but it started a feud between them."

She pauses, taking a swig of her tequila, and we both follow her, taking a drink.

"We were both just so tired of dealing with our families. Having to put on this front, looking over our shoulders all the time. Then when his father wanted him to divorce me, things went south real fast."

"How come no one knew about this? Did Marcus know anything?" Raydene asks.

Vi shakes her head. "Well, besides Sergio and Joe, who went everywhere with us, nope. Only one person outside our circle knew what was going on."

Raydene and I both murmur simultaneously, "Brick."

Tears well up, threatening to escape, as I think of her bodyguard Sergio. He was such a sweet guy—big and scary but loyal beyond belief. He died, saving Vi's life, and Joe was Tony's bodyguard.

Vi nods. "Yep."

Raydene fires back. "How? Why?"

"Ton' was concerned with his father's hatred for me, and with the family fighting with the Chingas, I was a target. Ton' and Brick have known each other since they were kids, and they did business together and were really close.

"One night, he had Brick come over, and we had a meeting. He told Brick he wanted him to watch out for me. He wanted me to be protected if anything happened to him, so he set up an account for me, but it linked through Brick. It looked like a business deal on paper, but it was actually money for me."

I jump in, asking, "Why not tell Marcus? Couldn't he protect you?"

"Ton' was worried not all of his members were faithful and his father would be able to pay them off. He was trying to find Ronny and run his own business. Ton' didn't want to rely on them. Yes, it was my family, but money changes people."

We all lift our glasses, taking a big drink.

"So why lie? After Ton' died, why not tell us then?" Raydene asks.

"The night of the drive-by, we had just found out I was pregnant the second time. We were out to dinner, just the two of us celebrating." Vi pauses, getting choked up. She sets her glass down, grabbing more tissues to wipe her eyes. "We had just finished eating, and we were walking to the car when we got hit. Joe moved in front, getting hit first, then Ton' went for me getting hit himself. As you know, I got hit in the shoulder, but Sergio pushed me down, taking the rest of the hits.

"I was knocked unconscious. When I woke up, I was in the hospital, and you both know the rest, but what you don't know is that Brick secretly hired a guy to follow and watch me. He was there too and ended up saving me. I guess one of the guys came back to make sure the job got done, and Brick's guy killed him. That is how we know it was a contract hit, but who actually did

Dallas

the hiring has never been resolved. I guess the guy picked me up and rushed me to the hospital, dropping me off, saying he was just someone walking by. The police came later, along with everyone else, as you know."

"Again, why not tell us?" Raydene was starting to sound like a broken record.

"I don't know. Brick and I formed a secret bond. Yes, people like my cousin and Ton's father knew I knew Brick, but they didn't know I was secretly protected. He is the only reason I have found out who I can trust and who I can't. I have been living a lie for so long I just keep going along with it."

"What about the baby?" I whisper.

Vi takes a deep breath, letting a few more tears escape. "Sal found out I was pregnant in the hospital. He told me not to breathe a word of it, threatened the hospital staff to keep quiet. I thought Sal was protecting me, but I knew better. He hated me. A week after Ton's funeral, I lost the baby."

"Jesus, Vi," I choke through tears.

Raydene wipes her tears away too. "No wonder you withdrew from everyone and everything."

Vi nods, grabbing her glass of tequila, killing the remainder before reaching for the bottle.

"So, what now? It's been years," I ask, leaning forward, pushing my glass out for her refill.

"Ton's family pretty much disowned me. I'm cut off from any of their money, but I have everything Ton' left me. Yes, I have his name. And, yes, I'm still living the life, but it's all a lie. They will have nothing to do with me. The threats didn't stop even when Ton' was gone. I had to become brutally vicious with the kill or be killed attitude. I've had to watch my back every step of the way." Vi's voice became strong and stiff.

"And Brick?" I ask.

"He and I have become close. He's gotten more attached

this last year. I'm just tired. I'm tired of living in Chicago, where I have to watch my back all the time. I want to move on and be happy." Vi takes a big gulp.

"Jesus, then do it. What's stopping you?" Raydene exclaims, lifting her glass. "Shit, is that why you've been more into DJing again. I think you should get back into it and travel with me."

I finish my second glass and feel the alcohol starting to work its magic as I start to relax.

"Marcus and Brick won't let me move away or do anything like that. Marcus knows that Brick has been protecting me. How much he knows, I don't know. I've never talked to him about it. He just seems glad when shit goes down, and somehow Brick is always around. He doesn't ask, and I don't say, but lately, he just deals with Brick."

"Are you hitting it?" I spout, only to realize what I've said and slap my hand over my mouth.

Vi and Raydene laugh.

"Yeah, I have, but it's not like that, or at least not for me. I don't know. We've never really talked about it, but the way he's been acting lately, all bossy, I think we need to have a little talk," Vi says, leaning back on the couch, looking more relaxed.

"I'm glad you told us. You really need to get that shit off your chest, and girl, we are your best friends. You can tell us anything. I mean, who the fuck am I gonna tell?" I rant, throwing my hand up.

Vi smiles.

"You." She points to me. "I can trust." She looks to Raydene. "You." She pauses. "I don't know. You tell Dexter everything, and I don't like your family or him knowing my business."

Dayum.

We sit in uncomfortable silence. Raydene looks hurt but she doesn't say anything, looking down at her glass before finishing it. So, I just wait and watch the two of them.

Okay, what am I missing here?

Dallas

"What? What are y'all not telling me?" I ask, looking between the two.

Vi breaks her stare at Raydene and smiles at me. "Nothing. She just can't keep a secret, and Dex has the biggest mouth." Crossing her arms, she looks back to Raydene. "Plus, lately, he's acting weird. Something isn't right with you two."

"Things have changed." Raydene's voice is low. "I've changed."

"Really? You don't run to Dex or your family and tell them everything?" Vi demands.

I'm waiting for Raydene to fire back and defend her man, but she doesn't. She grabs her phone and looks to see if anyone has called or texted.

What the fuck is going on...

Pounding at the door has us all jumping in our seats.

"Bitches, open up! It's time to go upstairs," Ginger yells from outside the door.

"And our escorts need to leave, so hurry the fuck up," Izzy yells sarcastically. I'm sure she's annoyed with Redman.

I look over and see Raydene and Vi giving each other a stare down. Something is for sure going on between the two of them, but I don't know if I want to push. I'll talk to them one on one and see if I can figure out what is up with them.

I jump up off the couch and head for the door, leaving the two to stare at each other. The alcohol rushes to my head, making me sway as I open the door.

"Goddamn." Izzy pushes past me, making me lose balance, falling back. Luckily the wall behind me catches me. "Are you ladies drinking without us?"

"Bloody hell, Legs," Redman shouts at Izzy, reaching out to help me. "Doc, ya alright?"

I giggle.

"Jaysus Christ, *ye betties are off your nut.*" Redman laughs, moving me aside so he can shut the door, keeping a hand around my arm just in case I fall.

"Betties? Off our nut?" I look at him weirdly, not understanding him.

Redman stands enormously taller than me. He looks down with his gorgeous eyes and fire engine–red hair. "*Ye* ladies are *fuckin'* crazy."

Goddamn, he's sexy as fuck!

I break free of his hold as I turn to walk away and say over my shoulder. "Crazy? I'm fine. I just got up too fast, and all the alcohol hit me. I'm fine. I'm not crazy."

Okay, that sounded crazy, and it came out way too slurred.

I giggle again.

Ginger and Izzy take shots with Vi and Raydene, as I hold on to my almost empty glass. I think I've had enough. I want to stay alert in case something happens.

"Okay, we gotta go," Redman says, standing next to me. "Mia is waiting, and I have to head back."

"Then go. We can find our way upstairs," Izzy says snidely.

She's not happy.

"Doll, I'm not gonna say it again. I'm takin *ya* to Mia's, where *yer* gonna stay until one of *me bois* or I come and get *ya*. I don't want any of *ye* walking around without a man with *ya*."

Vi gets up. "I'm sure we'll be fine," she says, pulling a gun out of her boot.

Holy shit!

Ginger scoffs, pulling her gun from her ankle holster. "See, what did I tell you?" Ginger says to Redman, waving her hand between the two guns. "We got this."

Raydene huffs, "I want a fucking gun. Why can't I have one." Sounding like a little kid who didn't get her piece of cake.

"He won't let me have mine." Izzy pouts.

Dallas

I start to laugh but cover my mouth, not wanting to piss him off even more.

Redman rubs his face, irritated.

"Quick let Ruby have hers. I don't understand why I can't have mine." Izzy keeps poking the bear.

I'm ready for him to snap, but all he does is look up to the ceiling, muttering some Irish gibberish.

I feel bad for him, so I try to help. "Come on, girls, let's go eat. Izzy, aren't you supposed to be working on music with Alex right now?"

Sure as shit, that gets them moving. We all pile out of the apartment with the bottle of tequila in hand.

At least it's keeping me from thinking of Dallas or what's happening with Ronny.

When we arrive at Mia's house, she welcomes us all with hugs. The place smells amazing, and my belly rumbles.

Maddox, Eli, and a couple of other guys are all in the living room waiting. When they see us walk in, they all get up.

"Where's Alex?" Izzy asks.

Maddox smiles. "She's in the studio waiting for you."

Their penthouse is the whole top floor, and Luc has a state-of-the-art studio in his house.

Izzy gives Redman a quick kiss, excited to work on music.

"Wait, before you go, I want to introduce everyone. This is Roc, Ace, Hunter, and you all know Eli," Maddox says to all of us. "They will be staying with you until we return."

Izzy laughs. "Um, I know them."

Maddox smiles. "I know you do, but let me finish. We've got men on every floor and eyes on the videos. I don't want any of you leaving here unless one of them is with you. Just call or let Eli know if you're going to go back to your place."

"Wow, all of this for little ol' me?" I say softly.

Maddox turns to face me, squaring his shoulders. "It's for all of your safety. We usually always have eyes on the videos, but we have a guy on each floor monitoring since you're all here. You're safe, and it's their job," he finishes with a beautiful smile.

Holy shit, he's gorgeous.

Everyone seems to disperse, just as I'm about to head into the kitchen with the girls, I hear Maddox call my name.

When I turn around, all the men are standing there with eyes on me. "Doc, hold on," Redman speaks up.

Maddox takes a step closer to me, lowering his voice. "Dallas wanted me to let you know that he'll text you every hour to check in and to remember you're safe. He has links to the surveillance here too. These guys I'm leaving here are well-trained men." I look over his shoulder, and the big scary guy they call Roc smiles.

I smile back sheepishly. "Oh-kay," I draw out slowly.

They all smile at me but don't say anything. I'm sure it's the alcohol, but I need to know, so I ask, "Is Mac okay? Is he back from where he went? I know the girls were worried he left in a hurry." I look to Redman more than any of them, but Maddox is the one that replies.

"He went to scope something out. He isn't in harm's way, but he is watching something important and getting intel to bring back to us. Like Dallas told you, we're trying to get all the information we can before we take action."

"Oh-kay. Thank you," I say, nodding my head before turning to head into the kitchen. As I enter the vast room, the delicious aroma coming from the table makes my stomach growl. My phone begins to vibrate.

Pulling it from my back pocket, I see it's a text.

Dallas: I'm thinking of you. I can't wait to hold you in my arms.

Well, damn, that was fast. Maddox must have just texted him, telling him he talked to me.

Dallas

Lee: I'm thinking of you too and doing good. Just about to eat some heavenly food. Thank you for checking in. It helps with my anxiety. (kiss emoji—heart emoji)

Dallas: Hmm, I can think of something heavenly I want to eat. When I'm done, you will be my dessert.

I smile ear to ear.

Dallas: Fuck! My buddy's hard just thinking about you.

I cover my mouth as I laugh out loud.

Lee: Well, let him know his girl is all wet and ready to go. Now get to work, so you can ravish me sooner.

Dallas: (emoji kiss) I'll hurry.

Mia walks in, clapping her hands, *"Bien, chicas, es hora de la fiesta. Sirve una scopas, sube la música y comamos."*

Luckily, most of us know Spanish, so we know that she told us it was time to party, pour some drinks and let's eat. We hoot and holler at her from around the table as Izzy and Alexandria come from the other side.

Jesus, this place is enormous.

"Where's Ruby?" I ask, pulling a seat out next to Raydene.

"She's waiting on the babysitter to get there, then Hunter will bring her up here," Mia answers, picking up a dish to pass around.

Once seated, I lean over and say in a low enough voice—only Raydene can hear. "I found out Mac is doing surveillance, getting intel to bring back to the club. He's not in harm's way, just watching, and that's why he can't talk."

Raydene's face lightens. "Thank you."

I smile back, reaching for the dish Ginger hands me.

My mouth is watering, the food smells so good. It's time to eat.

23 | The Timeline

Dallas

ONCE THE GIRLS WERE GONE, WE OPENED UP THE CONFERence room and spread out, giving us more space. Maddox's three guys, Ethan, Isaac, and Chad are here, while Maddox went with Redman to drop the girls off. Along with Luc, Beau, and a guy named Reed, who I've met a few times since he sets up most of the security surveillance feeds and helps monitor them.

Wolfe, Cash, Shy, Quick, Tiny, and I are the only members in here. People keep filtering in and out now that we opened it up. Mostly everyone is trying to figure out what's going on while I get Ethan and Reed set up.

Ethan and I decided we needed to put together a wall of intel. Since I wasn't involved during the Emmett stuff, Ethan is starting there, and then I'll add in all my stuff.

When Mac and the others got to the auto body shop, we set a guy at each corner to see every view. That way, when one of the parties leaves, we'll have someone on point to follow them.

We've been watching Ronny now for almost three hours. An hour after the girls left, Ronny's little meeting ended. Jammer, his brother, and his cousin took off following the Russians. Tiny brought in another TV, so we have Jammer's live feed going on that TV.

We found out the two men with Dexter are Jesse Johnson, known as JJ, a big-time drug dealer out of Chicago, and the other

Dallas

man is Sonny King, known as King, a high-ranking weapons dealer. I'm still running a background search on them.

I told them not to call Brick just yet. I think it would be in our best interest to wait till he gets here later tonight and tell him about this information in person to see his reaction. I don't think it's coincidence that all this trouble has emerged from Chicago.

Before Viktoriya left, she and Dexter had an intimate conversation. She was caressing his arm, kissing him on each cheek. They clearly know each other on a more personal level.

When it was time for Dexter and his guys to leave, Mac and Trey followed them. Since Dexter hasn't ever met either of them, we thought it would be good to send them. We have his live feed on our TV that usually plays our club security—leaving the big-screen TV to watch inside the shop where Ronny and Lenny are with the product. And, of course, the Devil Duos and Devil's Dames are having a party outside where Blaze and his sister Karma are hanging out.

"I can't fucking believe this is happening again. I looked into Dexter and Ray. I've been around them, talked with them, and they don't do anything but DJ. They were clean," Luc states more to himself but says it out loud, sounding defeated.

"Who is doing your searches?" I ask the room.

Luc looks to Beau then to Reed. "I have a few different people that do my background checks."

Wolfe says what I think everyone is thinking, "Well, why aren't they here? It seems they aren't doing their job. If we're all going to be working together, we need to trust each other. We need to lay everything on the line *right now*. Because this" —Wolfe turns to the big screen and points to all the bikers partying—"isn't just coincidence. All of this shit keeps bringing us back together. So, tonight we need to lay it all out on the line and figure this fucking shit out."

Most of us acknowledge him in agreement. Luc looks to Beau and then back to the TV.

"Chiv, are the men in position?" Cash speaks for the first time in a while.

Chiv exhales, sounding annoyed. "I've got the front, as you can see. Worm's to the left, Dasher's to the right, and Phil'em-up has the back, of course."

Everyone chuckles, throwing in their comments about Phil'em-up Phil.

"Plus, we have a couple of men a few blocks away in case the bikers split up. They can follow."

Cash laughs. "Thanks, brother. We just don't want to lose the slippery fucker."

Chiv laughs. "One thing I learned from my brother is how to track a motherfucker. We're good over here."

We all nod, agreeing. His brother Blink is the best bounty hunter around, it's why he's so in demand.

Ethan and Reed come up next to me, looking at the massive wall of photos and intel.

"Okay, I think we got everything, but once Maddox and Gus get back, we'll have them look it over too before we dive into details. But here—" Ethan points to a photo of Emmett. "It all starts with his infatuation with Alexandria, and then he gets a job with Spin It, linking himself to Luc. Dominic and Emmett's meeting is still a mystery, but I'm thinking Dom initiated it." He points to the picture of Dominic. "They became roommates and started kidnapping girls. Alex comes back—Emmett takes her—Ginger kills him. But we still didn't know about Dominic's involvement with the girls being taken until later with Izzy's incident."

Ethan moves to the next group of photos that I put up of the MCs. "Now, this is where I think things get confusing, or we might be missing something." Ethan pauses, rubbing his chin.

Dallas

"Izzy said Kirill made Dominic admit to hiring bikers to send the hands and letters, right?" Ethan looks at me.

I agree, "Yes, Izzy said Dominic was behind it all."

"And we automatically thought it was Snake they hired, correct? Well, maybe it was Ronny or the Devil Duos?" Ethan looks at Reed and me. "How do we know?"

I try to think of what Snake told us when we interrogated him.

Ethan motions to me. "I know you weren't around, but Alex and Madd Dog said Emmett told them, *'they would get what is coming to them.'* What if Emmett had hired someone to fuck with them as well? Now, it's just a theory. So, let's come back to that." Ethan points to Ronny's photo.

"Raven said the same thing to Snow when she was with Snake. It could be true," Shy announces from behind us.

I look over my shoulder, not realizing all the men are watching and listening to us.

Ethan nods his head. "Yes, so we'll have to look deeper into that because looking at it now" —he points to the TV— "both Devil MCs are involved with the rogue Black Crows. Maybe Snake was a pawn or decoy. Since Snake's only motive was to get back at you, Shy, for killing his father, maybe they used him. So, we need to figure out who was really pulling strings there."

Ethan moves to Dominic and the Russians' photos, but I step toward the MCs' photos, cutting him off. "Hold on, let's go back. Reed, get some paper. E, get some tape. Let's put up a timeline above all the pictures. We need to think of it as one individual incident. We've had, I think, eight incidents happen so far, linking these people. I think we may be dealing with more than one person making the calls."

"Eight? What are the eight?" Luc moves forward to stand closer to the wall.

I turn to the room, which has filled with more men all

listening in. "Reed, write these down, each on a separate piece of paper. One, Alex was taken—Emmett getting killed—Snow was shot—the girls were found." I raise two fingers. "Two, Snow receiving a hand at the clubhouse." I lift another finger. "Three, Snow receiving another hand—her hotel was trashed—then three Scorpions get killed."

"Wait, you forgot Snow and Brant had bikers chasing them while we were out looking for Snake. That happened after the hand incident at the clubhouse," Shy points out.

I turn to Shy. "Yes, that is what I mean. So many things happened in this short amount of time, it could have been related to something completely different." I turn to Reed. "Add that one too—Snow being chased."

I grab the pages Ethan has put tape on but stop. "Wait, I think this incident is what started all of these chain reactions." Holding the page that had Alexandria, Emmett, and Snow. "Break this up into three incidents—Alex taken—Emmett killed—Snow shot." I hand the page back to Reed.

Turning back to the wall, I hang up Snow, receiving a letter and hand at the clubhouse. Snow being chased. Before I put the other one up, I stop.

"We need to separate this one too. Hand, letter, and room together, but put Scorpions killed by itself and MC going after Snake another."

Luc adds, "I think we should put Dom getting arrested that night too."

The room all agrees.

Ethan moves to put up the first pages we separated. We all stand there looking at what we have so far. I grab a pen and add on Snake down south.

"I think we also need to have a picture of Sasha up because she was in the middle of all this and then gone," Beau says to the room.

Dallas

"Yeah, I went to B that night in LA and told him we needed to check into her, and then she was gone," Shy tells us all.

"Is that where Brant's at right now?" Wolfe asks Beau.

The room gets quiet because we've all been wondering where he's been. After Izzy's incident, he kind of just quit coming around here.

"B's taking some time off. He was taking care of Ghost, and then they went on a trip," Beau explains, but I'm sure he's leaving out more details.

We need to stay focused, so I continue, "Okay, next is the incident in Miami. Let's separate this one too. Snake and his men come to the club—Sasha goes missing—Austin killed—Snow getting a text—we take Ball Z, a former Scorpion. We need to find a picture of Ball Z or just put a page up for him."

I step back, taking my ball cap off, running a hand through my hair, taking a minute to clear my head. Ethan moves to put up more pages.

"Okay, then Snow gets into a fight with Raven." I turn to Reed. "We need to add a picture of her too." I turn back, folding my arms over my chest, rubbing my chin. "We need to pull videos of that night and get IDs on all of those girls and guys that started the fight. Were they Devils? Randoms? We never looked into it because we got Snake that night and Raven."

"I'll get Hawk on that right now," Wolfe announces, pulling his phone out.

"Nah, I can get it. Give me a second," Beau says, moving over to Reed's laptop.

"Cash, or someone write this down," I ask, pinching the bridge of my nose as I try to think of what else happened around that time. Anything that we may have missed. "We need photos of Raydene and Dexter because they enter the picture

221

around this time, linking to Alex and Madd Dog. Oh, and also, Vi, Doc, and the new guys from today."

"*Quel figlio di puttana*, Dom, was arrested again, but here. Then those Russian guys came looking for him. That is when Dom started going *pazzo*," Luc grounds out, becoming more agitated.

"English?" Wolfe snaps back.

Luc, who we all know has a temper, turns to his native tongue when he's pissed.

"I *said*, that motherfucker Dom started going crazy, *capisce?*" Luc says to Wolfe, waving a hand.

Wolfe laughs. "I need to learn some of these fucking words."

"Okay, Reed, put up there that Dom was arrested in NY and the Russians came looking for him. Oh, and we had some guys try to convince him to leave Izzy alone, but I think that's what made him flip, yeah?"

"Uh-Uh. Nah, Dom flipped way before then," Luc says, waving a finger. "But that's when he went back to Russia. We thought he left to get away from the court dealings, but now I'm sure it was because his uncle called him back. *Futtuto puttana!*" Luc crosses his arms over his chest.

I chuckle.

"To be clear, I said fucking bitch." Luc drags the two words out, looking over at Wolfe with a smile. "I'm glad that piece of shit is dead."

"*Futtuto puttana!*" Mac's voice echoes across the room with a laugh. "I need to remember that one."

"*G'Lawd, wat* me miss?" Redman announces, entering the room.

"Fuckin' hell. What is all this?" Maddox follows him into the room, looking at the wall.

Dallas

Cash replies comically, "Well, Luc is giving us all a lesson on Italian."

Luc scoffs, *"Vaffanculo!"*

The few of us that do know that one shout out simultaneously, "Fuck off!"

The room erupts in laughter. Redman and Maddox make their way to the front, looking at all the intel we have put up.

"Well, since you've been gone." I point to the TV, where we see the front and back entrances of their hotel. "Mac and Trey are outside the hotel where Dexter, JJ, and King are staying."

"Then over here." —I point to the other TV—"this is where Jammer, his brother, and cousin are sitting outside the Conrad where the Russians are staying."

"And finally" —I point to the big screen—"we've got Ronny, Lenny, and the Devils."

"And here?" Maddox says next to me, not taking his eyes off the wall.

"This is our timeline of incidents and people involved." Ethan puts up pictures of Raydene, Vi, Doc, Dexter, JJ, and King. When he's done, he turns to Maddox. "We think we missed something around the time of Ginger's stuff."

I let Ethan bring them up to speed and return to my laptop to ensure nothing else has popped up on my searches.

Beau is on Reed's laptop next to me as Shy, Wolfe, and Luc walk over, talking about tomorrow night. "We need to keep those girls in our sights," Wolfe mumbles.

"Yeah, but we can't keep them here. They're supposed to leave Sunday," Shy informs them.

"We can't act like we know anything. We need the girls to DJ tomorrow like nothing is wrong. We can double the security and see if any of these people make a move," Luc suggests.

Are they going to use the girls to draw out Ronny? *Or the Russians.*

"Fine," Wolfe snaps. "But you need to talk to your *contacts.* We need to go over all this fucking shit with them, and they need to explain why they're giving you false information."

Them? He must know who Luc's contacts are. *Maybe Frank?*

"Yah. I'll put in a call. Let's get through tonight and tomorrow, yeah? I think a lot will reveal itself," Luc says in a monotone voice.

"We've got movement." Jammer's voice booms through the room.

All eyes go to the screen showing the Russians entering their SUVs.

"Josh, Cam—are you both ready?" Jammer asks his brother and cousin.

"Yeah, we got 'em."

"What the fuck? They're stopping," Jammer says.

"The Russian Tea Room," Luc announces.

"To eat or meet someone?" Shy asks next to him.

Mac speaks up, "Hey, maybe you should have someone bring over some clothes for us in case they go to a club. I'm not letting this *futtuto puttana* out of my sight."

Luc smiles. *"Perfetto."*

"Seriously, if they leave this place, I'm going inside to see what the fuck they're doing. None of these people know what Trey and I look like," Mac demands.

"Well, unless they've looked into all of us, but it is a club. It wouldn't be out of the ordinary," Luc puts in his two cents.

Jammer says, agreeing, "Yeah, we can't see shit out here, and we're not dressed to go into this place. Cam, come back around and try to park your bike in that construction site across the street. See if you can get a better view of the door. I'll be back around."

Dallas

Shy says, "We need someone inside to see if they are having a meeting."

"I'll go," Luc interrupts. "I know the owner, and it wouldn't be out of the ordinary. The only problem will be if they are meeting someone I do know, like Dexter."

"How can that be a problem? The cunt must know he might run into someone. I mean, what if he ran into Ray?" Redman points out.

"I'll head over there." Luc grabs his suit jacket and starts for the door.

"Wait, I'm going with you." Beau jumps up from next to me.

"Fuck, alright. Quick, get some clothes for Mac and get dressed. You're going to meet up with Mac and Trey, just in case they go to a club."

"It looks like we're in for a long night over here. Anyone want to bring me some food and drinks." Chiv chuckles. "That candy sure does look good."

We look over and see that the party has trickled inside. Ronny's fucking some bitch. Lenny's at a table with someone lining up drugs, with a couple of club whores next to them.

"Wait a minute." I jump up. "That's Rayaan! Fuck, when did he get there?"

Chiv chimes in, "About thirty minutes ago. He came in with some bitches, laid out some drugs, chatted with Ronny and Lenny for a few minutes before the party moved inside. Ronny grabbed a bitch and started fucking her." Giving a detailed play-by-play.

Okay, he's definitely his brother's twin.

"Did they ever go to the back bay where the product is located?" I ask.

"Nope, where they are is where they've been. Dude just came in ready to party."

"Chiv, have one of the scouts go grab all of you some food and shit," I say, moving toward Luc and Beau. "It looks like we're in for a long night."

I hand them a tablet. "Here, I'll send you a link so you can see what's going on at the auto body shop. We won't be able to see you or hear you unless one of you links to us, I'll send you that information. Otherwise, text or call us. We'll have eyes on you from the outside."

Beau grabs the tablet, and they both say goodbye. The room erupts with 'be safe' and 'good luck.'

Once they're gone, I pull my phone out to check in with Doc.

Dallas: I miss you. (kiss emoji)

She replies instantly. I smile.

Lee: (happy emoji) I think I miss you more. I'm thinking of all the dirty things we could be doing right now. (kiss emoji)

Fuck me!

Dallas: Mmmm. I would ask, but I'm already hard thinking of you. I might cum in my jeans again. (Sticking tongue out emoji)

Lee: When are you coming here to get me? How is it going?

Damn. She's going to be upset.

Dallas: Ronny is partying for the night, not going anywhere. Still figuring shit out. It's going to be a long night. I probably won't see you until morning. I'm sorry.

She doesn't reply right away. I look around the room, and

Dallas

most of the men are at the wall, listening to Ethan. I know I need to get back, but I want to be sure Doc's okay.

I push the call button and step into the hallway. She answers on the first ring.

"I was just responding to you." She giggles.

"I needed to hear your voice." My voice comes out sounding needy.

"I'm glad," she confesses. "I've wanted to call you all day, but I didn't want to bother you."

"Doc, you can call me anytime. You're not bothering me at all. If I can't answer, I won't, but you could never bother me. If anything, you're making my day," I say warmly.

"I'm just not used to this," she breathes.

"Used to what?" I ask, confused.

"Well. I'm not used to having someone to call or bug. The not knowing if it's okay or not okay to call. Plus, all the club rules and stuff," she explains, sounding unsure of herself.

I just want to hold her in my arms and never let go.

"Doc, I'm yours, babe. You can bug me anytime, and I will never get mad at you for wanting to be with me. If club business is going on, I will text or get in touch with you as soon as I can. Sure, there will be club business, like right now, that I can't explain to you."

Silence.

"Plus, I've never been in a relationship before, so we can wing it together. All I know is I want you in my life." Jesus, I sound like a pussy-whipped kid.

I hear her intake a big breath.

"Remember, we got each other, right?" I tease.

"Thank you." She sighs. "I just can't wait for this to be over."

I see Shy come out the doors, so I hurry the conversation

up. "I know, Doc. I promise it will be soon. I got to get back in there. I'll text you later."

"Okay. Thank you," she says cheerfully.

"Anything for you, Doc," I reply before hanging up.

I put my phone back in my pocket, giving Shy a head nod. "What's up."

"We got something. Tiny was going through Ethan's folder on Emmett. I guess he used to come around the Scorpion's clubhouse back in the day, way before he met Alex when he was a skinny little geek. He used to buy steroids off the club." Shy smiles.

Fuck yes!

"Let's start digging. I know we'll find more connections that we missed."

Finally! Something I can work with… time to search and find!

24 | The Club

Dallas

"YOU REALLY THINK HE'LL SHOW TONIGHT?" I ask Mac, who's sitting next to me at Club Spin. We've been here for about an hour, Raydene and Vi are about to go on. We pretty much pulled an all-nighter last night, only getting a couple of hours of sleep. Well, I didn't sleep much. I mainly had lain in bed going over all the intel we got, trying to put the pieces together. It probably didn't help that I was high as fuck from doing some coke, drinking whiskey, and smoking some pot.

"Yeah, that fucker was shocked when I told him she was playing again tonight. He didn't seem happy," Mac tells me, eyes glued to Raydene on stage.

Mac and Quick went to a club on W. Seventeenth Street and 'accidentally' ran into Dexter in the VIP area. Once Quick mentioned his fiancée was Ruby, Dexter invited them to party all night.

We've been hanging out watching all the girls dancing around on stage to "Ride it" by Regard, behind the DJ booth. My eyes are locked on my girl, though. "Are you going to talk to Raydene about running into him and what went on last night?"

Doc's eyes lock with mine. She smiles and mouths the words *ride it* while swaying her God-given hips. *Fuck me!* My cock's ready to combust. I still haven't got my fix for the day. I need to get her in the bathroom for a quickie and soon. I smile back before finishing my beer.

"I don't know. Ray already told me they had an open relationship. So, I don't think him fucking around is new to her." He chuckles. "Plus, she isn't innocent either."

"You mean since you're fucking her too?" I laugh, taking a swig of my beer.

Mac nudges me, and I turn to see Chiv, Worm, and Tiny walking up to the VIP area.

"The Russians still haven't left the hotel, and Ronny is still at the Devil Duo's clubhouse. All teams have been relieved, so surveillance is still going," Chiv informs us, grabbing a beer from the bucket of beers we have on the table.

I grab my phone and log in to the system so I can see the surveillance on Ronny.

Still no movement.

Something doesn't seem right, and I'm on edge. Usually, I would think it's from being up for so many days and doing some blow, but the feeling is in my gut.

Ronny's group partied all night into the early morning. Then he and the bikers took off, leaving Lenny and Rayaan at the shop. The bikers headed to the clubhouse, where I'm sure they're sleeping after partying all night long, but for there to be no movement has me on edge.

We started rotating teams to watch Dexter's group, the Russian, and the bikers. We don't want to lose track of any of them.

I reach for another beer when my eyes catch Luc moving to talk to the DJ finishing up as Raydene plugs her headphones in.

Luc didn't find out much last night. Luc and Beau had dinner, but with no incident. Viktoryia and the men were seated in the back, but they were alone. The Russians had dinner and after they went a few blocks away to the Russian Vodka House to have a couple of drinks.

Dallas

Luckily Beau heard them say something about the place, and we placed Jammer and his brother inside before they went there, so at least we had eyes on them. They didn't stay out late, only having a couple of drinks before heading back to the hotel.

"Wolfe and them still at the clubhouse watching, or are they coming here?" I ask.

Worm finishes pouring himself a shot. "Yeah, he said he was going to hang there and keep an eye on everything and for us just to take care of the girls."

I nod my head, letting him know I heard him.

"Jesus Christ. What the fuck are they wearing?" Chiv grunts, sitting next to me, eyes glued to the DJ booth. "Or not wearing. Fuck!"

Mac and I both laugh.

All the girls decided to dress up, meaning wear little to nothing. They all are in tight, very short dresses with heels. I guarantee every motherfucker here has a boner for Raydene and Vi up there. Luckily our girls are behind the DJ booth, but I still don't like that everyone can see them. We planned to act normal and be seen like we didn't know any better.

"Believe me, brother, I wanted to rip that little thing she calls a dress off the minute I saw her. It's taking everything I have not to go fuck her right now."

"No wonder Maddox, Shy, Redman, and Quick are glued to their women up there." Tiny laughs.

Raydene drops her first song, "Free Your Body," by Chris Lake and Solardo. Raydene bounces, shaking her head, singing the words. When the beat hits, Vi moves up next to her with one arm in the air, and within seconds, they're moving together as one, dancing.

Mac breathes. "Jesus Christ."

I look over with a smirk. "You good, brother?"

He laughs. "I'm good. My dick, not so much."

"Right there with you, brother. Fucking fine as fuck," Chiv announces.

"What the fuck?" Mac growls.

"Just saying, those bitches are fine as hell."

"Why aren't you up there with Doc?" Tiny asks.

"Because if I touch her, we'll be fucking, and right now, I need to stay focused. I told her to go have fun with her friends."

"Brother, go get some. We'll be here watching over everything." Mac nudges me.

"What time did Dexter get back to his hotel this morning?" I ask Mac.

"He left Viktoriya's hotel a little before noon."

Mac and Quick were with them when Dexter got the text. He left the club alone, and Mac and Quick stayed with the other two men partying. Trey was sitting outside waiting for any of them to leave, so he followed Dexter. He followed him to Viktoriya's hotel. So, we know they're fucking for sure.

I know there is double security tonight, but something just feels off. I look across the club to the other VIP area where Maddox has his men, along with some of Beau's team. We decided to spread out so we could cover more of the club if anything should happen.

The club is packed, shoulder to shoulder. As long as we have eyes on Ronny and the Russians, I'm okay. Dexter, I can handle. Mac said JJ and King were cool last night, and they acted like they were on vacation and just wanted to party and get laid.

Then again, they didn't know we knew who they were, but Mac said they didn't have an attitude or start any shit. Mac said he actually had a good time after Dexter left.

My eyes catch Doc moving toward the exit, so I stand up,

Dallas

ready to go after her when Shy and Ginger follow. I move to the railing that's between me and the dance floor, waiting for them to come down the stairs. When they emerge, she locks eyes with me, and I see they're making their way over to us. I relax.

Doc is wearing a black Body Glove strapless dress. It's so short I guarantee if she bends over, her ass will pop out—her long luscious tan legs on full display.

Almost, buddy. Almost.

I greet them at the entrance of the VIP area. When she's in arm's reach, I pull her against me, and she giggles.

I lean down, kissing her neck. "Goddamn, Doc. You look so fucking good in this dress." I suck her earlobe. "I don't think I'll be able to keep my hands off you any longer."

Lee lets out a moan. "I thought maybe you didn't want me around."

I pull away, looking into her eyes. "Why the fuck would you think that?"

She shrugs.

I move us to the plush velvet couch, where I sit down and bring her down onto my lap, making her squeal.

"Doc, baby. It has taken everything I have not to go up there, throw you over my shoulder, and go fuck you in the bathroom. Jesus." I lean forward, kissing her neck and grab the mound of her breast bulging out of her dress. "Christ, this dress fits you perfectly. Your tits look like two mountains, and your cleavage's the slope. My dick wants to ride up and down that shit."

Lee laughs, turning her upper body, giving me complete access to her chest. She slides her hands around my neck up into my hair, gripping the back of my head, shoving my face deep into her cleavage, holding me there.

Time to motorboat these babies.

I tongue fuck her cleavage, sucking, nipping, biting, and kissing them. She wiggles her ass over my dick.

Christ, I'm about to nut in my pants.

I lift my head from her breast.

"Okay, time to fuck. Let's go," I demand, standing up and placing her on her feet.

"But—" I cut her off with a kiss.

"Don't worry. They have a private bathroom for the DJs. We'll be quick." I give Mac a head nod and when we pass Shy, he laughs, announcing, "I'm right behind you. Hurry the fuck up."

I practically drag Lee down to the private bathroom, pulling her inside. I slam the door, shoving her up against it, pinning her. I grab both her hands, lifting them above her head, securing them with one hand. I lock the door before grabbing her around the throat, holding her in place.

The bass from the music vibrates the walls as "All I Need" by Shiba San and Tim Baresko erupts through the speaker.

"I will always want you, Doc," I growl, and I probably look like a crazed man needing to get high. "Fuck, baby, I need to fuck you so fucking bad." I slip a leg between hers, spreading them, rubbing my thigh up and down, making friction against her clit.

Doc moans. "I missed you so much."

My hand around her neck slowly moves down, kneading her breasts before moving down her belly and finally slipping under her dress.

What the fuck?

I let go of her hands, leaning back a couple of inches, looking her in the eyes. "Commando?"

She smiles big. "I wanted it to be easy for you." Doc reaches for my jeans. "I think I need you just as much," she purrs, biting her lower lip.

Dallas

When her hand grips my buddy, I lose all control—slamming her back against the door with urgency, yanking the paper of a dress up to her waist, exposing all.

Lee grabs my neck with both hands, forcing my face down, kissing me hard. I lift her, moving to the closest counter, setting her down. I break the kiss, dropping to my knees, spreading her legs, then her folds before beginning my assault on her. She's soaked. I suck her clit before tonguing her opening. Lee drops her head back, hitting the mirror with a loud moan.

"Yes, baby," she cries out in ecstasy.

Hmm, baby. She must really like it because that's a first.

I place her legs over my shoulders and work my magic, sucking, licking, flicking, and working her clit. Doc's hands are pulling and tugging my hair, moving in motion, trying to catch her release.

When Doc screams, slapping her knees together, I know she's coming. Dipping a couple of fingers into her pussy, she spasms around them as I continue a slow, torturous flicking of my tongue on her clit.

My turn.

I stand up, holding her legs. I move in, gripping the counter before slamming into her hard. "Fuck yes," I roar, but the music vibrating through the club muffles it.

I start to jackhammer into her fast and hard, each thrust slamming her against the mirror.

We're like two animals in heat, moaning, grunting.

"Fuck me," Doc demands.

I can't get deep enough, ramming her harder, gripping her hips. I slam into them roughly, needing more.

"Yes. Oh, God. Yes." Her walls clench down, spasming around my cock as another orgasm explodes inside her.

Almost. Fuck yes.

"Mine," I growl.

Lee's tits burst out the top of her dress, bouncing up and down as she screams, her cunt milking my dick.

"I need to be deeper, baby." Lowering her from the counter, I flip her around, grabbing her waist, and slam into her from behind.

Fucking heaven.

My eyes roll back in my head, and I commence pounding her sweet, heavenly pussy. Lee puts both hands on the mirror, giving herself leverage, and starts ramming her ass back, meeting me thrust for thrust. The tip of my cock hitting her cervix. When I open my eyes, I see her smiling in the mirror, watching us.

Yes! Now I'm deep enough.

"Fuck. Yes." I slap her ass. "You like that? Fuck me." I slap her ass again, not taking my eyes off her beautiful face as she slams back hard with a smile. "That's it, baby, fuck me!" I grunt breathlessly.

"Yeah. Fuck, yeah," she moans, slipping a hand down, touching her clit. Another orgasm rips through her, clamping down on my dick, pushing me over. I drop my head back, seeing stars. My body goes taut, and I release a guttural moan as I fill her pussy with cum.

Jesus Christ.

Watching us through the mirror, I pull her up against my body, gripping both breasts, kissing her neck, never taking my eyes off her.

"Fuck, I needed that. I can't go that long without you, baby." I nip her ear, making her giggle.

"I agree," she coos.

I release her, and when my dick slips out, cum rolls down her leg.

Fuck yes.

"Let me get you something. Hold on." I turn around to the

Dallas

sinks behind us, grabbing some paper towels. "I'll be draining from you all night," I tease.

Lee turns toward me with an ear-to-ear grin. "I don't care." She lets her 'just-fucked hair' down and redoes it before fixing her makeup. Once we're all put back together, I grab her ass, pulling her up against me, giving her a passionate kiss.

"Thank you. That should hold me over till we get home." I chuckle.

"Hopefully, that will be soon," she says with a devilish smirk.

But I feel so fucking good blares out of the speakers just as we exit the bathroom. "Right Now" by Anti Up, Chris Lake, and Chris Lorenzo.

Perfect song.

"Well, I feel so fucking good! Next!" I announce as we pass Shy, who has Ginger pinned up against the wall making out.

25 | The Curveball

Lee

"DOLL, I THINK IT'S OUR TURN," REDMAN GRUMBLES to Izzy next to me.

It seems Dallas and I started a fuck frenzy. Shy and Ginger went after us, then Maddox and Alexandria disappeared. After they came back, Quick and Ruby went missing, but they are now back in the VIP with the others. All of us are looking well fucked. I giggle, grabbing my shot of tequila.

Vi is DJing and killing it. I came back upstairs to be with the girls. Dallas got a call and had to go outside so he could talk. I see the men scattered throughout the club watching over us, but I don't care. I just got fucked really good, a bomb could go off, and I'd still have a smile on my face.

When Dallas first got here, I didn't think I would be able to hold myself back. He looked so good in his jeans and button-up shirt. This club has a dress code, so when he came in with no hat and dressed up, I damn well almost lost my shit. Don't get me wrong, I love his bad boy look, but goddamn, he cleans up real nice.

"Okay, Red, let's go." Izzy grabs Redman's arm, pulling him down the stairs to the private bathroom.

Raydene looks over and shakes her head, laughing. I shrug, putting my finger to my lips to shh her. I grab the bottle of tequila and move to the booth so I can pour them a shot.

"Turn Off The Lights" by Chris Lake, and Alexis Roberts drops, and Vi turns around bouncing to the music.

Dallas

"All you bitches getting fucked is making me jealous!" Vi exclaims.

"I know. What the fuck!" Raydene laughs.

"Have you seen my man?" I take my shot and wave my hand toward the VIP area. "They all cleaned up looking really nice and fine as fuck." I giggle, pouring another shot. "It has me turning animalistic. Shit, I'm ready to pounce on him again—round two."

"Round two sounds good to me. Shit, round one was like a teaser and shit," Ginger announces, coming up next to me, sticking her glass out for a shot.

We all laugh as I refill all our glasses. I look over to the VIP and see all the guys huddled together, looking at something.

"What's going on?" I ask Ginger, motioning to the men.

"I don't know. Shy said for me to go back where the girls are and he'll be up here in a minute."

We both scan the crowd, and I'm sure we're looking for different things. I'm always looking for Ronny, especially now that I know he's in the same city.

Ginger squints her eyes, but when I look to where she's looking, I don't see anyone I know.

"Holy shit. B?" she breathes.

"What?" I would panic, but she's smiling ear to ear.

"She shakes her head. Nothing."

Bullshit.

"I thought I saw an old friend, but it's just a ghost."

I know she's lying because she hasn't stopped looking at the crowd dancing. I don't see anyone I know, so I slam my shot back, turning back to the girls.

I notice Mac out of the corner of my eye, and he is beelining it to us, and Raydene's face lights up.

"Bitch, you better not go fuck him, or I'll lose my shit," Vi hollers from the decks where she is setting up her next song.

What is she talking about? She and Mac? No.

"How much longer is your set?" Mac yells.

Okay, he doesn't look like he wants to fuck. He seems pissed off.

Raydene's face falters, but just for a second. "We got about twenty minutes left. Why?"

"Because we need to get back to the clubhouse."

"Well, then go. We can handle ourselves, and we don't need *you* watching over us," Raydene snaps back.

I look over Mac's shoulder and see Brick just showing up, heading straight for us.

Something must be going on. Ginger is still staring off into the crowd.

"Okay, you two can go fuck now. I got a partner." Vi laughs, seeing Brick charge our way.

"Vi, shut the fuck up. I'm not fucking him," Raydene says, folding her arms over her chest.

Brick comes to stand next to Mac, glaring at Vi.

"What the fuck is wrong? Why are you two acting all caveman-like?" I demand.

"What the fuck are you wearing, Vi?" Brick yells, but Vi has headphones on to mix the next song.

Brick moves to the other side of the booth so he can be right next to her, so I'm sure when she gets done, he'll snatch her.

I giggle to myself, knowing we did this on purpose. We decided to wear little tiny black dresses to piss off the men. But, so far, it's only made our men horny as fuck. A win for us, well, not Vi and Raydene, it seems.

Then I remember Ronny is out there, and I start to panic. "Where is Dallas? Is it Ronny?" I search the crowd, and I don't see Dallas.

Mac grabs my arm. "Don't panic. He will be right back. He sent me up here to watch over you girls."

"Why? Is something wrong?" Raydene grabs his hand, removing it from my arm.

Dallas

"No, we just need to leave and soon," Mac tells her.

I'm scanning the crowd. Everyone looks normal, I'm the only one freaking out, but then I see it. I see Dexter with a group of people moving through the crowd, and he's with men I've never seen before. I'm about to say something, but Raydene says, "Fuck. What the fuck is he doing here?"

Yep, she sees him too.

Dexter isn't a threat. I don't understand why everyone is on the defensive. I turn and watch as all of our men have glued themselves to their women. Well, everyone but me. Dallas is nowhere to be seen, but Mac places himself between Raydene and me.

Dexter's eyes are glued to us on stage, but he moves to where a woman and several men are standing. They're toward the back of the club, Raydene doesn't move, as we both watch him.

"Ray, what's going on? Did you know he was in town?" I ask her while still watching Dexter greet this woman, kissing her on each cheek.

Even though Raydene's on the other side of Mac, I can feel her tension. "Don't know, and nope!" She pops the 'p,' sounding pissed off.

Mac doesn't say anything either as he watches Dexter and his group.

Something isn't right.

Mac turns to Raydene, breaking us both out of our trances. He asks her, "Did you know he was in town?"

Mac grabs her waist, pulling her up against him. Raydene's lost in thought, like she's seen a ghost.

"Shut the fuck up," Vi yells at Brick, turning to us, "No, she didn't know. He hasn't returned any of her calls or texts the last few days we've been here."

Arms wrap around me from behind, and I squeal, jumping forward. "Doc, it's me," Dallas yells, pulling me back against him.

I sigh in relief.

"We need to go," Dallas demands. I turn to face him. "Is it Ronny?"

Dallas scans the crowd, and when his eyes stop in one direction, I know he's focused on Dexter. He turns my body away from the crowd, locking eyes with me. "Ronny isn't here, but we don't know exactly where he is."

My heart starts to race.

Raydene and Mac are next to us, whispering to each other, while Mac moves us toward the back of the stage area. I see Dexter come up the stairs, along with four men. His eyes are glued to Raydene in Mac's arms and he doesn't look pleased.

Oh, shit.

"What the fuck? We met last night, and tonight you have my girl in your arms?" Dexter yells from the stairs. The four men behind him look like security guys dressed in all black with headpieces.

Raydene moves toward Dexter. "What the fuck are you doing here?" She stops midway, realizing what he said, and turns back to Mac. "Wait, you met him last night? Where?" she demands.

Dexter steps forward, grabbing her by the arm yanking her to him forcefully. She squeals, pulling her arm from his death grip. "What the fuck, Dex. Let me go, Jesus!"

Mac steps forward, hands clenching. "I guess I forgot to tell you I knew her," Mac says with a cocky smile.

Dexter doesn't let her arm go, pulling her to his side. "We're out of here."

Raydene starts to fight him, but he whispers something into her ear and instantly she stops fighting. Her whole demeanor changes, losing all life.

What the fuck.

"I have to get my stuff. You need to let go of my arm," Raydene replies, sounding dead with no emotion. She won't make eye contact with any of us.

Dallas

Something's wrong.

Dexter doesn't release her right away, keeping his standoff with Mac when he finally lets her arm go.

"Ray, you *outa* your damn mind if *ya* think *I'ma* let *ya* leave with *dese* motherfucker," Vi announces from behind us. She's packing up all their stuff as the new DJ enters the booth.

I look out to the crowd, and no one suspects a thing. Music is blaring, people are dancing, and if you are out on the dance floor, you'd never know what is really going on up here. It looks like we just have a big group of people in a circle.

"I'll have someone come pick my stuff up tomorrow from the apartment. I have to go with Dex. Please don't fight me," Raydene pleads with Vi, and I don't watch her because my eyes are glued to Dexter. He seems so different. I haven't seen him in a few years, and I've only seen the girls each time I visited. Something's off.

"We have to go. People are waiting for us," Dallas murmurs into my ear.

I turn to Vi, being held back by Brick. He's trying to calm her down. I move toward Raydene. "Ray, are you sure?" I beg her, but when I see her face, I know she's gone. Emotionally and soon physically.

She grabs her stuff, hugging me. "Yeah, I'm sure. I have to go. I'm sorry. I love you."

I hug her back.

Mac turns, grabbing her arm. He demands, "You don't know him. Stay. I need to talk to you."

Dexter starts to move toward him, but Chiv and his men move in, blocking him.

"What the fuck?" Dexter demands. "Move, that's my girl." The men behind him don't help as they stand there and watch.

Mac tells her softly, "I need to talk to you. You need to know what I know, you don't know who he really is."

I think he's gotten through when she smiles up at him. When

she reaches for his face, she stops, hearing Dexter yell for her. Ray drops her head, and before walking away, she replies. "I know exactly who he is."

"What the fuck?" I huff.

Mac doesn't turn to watch her go, he just looks at me with empty eyes. We're both shocked just standing there. Brick yells, "Time to go."

I look over and see a very angry Vi who's trying to get to Raydene. The stage has cleared out with Raydene and her group leaving ahead of us, with Chiv and some of the members following. I see Maddox and his group move toward us, but I don't see Izzy or Ruby. Dallas grabs my hand. "Let's go, Doc. Everyone is outside waiting for us."

Once we're outside, I see Izzy is crying in Redman's arms. *Jesus Christ. What now?*

We rush over to the group when I notice the woman Dexter kissed inside is standing with two other prominent men facing off with Redman and Luc.

The woman speaks in a Russian accent that fills the air. "I'm here to find out what happens to *moy kuh-zn* Dom." She slowly pronounces cousin.

"Viktoriya, ask *yer* brother, Kirill," Redman fires back.

Viktoryia? Who are these people? How does Dexter know them?

Viktoriya takes a couple of steps closer to them, lifting her hand, waving her pointer finger, signaling no. While saying, what I assume is no, "*Net. Net. Net.*"

The two men behind me move as one, staying within hand's reach of her.

"See *moy kuh-zn*," again she says, cousin slowly. "He would *never* leave his…" She pauses, rubbing her chin, thinking. "What did he call you? His *zvezda?* Why would he leave his *star?*" Viktoriya smiles, but her voice is dripping with disgust.

Izzy starts crying harder. Redman motions to Chiv, who

Dallas

comes to his side. Redman says something in her ear before handing her off to Chiv, putting her in the SUV waiting behind them.

"You can hide, *suka*. But I will find out," Viktoriya yells after Izzy, but Chiv already has her inside the vehicle.

Luc chimes in, getting her attention again, "Yeah, like I told your father. He went back home, your men came for him after he was arrested here. We haven't seen him since he went back to Russia," Luc explains calmly.

"*Fignya! Pizdlo!*" Viktoriya snaps in Russian, but stops, pinching the bridge of her nose. "Bullshit. You are lying," she says through clenched teeth, pointing toward Izzy in the SUV. "That *fucken suka* knows where *moy kuh-zn* is. I will find out. *Da?*"

Viktoriya turns to leave with the two men following but stops when Redman yells after her. "She's mine. *Yer* cousin is gone, an *yer cunt* of a brother knows *wat* happen. I promise *ya*, Izzy ain't fibbing. She had nothin' to do with it, but if *ya* come at her again." He pauses, waiting for her to turn around and when she does, he finishes. "*Ye'll* have to deal with me."

Viktoriya gives him an evil smile. "*Togda, do vstrechi.*"

Nobody moves or says a word. She laughs. "I say, yes, I see you soon."

Redman gives her a nod when the Russians turn to leave, Redman gets into the SUV.

"What the fuck just happened?" I say more to myself, but Dallas answers, "More fucking balls dropping."

A male voice yells from behind me, "Why the fuck did you bring her here. Why would you do that knowing they were here?" I turn to see a man and woman charging toward Luc and Beau.

"B, you and Ghost need to calm down. We're heading to the clubhouse, let's talk about it there," Beau tells them as he moves to the SUV.

Ghost?

I look for Ginger but realize she's already gone. *Well, fuck!*

245

"Come on, Doc. Let's get you back home." Dallas pulls me into his side, trying to warm me up as we walk to where our ride is waiting.

"Home. Where's home?" I murmur.

Dallas stops, pulling me to face him. He cups my face with both hands. "Home is wherever we are together." His eyes are wild with all the excitement.

I don't reply.

"Doc, believe in me. Believe in us and believe things will be over soon. I promise you will have your life back, and it will feel like home. Trust me." He leans in, kissing me. "Now, let's go." He swats my ass to move me to the truck waiting for us.

What life? I hadn't had a real life since before Scooter died.

The door flies open. "Christ, did you two get lost? What the fuck," Quick yells from behind the wheel. Ruby, who looks like she just got fucked again, laughs next to him.

Well, at least they missed all the drama.

"Nah, just more motherfucking curveballs. I'll explain once we get in."

I seriously need to tell him I hate baseball talk.

26 | The Release

Lee

"You're quiet this morning," Dallas says, looking at me through the mirror, where we're both getting ready.

I smile, putting my hair into a messy high bun. "I wasn't quite a few minutes ago when you were ravaging me in the shower," I tease.

Dallas grins with a mouthful of toothpaste.

Once I finish my hair, I head back into his room, plopping down onto his bed. Since it's Sunday, I put on lounge clothes, and we don't have any plans except meeting up with everyone here later.

I know what he's talking about, but I'm trying to act like I don't. I'm still reeling from last night's sit-down. When we got back here last night, everyone was here except Izzy, Ruby, and Alexandria. Ruby and Alex decided to stay back with Izzy and make sure she was okay. Vi and Brick went somewhere, but Vi hasn't responded to my texts or calls.

Dallas walks out of the bathroom, throwing his towel in the hamper. "Doc, I meant, are you okay with everything you found out last night? I mean, it was a lot to take in. Have you talked to Vi or Ray yet today?" Grabbing a shirt, he turns to face me. "Do you want to talk about anything before everyone gets here today? I just don't want you overwhelmed like you were last night," Dallas finishes, standing shirtless in front of me, looking sexy as can be. He smirks, knowing precisely what I'm thinking. "Babe, I just fucked you senseless, but if you keep looking at me like that, I'll fuck you into a coma," he teases, putting on his shirt.

I put my hands behind my head and get comfortable.

Dallas puts his hands on his hips, looking hot as fuck. "Lee, do you not want to talk about it? Is that why you're not answering me?"

Yes! I don't want to think about it. I'm freaking out!

I'm screaming in my head, but I try to be calm when I answer. "I'm still processing, and I just need some time alone to—" I shrug. "I don't know, get my thoughts together."

Dallas crawls up the bed, situating himself beside me. He doesn't say anything but as he stares at me. I know he's waiting for me to spill. He's analyzing me, it's what he does.

But truthfully, I don't know what to think. I turn to my side, stuffing a pillow under my head so I can look him in the eyes.

"Alec, I really don't know what to think. It was so much to take in, and I don't know what to say about Raydene and Vi. I mean, I know Vi's husband and cousin deal in illegal shit, but I've never seen it or been around it. Yes, we party, and we party hard sometimes, but I've never seen drug deals or anything at the level you're explaining. It's crazy what all of you have been through. I mean, I can't even begin to understand what happened to the girls, especially Izzy."

Dallas springs up to a seated position. "What do you mean you can't even imagine? Doc, you've been terrorized, raped, and beaten by Ronny for years. *Fucking years.* A fuck of a lot longer than any of those girls. So, if anything, I think *you can* relate." His voice is filled with emotion.

I pause, thinking he's right. I don't say anything right away as he lies back down, face to face, in silence for a few seconds.

I break the silence. "Raydene hasn't replied to any of my calls or texts. I don't know what's going on with her or Dexter. When I moved here, I threw myself into my work, so I wasn't

Dallas

always in touch with them, but it's always just the girls when I was around them.

"Raydene acts like she and Dexter are fine. But being around the girls lately, I've found out they both have been keeping secrets. I think even from each other. They've been at each other's throats this whole time. I thought it was because we didn't know about Brick, and Raydene was all up on Mac. Now all of this with Dexter, I don't know."

Dallas reaches out, caressing my face. I close my eyes and tilt my head into his hand.

"Doc, I just want you safe. I'm sorry if we came off aggressive last night, but I just needed to know what you knew about them and how it's all related," he says softly.

I sigh. "It's crazy that I'm linked to all of this, but I think Ronny is what's linking me to it all. I really do. He's been infecting my life with every turn I make. If he isn't taunting me, he's infiltrating every aspect so he can be around me. I think it all stems from Ronny, so once we find him, we'll know. Until then, I think we're just drawing straws."

Dallas smiles.

I laugh. "What?"

He leans in, giving me a brief kiss. "You are just so beautiful and a survivor. You're handling all of this so well, I'm just impressed."

I fall onto my back, looking up at the ceiling, trying to keep the tears from falling.

"This is my life. This has always been my life. Ronny has ruined anything and everything good in it. Family, friends, even places I called home—gone because of him. He fucks it all up for me." Tears run down my face as I throw an arm over my eyes, trying to control myself and hide the tears. I don't want to lose it again in front of him.

My little analyzer is on top of me, pushing my arm away so he can look me in the eyes.

"I told you last night, that's all going to change. You are not running, hiding, or changing anything ever again for him. I've got you now, and it will end soon. I promise you that, and you'll have your own life again."

Tears are running freely down my face now. I'm so afraid. I want to believe him, but after hearing all the things about last night and what Ronny was doing. How he has infected every place I've lived and people I've turned to. All to what, hurt me? Get me back? Hurt the ones I love?

"Talk to me. I see that beautiful mind of yours spinning. Let's figure this out together," Dallas murmurs, inches away from my face. I open my eyes and see that gorgeous smirk of his.

I chuckle.

His phone rings, breaking our connection. I'm thankful because my thoughts and emotions are all over the place. I just really need to have some time alone, and I need to go for a run to clear my mind.

Dallas gives me a quick kiss, popping off me to grab his phone. "Yeah?"

Silence.

Dallas turns, looking down at me. "Yeah, I'll be down. Give me five. No, she's relaxing."

"What's going on?" I ask.

"Shy and the guys want to meet before everyone else gets here. Kind of a club meeting."

I roll back to my side, fluffing my pillow. "Church, I get it. Perfect. I'm just going to lie here in the quiet, alone, and try to clear my head."

Dallas puts his hands on his hips, not saying anything as he watches me.

"I'll be fine. I just need to be alone. What I really wish I

Dallas

could do is go for a run, but I know you won't let me." I pout, teasing him.

He laughs. "I'm sure we can arrange that. Jammer's cousin or brother, I think, runs. I'll figure something out before we lock ourselves into our meeting. I'll give you some time alone and text you when I figure it out. Just relax right now." He leans down, kissing me before grabbing his cut and heading out the door.

Once the door closes, I let out a few deep breaths and let the tears flow.

I let it all out, flipping over, trying to calm down, breathing through my nose and out my mouth. I need to get it together. Last night was just so... so much.

For ten years, I've been alone. When I lived with Marcus and his group, I stayed in my room, recovering from Ronny beating me. I was scared for my life, shit, I was scared of my own shadow. Plus, I was studying and trying to finish school.

I never felt that attraction toward Marcus like I do Dallas. I know Marcus has feelings for me. He told me straight up that I could have the world, but I didn't feel that way. I never thought I would feel like this toward a man again, especially with Ronny terrorizing me every few years.

From the very first day being here, I've never felt overwhelmed, and I thought I would with so many people around me all the time. I'm used to having alone 'zen' time. I live and breathe my job, and I'm good at it, but it also brings stress to my life, so to escape my job and daily life, I run and listen to music.

I bolt up when I hear a knock at the door. I don't move or say anything.

"Lee, are you awake? It's Snow."

That's the first time she's introduced herself as Snow and not Ginger.

Is that a code? Is she alone? Fuck.

I hear a thump against the door, like a head hitting it. Then, the sound of something sliding down the door.

I panic and grab my phone, ready to text Dallas, but I stop when Ginger speaks.

"Listen, I just wanted to talk to you. My mind is going a million different ways, and I could really use someone to talk to." She pauses. "—that isn't in my day-to-day life," Ginger explains.

I'm off the bed in an instant, throwing open the door. Ginger falls back, landing on her back, looking up at me.

We both start laughing.

"Sorry. I guess I should have said something before opening the door." I reach down to pull her to her feet.

When she's fully standing, she turns toward me, yanking me into a big hug. At first, I freeze in shock but then I hug her back.

We both start crying.

"What the fuck?" Tiny barks out. "Are you two okay?"

We both start laughing, releasing each other.

Ginger turns to him. "Yes, Tiny. We're good. Just girl shit," she says before slamming the door, shutting us in Dallas's room.

When she realizes what she did, she asks me. "Do you want to go to Shy and I's room? Will you be more comfortable?"

I shake my head. "Nah, he trusts you. I feel comfortable here."

She beams. "Good, because Shy can't get in here, and I need to get away from it all. If you know what I mean."

Fuck yes.

Ginger's so beautiful in like a bad boy biker girl kind of way. She has always made me feel so welcome. I've always seen in her eyes she's been through some shit, and after hearing the stories last night, I understand.

Ginger and I were the only women in the room last night with all the men. I know she was overwhelmed too.

I sit at the head of the bed, leaning against the headboard,

Dallas

pulling a pillow onto my lap. Ginger sits across from me at the end of the bed with her legs crossed.

We don't say anything but just smile at each other.

She grabs her sleek black hair and throws it up in a messy bun matching mine.

"I'm sorry for everything that's happening to you," Ginger starts, but I interject

"You mean to all of us. It seems you, Izzy, and Alex have had your share of fucked-up shit." I try to laugh, but it comes off wrong.

She looks down to her lap and picks at her leggings. "Yeah, I guess you could say that." She pauses. I'm about to say something because she just looks so sad, but she snaps out of it, tilting her head up, saying cheerfully, "Well, I'm sure you have lots of questions. I mean, who wouldn't. Me and Shy—and then me and Brant."

That wasn't what was on my mind, but I could tell she needed to talk, so I let her have her moment to vent. I'm sure we will be taking turns.

"Shy was my first and only true love. We met on my sixteenth birthday."

She dives into her life story. The one she told me a few days ago she would say to me one day. I lean back and watch her tell her story. She's so animated, and I laugh when she laughs. Our stories are the complete opposite, but heartache is heartache. I have so much respect for her and her strength. She and Shy genuinely do have a happily ever after. They went through some fucked-up shit, but they made it.

"Wait, so Brant from last night, is the only other person you've been with?" I look at her like she's crazy.

"Yeah. I know, pathetic, but it's always been Shy for me," she answers with a smile.

"Jesus, he was hot as fuck. No wonder he was acting all caveman over you girls." I laugh.

My phone goes off and I grab it, seeing it's Dallas. "Hi."

"Are you okay? Is Snow still with you?" Dallas barks into the phone.

I look over at Ginger and smile. "Yes, she's still here with me. We've locked ourselves in here to have quality time, and we're good." I giggle.

I hear him let out a big sigh. "Thank fuck. That sounds perfect. I'm glad she has you, and you have her. I'll text or call you before we head into our meeting. We're waiting for everyone to get here." His voice sounds more chipper.

"Okay. Don't worry about us. We'll be here." I end the call, laughing.

"See!" She throws both hands at me. "I can never get away."

Her face becomes stressed, so I bring her back to our conversation.

"So seriously, B is hot as fuck. Was he all caveman over you?" I give her a devilish smile.

She waves her hand. "Girl, when he and I hooked up, he looked nothing like he does now." She giggles. "He's always been a caveman, that's just B. He hasn't been good since Sasha was taken and Austin was killed."

I hold up my hand. "Wait. What *did* he look like?" I demand.

"He looked like a cop, buzzed head, cleanly shaven and a whole lot nicer. He's always been big but, fuck me he's a whole lot bigger. Plus, he's grown his hair out with his hot as fuck beard. Oh, and yes, a shit ton meaner. Jesus, he's mean." Ginger winces.

"Why is he so mean? I could tell he was pissed off, but I thought it was because of the Russians."

She waves her hand. "No, after I got shot, I went back to Shy. Then Sasha was taken, and his friend got killed, he lost his shit.

Dallas

Literally. Then no one told you this last night, but…" She leans in like she's going to whisper a secret.

"Ghost, the badass bitch he was with last night."

I nod, getting excited.

"Yeah, well, *she* saved me, *and* she saved Izzy."

I throw my head back. "Shut the fuck up. No way."

Ginger starts nodding her head, laughing. "Talk about a buzz-kill to our men's ego. See why B's all pissy. That bitch has saved all of us."

I hold up my hand. "Wait a fucking minute. You saved Alex. Um, hello, you were shot."

She throws her hand out like it's nothing. "I protect my family."

We both start laughing.

"Okay, so back to real talk. Do you think we can trust Vi and Ray? I mean, I'm pretty good at reading people, and I didn't feel any bad vibes with either one of them. But they're your girls. After hearing all that shit last night, talk to me. How are you feeling?" Ginger turns her attention away from me, extending her legs, giving me time to think. She moves to lie on her side and once she gives me her full attention, I freeze.

Then scream, "Fuck!" at the top of my lungs.

Ginger leans back with a smile, like I blew her away.

"Girl, let it all out. It's your turn." She laughs.

"Fuck! I don't know. I mean, you know my story. I don't have one. I have lived my life in hiding. Busting my ass to become the best doctor I could be. If I didn't have my job to focus on or my hatred for Ronny, I… I would probably be dead by now. Seriously, I just don't know."

I get up off the bed, throw the pillow. Ginger gets up, taking my spot at the head of the bed, pulling the pillow onto her lap as she leans forward. "Go on. What? Tell me. What the fuck do you want?" Ginger demands.

I'm filled with excitement and joy, but when I start to think about what happened last night and all the things Ronny is doing and how Vi and Ray, my only two friends in this world, might be involved, I stop.

My back to Ginger, I drop my head.

"Wow! What just happened? Talk to me." Ginger crawls to the end of the bed, sitting on her shins.

"I don't know if they are involved. I don't know anything. I'm always ripped from my life. I'm always in the dark. Vi and Ray are *the* only two lifelines I've had. Without them these past ten years, I don't know if I could've made it. And now hearing they might be linked to him…" I can't finish, I drop to my knees and lose it.

Ginger is off the bed, pulling me into her arms. "Shhh, I've got you. I know for a fact those two women would die for you. I know it to my bones. I've got you." Ginger leans back so she can face me. "I promise on my life. You'll be okay. You are strong, just like all of us girls. Plus, these men. My Wolfemen are protectors. Why do you think they call me Snow?" she pauses. "I'm motherfucking Snow White. And these guys are my Wolfemen not dwarfs but my Wolves. They protect what's theirs." She pulls me into a hug, squeezing me hard. "And you are one of theirs now."

"Vi and Ray are true friends. We'll figure out why all this shit is fucked up. You just need to talk to them. You and I will deal with all these Wolves downstairs. We've got this. Plus, I called in reinforcements." She laughs.

I lean back, breaking the embrace, wiping my nose. "What?"

She smiles ear to ear. "Oh, they think they're the only ones who can call in their reinforcements, well, so can we. I've called in the aunties—mine and Ruby's auntie. You just wait. Shit's gonna hit the fan."

Dallas

I sit back, trying to compose myself.

"What do you mean?"

Ginger sits back, leaning against the bed. "Lee, you were raised differently. In my world, women are treated like queens. Well, the ones who deserve to be. My mom died when I was young. These men raised me, along with my auntie, my daddy's sister. They're big, bad Wolves, but you fuck with their mates and all hell breaks loose. We keep quiet most of the time, but if we lose our shit, they sit back and let us take the reins. You watch."

I laugh, remembering Storm walking around, throwing orders, and taking Bear down the hall to fuck him.

"Who is Ruby's aunt?"

"Oh... you don't know. So, Ruby's aunt is a well-known madam. Her name is Mistress Z. She runs a high roller strip club down in LA. The best part is that one of the characters she dresses up as for a client looks like my mom, like the spitting image. She puts a wig on and I'm even doing a double take. So, she's my ammunition. Bring her around, and all the men buckle. Don't say anything to Dallas, but you watch." She gets up, giving me her hand to pull me up. "As I said, us girls take care of our own. We love our men, but I've been raised with a pack of Wolves and know how to take care of myself. Just like you."

I'm up and in her arms for a tight hug.

I let out a deep breath and relax into her. I feel safe, and I don't want to let myself feel it, but I feel hope.

We both pull away when my phone chirps.

I grab it and read the text.

Dallas: You want to go on a run be down here in 10 min.

I beam.

Lee: Fuck yes! Be down soon.

I clench my phone and squeal.

"I get to go running. Do you run?" I ask Ginger.

Her smile goes big. "Fuck yes, I do. I even have a route around here. Let me get my shoes."

Ginger is out the door, and I move around the room to get ready.

My heart swells with joy. *Can this indeed be my life? Will everything be okay?*

"Fuck yes!" I say aloud to myself and the universe. I'm taking charge of my life.

27 | The Interrogation

Dallas

"LOOK, I DON'T KNOW WHY Y'ALL HAVE ME ON *DIS FUCKIN'* timeline. I told *y'all* that the Chingas coming here had to do with me, not you. I don't have any idea why *the fuck y'all* think I'm linked to any of *dis shit*. I'm Lee's best friend. I would kill to save that bitch." Vi leans back in her chair, crossing her arms.

"Vi's right. She would die for Lee," Brick explains. "And the Chingas are a problem, but they aren't linked to any of this shit." Brick waves at the timeline. "If keeping her here is a problem while I deal with the Chingas, then I'll find somewhere else to keep her," Brick yells, sounding defensive.

"That's not what we're saying," Wolfe interjects. "She *is* safe here. We just want to make sure because—" Wolfe gives me a nod, and I start the video from the other night showing Dexter arriving. "When we saw this, we just didn't know who was involved."

Everyone sits there, eyes glued to the TV. When Dexter gets out of the SUV, Vi stands up. "*Dis motherfucker!*"

Brick follows when he sees the other two men. "What the fuck are JJ and King doing with him?"

Thank fuck. They didn't know.

Brick and Vi look at each other and then back to the TV. When they both see who they're meeting inside, they go ballistic.

"Has Lee seen *dis shit*? Or Ray?" Vi demands.

"Yes, and no. We showed Lee last night, along with Snow, but none of the other girls have seen it," I say.

"Is she okay?" Vi says to me, eyes frantic.

"She needed time—hence why we let the two of them go on a run today."

Vi looks to Brick. "You need to call JJ and King, find out *why the fuck dey* at that meeting, and what the fuck *dey* doing with Ronny. If Marcus finds out *dey* was with him." She pauses, making a tsk-tsk noise, looking back to the TV. "It just doesn't make any sense." Vi waves her hand at the TV. "Who *dey*?" pointing toward the Russians.

"They're Russians," Shy answers. "Russians from the timeline."

Wolfe jumps in with questions. "This is why we're all worried this shit's linked. Do you know why Dexter's with them? What they're doing or why they would be meeting with the Russians and Ronny?"

Vi spins around, furious. "Fuck no! I'd kill Ronny myself if I could find him. *Dese* men… JJ and King worked with my late husband and my cousin. Shiiiiit, *dey* work with Brick." She waves at him standing next to her.

Brick pipes up, "I transport shit for them."

"Do you think Ronny's trying to take over your territory?" Wolfe asks Brick.

"He doesn't have the numbers or the power to do that. I'm locked in with the Chicago Outfit, the Reapers, and before last week, The Chingas. Who we're dealing with now. Nothing goes in or out of Chicago without my hands touching it," Brick explains, moving closer to the TV. "So, Ronny's in with the Devil Duo and the Devil's Dames? Shit, if the Chingas were there, they'd have all our sworn enemies in one place," he says to the room.

"I just don't understand why Dexter's there," Vi murmurs to herself. She rubs her lips, deep in thought, moving around the office. All of the officers from both West Virginia and New York are in here. She stops looking at me. "How'd Lee take it?"

Dallas

I shake my head. "Not too well. She kind of lost it when she saw him with Ronny, pretty much the same response you had. Then she started crying, thinking Raydene knew about it, but I told her Ray was with you two the whole time and Ray hadn't seen this. Dexter took her before we could show her. So, we don't know if Ray *is* involved or not."

"Fuck no, she isn't involved. Raydene's the one who got her a new identity. For *dese* past ten years, we've been *the only* two people protecting her. Why would you ever think we'd go against her? She hates Ronny just as much as any of us. If Ray saw *dis*, she'd lose her damn mind too. I don't know what Dexter's doing there, but I pray for his sake it's for intel because once Marcus finds out all three of them were there *and* didn't inform him, shit's going to pop off in a bad way."

I let out a big sigh of relief. It would kill Lee if one of these girls knew or was involved with Ronny.

Loud commotion comes from down the hall, causing men to rush out of the room to see what's going on. I click on my laptop to pull up the security cameras, my heart stops. "Lee!"

I jump from my seat and run to the front door. Two brothers walk in covered in blood. Jammer's barely stumbling behind Redman, carrying Cam, Jammer's brother. "Stitch, he's hit bad."

"Chain ran down to help the others," Redman says, putting Cam down onto a table as the brothers move chairs out of the way. "I need to go back," Redman tells us, turning to leave.

"Others? Go back where? Where's Snow!" Shy yells.

"I don't know. We saw Jammer trying to carry his brother a block away, and Chain took off running to find the others," Redman explains.

"Where's Snow?" Wolfe demands, walking up holding his gun.

Jammer's eyes fill with tears. "They got 'em. Fuck, I'm sorry. They got 'em."

Stitch starts to work on Cam as I grab Jammer. He winces,

and I realize he's shot too. "They ambushed us. There were two vehicles, one came at us and started shooting, the one came at us from behind, we didn't even see it coming. The van pulled up and grabbed the girls."

Wolfe roars, gripping hands full of hair in frustration. "Not again! Fuck! Call everyone. Lock everyone down."

Cash grabs his phone.

I look around. "Where's Josh? Where's Pete?"

Tears fall down his face. "I don't know. I just needed to get Cam here. We all got hit. Chain went to find them."

Shy snaps his fingers, and men run out the door, following Redman.

I move Jammer to a table. "Are you shot anywhere else? Was it Ronny? Did you see Ronny?" I ask, applying pressure to his shoulder.

"I saw Ronny and Blaze grab the girls. We got a couple of them coming at us. Snow was covering Lee behind us. We moved in on the car in front of us but didn't see the van. It all happened so fast. I'm so sorry." Jammer loses his shit and starts to cry. "Stitch, please save my brother. I can't lose him." He drops his head back, and I move so Tiny can start stitching him up.

Video. Fuck, the video.

I jump up. "Fuck, the surveillance. We still have eyes on them." Running for the office, I grab my laptop. Frantically, I pull up the auto body shop—nothing, and no one around. I pull up the clubhouse, there's no movement. All the bikes are still there. *They'd be stupid to take them back to their clubhouse.* "Fuck!"

I fall into the nearest chair. *Think, Dallas. Think.*

When I open my eyes, Vi, Mac, and Brick are standing in front of me, with Quick, Shy, and Wolfe on their phones behind them. "Vi and Mac try to get ahold of Raydene or even Dexter. Let them know Ronny has her. Brick, you need to contact JJ and King. Get them here if they're still in town. Explain to them we

Dallas

know they had a meeting with Ronny, and we need them to get in touch with Ronny again. We need them to meet up. We need to get Ronny," I demand.

Everyone starts moving, pulling out their phones.

I can't let her down. I need to save her. *Fuck!*

Lee

"I need to stop the bleeding. Please let me loose so I can tend to her wound," I yell at Ronny.

"Fuck you." He sneers.

"Fuck me? Fuck you!" I cry out. "What the fuck is wrong with you, Ronny? Are you that fucking delusional? Why do you want me so fucking bad? Just let me go, for fuck's sake," I scream—fury taking me over for the first time, and I'm not cowering down to him.

A sparkle ignites in his eyes. "I like you feisty. Keep it up, and I'll be fucking that dirty mouth of yours right here and now."

Ginger's knocked out cold. When they grabbed us, she was shooting at the car in front of us. There was a shot from behind me, hitting Ginger in the leg. I went to help her but was yanked back by Ronny just as a man came out of nowhere, hitting Ginger so hard in the face, knocking her out cold. I fought Ronny, but he had my arm pinned behind my back, wrenching my wrist to the brink of breaking. They grabbed her gun and threw her into the van. Ronny said into my ear, "if you want her to live, don't fight me," causing me to freeze. They tied me up and threw me in next to her, with Ronny and the guy jumping in behind us. She was shot in the back of the leg, and it doesn't look life threatening, but I need to check to make sure.

"Why, Ronny, why?" I plead with him. "Please, let her go. She needs medical help. I won't fight you."

"I wish I could, *Har*-baby, but she's for someone else." Ronny laughs.

Oh, God.

"What do you mean? Who?" I cry.

"None of your goddamn business," the other man yells, back-handing me, sending me flying to the side, hitting the van wall.

Ronny gives the man a lethal look. "You fucking touch her again without my consent. We'll have a problem. You got that, Blaze?"

"Then shut her the fuck up," Blaze fires back.

Ronny says through clenched teeth. "Blaze, you can do whatever the fuck you want with *that one*, but if you touch what's mine again, you know it won't end well." Ronny picks me up, helping me sit up.

"I'm not yours," I huff.

Ronny keeps looking at the other guy. "Don't touch her again." I look at the man, but Ronny hits me with something so hard my head smashes against the wall, and everything goes black.

"You killed Emmett. Admit it," a woman's voice yells from afar.

I try to open my eyes, but pain erupts in my head. My eyes are blurry, blinking rapidly, I try to focus them. My head hurts so bad I know I have a concussion. Everything's blurry, and I can barely keep my eyes open.

"I shot him, yes, but I didn't kill him." Ginger's voice is weak and broken, but my heart races hearing she's alive.

I hear what sounds like someone getting punched and grunting sounds. Then the same woman's voice seethes, "I saw the reports. The two of you got into a fight, you both got shot. He's dead, and you're not. Explain to me how you didn't kill him."

I'm dangling with my arms above my head, handcuffed to a

Dallas

rope. I try to move my feet, but they are bound to something. The handcuffs are cutting into my wrist, same as my feet. I'm stretched to the max. I try to see again, blinking to clear my vision, but I can't see clearly. I can only see silhouettes moving around in front of me. My whole body hurts like I've been beaten on for days. I lift my head again and see someone is in a chair, with their head slumped down.

Oh, my God, Ginger. They're beating on her.

I glance around, seeing we're in an empty, dark warehouse. Ginger coughs up blood. "I promise I didn't kill him."

"Liar!" she spits. "You took him from me. You and that fucking bitch Alexandria. He was mine. Well, you won't be so pretty when I'm done with you."

"Ah, she's awake." I hear Ronny moving up next to me. "I'm sorry about the head. He wasn't supposed to touch you. Then you had to mouth off, so—I knocked you out. I'm sorry for that. You know I have a temper." His laugh sounded so sinister, making my hair stand on end.

My voice comes out choked. "Ronny, let me down. Please. It's hurting my wrist and ankles."

"I don't know. I kind of like you all tied up. It's fucking hot." He grips my face hard, licking the side of my cheek. "My dick's hard just standing next to you. So many nights, jacking off to pictures of you." He laughs. "I'm going to have my fun with you first. I will make you submit to me. You're mine, Harley." His other hand slides up my body, cupping one of my breasts as he licks his lips.

"Never." I scoff in disgust. "Who's hurting Ginger?"

"Oh, you will. That's Karma, Blaze's sister. She doesn't like the Wolf Princess very much. It was kind of perfect that you two went for a little jog together. It saved us from having to get her later. You're so predictable. I knew one of these days you'd go for a run again. It's always how I get you."

265

"Fuck you," I spit out. "I'm not yours."

Ronny's eyes become as black as an abyss. He backhands me before gripping my face harder. "You are mine. You always have been and always will be." He moves his face inches from mine and whispers, "Submit to me, and life will be good for you." He grabs my crotch, making me wince in pain. "Fight me, and I'll make your life hell, taking what I want anyway. The choice is yours." He releases his hold on my face, throwing my head back, and my body follows, stretching my limbs. I cry out in pain.

I cry out in pain, but anger ignites inside me. When my body swings back toward him, I spit in his face. "Never."

I will fight. I will not submit to him.

He reaches back and punches me, breaking a rib. I scream in pain, but he can't hurt me mentally anymore, so I laugh at him, making him angrier. I've lost my mind. He grabs me by the throat, stopping me from breathing. I smile. He roars, frustrated, swinging me back again, and this time, I hear a crack, and pain ignites in my ankle. I keep laughing, spitting the blood dripping from my mouth right in his face. His next punch to the face knocks me unconscious.

I'm aroused, heat rising throughout me as my body comes alive. I moan, "Dallas."

A slap to my face brings me back to reality. "Wake the fuck up," Ronny breathes into my ear.

I silence my cry, realizing Ronny has my leggings shoved down, fingering me. He's torturing me, slowly slipping them in and out of me.

"Ronny, please, stop. What are you doing?" My voice, broken.

"Just having a little fun while no one's here," he whispers.

Dallas

"I'm going to fuck you real quick before we move you. I've waited long enough but wanted you alone," he grunts.

I start to cry and gurgle through the blood. "Please don't."

Ronny's cock is hard, pressed against my belly as he jacks himself off while he fingers me. I try to squirm out of his reach.

"Stop fucking moving, or I'll knock you out again and take what I want."

Loud voices break the silence. "You just need to kill the bitch. Why sell her, she can't talk, and she'll probably bleed out before she even gets to them?" A male voice yells from behind us.

"Goddamn motherfuckers," Ronny grunts, putting his dick away.

"Because I want her to suffer. I don't want to kill her. I want her to feel what I've felt since Emmett died—pain and suffering. Plus, the Wolf Princess is worth more alive than dead," the woman yells.

"Seriously, Ronny. Fucking open the door, they rattle the doorknob. Fuck her on your own time," the bitch demands. "Will you two just fucking get her ready? I'll be back."

The door rattles harder.

Ronny bends down, licking and sucking my pussy before slipping my leggings back up over my hips. "Fuck! *Har-baby*. Soon, I'll have you." He grabs my face by the cheeks, making me pucker, kissing my bloody face. As soon as he releases me, I spit.

Ronny moves behind me just as the door gets kicked open.

Ronny roars, "What the fuck, Blaze?"

"I don't have time for your shit. I'm here to get the bitch ready to move," Blaze announces.

I try to find Ginger. When I see Blaze and another man move across the darkroom, I see someone slumped over.

She said she didn't want to kill her. Please, God. Ginger, please be alive.

Ronny moves in behind me, wrapping his arms around me, swinging my body up against him. His hard cock poking my ass.

Tears run down my face as I see the other guy lift a lifeless Ginger over his shoulder. Blaze moves to a table near the wall as the other guy takes Ginger somewhere behind me.

Suddenly, I hear an oof, along with bodies dropping. I try to look around to see what happened when I feel a knife pressing against my throat.

"One more step and I'll slit her throat," Ronny breathes, swiveling me around. He pulls down on me, and I cry out as my shoulder pops. I almost lost consciousness, but when I opened my eyes, I came face-to-face with the petite woman I was introduced to the other night as *Ghost*. I cry out in pain.

Ronny is frantic, swinging me around. "Blaze!"

Blaze turns around and sees Ghost with a gun aimed at both him and Ronny. He looks around the room and laughs. "Who the fuck are you?" he asks, moving toward us.

"I'm here for the girls," Ghost replies.

Ronny keeps swiveling me around, making my limbs stretch, searching the area for more people.

The place is dark, and God, I wish I could see Ginger.

Blaze raises his gun, pointing it at Ghost, but she doesn't move, only smiles at him. I throw up from the intense pain, distracting Ronny just enough.

There are two popping noises, and both Ronny and Blaze go down, crying out in pain just as Ghost reaches for me. Ronny's knife cuts into the side of my neck when he goes down.

"Goddamn it, Maggie, you didn't let me get close enough to her." Ghost shushes me while wrapping something around my neck. I start crying hysterically.

"Shh, Lee. We need to get you out of here," Ghost says calmly to me.

"Ginger?" I choke out.

Ghost smiles. "B has her."

Relief washes over me, but when I hear Ronny groan, I freeze.

Dallas

They're not dead.

I look over to see another woman pulling Blaze up, moving him. Ronny's lying on his side, bleeding. Ghost reaches above me, cutting the ropes, but my hands are still handcuffed. I cry out in pain as my arms fall. I slump over her back as she holds me around the waist, lowering herself to cut my feet free. There is so much pain I'm going to black out. My head becomes fuzzy, I'm light-headed, but just as I'm about to lose consciousness, Ronny smiles at me from the ground.

He has to die. Kill him.

Ghost is still working on freeing my feet while trying to hold me up. Without thinking, I use my good hand that's still cuffed, grab her gun from her holster, and shoot. Ghost snaps up, snagging the weapon from me just as I lose consciousness.

"Jesus fucking Christ!" Ghost yells, grabbing me.

28 | The Affirmation

Dallas

"**We got 'em!**" Brant bellows into the phone. I jump up from the table, snapping my fingers. "What do you mean 'we' got them? Who? Where?" I demand.

The room erupts in chatter. "I'll explain at the hospital. Ginger and Lee are alive, but they're in bad shape, Ginger more than Lee. Lee was conscious when we got there, but Ginger has been unconscious the whole time. I can't get her to wake up. Just get to the hospital," he barks, hanging up.

I grab my cut and head for the door. "They got 'em. Call Redman. They're on their way to the hospital."

"Who's got them, and are they okay—is Snow okay?" Shy roars.

I rush down the hall and yell over my shoulder. "Brant said he got the girls and for us to get to the hospital."

Jumping on my bike, I take off, breaking every law there is to get to the hospital, including the chain of command, leaving my president behind me. They're all behind me, I'm sure, but all I can think about is Lee.

Please, God, let her be okay.

So many questions fly through my head.

How did they find them?
Why didn't he call us?
Where did he find them?

It's been five hours since they were taken.

Dallas

Flying through the ER doors, I see Redman, who's in a huddle with Brant, Ghost, and what looks like cops talking to a doctor. Our men have been here since they found Josh still alive. We rushed him and Cam to the hospital along with Jammer, who only had a flesh wound but wanted to stay with his brother.

When I look closer at the men in black, I see they're FBI agents and they're all talking to Greg, Lee's doctor friend.

Fuck!

"What the fuck?" I fire at Brant.

Just as the doors fly open, Wolfe yells, "Where the fuck is she?"

Brant stands his ground. "They have been taken to the back."

When the FBI agents turn toward me, I recognize them from when Izzy was taken. Greg excuses himself, and I move toward him.

"Is she okay?" I choke out.

"I've seen her worse, but she's pretty beaten up." I can see the anguish in his eyes. "What are you not telling me?" I demand.

"Lee has some broken bones and swelling to her face and head. Ginger's still unconscious and has some severe injuries that I'm more concerned with. Lee's in CT getting her head scanned right now. I need to get back there, but I'll send Nurse Cheryl out once we know more. Please stay calm."

He leans into my ear. "You better have gotten that motherfucker," he says, gripping my arm hard before walking away.

When I turn back around, B must be telling them what the doc just told me because Shy punches the wall, and Wolfe throws a chair.

Luc and Beau walk in with Maddox and the team following behind them. Luc's eyes scan the room, assessing the situation. When he sees the FBI agents, he beelines it straight to them.

I follow.

"What the fuck are you doing here, Maggie?" Luc demands.

She holds her hand up to the other FBI agents, stopping them from saying something. "I got this. Just secure the area and meet back at the office." She turns to us. "Not here, follow me."

When she passes me, she says, "Just you and your presidents."

I follow her, whistling, getting their attention. Shy and Wolfe follow, and of course, Mac and Cash linger behind Brant and Ghost. I give one of our prospects a nod, letting him know to stay. We placed men all around the hospital earlier when we brought our men here.

Agent Maggie leads us to an SUV, where she opens up the back.

"Fuck me." I whistle. The entire back is full of guns, files, computers, etc.

When she turns around, I notice an agent come out of nowhere. I would've pulled my gun, but I'm guessing he's friendly. He ignores us getting into the passenger side.

"Okay, I can't go into detail right now, but I've been working on this case for a while now. It seems you've been caught in the crossfire *again*." She looks to Luc. "Do you want to tell them?"

We all look toward Luc for answers.

Folding his arms in irritation, he grunts. "She's one of the people I get my intel from."

Shy laughs. "Seriously? And you believed her, why?"

"Because we go way back, he's saved my life more than once. I owe him." She smiles.

Wolfe doesn't say anything. He just looks between Beau and Luc. Beau, feeling eyes on him, turns and says, "Look, you knew we had FBI intel. They helped us with a few other incidents, including getting Izzy back. So, don't act like you didn't know. We've known Maggie for years. She's good people."

"So, what does this have to do with us?" I ask, wanting to get to the bottom of this.

"Look, here's a folder I put together for you. I hope it can

Dallas

fill in some missing parts to your timeline," she says, handing me a folder. "You're good, and you almost had all the pieces, so I hope this helps."

I smile, giving her a nod of appreciation because she really did help us put together Dominic being a Petrov and all that bullshit.

"How the fuck did you hear about our timeline," Shy demands, clenching his fist, moving toward Luc.

"It was me," Ghost announces. "I told her about it last night. When you told us about the vans leaving the clubhouse, I called her. I knew she was still working on the trafficking case and wondered if the vans were the same vans in her case—maybe they were linked. She asked me what I knew about the vans, and I explained what was going on. She found the vans—we found the girls."

"Are you fucking FBI?" I grit, knowing we had our suspicions, but Maddox vouched for her, so we let it go.

"No, but I've been helping them find girls for years now, and they've helped me when I need it. We all want the same thing, to get the bad guys," Ghost explains.

"Why didn't you call us when you found them?" Wolfe asks.

"When we got a hit on the vans, I texted them the location," Maggie tells us. "We didn't know the girls were taken. We were just following up on the vans' whereabouts. Once we found out the girls were taken, we went in. We saw our moment when most of the men left with the Devil's Dames' president, Karma. We wanted to sneak in and sneak out. We left no one behind. It will take them a while to figure out who took them. They'll probably think it was you, not us." She laughs.

Shy snarls. "I hope they think it was us too. We'll be ready."

"So, you let all the members go?" I ask.

"We got one, and he's in custody. We're keeping him for interrogation."

"Who, Ronny?" I seethe.

Maggie looks to Brant and Ghost.

"What?" I huff. "Fucking tell me."

"He's dead," Ghost says, emotionless.

Goddamn, she's a cold bitch.

I look to Brant. "You know we needed him alive to interrogate. We all need answers."

Brant shrugs. "It wasn't us, and we had no control over it. Believe me. We tried."

Wolfe chimes in, "What do you mean you tried?"

Maggie sighs, obviously wanting to end our little chat, "In short—we went in fast. We secured the area, while Ghost went in after Lee. Brant killed the member carrying Ginger out. Ronny had a knife to Lee's neck. Ghost distracted him and the other member while I snuck in behind, shooting them both, but only injuring them both. When I was pulling the other member out, Ghost was helping Lee down. Lee saw Ronny was still alive and I don't know how she did it, but Lee pulled Ghost's gun and shot him point blank before passing out."

My body tenses hearing her tell me what happened, but I need to know. "So, what's going to happen to her? Is she in trouble?" I question.

Maggie shakes her head. "No, in our report, we put self-defense. That he was pulling a gun, and she shot him." Maggie pauses, shutting off the SUV. "I've seen what he's done to her all these years, and I would've done the same thing. Sorry, none of us get our answers, but at least she can live free now."

"So, now what?" Wolfe asks her.

"I'm going to head out. We need to be far away from here when they find out what happened. We've secured the place. Gus has taken over placing men around. If you need anything, they know how to get hold of me. Let's just say this never happened." Maggie laughs, walking to the driver's side of the SUV.

"Wait! Who do you have in custody?" Shy questions.

"He goes by Blaze, president of the Devil Duos. So, shit's

Dallas

going to hit the fan when they find out their president and road captain are missing." Maggie laughs. "You might want to be prepared for retaliation. Again, we'll do what we can, but we were never here. Hopefully, we can wrap up this case soon and bust everyone involved."

"You mean bust us?" Wolfe laughs.

Maggie turns around, giving us her full attention. "Believe me. If I was after you—you'd know. And I sure as fuck wouldn't be helping you. So, unless you're a major drug smuggling dealer or trafficking girls, we're good. Keep your nose clean, and we'll be on the same side." She salutes us and jumps into the SUV.

We all stand there as she drives away. I grip the folder tighter, shoving it in the back of my pants, pulling my cut over it, hiding it from sight.

Wolfe turns to Luc and Beau. "We have a lot to discuss, but right now, I need to make sure my baby girl's okay. Can you help me get this place locked down? I don't want anyone going in or out without us knowing."

They both nod at the same time.

Shy looks to Brant and Ghost. "Thank you both for saving my angel." He pauses, looking straight at Ghost. "Again."

Brant shakes his head. "Don't thank me. We should have been there sooner. She's in bad shape." He pauses again. Wolfe and Shy close in, wanting more information. Brant clears his throat. "Prepare yourself. From just what I could assess, she has a broken jaw, major lacerations, a gunshot wound to the leg, and her face was completely swollen from being beaten. So, when I say be prepared, I fucking mean—be prepared. Seeing her like that will haunt me." Brant shakes his head.

Everyone gets back on their phones, barking orders and setting up a plan. Shy and Wolfe take a minute. Wolfe grabs Shy, embracing him like a father would a son, they murmur words of encouragement to each other.

I reach for them, but Ghost grabs my arm, stalling me. "Dallas, you need to be prepared too. She's got some broken bones, and her face was bruised and swollen but nothing like Ginger. Her scars are going to be more mental. Getting beaten is completely different from mentally being abused and killing someone on top of that—just keep her close. She wasn't even coherent when she pulled the trigger." She smiles softly, finally showing a soft side of her. Around us, she's just the badass bitch that will do anything to save our girls.

I smile back. "Thank you for always being there for our girls. I'm not letting her out of my sight for a long time."

Brant appears suddenly next to her. "At least the fuckers dead. Two less motherfuckers we have to deal with. If the feds weren't there, I would've taken them all out. Fucking pieces of shit."

I reach my hand out to him, giving him a handshake. "Thank you again. Sorry for flipping out."

He laughs. "It's my job to protect them. I'll always be here."

I nod, turning to head back inside.

I need to see my Doc.

Right when I walk in, I see Nurse Cheryl looking around for me. She finds Mac, and he points to me. She seems relieved at first, but I can tell she's stressed. I pick up my pace, hurrying to meet her. She hugs me, taking me off guard. "She's going to be okay. Thank God."

I release her. "Talk to me. What're her injuries looking like?"

"I don't know all of them, and I need to get back in there, but she keeps murmuring stuff. Her face is badly swollen, we're waiting for the CAT scan and X-ray results, but her wrist, ankle, shoulder, and ribs are badly bruised and swollen. Not sure if they're broken or just badly sprained. Her head is our main concern." She looks around, seeing who's listening. I pull her to the side. "She keeps calling out for Ginger, saying Alex's in danger from her karma or something? I couldn't make out all that she was mumbling. She

Dallas

keeps going in and out of consciousness. Greg's worried about a major concussion since we can't keep her conscious long enough to talk to her. He wanted me to tell you these exact words, '*He's been taken care of.*' I hope you know what that means."

Lee must have said Ronny's dead or something.

I nod. "Okay. Go take care of my girl, and please let me know how Ginger's doing."

"I'll go right now and find out what's going on with Ginger. Greg wouldn't let me leave Lee until he got back, and then he told me to come tell you what she's been mumbling."

"Thank you, Cheryl." I hug her before she turns to rush off.

Shy and Wolfe are next to me within seconds, both simultaneously asking. "What did she say?"

"I guess Lee's mumbling, in and out of consciousness. She's asking for Ginger, saying Alex's in danger from her karma."

Then it hits me. "Fuck! Karma left with men. Where's Alex?" I yell, looking for Maddox.

"Maddox, where is Alexandria? I think she might be in danger."

Luc and Maddox rush over, and I explain what Cheryl said. Maddox's out the door in seconds, followed by Redman and Quick on his tail. All the girls must be together if they're all rushing out. Luc gets on the phone.

"We need to lock down everyone until we can regroup. Everyone should go deal with their shit, either bring your people back to the clubhouse or Mancini building, then we'll plan to meet at the clubhouse once we know more about Snow and Doc," Wolfe tells the room of men.

There's a commotion coming from outside, where our guys just exited. Most of us pull our guns, ready for anything to come through that door.

"Where is she? Is she okay?" Vi yells.

Followed by Storm. "I need to see my niece. Where the fuck is she?"

"What the fuck're ya doing here?" Bear rushes her.

"My niece called me yesterday, saying she needed the girls and me. I show up and find out she's in the hospital. What the fuck do you think I'm doing here?" She pushes past her husband and beelines it to Wolfe. "Talk to me. What's going on?"

Wolfe embraces her. Storm starts crying. "Don't you hug me, Johnny. You better start talking before I lose my shit." You know she's upset when she uses his birth name.

He doesn't release her when he replies, choking up. "I don't know yet, sis. I'm waiting to hear."

Cheryl rushes back into the room. I tap Shy and head toward Cheryl.

She rushes, sounding out of breath. "I don't have all the details, but she's in surgery to stop all the bleeding. She's got a gunshot wound to the back of the leg. She's lost a lot of blood with deep lacerations all over her body. We still need to do a CAT scan and X-rays, but…" She pauses again, making the men become irate. I'm sure it would be scary for any nurse to see a roomful of bikers become mad. I grab her arm, reassuring her. Shaking her head, she says, "We're pretty sure she has a broken jaw and ribs. Once she's out of surgery and they stop the bleeding, we'll do more tests. She's stable right now. I'm sorry, that's all I could get from them. I promise to return once I know more."

Storm begins to cry harder, and Wolfe pulls her tighter to his chest. I thank her again, and she gives my hand a squeeze before rushing off again.

"Dallas, you best start telling me what's going on with my girl before I lose my shit too." Vi's voice cracks.

I turn around and see Vi's eyes fill with tears. When I tell her what I know, she grabs me and pulls me into a hug. "Thank you. Thank God."

Dallas

I whisper so only she can hear. "Ronny's dead. She killed him. Shh, not everyone knows yet."

Vi pulls back, eyes wide. "Ya fucking with me?"

I shake my head. "Nah, only a few of us know."

"Fuck. Okay, well, I'm not leaving anytime soon. I'm here to stay and help out." She gives me a brief hug again before walking over to Brick.

When another doctor comes out, he looks around the room. "Y'all must be Mr. Cameron Hill's family. Any of you his immediate family?"

Shy steps forward, answering him, "His brother Jamie Hill was admitted too. We're his family, you can tell us."

The doctor looks around, rubbing the back of his neck, looking uncomfortable. Knowing damn well he's not supposed to tell people unless they're immediate family. He lets out a long sigh. "Fuck it. He just got out of surgery. He was shot three times, but thankfully, no major arteries or organs were hit. He lost a lot of blood, but he's stable and in recovery."

A sigh of relief sounds across the room. Cam was in line to prospect once Jammer became a member and nominated him. After this, I think he'll be nominated no matter what.

"And his cousin Joshua Hill? Can you tell me how he's doing?" Mac asks, coming up next to us.

"I'll have a nurse find out and get back to you. I just got out of Cameron's surgery," the doctor says.

We all thank him before he leaves.

I look to Wolfe. "We need to make sure everyone is on the same floor. I know what Maggie said, but we need to make sure it happens."

When the elevator door chimes, we all turn. Chain and Trey stop in their tracks, seeing us all standing there. "What the fuck?" Chain murmurs.

"Where have you two been?" Shy asks.

"We've been upstairs with Jammer. What's going on? He just got out of surgery. Is it Cam or Josh? Are they okay?"

Shy proceeds to tell them about the girls and what we know. Vi taps my back. "What's all of that?"

I forgot I had the file stuffed in the back of my pants. I pull it out and open it up. The first thing I see is a recent picture of Karma and Emmett embraced in a kiss. This photo is clearly right before he died.

Well, fuck me.

I start to fumble through the file, revealing more secrets.

I look up to the room. "I need my laptop."

29 | The Details

Dallas

"**D**O YOU REALLY THINK SHE'LL WANT TO HAVE A PARTY when she comes home?" Vi says, sitting next to me at the bar.

I take a swig of my beer. All I care about is having my Doc back in my arms and in my bed. The last two weeks have been a shitstorm of events. Karma and her crew have gone radio silent. Wherever they were going to take Ginger, they must've gone because we can't find them, or Lenny and Rayaan.

We raided the auto body shop, but the shit was gone. I don't understand how we missed it. But going back when we were all at the club and the guys were mostly watching Ronny at the clubhouse, they moved the product to vans. But we didn't notice the vans until they showed up at the Devil Duos clubhouse. Plus, the intel from Agent Maggie showed pictures of the vans. They had been tracking them—thank God, otherwise who knows when we'd have found the girls.

The Russians haven't left yet, but still haven't moved on any of the drugs or investigated Dom's whereabouts. They've pretty much been partying at clubs and making themselves seen.

Maze pours herself a shot. "Well, I don't think she'll have a say. All these people have been on lockdown and need something to be happy about." Maze smiles at Vi, lifting her shot. "Plus, these ladies are heading home Sunday. We'd be having a party no matter what. So, she can go up to her room or she can hang out, either way… we're partying," Maze finishes, slamming a shot.

Thank fuck all the ladies are heading back. I feel like this place is crawling with women and not the one I want. Coming home from the hospital alone isn't fun. Shy and I have been taking turns staying the night at the hospital. Our girls have a room together, and they'll only let one guy stay. We fought them at first about staying there, but it got cramped. Plus, Ginger's been unable to talk with her mouth wired shut. Once she was out of the woods and able to communicate somewhat, we both felt better, leaving only one of us there. So, I've buried myself in work.

Vi turns to me. "What do you think Lee will want?"

I finish my beer. "I think she'll love it, and if she gets tired, we'll go upstairs. But, I agree with Maze, this club needs a good party. Be ready in ten. I need to talk to the boys real quick." I slide my empty beer over to Maze and turn to head down the hall.

Vi's been staying here with us at the clubhouse but says she'll be moving into Lee's apartment once Lee's out. I told her she's fucking high if she thinks I'm letting Lee out of my sight. Plus, she's supposed to be in hiding here from the Chingas. We're not letting either of them stay at the apartment unguarded. Fuck that.

Mac and Shy are in Shy's office. "I don't give a fuck. You're not leaving. She ain't your problem, and we have enough shit going on here," Shy yells at Mac.

I knock on the open door. "I'm headed out to pick up Lee. You headed that way to see Snow?"

"Can you please tell him he doesn't need to run off after Raydene. Romeo over here thinks Raydene's in trouble. Brick said when he got back, he'd check in on her. What do you think?" Shy asks, leaning back in his chair, folding his hands over his belly.

Raydene called a couple of times and spoke with Vi and Lee. She told the girls right off the bat, *'I know about Dexter's dealings with JJ and King. I don't get involved, so don't ask me.'* But, when they said, *'Did you know Dexter has been dealing with Ronny?'* She flipped out. She obviously didn't know and it made the girls feel better,

Dallas

but since that conversation, they've only talked to her two other times. Each time she was super short or quiet, saying Dexter and her are fighting and he won't talk to her about what he's doing.

"I think you need to wait to hear from Brick and let him check out the situation. There's a lot going on over there. If Brick needs our help, we'll go, but we have our own issues with the Russians and both Devil MCs. Plus, we have the meeting with Knight tomorrow. Raydene's a big girl. If she needs help, she'll call," I agree with Shy.

Mac's face hardens. Standing up, he storms out of the office saying, "Fuck this."

"Fuck, I don't know what has gotten into him. She left!" He throws his hands up. "She has a *fucking* boyfriend. I don't understand him. Get the fuck over her." Shy shakes his head. "Jesus Christ, is the infamous Mac Daddy pussy whipped? I mean, her pussy couldn't be *that* magical, can it? Fuck!"

I chuckle. "I don't know. He's set on something not being right with her, but who the fuck knows."

Shy leans forward, placing his forearms on his desk. "Okay, so tomorrow is a go. Any setbacks we need to focus on?"

He's talking about our meeting with Knight. Wolfe called Knight from the hospital, letting him know what happened. We've been in contact with them throughout the past two weeks, making a plan. He called a couple of days ago, wanting to set up a meeting, saying that he had intel for us.

"Yes, all is good. My inside guy says Knight is ready for this to be over, but still wants to deal with those rogue Crows. I've set up surveillance on all of the locations for both the Russians and the Devil MCs, so if someone leaves the clubhouses or the hotel, we'll know. Beau has men monitoring all video surveillance, so we don't miss anything again. We have everything feeding through his security office."

"Good. What else are we missing?" Shy leans back. "I want to be ahead of anything coming our way."

"Ethan and I both have facial recognition running nonstop for Lenny, Rayaan, and Karma. If they reappear, we'll know." I push off the doorframe. "I need to head out to pick up Doc. You coming?"

Shy stands up. "Nah, her dad's there with Cash. I have shit I got to get done before I head there tonight."

I shake his hand and give him a man hug. "Sounds good. See you back here soon."

"Glad your ol' lady gets to come home. Fuck, I can't wait for mine," Shy says, slapping me on the back.

I head back down the hall with Shy next to me when I whistle for Vi and head for the front door.

I have Doc's Range Rover. I picked it up this last week, so she'd have it at the clubhouse. I also pretty much packed up her clothes and anything I thought she'd need. My thought is, she won't be coming back. I want her in my bed with me at all times. I'm just praying she feels the same way.

We haven't had much time alone—well, actually, we've had none since Ginger has been in her room this whole time. We thought it would be good to put them together, but later realized it sucked for Shy and me, since we wanted to be alone with our girls but had to share our time with other people.

Not like any of us could do anything anyway. Both girls have broken ribs. Ginger's arms, legs, and face are cut up pretty badly. Lee's wrist and ankle ended up being broken.

We're in the car when Vi turns to me. "Your boy's trippin' on Ray, huh? To be honest, I'm trippin' too. She ain't been the same for a while. I didn't see it before because I've been goin' through my own shit after Ton' died, but now that I look back. Shit ain't right." She turns to look out the side window.

I glance over at her from the driver's seat, and I can tell she's

Dallas

genuinely worried. I give her a second to see if she's done. Vi and I have gotten somewhat closer these past two weeks. She's a good friend and overall, a good person. She hides behind this big badass persona, but I think she's a softy at heart.

"Well, I promise once shit settles down here." I pause. "Nah, fuck that. Shit's never calm here. Once I get Doc home and back in my bed, then we'll have a meeting tomorrow. I will personally dive into her life. We'll figure this shit out, but you're not going back there until Brick says it's okay."

She laughs. "You're a good man. But, to be honest. I don't want to go back. I want to find out what is goin' on with my friend, but I don't want to go back. I like it here."

"Does Brick know this?" I chuckle, shifting in the seat. I feel caged in this fucking car. I'd rather be on my bike than caged up. It's why I don't have a car. I use the clubs or ride with a brother. I don't need a car.

"He ain't my man." She waves her hand. "We're business partners."

I raise an eyebrow at her. "Does he know this?"

She turns to me. "Um, yes. I've told him several times. I'm not into him like that. And, if he's catching feelings, that's even more of a reason to move here. I care about him and all, but he reminds me too much of Ton." She pauses, looking out the window again, lost in thought. "Shit… all of Chicago does."

When we arrive at the hospital, we're greeted by Trey and Dasher.

"How are the Hill boys?" I chuckle. It seems our Hill brother and cousin are a hit on the floor. Sweet-talking the nurses, always making people laugh. Josh was shot in the shoulder, arm, and stomach. If Chain hadn't gotten there, he probably would have bled out.

"Schmoozing the ladies as usual." Trey laughs.

Walking into the girls' room, I take a deep breath because it's still hard to see them all banged up. We all freaked the fuck out when we first saw them with their faces swollen black and blue. I'm not a crying kind of guy. The last time I cried was probably my mama's funeral, but when I saw my Doc all fucked up, I lost my shit.

Then when Ginger was rolled into the room, everyone lost it. I don't think there was a dry eye in the room. Thank fuck she was unconscious so we could get our shit together before she saw any of us tear up. She'd never let any of us live that down.

She *is* and will *always* be our Wolf Princess, our Snow White. That bitch is one of the strongest women I know. I was practically raised with her, so to see my baby sister beaten was pretty hard on all of us big, bad Wolves.

Even two weeks later, her face is still black and blue. Her jaw's wired shut so we can't hear her talking shit, but she has a dry erase board.

"How are my ladies today?" I declare, walking in with a massive smile on my face.

"Ready to get the fuck outta here, and I love being here," Lee exclaims from the bed. I move to her, giving her a kiss on the forehead. Her golden eyes twinkle with excitement. My buddy is bursting at the seams wanting to share her love too.

Wolfe, Bear, Storm, and Cash are all crammed in the room. Ginger raises her good arm and shows me her sign, reading, "Fuck both of you." With a smiley face.

Wolfe and Bear stand, making their way to the door. "We're going to head back to the clubhouse and relieve Shy so he can come over here and get some alone time with Snow," Wolfe says to the room.

"I don't know what you're talking about, but I'm staying here." Storm huffs.

Bear turns, giving her an eye. She ignores him. "Come get me when Shy comes back because I'm not leaving her here alone."

Dallas

A sign flies up. "Auntie, the whole floor is filled with Wolves. Hello, Jammer, Cam, and Josh are on the same floor."

Even when she can't speak, she is still telling it like it is.

We all laugh.

Bear lifts a hand and fingers her to come.

Wolfe laughs. "Come on, sis."

Storm huffs but gets up, kissing Ginger, then hugging Lee. "I'll see you at the clubhouse."

When everyone is gone, leaving Ginger, Lee, and myself in the room, Ginger throws her head back, closing her eyes.

Lee leans in. "She's exhausted and ready for some alone time with Shy."

I whisper, "I agree. I'm ready for Doc alone time." Kissing her on the forehead.

"Can you give us a moment? Go get Cheryl with the wheelchair?" Lee says quietly.

I nod and make my way out the door just as Vi is about to enter. I stop her. "She wants to have a moment with Ginger, and we need to find Cheryl."

I'm shocked Vi didn't argue, but instead, she just followed me to the nurses' station.

"Those Hill boys are fucking fools—they crack me up." Vi laughs.

I'm about ready to reply, but Cheryl comes around the corner and squeals when she sees me. "Dallas! You ready to take our girl home?"

I laugh. "Fuck yeah. Give me the wheelchair and show me where to sign." I hug her.

"She's not leaving until I sign her out." A deep rumble comes from behind me.

Dr. Greg and I have become friends over the past two weeks as well. He's a pretty funny guy. Once I told him the whole story about Lee, you could just see he was so relieved. Since then, he's been all smiles and a happy-go-lucky guy.

"Well, you better get on that doctor because I'm springing her from here." I laugh.

Three hours later, we're finally in my room, alone, in each other's arms. We ducked out of the party to get some alone time, and I'm hoping we can stay up here all night. She seemed totally fine downstairs, laughing and mingling with everyone. I was worried she'd be exhausted or timid around a bunch of people, but no. She actually seemed more at ease, like that wall that was surrounding her was gone.

I swipe her hair out of her face and smile, "Hi."

She giggles. "Hi."

I caress my hand down her arm. "I've missed you."

She smiles. "I've missed you more. I've needed this, or I should say I need this from you."

"What?"

"You. This. Alone together." She takes a short breath.

"Well, you got me. I'm not going anywhere." I smile. "These two weeks have been rough not having you in my bed. I think you're stuck with me, Doc." I lean in, kissing her.

Her broken wrist is under the pillow stuffed under her head.

"Want to know what Ginger and I were talking about?" Her face is blank all of a sudden. I'm worried she's going to lose her shit, and then I will, but I just nod and say, "Sure. If you want to."

"I told her that she and I were bonded for life and that she will always be a sister to me. That I would do anything for her. And her reply was, '*Well, do this for me—live your life—free of worry*'."

"Oh, yeah." I smile in response.

She presses her finger to my lips, shutting me up. "Then she

Dallas

said that she really hopes that means living it with you, here at the clubhouse, so we could become like real sisters." Doc leans up on an elbow, wincing from her ribs, using her good hand to push me onto my back. When I comply, she slides on top of me, straddling me, Buddy pulsing beneath her heated core. All her hair cascades down around her beautiful, angelic face.

"And do you want to know what I said in return?" She smirks. I nod.

"I told her that's why we'd be sisters for life. Because I'm going to spend the rest of my life making sure you're the happiest man alive, even though I saved your life that day, you gave me mine back. I'm finally free, and it's all because of you."

My heart swells. "Doc," I breathe.

She starts to cry. "Let me finish." I close my eyes and try to control myself, letting her get out what she needs to. Like Ghost said, *Just keep her close*'. When I open my eyes, she's smiling down at me.

"I know you're worried about me. I'm not going to lie and say I'm not fucked up, but one thing I know is I don't regret killing Ronny. I'd do it again in a heartbeat. So, the point I'm trying to get across here is what I want and need is you—I need." She grips my chest and slowly rocks her core over me. "I need you to remind me every day that I'm alive and living my life free of worry."

I groan when she rocks against me again.

"Fuck, yes," I moan in approval, gripping her hips softly, encouraging her to keep going. It's her rodeo, and I'm just along for the ride. I just wanted to hold her and maybe make out. She has been through a lot, and I'm here to comfort her. So, for her to tell me she needs me to make love to her each day, I'm game.

"Alec," she moans.

"Yes, Doc." I lean up, wrapping my arms around her, careful not to hurt her ribs, embracing her for a deep kiss.

"Take me, please," she murmurs into my mouth.

I whisper, "No."

She pulls back.

I smile. "You're still hurt, and I'm here for you to do whatever you need. I'm all yours, and tonight's about you and what you need."

I kiss her neck, pulling her to me again.

Doc drops her head back. "I want to erase all the bad memories and start my new life right now with you. I never have to worry about looking over my shoulder again. I'm free because of you. I need you to make love to me. Slow and deep, so deep you hit my soul. Then I'm gonna ride you good and hard."

I laugh, sucking her neck, slipping her dress off a shoulder, suckling down, popping a breast out, engulfing it.

Doc cries out in ecstasy

"Are you sure you're ready for this?" I rasp out between sucking and gripping her breast.

She lifts my head, looking me in the eye. "You're all I need, Alec. Now and forever."

Yep, that did it.

I carefully flip her slowly and gently onto her back, making sure her ribs aren't crushed. She's in a dress, so it's one easy whoosh, and it's gone—panties and bra off two seconds later. I take my time cherishing each and every inch of her body. She's panting, clawing at me, begging me for more.

"What do you want, Doc?" I tease.

"I want your buddy to reclaim his forever home," she demands.

It guts me that motherfucker touched her there. I slide down her body, capturing her mound, sucking, slipping my tongue between her folds. *Heaven.* I devour her, gently holding her down, gripping her hips until she's screaming my name in her release. I keep going, wanting another. She thrives under me, shaking as she comes instantly again, harder as juices fill my mouth. It's so

Dallas

fucking sexy seeing her come alive. I come in my pants instantly. But I don't care. I keep cherishing her beautiful pussy. I kick off my jeans, breaking contact for a split second to rip off my shirt before diving back in.

"Alec, please. I-I can't. I want you," she begs.

I kiss her inner thighs, moving my way back up her belly, suckling each breast, nipping them before moving on to her neck.

"Doc, you are mine. I'll never let you go." I begin to emphasize how with each kiss.

"I'm." Kiss.

"Claiming." Kiss.

"Every." Kiss.

"Inch" Kiss.

"Of." Kiss.

"You." Kiss.

I kiss her mouth with a deep, passionate kiss. Just before I slip torturously slow into her wet ready pussy. *My pussy.*

Buddy can't take it and slams the last few inches before slowly sliding out. I rest my body on my forearms, so I'm not putting any weight on her. I lean down, sucking her neck. "You're mine forever."

I slam deep, hitting her cervix.

She throws her head back, moaning her approval.

"Yes," she breathes out. She's trying to control her breathing, not to hurt her ribs, but I think she's fucked because I'm going to have her panting in a minute, wanting more. I continue my slow but stern thrusts.

"Your." Slam.

"Mine." Slide out.

"Forever." Slam.

"Fuck yes, Doc." Slide out.

"I've never." Slam.

"Wanted." Slide out.

"Anyone." Slam.

"Like I do." Slide out.

"You." Slam.

Breathless. "Please, Alec. Faster. Please," she begs.

I laugh. "I thought you wanted." Slam.

"For me to." Slide out.

"Make love." Slam.

"Slow." Slide out.

"And." Slam

"Deep." Slide out.

Fuck, I'm not even going to last much longer.

Her mewling and nails clawing me have me giving in.

Slam. Slam. Slam.

Sweat beads across my forehead, and I'm inches from her face, breathing hard.

"You want me to ride you hard, Doc?"

Slam. Slam. Slam.

Lee screams, "Yes."

I sit on my knees, grabbing her thighs. I give her what she wants—fucking her senseless, hard and fast.

"Fuck yes," I roar.

"Yes. Faster. Oh, God." she pushes the words out, taking a small breath in between each word.

"You. Are. Mine. Fucking mine," I growl.

I release her legs, dropping down, hovering over her. I jackhammer into her, rocking against her clit, sending her over the edge and me along with her. I bite down on her neck, silencing my voice as I release two weeks' worth into her.

"Fuck!" I choke out.

And she answers. "Yes, we did."

30 | The Alliance

Dallas

WE'VE BEEN AT THE WHITE WOLFE LOUNGE FOR OVER AN hour. Knight has been straight up with us these past two weeks, so this visit isn't as stressful, especially since Doc isn't the focus anymore.

Doc's back at the clubhouse with all the ladies and the prospects, including Redman.

"JT reached out to us last week, telling us something happened to Ronny, and he needed our help. We played stupid, went and met up with him, and he confessed to everything. Pretty much, our suspicions were correct. Ronny's been transporting drugs across the US," Knight explains to the table.

"Is that why he's been visiting Lenny and Rayaan?" I ask.

Knight nods. "Yes, he's been working with them—they smuggle the shit in, the guy's set up all over the US. I don't know how Ronny got in with these guys, but they're big time. Ronny's been dabbling in a lot more than we thought."

Knight continues. "Ronny had that meeting because they're supposed to start moving weapons, not just drugs. JT says he doesn't know what happened to Ronny. The last they knew, he was going to go away with Harley for a few days."

"Going away, where?" Wolfe asks.

Knight shakes his head. "I don't know. JT said he wouldn't tell anyone. It took them a few days to realize Blaze and another member were gone too. When they found out the girls were in the hospital, they suspected that you had them. They all started to freak. He called for help, and we went along with it to get information. They think we're going to help fight against you. No one knows of our arrangement."

"What about Karma," Shy grunts out.

"What arrangement?" Mac fires off at the same time.

Shy's out for blood for what they did to Ginger. Seeing that Karma is all that is left, he's focused on finding her.

"He said she went into hiding, but she had plans to go to Europe with a batch of women. We think Ginger was supposed to be with them, but no one knows."

The table erupts with men expressing their fury.

"So, what now? What's your plan?" I ask Knight.

Knight leans back in his chair, crossing his arms over his chest. "Well, we've squashed our vendetta. I feel bad for all the bloodshed, especially since it came from one of our old presidents and rogue members. I want to make it right."

Wolfe interjects, "It took both sides to shed blood. You don't owe us anything."

Knight looks to me. "Well, JT and the others, including the Devil MCs, think we're getting ready to start a war with you over Ronny. Wolfe and I talked about maybe letting them think all is well and we're on their side. That way, we can infiltrate their club and find out what's really going on," Knight says calmly, looking around the room.

"How can we trust you? How do we know you won't double-cross us, setting us up?" I ask, knowing damn well we're all thinking it.

Knight looks to me before looking over to Wolfe. "Because a long time ago John and I used to be good friends and I hope we can be again someday. The war between us should have never happened."

Wolfe gives him a head nod in agreement.

"Yeah, but what about your other chapters. Are *they* all on

Dallas

board with this idea? Or are you going to have some more rogue members go behind your back *again* and get us all fucking killed?" Mac asks from beside me.

I was thinking the same thing because I know of two members that give me intel. How do we know they don't have other members giving the Devil MCs intel. He's got shit control of his clubs.

"Look, I know we all don't trust each other, but Ronny didn't just fuck with you and Harley. Ronny went behind all of our backs, making deals—deals he couldn't keep. Shit we've had to deal with, and we had to fight for him. He started shit all over, not just in New York and Chicago. I need to see who was helping him, who was in on it, and who the fuck I need to cut from my club." Knight is practically yelling now, slamming his fist down. "Why the fuck do you think I only brought a few members. The Black Crows are getting revamped from the inside out. So, I'm doing this not just for you, but for me. I'm asking you to become a friendly and help me weed out the bad motherfuckers while you get your revenge. That we become allies instead of enemies."

It's true. He only brought five guys with him. Big Black, who I've noticed, usually doesn't leave his side. Kind of like Cash and Wolfe. You will hardly ever see those two separated.

My phone vibrates in my pocket. I slip it out and see I have a text message. Unlocking my phone, I see it's an unknown number.

Unknown: I've got information. I'm 5 min away. Frank

Dallas: Frank Mancini? How do you know where I am?

Unknown: 3 min.

What the fuck?
I look over to Shy and say, "We've got incoming."
All eyes snapped to me. I continue, "Frank Mancini is almost here."
The room goes silent as everyone takes in what I just said.

When a whistle comes from the front door, all eyes snap to Chiv and his brother Blink.

Wolfe motions for them to come in, but only Blink takes a couple of steps in. Blink just got back from a problematic bounty, and he looks exhausted. "We got company."

Three minutes, my ass.

"What the fuck's he doing here?" Shy asks, getting up.

Blink announces. "It's Frank Mancini, and he wants to join your meeting."

Wolfe looks to me, and I shrug. "I don't know why he would be here."

"Let him in. Is he alone?" Wolfe asks, getting up and following Shy to the door.

Blink nods. "Yeah, just him and a couple of bodyguards."

Chiv, who's half in the door and half out, motions to someone outside.

Blink pushes the door open and stands next to his brother.

A few minutes later, in walks the infamous Italian mobster Frank Mancini—Luc Mancini's uncle. I really need to do my homework on him. He lives in Italy but is always here. I just don't know where he fits in with all the five families.

"I'm sorry to intrude on your meeting, but I think you'll want to hear what I have to say." Frank glides in, demanding the room's attention. No fear whatsoever and always with a smirk on his face. It's like he knows he's going to drop a bomb on us, and he can't wait. He's fully fitted with a three-piece suit, probably worth more than my bike. I'm sure it's fucking Canali, Armani, or Salvatore, one of those fucking big-time luxury brand suits. The fucking man emits wealth and power, and don't forget fear. The man radiates fear, making everyone submit to him.

Wolfe and Shy greet him at the door. Wolfe turns to introduce Frank to Knight, but Knight cuts him off, "Franky Boy," extending his hand to Frank.

Dallas

Frank smiles. "Knight," he says, greeting him, returning his shake.

Well, fuck! Didn't see that coming.

Bear pulls up a chair for Frank.

Frank unbuttons his suit jacket before taking a seat. The room becomes silent, all eyes on Frank.

He starts by saying, "Seems our paths keep crossing, yeah?"

"Oh yeah, how so?" Wolfe says, grabbing his whiskey, taking a sip.

"May I?" Frank motions to the bottle of whiskey on the table.

Wolfe nods, sliding an empty glass his way. We didn't know how many men Knight was going to bring, so we had a couple of buckets of beer and whiskey sitting around the table.

Frank proceeds to pour himself a whiskey on the rocks.

"I have some information for you." He leans back in his chair, crossing his legs, picking at what I'm thinking is invisible lint.

"What do you want in return?" Shy fires back, crossing his arms over his chest.

Frank laughs before sipping his whiskey.

"I don't like when women go missing. I'm not a fan of taking women by force or trafficking, to be exact. So, we"—he motions his glass between all of us—"we got a mutual problem."

"And what problem would that be?" Mac asks.

"Well, for one—I have the whereabouts of two women that you've been lookin' for," Frank says with a mischievous smile.

"What two women? And, how the fuck did you know we were meeting," Shy demands.

Frank shrugs. "I know lots of things."

"What the fuck do you want in return?" Wolfe asks.

"Well, for one, I need you to back off Lenny Costello. He's an associate of mine. And…" He pauses, swirling his drink around. "Let's just say it would be beneficial to the both of us that he is not fucked with, *capisci?*"

"So, who's our mutual problem then?" I ask, grabbing a beer.

"Well, I'm glad to see y'all made up *an're* friends again. Oh, but it seems that not all your members were so lucky. Isn't that right, Knight? Or the other MCs either, yeah?" Frank laughs, placing his now empty glass on the table. "It was for the best."

"How the fuck do you know all of this shit." I narrow my eyes at him, trying to figure him out.

He reaches inside his suit pocket, retrieving his phone. "I've got little birdies everywhere." Frank stands up, placing his phone back in the pocket before buttoning his jacket. "Now, would you like to know the whereabouts of Ms. Sasha Mendez and Ms. Camila Roberts?"

Holy shit! He knows where Sasha and Karma are!

Everyone's on their feet.

"You've got Sasha?" I rush out.

"Nah, but I know who does." His face becomes serious. "First—" He points to Mac and me. "You need to go handle Chicago. It seems your doctor's friend is in danger."

Mac flies up out of his chair, fisting the table. He leans over. "What the fuck do you mean, her friend?"

"*Oh!*" Frank puts his hands up. "Don't *fuckin'* come at me all *pazzo* for helping. As I said, I don't like when women get taken. You really need to take better care of your *bellissima*."

Mac tries to go after Frank, who just stands there, not threatened at all by the number of men in the room, furious with him.

"What are you talking about?" I demand.

Frank looks bored. "Oh, she's going to be, how do you say, in the wrong place at the wrong time—if you don't go and get her. That's all my little birds have told me." He turns to leave but stops.

"Also, keep my great-niece under watch, *capisci*? She's on that little *puttana pazzo's* list as well. I'm doing what I can to protect everyone, but *fuck me*, I can't be everywhere."

Dallas

"What fucking list? Where's Sasha and Karma?" Wolfe questions.

"I'll send my info over to Alec." And then he's gone.

Mac's and my phone go off simultaneously.

Motherfucker. This can't be good.

Mac looks at his phone, and it must be a text because he punches in his code just as I answer Lee's call.

"Are you okay? What's wrong?" I ask her.

"Something's wrong with Raydene." Lee's voice is filled with worry.

Mac's face becomes enraged, not taking his eyes off his phone. I know it's not good.

"Why would you say that?" I try to keep my voice calm.

"She texted us girls, saying she needed us."

I move closer to Mac to see what he's staring at and when I look down, there's a picture of Raydene with a black and blue eye and a message saying, I need you.

"Okay, Doc. We're on our way back."

Mac's going to lose his fucking mind.

Fuck, here we go again.

The End

... Stay tuned for more of the Wolfeman MC series, with Macon's story coming up next.

About the Author

Crazy, outgoing, adventurous, full of energy and talks faster than an auctioneer with a heart as big as the ocean… that is Angera. A born and raised California native, Angera is currently living and working in the Bay Area. Mom of a smart and sassy little girl, an English bulldog named Ruby, and a spunky Siamese cat named Minnie. She spends her days running a successful law firm but in her spare time enjoys writing, reading, dancing, playing softball, spending time with family, and making friends wherever she goes. She started writing after the birth of her daughter in 2012 and hasn't been able to turn the voices off yet. The Spin It Series is inspired by the several years Angera spent married into the world of underground music and her undeniable love of dirty and gritty romance novels.

FOLLOW AND CONNECT

Email ~ authorangeraallen@gmail.com

Website ~ www.authorangeraallen.com

Facebook ~ www.facebook.com/authorangeraallen

Instagram ~ www.instagram.com/angeraallen

Twitter ~ www.twitter.com/angeraallen

Amazon ~ amzn.to/2A6dX8L

Bookbud ~ www.bookbub.com/profile/angera-allen?list=author_books

Goodreads ~ www.goodreads.com/author/show/16200622.Angera_Allen

Facebook Reader Group ~www.facebook.com/groups/235049216705223/

From the Author

Hi, I hope you enjoyed Dallas. I'm sorry it took so long to write. I promise the following three books will be out soon—2020 kind of knocked me off track. I'm excited about what's to come. Ideally, each series should be read in order to follow along with the storyline. Yes, each book is its own couple's story, but the storyline all starts with Alexandria. All the series intertwine with each other, so if read out of order, secrets will be leaked. (Recommended reading order at the beginning of Dallas.)

SPIN IT SERIES
Alexandria – Book One
Ginger – Book Two
Izzy – Book Three

STANDALONE
Firecracker

WOLFEMAN MC SERIES
Quick – Book One

COMING SOON
Violet – Book Four – Spin It
Macon – Book Three – Wolfeman MC
BB Securities – Book One (Brant's Story)
Franky Boy – Book One (Mafia Series)

Acknowledgments

Cheers to all of us that made it through 2020! Now, for 2021—where did the time go? Shit, I can't believe it's been over two years since Quick was released. Damn Covid pandemic! You would think being locked up at home, that I would have been able to push out books left and right—yee-aah, NO!

Seriously, I didn't even write one word during 2020. But, once I started, Dallas was fun to write, but damn, it took forever. After a year of not writing, the voices and stories were overflowing, so I took extra time writing this book. I introduce so many new characters, and if you have an imagination like me, you will see where I'm going to branch off to new series. I hope you enjoy Dallas!

To my beautiful baby girl—We made it! Fuck 2020. I'm so proud of the sassy-as-hell and unique young lady you're growing to be. You're reading up a storm now, making it harder for me to write at night because you like to 'sneak a peek.' The love and support you give me definitely keeps me going. I love you, my little sunshine.

To my parents, who love and support me each and every day. I really don't know what us Allen girls would have done without you both during the pandemic. We made it, though, and I love you both so much. My mom for loving me unconditionally. Thank you for pushing me to be the best I can be. You are, and will always be, my best friend.

To my Sistas from another Mista—Sonya & Sharm. Thank you for saving me from myself. If you both didn't shove me into your bubble during 2020, I would have lost my damn mind. This pandemic has really made me do some soul searching. I'm glad you both were by my side. I am truly blessed to have you in my life. I love you both so much.

Jennifer G—Gurl, thank you for letting me be in your bubble

this pandemic. Family is everything! Thank you for pushing me. I love hearing... *I need more—Where's my next chapters—Hello! I'm waiting!* It definitely made me not give up. For always dropping everything to answer my calls or text to calm me down or helping me work through something in my head. I love your opinion, the ideas, and the advice you give me. The best is when you get excited about the story. Best Jen quote—"Aw, shit! This gonna be good." You are critical to me during the writing process, and I hope you know it. Love ya, Jen.

Michelle K.—BEST PA EVER! Seriously, you always go above and beyond for me. You're the yin to my yang. Always dropping what you're doing to take my frantic calls or edit a chapter. You are always there for me. Thank you for helping me keep my Angels group going strong and for continuously checking on me. Your love and devotion to my family and me is unbelievable. This pandemic fucked up our travel time together, but I will see you at SBC. Love you, girl!

Kim H.—Thank you for your service during this pandemic. I am so glad you're healthy and safe. I'm sorry for bugging you so much these past few months, but you know I can't turn this in until it's Kim-proofed, cuz we all know you fix my shit. Love you, girl!

To my beautiful Russian bartender—Rus. I wish I could have acknowledged you in Izzy, but we had met right after it was published, and Quick was coming out. Picking your brain has helped me understand so much of Russian culture. Thank you for the strong drinks, amazing conversations, and most of all, the gorgeous photos. I can't wait to put you on a cover of one of my books. Cheers, my friend.

To the clubhouse next door— LO. When I first met you all those years ago, you were a prospect, and look at you now! I'm so proud of you. Thank you for the endless advice, great conversations, and of course, for always inviting me to come do 'research' at the clubhouse. You and your brothers will always be in my heart.

To my editor, Ellie—Seriously, you fucking rock! Not just for being so damn good at what you do but also for being a fucking great person. Your FB posts through this pandemic have been a lifeline for me, so thank you. You are the best!

To my Angels—thank you for all your endless love and support during these past couple of years during this pandemic. I was lost for a bit, but y'all brought me back. I love my group!

To my street team—get ready! I'm back.

To my bloggers—Thank you for taking the time to read and review my books. I appreciate you helping me promote them.

To all my friends and family—Thank you to those that reached out to me over the last two years. I see and acknowledge each and every one of you. I just want you all to know I love you and thank God every day for you. Without your love and support, I wouldn't have been able to make it through 2020, let alone finish this book. I know I'm going to forget people, and I'm sorry for that, but just know I'm so thankful for everyone that had a part in making this dream a reality.

Last but definitely not least, to my fans—I hope each and every one of you is safe and healthy. The 2020 pandemic shook so many of us. I know so many of you have lost someone through this, as did I, and it was a hard year. I can honestly say most of 2020 was spent finding myself and learning to adapt to the new normal. I tell people I should have written Izzy during 2020 because I was in a dark place. But y'all know me, I always find the light. I'm sorry it took me so long to finish this book, but I promise the next ones will be coming soon. Thank you for all the emails, messages, and, most of all, reviews. They all mean so much to me.

I love each and every one of you.
With love, Angera

WOLFEMAN MC

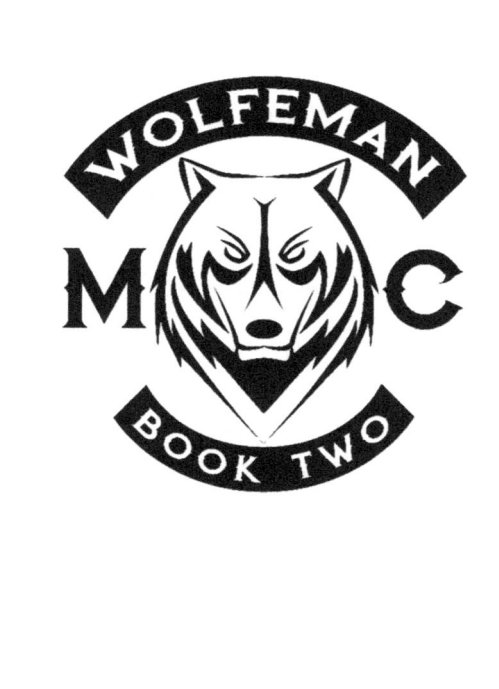

BOOK TWO

Made in the USA
Middletown, DE
12 March 2024